THE SPOILS

THE SPOILS

a novel

Colin Thompson

Burlington, Vermont

This is a work of fiction. Names, characters, places, and incidents are products of the author's imagination or are used ficticiously and are not to be construed as real. Any resemblance to actual events, locales, organizations, or persons, living or dead is entirely coincidental.

Copyright © 2024 by Colin Thompson

All rights reserved. No part of this publication may be reproduced, distributed, or transmitted in any form or by any means, including photocopying, recording, or other electronic or mechanical methods, without the prior written permission of the publisher, except in the case of brief quotations embodied in critical reviews and certain other noncommercial uses permitted by copyright law.

Onion River Press
89 Church Street
Burlington, VT 05401
info@onionriverpress.com
www.onionriverpress.com

ISBN: 978-1-957184-94-4

Library of Congress Control Number: TK

for jess.

I want it all.
—Katie Crutchfield

How dare you want more.
—Jack Antonoff

INTRO

THE INTERVIEW WAS ON A MONDAY. NOT THAT THAT MEANT ANYTHING to me. But I had treated the weekend like I'd earned it and now approached the interview with a belly full of Manhattan silly, even though a.) it was not a corporate gig and b.) it was the only job I'd ever been overqualified for. I had tremendous babysitting faculties and I was much better at lacrosse than 99.5% of the U.S. population (the math checked out). Silly nonetheless as I wound my bicycle through the crepe myrtles and California live oaks to the terracotta clay-roofed, stucco'd Escobarian estate that was The Brentwood School. The bike ride from Venice was trying. Not physically—I relished an arduous and pesky incline. After the hard part, where things flattened out and I pedaled past Bundy, past the place where OJ got really mad and so rudely interrupted Game 5 of the 1994 NBA Finals between the Knicks and the Houston Rockets, I started to think. And that never ended well. Yes, sure: the Knicks would win Game 5, but OJ and the Bronco interruption cast a strange, unsavory pall over the series. The Knicks lost in 7 and there I was, nearly twenty years later. It didn't take a conspiracy theorist to pin the tacks on that one.

The *what-could-have-beens* rained down on me like frogs and out from the privet hedges popped former selves, the Me's of yore I'd have to plead my case to, reason with and explain to them where I was going. They popped out like shooting targets or Fun House hobgoblins. The eleven-year-old Me was nice, just wanted to talk about that series he was still grappling with, reminding me that *two inches* in the final seconds of Game 6 was all that Starks needed to be a hero, so he's still one to us, never forget. But everyone else was a prick. And who could blame them? At thirty-one-years-old I was on my way to interview for a gig as a middle school lacrosse coach, a position that is, historically, a volunteer role. But me? I was not doing it to give back. This was not charitable. I could not afford to be a "good person". I just desperately needed the very little money they were offering.

"So heckle away!" I yelled at nobody as I chugged up Barrington, all the while outlining, in my mind, a pilot script for this exact scenario. And for *that*, I wished to be stabbed. Another small, sad circle.

Everything is prologue to this, but here is where the story starts. My bike was nice and I loved it—a Carolina Blue Fixed Fuji Feather—but the things that I loved were even starker reminders of who I wasn't, or worse: who I was. I had my own apartment and I was lucky and happy about that, or, rather, not happy but worried because those days were numbered. Luck made me fuck it up. I had a dog and I loved him and I had…my bike? And a La Creuset that wasn't mine? I was supposed to have *things* by then. Tennis lessons and Aesop hand soap. New restaurants I just *had* to try. The finer things. Thread counts. Seven years I'd been here! I could blame this town, the city of desperate hopeful hopelessness.

Or I could curse myself for not getting into finance out of college. But I would have fucked that up, too, chuck another punky log on the sad fire of things I never thought I was smart enough to do so subsequently never considered trying. Unsurprisingly, somewhere back there, I thought I was just not dumb enough to be a screenwriter. It felt like the dullards' medium. So all of my Simpleton Road led me to San Vicente Blvd., biking to The Brentwood School in the early spring of 2014, plenty written and nothing sold, wondering how everyone had a Range Rover and if there were any minor adjustments, little tweaks, tiny rumples in the fabric I could make if I, in the far off chance, happened upon a time machine.

ONE

Everyone gets to Los Angeles through New York and I wasn't special. 2007 had me living in Brooklyn. I was dating a girl (woman, I suppose, as she paid a mortgage) I had met in Lake Tahoe the previous winter. The move to New York was borne from thinking I wanted to be an A&R guy. I didn't know what "A" or "R" meant but I wanted to be the guy at the end of those letters at a time when that profession was becoming fossilized, the whole industry fucked on its ass because of Sean Parker. But, still, I thought that a world existed where I could drive into New York City, get a job I only knew the initials of (which didn't really exist), find a place to live (which I couldn't afford) and feel comfortable in my own skin because once you cross the _____ Bridge and commit to New York, you get an automatic indoctrination of confidence, a swagger-scan as you roll through the EZ Pass lane. Alas, no such scan. Two meetings in the morning, one in the afternoon—all of which my Uncle (who worked in Sports Marketing) had set up for me, none of which were for jobs I wanted to have, all of which were not actually interviews for jobs I didn't even want. They were favor meets ("meeting" seems grossly official to what they ended up being) because my Uncle was well liked. As a goof or actual advice, an older, employed friend told me to wear a suit. I didn't have a suit. So I borrowed one from a big person. It was a Friday in the Summer in the City and the workplaces I walked into for these pity-meets employed a "Casual Friday" option. This was the original trace of Manhattan silly—the Wuhan Guano, as it were—I felt searing my guts. Silly dude in a silly suit, nothing but the distortion of shame, the flange of humiliation zing-zanging around my head as I sat there looking like Tom Hanks walking home at the end of Big, trying to explain to a girl at a PR firm who was maybe two years my senior that I dug music? And just like that, offices were not for me. A body riddled with indignity, too far gone, too much silly too quick to ever recover, like Lyme or Syphillis gone untreated. From that day on there would not be a corporate place of work in which I set foot where I did not feel like the Silliest Boy in New York.

I loosened my tie, cleared my afternoon of the remaining courtesy meets, drank four Guinness' in a dark midtown basement bar and recalibrated the trajectory of my life. Jen (girlfriend) had been back in Tahoe for the summer, readying the big move, tidying up her estate. It was, for me, the summer of Love. One month into our consummation and we separated for the summer. I'd never been so smitten, so sure. Three thousand miles and limited texting capabilities is all it takes to make the heart grow dumb. That I'd learn later. But as I homelessly necked Guinness' at a cop bar, she already had a place to live in Brooklyn and a waitressing gig lined up. I was getting day-creamed in a Big n' Tall while I should have been hustling East Williamsburg, ear on the streets, sniffing out the next Strokes. But, alas, my A&R days were done. Of that I was certain.

So I slept on some couches, worked with my hands, figured it out. Found a sublet with paper mâchè walls for seven-hundred bucks a month in Williamsburg. Jen arrived, worked nights, I worked days and nights like a mule on meth, so we didn't see each other enough to know the fault lines and we carried on, deafened by the noise pollution of the hustle. I perhaps could have gone to work in Sports Marketing, but my jib was off. I lived in a wacky musician compound, a building full of hip heads and grass-hounds with a warted Russian ogre in the basement collecting rent. It was heaven. Bands would pass through, sleep in the hall if they got in a pinch. Twelve-year-old Kevin Morby bobbling around eating grilled cheese, borrowing undies. We had Honky-Tonk Wednesdays and I played a scream therapy version of Coldplay's "Yellow" and a Lucinda Williams tune and felt the glowing absence of silly, felt of the moment, with the times, of and in the times—we were the times!—part of an ecosystem of what it was supposed to be, of what *mattered*, knowing nothing did so fuck it, it's okay, and there was no pretense, no posture, just two dollar PBRs as far as the eye could see. I was happy. I felt cool.

All things must pass.

Paying mortgage in Lake Tahoe while living in New York proved unsustainable, so Jen had to return West. I stayed put for a month or two, a few more Lucinda songs, a hundred thousand PBRs and then, as I've said, as it does: absence (+ distance + T9 texting) makes the heart stupid. So. I packed up the Subaru and drove across this great and awful Nation once again.

The loose plan was to start a house painting company in Lake

Tahoe. Have a kid. My Old Man had had me at twenty-six and I was that age so that made sense. Luckily, within three minutes of arriving in Tahoe, it was clear how much sense my father's decisions failed to make. My brain called my heart a retard, my heart capitulated, and every part of me—every organ, every cell—was on board to *not* follow through with any of those terrible mistakes. As much as I wanted to about face and go *back* to New York, I knew that a.) a dude from Akron/Family saying I sounded good singing someone else's song when I was drunk one time did not justify a pursuit in the field of rock n' roll and b.) I didn't feel like driving back. c.) for whatever reason I had been writing a story (short story, essay, zine—who knows. It was early germination). And what with Los Angeles a short six down the 395, it occurred to me that it could be a script. I was already in California, I had watched a few seasons of *Entourage*, I was a decent surfer, and the design/build outfit I had been working for in New York had opened a studio in Los Angeles. I was lucky to have work in those big-little, and at times, good recessions. And, I thought, what's another half-drunk twenty-something trying to tell their three-quarters-baked story in what I didn't yet know to be a vapid, meritless, garbage heap of a town?

Look out, Hollywood, Here I Come.

Aimee Mann sang *kicking is hard, but the bottom's harder*. So I listened to her a lot and, again, I hustled. Made enough money to pay rent. Jen moved down and we had an apartment home in Venice beach. Succulents and a Bialetti. I bought a surfboard and paddled out and the first wave that agreed to have me, I hopped right up, made a late bottom-turn and the wave was gracious, allowing me to pump down the line for a few Mississippis.

I was going to sell scripts and this whole thing was going to kick ass.

It's Like Another Perfect Day…I Love L.A.!

However. The next paddle out, I'd get threatened by a local (whatever that meant), decked by a mean six-foot wall of a wave, voo-doo dolled by the great Pacific to finally come up for air only to get hit in the mouth with a diaper. I would not sell scripts. This would not kick ass.

THE PROBLEM WITH writing for the screen, or, moreover, doing anything at all, is that if you're just north of good at it, you'll fail, and if you're just north of bad, you'll be fine. If you're pretty good, the people who don't really matter will stoke the embers of your ego just enough to make you stick around. The people who matter will stay mum or discourage you because there's not enough room at the table and they just sat down, regardless of how long they've been there. If you're a skoasch better than bad, the people who matter will give you a booster seat because your shit's not a threat and the people who don't matter will give you their honest opinion but you're not listening to them because you're at the table. If that doesn't make sense, that makes sense. If the words make sense but the ethics or fundamentals don't add up, that is correct.

The first few scripts I wrote were eating-disorder-themed because my sister's eating disorder was by far the most interesting thing that had happened to me since my parents' divorce, and divorce you can always use as a universal seasoning to taste. Highly inoffensive. At this point it's just parsley. No one is going to send back a dish because of a divorce thread. Furthermost, though, if my sister was gonna muck up everyone in our immediate family's shit for a decade and counting, I was gonna try and squeeze some MiraLax™ from that stone.

At the very most it would be interesting to a small demographic, the very specific sect of people that had had brushes with that particular disaster. Also known as: Unsellable. At the very least it would give me something to blame my lack of traction on (the Eating Disorder Dramedy sub-genre hadn't quite caught yet). So I ran it back a few times. A few different spools and wonders, a meager stack of scripts piling up and *just* enough people giving me *just* enough encouragement to not blow town, disappear maybe, stumble backwards into a Zydeco band, a washboard percussionist in New Orleans. There were other daydream scenarios, which, for many reasons, I kept to myself. One main reason being that I had a girlfriend who I was too lazy and too spineless to break up with. So I just set about being not very nice most of the time. I was a real asshole all of the time except for seldom. I loved her or something but couldn't stand anything that came out of her mouth. "I *love* David Bowie" I might hear her say to someone. My response would go something like: "No shit? What's your favorite Bowie record?" I don't know. I've always been a hopeless romantic when it came to the idea of romance.

She broke up with me. And good for her! I, however, spun into an abyss of self-imposed sadness, typical of a twenty-seven year-old who thinks things are a certain way. It was bad but how bad could it be? It's like a dog rolling in a dead bird—"You dummy." I wanted to be there. I wanted to be alone and feel the pain, really feel it, deep down in my appendix when Rick Danko sings: ...*that I've never felt so a-lo-o-one be-e-fooooore.*

I thought that was where the good stuff grew. But it turned out it was just where three and a half years went.

So, yes, I forced her hand and she broke up with me and we sorted through some items. I got the dog in a very easy and amicable custody discussion, packed a bag, walked over to a friend's house and zip-zap, I'd get my LPs later. This is after we fucked late on the living room floor. If that "fucked" felt abrasive, good. As a Dude, that's the only true fucking—the last impression fuck. You *gotta* fuck that last fuck outta the park or your brain's gonna rot with all those fictitious dicks coming for you, through her. They're coming for you regardless. But if you get lucky enough to secure a boner to hang your hat on, one that requires no touching or teasing, a strictly business boner of forgotten pride and purpose and *toughness*. One of them Josh Brolin boners. You close with that? Fuck with one of *those*?!? That's when you can walk away, head high and sure and full until a few hours or days later you strap in, shackle up and batten down the hatches on your confinement of melancholy and listen to songs for a while.

Oh, Little Boy Lost—he takes himself so seriously!
He brags of his misery—he likes to live dangerously!
And when bringing her name up, he speaks of a farewell kiss to ME.
He sure got a lotta gall; to be so useless and all; muttering small talk
at the wall while I'm in the hall...

Sam (dog) never tired of my crying these songs into his neck. Or at least he never made me apologize. He had Husky somewhere in him, a dark shepherd's snout, respected deeply people's personal space, yet had a smile that let you skip the hand-smelling formalities. He knew I loved a wallow. A sunset run on the Santa Monica bike path, something so sad and so pretty in my ears that I loved this whole being alive thing more than anyone who had ever blown their brains out couldn't stand it. Tears were just more attractive to me, the laughter on the come-up from deeply downhearted bona fide even if the tears were syndicated, reran within my networks. But how many times can you watch the five season run of *Friday Night Lights* or *The Wire*? Two, three? Tops? It was perfect when it was. But those shows, like my tidy island way down in the dumps, well: shut up and find a new show.

Hindsight is an old woman with pretty good eyes for her age and three and a half years is a pretty long time to listen to songs. But I got it together. On the bright side I was in terrific shape and the argument could be made that the sentence had owl'd my hull, regardless of its self-sanction. I was arguably better for it. Arguably because I was arguably worse for it, as I had a sociopath's relationship to feelings toward those of the opposite sex. Either way, it needed somewhere to go before I got nice. Which I figured would probably happen. Thirty-one years old, financially still never having made enough money to ever use the word "financially"; professionally nothing, spiritually middling, I needed to brand something, scar it with my fucked up fire iron before it cooled for all time. And that's when it occurred to me. I had a harried relationship with the game, had sworn it off, cut ties with it like a lanced boil. But it came to me clear as a bell, sound as an old engineer. Branding iron still hot enough to irritate if not lightly scar, I found on the local internet, an innocent, malleable herd with which to point it: The 7th & 8th grade Brentwood Boys Lacrosse Team.

TWO

The middle school was connected to the high school and the rich kids were making me sweat. I envied youth, though I didn't want to be young. I just wanted a talking to back then, at some point in the late 90's, something that would right my posture, slap the bubbler out of my hand. No DeLorean in sight, as I now felt late 90's stoned, walking around, looking for a place to lock my bike even though I knew it was painfully safe. These kids had never been found wanting. I had to pinprick the ballooning intimidation these beautiful teenagers and their immaculate Spanish-style noble estate were imposing on me, and quick. I couldn't give it credence. I caught myself muttering chides to myself, patronizing insults that were clinically abusive. The Olympic sized swimming pool and the Bermuda grassed athletic fields made me feel all of the lesser that I was. These kids and this place were better than me. Simple as that. Just another place on the ever-expanding list of places I didn't belong. I would have been a terrible rich kid. I never could take advantage of looking the part.

My pulse threatened to pop out an eyeball. I double-checked my calf muscles—Lord knows—and my Aviators slid off my nose, clattered on the cement and I wanted to die. A teenaged girl and boy—genome alignment odds unfathomable each—tussled playfully as I tried to lock my bike, but I had the wrong key for the wrong lock, a man of many blunders. I reminded myself that the bike was safe, but I badly needed something to do. The sound of my Ray-Bans hitting the concrete coupled with the Abercrombie hormones barreling down the breezeway—my inappropriate tachycardia—all of it battered my pride like a wintry mix on this seventy-seven degree miserably perfect day. I couldn't go through with it. What was I thinking? The money was peanuts, the thought of speaking to any of these people felt fraudulent. I hadn't sold a script not because my time had yet to come, not because I hadn't met the right like-mind, no: I hadn't sold anything because I simply lacked the talent and/or the hustle to make it work. I was stupid and lazy, the two things that I joked openly about and secretly white-knuckle prayed weren't true. But I saw it in the reflection of my scratched-to-hell Ray-Bans. I was thirty-one years old. And I had lost.

Accepting defeat, my pulse slowed and a more adult hue returned to my face. It was okay. I had tried. It was only fair to myself to fold, to throw in the chips and move back east. Real estate or solar or coffee. A "start-up," any start-up will do. Start it the fuck up. Slap **Vermont** on the label and units move. Beanies, bread, burlap sacks—and those were just three b's off the top of my head! I giggled to myself. Giggled! I hadn't giggled in years. What a re*lief*. I could go back to Vermont, I could go *home*. Fuck Thomas Wolfe I liked Tom Wolfe better. I'd be respected for trying, doubly respected for reading the tealeaves. Humbled but stoic. Weary but content. The next chapter would unfurl and cooly present itself like a casual hammock boner in the summer shade. Organic maturation. This was psychedelic in its own right—I was out of body, watching myself become the Man I didn't necessarily want to be but who was I, anyway? If I didn't want to be him, all the more reason to go all in. I saw the road from above, and it led to Vermont. Part of me wanted to just start biking back. Earn it all, reborn back through the HPV pocked cervix of America. But the dog. We could hitchhike. Get rid of all our earthly possessions. Man and Dog. And drugs. Get a sheet of LSD and ride boxcar to boxcar, figure this country out once and for all, cure it of its ghastly ills from the inside out, from belly to shore. Get into politics. Last stop, District of Columbia. First stop—

A lacrosse ball scooted under my front tire as I mounted my bike to take the first pedal toward Capitol Hill. A kid—no more than thirteen, no less than five—crossed in front of me to retrieve it. He wore cargo shorts and Vans, smiled at me self-consciously and I loved him immediately. Lacrosse stick in his left hand, he grabbed the ball from the mulch under the juniper bush with his right.

"Don't do that." My political aspirations would have to wait.

The kid froze, looked at his hand and looked at me.

"What?"

"Don't use your hand."

He put the ball in his stick, with his hand, and I gave him a look that made me remember that nobody would be better at this than me. His shoulders slumped and he tossed the ball back under the juniper. On his third try he scooped the ball into his stick, turned to me with a "happy now?" showcasing that made me hate kids that age as a people. As he trotted off, back toward his friends, he ran with such a posturing lurch of self-doubt, an intentional hitch, thinking the high school kids were watching. I loved him again. The beauty in watching this kid think that anybody gave a shit about him, you, me, was staggering. I thought about it all and thought probably I was the next John Wooden.

Nobody cares about lacrosse. You can't make any real money playing professionally and its associations are garish and rapey.

So I dedicated some twenty years of my life to it.

There's more to it than that, of course. More to the game and more to my relationship with it than that ha-ha overview for the cheap seats. But for years I'd been mad at the sport, Duke rape-case optics aside. I had a grudge. It had done the opposite of what it had advertised. Sports were supposed to provide discipline and structure, focus and comradeship—especially at the collegiate level. But I walked away from the sport dumber, drunker, aimless and misanthropic. The argument could be made that I'd be fat or dead from the opium molecule if not for lacrosse, though I chose to look the other way and use it as a fall guy for my follies. But, as years and options fell by the wayside, I emptied my empty sack of skill sets to find only a lacrosse stick and was forced to let it back into my good graces. I would nullify all of the blow-hard ass-hats and schmucks I played with, all of the doughy losers who got a life of opportunity because of pigments and districts; the mulleted twits with their chillied post-game peckers and khaki pants; the Duke boys who didn't rape that woman but who certainly weren't gallant in their transaction. I'd right all the wrongs and absolve this popular, un-beloved and lampooned prep school sport by coaching...at a prep school in one of the wealthiest neighborhoods in the country. THAT BEING SAID. If I got the gig, I vowed to coach and mentor these rich kids while moonlighting on a script about a guy kinda like me coaching lacrosse at a public school in South Central. And when that script sold, I would then coach a real high school team in South Los Angeles not because I had to but because I wanted to, *needed* to, and we would beat Brentwood, beat the same kids I had molded into champions not four years earlier, and another script would rear it's worthless head, this scatterbrained snake eating its own tail from inside the eggshell.

INJURIES HAD PLAGUED my lacrosse career (two ACL reconstructions, broken collar bone, a bevy of concussions, all of which led to playing semi-professional drugs, a disabling obstacle in its own right) yet I somehow managed to hardscrabble my way through a par to sub-par D-I college program without quitting. Not out of perseverance or moxie or any of that honorable crap. The lift of quitting was just too heavy, and, frankly, out of the question. My Old Man would have been heartbroken. Angry, yes, but not Great Santini style. He took my brother and me to a Dead show the summer before fourth grade so staying mad wasn't really in his code. He had that marriage of Hippy & Jock borne out of mid-70's Long Island. John Prine and a blast of cocaine. Did he love the game? Sure. But what he really loved were the *fellas*.

He loved buying ten pizzas and a keg for the team after a game, win or lose. He loved putting ten thousand miles per season on his Cherokee, loved being the only parent in the stands for a fourteen degree pre-season scrimmage at Canisius, loved being the one constant for a group of B-list (C-list) knuckleheads who were underfunded, overworked and everdrunk. It was his *shit*. So, sure: he would have been angry with me for quitting. But he would have been straight-up, Elliot Smith-style, katana to the heart, *bummed* to lose that world whose expiration date was already right there within spitting distance. Thus, I played. It would have been so much work consoling him that I figured a few years of getting raped spiritually, mentally, and physically seemed the better option. Ever-selfless. Then, go figure, I find out years later that he had quit in the fall of his sophomore year (lacrosse is a SPRING sport, mind you) and blew the country to bone fish and smoke thai sticks in St. Croix for a semester. I was so baffled at this omitted nugget that I actually admired the hypocritical bastard. It was laugh-it-off or zip-tie him to the cross and slowly disembowel him for conning me into giving a sport with zero earning potential my life, and for what? The "camaraderie"? I laughed it off. I'm laughing now. I'll die laughing.

"WHERE'D YOU PLAY rugby?" I blurted out, asking the Athletic Director this question with no rugby leads or clues whatsoever. Well, none that I cared to admit. She reminded me of a faceless wookie I had stood behind at a Phish show in the summer of 1999, miserably tripping on equal parts ecstasy and LSD. She wasn't dirty and they were of opposite sexes, but they had that same squant get-up, like a dwarf that mostly kept growing.

Her desk I sat before was in a small, windowless office which became even smaller as her freckles came together, nose scrunched, trying to locate where this information—the "rugby" assumption—was gathered. The barometrics of the room grew so thick with the knowing that I figured her a lesbian, it felt like we were on Venus.

She eyed me, challenging, a dare to explain myself.

"*Bugsy* I think I said," I said. "Barry Levinson had quite a run up until *Toys*—"

"Bates," she replied, flatly, scanning my resume, which included my first job in fourth grade working at an apple orchard. I needed to cover the real estate of the page.

"You went to UVM. That makes sense," she said as she handed back the resume. There seemed to be a lot of stereotyping going on.

"So here's the thing," she began. But I didn't care. I felt stupid for feeling silly going into this thing. I was better than her; I had more things that I wouldn't live up to. "There's this other guy who came in to interview and I told him that I had to meet with you before I made a decision and you both are great—or good enough—and you probably need help, right? Whichever one of you, like…maybe you guys could be co-coaches."

"'Co-coaches'," I repeated as if she were suggesting we get delivery from a fast-food chain.

"I know it sucks, but…the pay's the same and you have somebody to pick up the slack if you have to go to an audition or something."

"I'm not an actor," I said as if she fingered me a Republican.

"Well he is, so…you guys can work it out," she said, as I sat before her, displeased. "Or…" She held onto the "r" in "or" for long enough for me to delineate that what followed, what was implied in the long "r" was: "(or) you can fuck off."

I let out another of my all-too-common defeated groans. "Who is this fffff…did this dude even…does he know lacrosse?"

"Yes."

"Did he play?"

"Yes."

"Where."

"Ummm….Drexel…no, Delaware."

Fuck. They beat us Sophomore year.

"Okay."

"Okay?"

"Sure I'll do it." I'd hate this dude or we'd be best friends. My money was happily, angrily on the former. But this was about the kids. Or whatever. I would inevitably make it about me and the sooner I came to terms with that the better off they'd be.

THREE

VENICE, CALIFORNIA IS THE WILCO OF LOS ANGELES NEIGHBORHOODS. Everyone moved there before it got gauche, everybody was listening before they got Dad Rock. But, as the thresholds of gauche vary among us; every Wilco nerd has their own origin of integrity. The sun raisin'd once-punks lauded the grubby gilded age of the 90's when it was only Shoreline Crips, crack, Hal's & The Brig. These are the nerds that wish Uncle Tupelo never broke up. Then, as they (we, she, him) do, entitled Caucasians took over the joint, pushed the Crips and the crack south to Inglewood and slowly started the evolution of insufferable, which would culminate in the twenty-five dollar loaf of bread from Gjusta, 2020. *Bread*.

Gjelina, Gjusta's beautiful bohemian Mother, opened in 2008. So those of us who moved to the neighborhood BG (Before Gjelina) could proudly lament: "Man, the old neighborhood's really changed." Those lucky ones who heard *Being There* from a friend's older brother or a hip English teacher. The Raisins and Latinos who stuck around could make people like me feel awful for moving there and did so at their ornery leisure. So I'd offer a cold Bohemia from my frequent six-pack bought at Windward Market as an olive branch, casually mention an X record and keep my head down. But if anyone moved to the neighborhood after Gjelia opened, or, God save you, after the Cafè Gratitude epidemic, myself and my '06/'07 post-Crip, Jay Bennett-era-preferring peers could tell them they ruined the neighborhood we had already started ruining. But I've *always* said it: Nels Cline fucked it up.

In and around 2010 Gjelina was the greatest restaurant in the world. God, that place could piss you off. The food was terrific and you wanted to fuck everything in the place, the dude servers notwithstanding—hell the dude servers most of all! They were so good looking and good at their jobs that it turned everyone into some variation of vaudevillian buffoon. They made you feel cool because they were decent actors with perfect shirts and hair and jewelry, and their making you feel cool gave you an immediate speech impediment, and as a result, nullified the cool they had let you feel, so all you could do to make up for it was to spend all the money you didn't have. It was a beautiful scam.

Venice, 2014, saw the neighborhood fully ruined, but, you know, still awesome, and if there was ever a place to get back on the humping horse, Gjelina was the stable. An actor friend of mine—Paul Everett, ever philandering family man—could always squeeze in a quick seventy drinks and dinner on his way home from Studio City. This made no sense, geographically, as he lived in Brookside or Scrimshaw, some middle neighborhood where people started moving to. But sometimes it's hard to go home. He made the time and the trip, though, and our full-throttled idiocy found a long-shot nexus of endearing and what some-even-found-cute, so we couldn't afford to not hang out a few times a month. He was an actor who people outside of New York and Los Angeles recognized because he was on network television; the firehouse spin-offs, pick-your-city PDs or SVU's borne from the Grey's Anatomies that ran amok on the big three's. But nobody in Los Angeles knew who the fuck he was, which was great. He was rich and he didn't have a bunch of nit-wits frantically trying to avert their eyes while he waited for his Americano. But he could go door-to-door and get blown by every soda sucking land monster in the greater Kansas City area, which was pretty neat.

Beautiful bastard, though. Racially enigmatic, freckled with a Guamanian or Laotian vibration. Full head of hair that looked as though he snapped it on in the morning like a Lego piece. He was on the juice, though: weekly scalp injections, daily Finasteride mgs, back of the scalp stripped, plucked, repurposed to the frontal vanity plate. And this was just to get out ahead of the far off maybe that he might lose his hair. I'd known him since before he started juicing and re-follicling and, as a professional, I knew his hair was here to stay. Maybe sometime two or three decades down the road his hair would follow suit with the rest of his being and quit on him, but he was better than good for now. Of course, this was the business; that was this town and that's why I wasn't an actor, for I was bound for bald. I had a few phony years of desperation before I had to start phoning in the comb-overs, musses and forwards', but I'd soon have to hang my hat on my head and just try to look good naked. It sucks, going bald. But it's sometimes funny and there's nothing funny about a full head of hair that you borrowed from the back of your own head. Plus we had Woody Harrelson, Tucci, Corey Stall and, of course,

His Airness, so LeBron could certainly eat a dick. On top of it all was the reality that I couldn't even afford to offer to split half of the bill we were about to run up, so fuck my hair, even if I'd go to disturbing lengths to save it, naturally, hypothetically.

The women who flocked to Gjelina were in a different tax bracket, fiscally and physically, up in the Exosphere, notes in the range only Mariah Carey had access to in the mid 90's. It was like *The Adjustment Bureau*, though. A lotta hats. It made me nervous. The repurposed wood planked ceiling. The brick floor. The floor to ceiling windows with the shades drawn come sundown. The lighting burnt orange and dim, bouncing off the copper wall paneling just so. There was no real bar so there was no good place to stand while you waited for your table; you were left with no choice but to guzzle by the wall. The escape route was blocked and besides, having drummed up the druthers to cross the threshold into this abominable soup of egomaniacal one-percent-beautiful-boho-fuck-monkeys, it was too late to reroute to Hinano's for a turkey-swiss burger and twenty pitchers. Get comfortable being uncomfortable and this will all be over soon.

On a night like this, though, things weren't so bad. I had marketed it as one of those "I'm gonna get back out there" nights, omitting or misremembering that I'd kinda been out there all along, a chagrined school of 24-39 y/o women broiling in the wake that was the years of my forcible sorrow. I had never really been a rah-rah, rock-'em-sock-'em "pussy" guy. It's part of life, and that's cool. But so much seems to make Dudes seem pathetic. I tried to keep a low profile. That night, however, I set out to be *One of the Guys*. The next day I was to start a new, tragically underpaid job which I was too old for, alongside a dude I would probably hate. I needed a woman to like me immediately. Somehow the two were connected. Paul ordered everything on the menu because he had that steam engine Southeast Asian metabolism. I was okay with it because it lowered the odds of another tactless blackout and I hadn't eaten anything but eggs, spinach, bananas and peanut butter in weeks. We batted some witty repartee back and forth with the waiter who wore a hat that cost a month's rent and then cased the place for anyone who would have us. Paul was in a jovial loveless marriage with his really good pal and they had two kids. He didn't want to break up the nucleus and he definitely didn't want to have sex with his wife-pal, so when he was filming away from home—which he was for a quarter of most calendar years—vaginas and mouths sometimes slipped and fell smack dab onto his cappuccino dick. He was charming like a young Vince Vaughn and had a humility so fraudulent that you couldn't help but love him for trying. He made me look reserved and introspective or whatever and it worked.

"I can't do it, I can't do it, I can't do it anymore I WON'T DO IT," he said without any spaces in between the words.

He signaled to our new friend with the hat, indicating we needed more cocktail and the dude nodded solemnly, leaning into the bit, respecting the medicine. He was awesome.

"The acting or the…acting," I asked.

"The acting and the acting."

"Yeah that's tough," I said, implying things—all things—were tougher.

"I just wanna go back east. Do some *theater*. Have a house at the base of a mountain, on a river, with a little footbridge to go to your thinking place."

"You actors all think you just want a footbridge," I said. "But it's never enough. You'll get a lap-pool and something you won't keep up the upkeep with. A pickling barn." I did love the idea of a thinking place. Sanded stumps and the whole area insulated with peat moss.

"Pickling takes time, not upkeep. Jeff Daniels knows how to do it."

"I think he lives in Detroit."

"AH! Even better!"

I started singing "Nothing is Good Enough" by Aimee Mann. Our beautiful friend came back with drinks and sang a few lines with me. It was cute but it exposed the fissures in our relationship and now I just wanted to keep it above board. Was I singing a song more people knew than I had thought or did we have a connection that he was now exploiting to get a bigger tip? I wasn't paying but that wasn't the point. We were through. We never had a chance. He walked away and I prayed his shift was done.

"And there it is," Paul whispered with lecherous grit.

"What? Where?" I followed his eyes to a table of two women, one of whom was looking at, dare I say it: me. I grabbed my drink too quickly and my mouth was late; dribbled my chin, onto my shirt.

"It's so fucking on," Paul stage tittered.

I was less sure, but I wasn't there to not throw it at the wall. So I said: "It might be moderately on."

"The hot one's looking at you," Paul said, excitedly, which

seemed rude.

"Well, she's racist." But he was looking at his phone. I almost repeated myself but thought better of it.

We continued to stuff our faces and drink hundreds plus dollars' worth of cocktails as we played peek-a-boo with the ladies across the room.

"We send them a drink," Paul concluded, and he wasn't wrong. But that seemed so clinical.

"That's kinda corporate," I said, as I dreamt of corporate benefits.

"Yeah, *man*, but there needs to be, you know, something to broker the deal."

"A courier."

"A courier indeed."

We sipped, thought.

"A dessert," I ventured.

"That's the Jedi Mind shit," Paul kicked me under the table. Our act was played but we couldn't help it. We were committed.

We proceeded to pour over the desserts, running numbers and figures on which one hit the Venn Diagram bulls-eye of benign, interesting and over indulgent.

"You don't want anything too rich," Paul began.

"For the obvious reasons."

"For the obvious reasons."

"But you also don't want the lightest fare because that sends a hidden message that could be taken for what it is, for what we are," I expounded.

"Vain, superficial."

"Shallow, shitty."

"Can't show that hand. You wanna send something that says 'I can party—I'm HERE to party'—"

"But let's not get grubby."

"Let's not. Get. Grub-by," Paul sang.

And, mind you, we were two dudes who had just split at least ten thousand calories in food and drink.

It was crème brûlée we landed on, though not until after we huddled up with our old friend in the hat. I felt weird consulting him on which dessert to send, but he knew the menu and I think he had accepted our fate as I had earlier, after the Aimee Mann kerfuffle: it was too perfect or too much. Either way, unsustainable, not to mention we were both quite heterosexual. Clearly not *entirely*, but we agreed on the crème brulee.

And that was that. We sent over that decadent little ceramic dish, they waved to us, we raised a glass, they came over after they paid their bill, sat with us for a drink, Paul went home and the cute one with the mussed pony tail came back to my apartment to listen to records and have nightcap or two. It wasn't easy because it was never that easy but Paul Molitor is one of the greatest hitters of all time and he had a career batting average of .306 so you do the math.

I FORGET HER name but she was from somewhere you could have guessed if you had a ton of guesses: Chicago, Houston, Orange County, San Antonio. She was probably from San Diego. She wore a leather jacket that seemed a bit much but I had a framed Carl

Banks poster on my wall so I curbed my judgments.

With fifty-eight drinks mixed from an array of spirits, it would have taken a professional to cajole a boner out of me. But I didn't want to count her out because Paul had put in the hours and was probably getting a DUI. Luckily, I didn't have to worry about not getting a boner because she promptly picked up my guitar and began playing a ghastly original of, um, acoustic rap? Think Lauryn Hill Unplugged No. 2.0 but flopping around on air dusters. She then cracked my headstock on the coffee table, spilled a glass of Wolftrap on the dog, moved in to kiss me and off my stony lips asked:

"Are you gay?"

"Yes."

"I knew it! I told Liz that when you guys sent the dessert."

I was equal parts flattered, offended and didn't give a shit. I told her we'd get together soon and eat popcorn or something, gave her Geordie Smith's landline number from when I was a kid and sent her on her way.

I opened a relieved if celebratory Sierra and cleaned the dog.

FOUR

COLBY CUTHBERT WAS FROM NEW JERSEY AND HAD GONE TO DELBARTON, an all-boys Catholic prep school where he played lacrosse and cracked-wise in a style deeply unfunny. "Cutty" was his nickname and what he introduced himself as, so my mind was made up. He was shorter and tightly wound and rehearsed and crass and let you know he was a comedian within minutes of meeting him. You felt like the better person in his presence, that's the best I could say for his character. His brother was a marine and his old man was probably a fucker and his mother seemingly nice, having gotten him to really believe her when she said "oh, honey, they're just jealous" in regards to all the kids who razzed him. I saw firsthand how this caused irreparable damage as he removed his hat to showcase a dyed blonde mohawk. It wasn't a proper mohawk, but some sort of Zippy-the-Pinhead front-hawk that he had grown out and slicked back. I think Macklemore had a similar do' but I wasn't exactly sure who Macklemore was. I had a hunch. Was its intent irony? Because he wasn't running from hair-loss and he didn't have an iota of cool about him (see: cargo shorts, funny t-shirts) or anything that could permit an attempt to pull off a Pinhead-hawk such as his. He was just an asshole. After five minutes of small talk, I wondered when it happened. To people, specifically Dudes. I wondered at what age, what moment he went all in on being a dickhead. Because that was a much bigger commitment than the one I had had to make. My moment came when I ate way too many mushrooms in my fifteenth year and on the comedown broke down sobbing because my arms felt bigger than my brain was ready for and my life was flying by and I loved and resented it all so much and was so deeply terrified and a little psyched and that was just who I was going to be forever.

"Did ten minutes last night at Bar Lubitsch. Killed," he said after he shook my hand too hard, sized me up. He swatted at my mid-section, snickered: "You slay down in Venice? I bet." It was maybe a compliment but it made me feel weird about being male.

We stood on the field watching the kids leaving school as the bell rang.

"Jail BAIT. Jesus. Right?" This dude was bumming me out. But I didn't know what was worse: his being a creep or me not wanting to be seen with him as the cool kids got let out of class.

"So you played at Delaware?" I felt an obligation to steer it back to what we were there for.

"Yup-yup. With Konkie and BelMar and those boys."

What the fuck. "Right on. When'd you graduate?"

"'04." This made him a year or two older than me and that made me feel better—it always does, always will.

"So we played against each other," I said, seeing something flicker across his ass-wipe veneer. But he was ass-wipe underneath and all around, so giving him the credibility of a façade was a slap in the face to those of us who could actually act unlike our own selves from time to time.

"Maybe."

Maybe?

"No that's right!" He doubled back. "'03, '02. That's a blur," he looked off, out into the vista of his stupid fib.

"You guys beat our balls in," I dangled.

"Oh that's right! We probably played our scrubs."

"You beat us in overtime." None of this was true! Everyone was lying! But I was gonna full-nelson this phony in a grapple of dim-wits even if it killed me, which it would not.

He turned his attention to the kids, our kids, ambling onto the field. 7th and 8th grade was insane. There were kids with mustaches and kids in diapers. Kids with zits and kids who still wanted their crusts cut off. You could tell right away which kids would ball and which kids' parents were making them play. Either way, everybody needed to tighten up.

I started to corral, but the imposturous skunk cut me off.

"Well, well, well…" And that was all he had. The kids started haphazardly putting their shit on in the middle of the field and I let it piss me off too much, too soon. I wasn't nervous anymore, just upset about how bad we were going to suck.

"Dudes. There's a sideline, there's a bench. Let's have some respect. For ourselves." I had a sinking feeling a lot of these kids came cleat-less. Filthy rich, cleat-less kids I would not abide. I was getting angry and I didn't even know anything yet.

"Yeah, c'mon girls," Cuthbert said. I saw a few of the kids make up their minds about him. Which made me quickly choose favorites. I noticed the kid from the other day—the hand scooper—making his way across the field, not late but lagging.

"Hey, Crothers," I said. He looked Crothers-ish.

"My name's Bennett," he half asked.

"Crothers it is." Camaraderie was built on nicknames. The kids immediately took to it and started calling him Crothers and Crothers didn't mind. He liked it. He was Crothers.

Cuthbert ran his mouth for a while and I silently took stock of our squad, discomfiting most of the kids. They'd look at me and quickly look away, but check back in a few seconds and I'd either wink or try to squirt my eyeballs out of my head without widening my eyes, a look much more uncomfortable to give than to receive, turned out.

"Coach, you're creeping me out," squonked a pimply kid with a sweaty mustache who was going to be good looking on the other side of this mess. His name was John. Just John, in a land of Coltons and Braydons and Ampersands. He smirked like those who were forever unafraid of authority only could. God, I admired those fuckers. But this kid was going to be a pain in my ass. I gave him a conciliatory wink and moved on.

Huddled up, Cuthbert introduced himself the same way he had with me. Nickname, military style: "Coach Cutty." Rank and honors, yanking himself off in staccato. Then, once again, announced his unpaid occupation in the comedic arts. Some of the dumber kids laughed at the word "comedian". Just John snickered knowingly, looked at me conspiratorially and I quickly looked away because once that's breached, the whole system can collapse. This kid was going to be tricky, but I was going to run him till he crapped tears, cried blood, begged for his Mommy or God, but the catch? I'd run every sprint with him. With them. I had been trying to figure out what my *thing* would be; one needed a thing as coach. Something insane but respectable, both on the surface and down in the meat. I could already see the bowed, sagging ceiling of the majority of these kids' talents, and I didn't have the time or resources to raise the roof. But. I could get them in dangerously good shape. We would run all over everybody. Plenty of teams would be *better* than us. Maybe most. But none, I promised myself then and there, *none* would be in better shape. Run all-over, around, under and through. Teams would marvel at our wind, at our fitness. I'd hardly seen any one of these kids catch or throw but my mind was made up! Tyrone Willingham had done this at Notre Dame and Stanford. Everything was borrowed, and Tyrone Willingham was good company. I chortled in the middle of the thought on just how much we were going to run, but, judging by Just John's pubescent whinny it sounded like I was taking the piss out of Colby.

Cuthbert wrapped it up and nodded to me; "Coach."

I smiled, looked around, got a little nervous but manageably so. I would be their R.P. McMurphy, their Ty Willingham. R.P. McWillingham.

"Fellas," I started and stopped, remembering they were twelve and thirteen and had just listened to Cuthbert's pointless life's story.

"Where you played, why you're here, goals for the season," Cuthbert said in Marine, thinking I needed his direction. He made it easy to not feel bad about putting on airs.

THE SPOILS

"Oh, I don't know. I think I'll preserve the mystery a little longer."

I let the silence hang, let them wonder if the "little longer" was twenty seconds or a few weeks.

"AAAHHH!" I grabbed a little kid and screamed, scared the shit out of him. "Let's see how bad we are."

WE WERE BAD. Just bad enough, rather, which was good since I was committed to the wind. Just John was going to be really good. I knew the type of player he'd become: A little stiff and tinny up top in his dodges, grace never gracing his future superlatives. But the kid could fly. His legs blurred up into Road Runner's motor-wheel when he got going, and he slid around at full speed like he was on skates, which in his heart he was, hockey being his first love. But I would muscle this game I ended up hating into contention with that love of his. Hockey would hate us for it, but respect us in the end.

The rest of the kids were mostly going to be only okay; I'd put a long stick in Crothers' hands, a kid named Maybelline—Abe→Abelline→Maybelline—had good genes and could be a utility guy. The late addition of a husky black kid named Kumal (I started to call him Pepper Johnson but had thought better of it) had the double-reverse, unconsciously-over-alert racist in me trying to suppress my glee. A little munchkin with braces and a young Stephen Stills haircut—I forget his name but we called him Manassas—welled up and had to bite his lip when I gave him grief for coming to practice in skate shoes. I almost picked him up, nuzzled his neck and kissed his cheek to get him to giggle his way out of it but it was the first day and I could make it up to him in other ways. There was a little fellow named Tom but we called him Burt. Burt hadn't hit puberty, yet he still looked like he would in fifty years, ordering the latkes and matzo ball soup from Nate n' Als thrice weekly. He wasn't fast, wasn't slow, would be hard on himself, someone I could trust. He'd play attack.

In lacrosse, there are three general positions (four if you include the goalie). Attack, midfield and defense. The attackmen have to stay on the offensive half of the field, the defensemen on the defensive. There must always be three offensive bodies and three defensive bodies on each side of the midfield line. Midfielders are the horses and play both sides of the ball and substitute often. There is a long-stick midfielder option to play on defense, but those are particulars and after that and a few others, that's pretty much it. It's a simple, violent game in which you can use your stick as a weapon as long as it seems like you're going for the ball, which is in the stick, which is attached to your hands and arms. This is me, beating the hell out of your arms, trying to get the ball. Open field hits are fair game as long as they're not from the back; you can line someone up and Ray Lewis them into a million little pieces. You can push on defense (again, as long as it's not from the back). The thing that would separate this sport from others, such as basketball or hockey, are groundballs. The ball is on the ground a fair amount (getting checked out of sticks, missed shots, dropped passes) and the team that is more deft at scooping the ball and maintaining possession has an advantage. Ground balls are important. Which is why I chastised Crothers before I knew him.

AFTER PRACTICE, CROTHERS, Burt and myself hung around playing catch. They were both 7th graders and would be good enough to play a lot and I knew early that I enjoyed their company more than most of the others. I needed to let the dog out, but we had a parent meeting in an hour and it didn't make sense to go all the way home just to double back. He was fine. I didn't love it, though.

"Coach," Burt asked after he cursed himself for a dropped pass.

"Yeah, Buddy?—stick on the outside, please; lemme see your right." He was left-handed.

"Oh, shit—"

"Dude."

"Sorry, sorry—about…both--"

"It's fine. What were you saying?"

"Oh, right…um…when you said that you were gonna have favorites you were kidding, right?"

I had said that. And I wasn't kidding.

"You have nothing to worry about, Pal." But he was uneasy.

Coaches are human and humans have favorites. It's innate, it's science, "attraction" not a word I wished to use in my explanation to this child as to why certain kids would play more than others. There were poles and ions, maybe, but mostly, as a coach, you want to on the field—with a few minor or glaring exceptions—the players who gave you the best chance to win.

Just John wasn't going to be my favorite kid to coach, but he was going to be the best player, and the ball would be in his hands in crunch time, unless he told me to go fuck my Mother in front of a large crowd and even then, it wouldn't be a no-brainer. Burt and Crothers—they'd be my favorites in a different way and would play because they tried, they didn't suck, and they made me laugh. Kumal would play because of his linebacker thickness but also because of Reparations. The X factor, though, or deciding factor, rather: if any of these kids' parents happened to be powerful Hollywood folk—hell, even a location scout or a grip—then none of the above matters and that's a whole different way to field a team, a whole other way of life. But, you know: *kinda* similar.

SOMEHOW I WAS late to the parents' meeting even though I was already there. Cuthbert and Keri—that's what the athletic director's name ended up being—leaned on the front of the desk of the teacher whose classroom we were in. Cuthbert said something to her and laughed, and she laughed because she was being courteous or she actually enjoyed the company of this chum bucket of useless dicks. Either way, it didn't bode well for me. I futzed around with my phone so they could finish their stale jousting. I had nobody to text and no news to read so I took in the room from my periphery. It felt like I was in the VIP lounge in the USS Enterprise. The desk chairs were hard, yes, but the seats and back boards were almost suspended, two pieces of half or three-quarter inch birch plywood sandwiching halved tennis balls. Some seats rested on only one (halved) ball. Probably to encourage balance, ergonomically? I was thinking out of my ass.

All of the parents seemed to understand the seats. My guess was that a student, some lithe, hyper-dimensional tennis player, had fashioned them as some sort of a senior project. And then, go figure, the fortunate get lucky or maybe you just have to do one good thing before you start chasing sips for a living. Somebody had to figure out what to do with all those old tennis balls. This young inventor was killing me. The poise! The *conviction* he or she awoke with every morning at such an age. Twice their age and I had yet to have an original thought let alone *invent* something. You can't be *ingenious* if you wake every day serving yourself second-guesses and grief before you've even looked in the mirror. A cautious, cautionary tale is all I was, all I'd ever be, and maybe that was my legacy—that's what I could give these kids, if I even made it that far. I needed to not drink for a couple days. Or drink harder, everyday, forever.

"Bro. You're creeping her out." Cuthbert snapped me out of my trance, his lone contribution. I looked at who I was looking at and quickly looked away and looked back and in all that glance darting my palms had gone clammy and my phone squirted out of my hand like a greased turnip. It was a woman I'd been looking at and she looked Croatian, although I didn't know what that looked like. She looked like she'd recently swum in the Aegean. Plus, I looked at everybody, always! I was sick of explaining myself. I wasn't creeping her out. This was a woman who was professionally creeped out. It was clearly what she did. My lolling in space wasn't going to move the needle. As the other Dads continued to file in, they all either registered her in creep or said a genial hello, made brief small talk in an overblown cover-up.

Those were the creeps. I was just a neurotic waste, sweating his way through the scenes.

"Hey guys—I have to run but I wanna introduce you to Coach Cutty here. And if you could fill these out by the weekend," Keri held up a stack of papers which she set down on a desk in the front row. "That'd be great. So...here's Coach Cutty!" She got a light courtesy laugh from the room, for existing I guess, smiled and walked out. She paused slightly, a minor hitch in her step as she passed me, clearly thinking: "shit...oh, well" in regards to my forgotten intro. Thank God Cuthbert was such a stain. What a blessed foil. Even at my absolute worst I could muster more charm than that bungled conception. Miracle of Life. What a fucking disaster.

Not seven seconds in had Cuthbert, again, mentioned that he was a comedian. I tried to back out at the last second but I let go a "HAHAhaaa..." The Croatian laughed and muzzled her mouth with her hand. Clearly, she was not ESL.

Cuthbert ignored me and barked on about himself and I tried to figure out what I was going to say. The ever-crept upon woman caught me mouthing potential openers to myself like Twelve Monkeys. I shrugged, smiled. She couldn'tve been much older than me, somewhere between twenty and forty? Was she one of the boys' older sisters? *Was* I a creep? Maybe she was an au pair. It was fine, that didn't matter because "Cutty" had given me my opener.

"...played four years at Delaware...worked in New York for a few years and came out here to get into the comedy scene." Here he put hands together, one fist in the palm of his other hand like some sort of motivational cross-fit speaker. "Lacrosse has always been a constant for me—gotten me through some rough times," followed by some drivel about wanting to pass that down to the youth, yadayadayada. "Now I'm gonna pass the mic over to Coach," and he introduced me by my first name, which I hate. So I introduced myself as "Coach", followed by my last name—Wilson—as any respectable coach has ever done.

"Before I get into anything about me," I began, shakily. "I just wanna be clear here: Colby played *club*."

I got a guffaw from someone, a Dad who understood, but let me be clear *here*: In between practice and the meeting I had done some digging. A friend of a buddy of mine had played at Delaware—*suffered* at Delaware, rather—and, by the hair of my chinnie-chin-chin, the better to see you with my pretty, turns out: Cuthbert played *Fall*-ball his *fresh*man year and had either quit or gotten cut by Spring and then played club ball for who cares, whatever. Fine and respectable either way: You tried and failed OR you realized you weren't a sad and angry masochist, bailed, played club, had some smiles. And good for you! He probably had a great college experience. But mother*fucker*, do NOT go around posturing that you've been through the shit. That you've heard a soul break. That you, too, have seen even the most abhorrently homophobic of your teammates jump in on the hypothetical barter regarding the dicks they'd put in their mouths just to not have to go to practice this one godforsaken time. That you, too, had had a strength and conditioning coach who was a legitimate award season villain, fired from the Wisconsin Badger football program because he was too hard-core, too *mean*. Plus the hangovers, the tears, the blood pissed, the blood shed, the injuries you could *probably* play through, fighting for playing time, dreading practice so deeply, so deeply consumed with that dread that nothing, not one thing, could ever get learned in the classes which, in an alternate reality you maybe would have enjoyed taking, but you don't know what "enjoy" means anymore; "relax" or "enjoy" are just words you repeat in the anxious space between the pride-eviscerating time-pockets known as "practice". Fundamentals turn to stone; you dissolve and all you hear is the fizzle of fear and oops! forgot how to *catch the ball* and any love for the game is just a campfire tale you try to muster for the kids; a time of promise before the plague. Before the world burned. Nobody *wanted* it. But we did it, saw it through, benefitted net zero, the only consolation prize being that *We* did it and *you* did not. And that is still quite the Necco Wafer of a prize because most people will say, confused: "But I only asked if you played little league"—which is true, it was a stretch, but look how long we were in Afghanistan. "Ha-ha" we try to laugh as we sip our pints of irrelevance, evaporating before it even hits our lips until finally, thank Johnny Christmas, some asshole claims to have been there.

"Not that there's anything wrong with club! I wish I had gone the club route!"

I could feel select parents scanning the kid-friendly credentials of my aura.

I continued: "I played four years of division one lacrosse at a mediocre school in a mediocre conference and it was *awful* and taught me to think very little of myself and that is why, at thirty-one-years-old, I'm coaching your middle school kids."

The Au Pair liked that one, too, but I was losing the rest of the crowd.

"But, really: I wouldn't change a thing. Suffering…is…the only way to dig the fruits." My pitch was wilting. "It is my privilege to coach your sons. They're gonna learn a lot and we're gonna have fun." Good enough.

Cuthbert wanted the fuck out of there and who could blame him? What a dick I was! But he did it to himself.

"Coach Cuthbert," I went forth, trying to fix the hole, Dear Liza, "has your sons' best interests at heart." Cuthbert nodded, agreeing. "That's in no small part because he played club—he's still got love for the game." Dear, Henry. "The club effect," I punctuated. How I had ever had a friend is beyond me.

"He will get them to love the game, and I'll make sure they're tired when they come home." That sounded predatorial. I flipped it back at them: "One last thing. Cleats are mandatory. A few kids were out there practicing in skate shoes and I almost went postal. You guys," I looked around, gestured outside, around the haloed grounds of wealth, this fortress of opulence, "can afford cleats. Get some cleats."

I put a fist in the air in unity and adjournment. Or something. Cuthbert brushed past me, grumbling a muffled threat, lite-if-inappropriate-but-understandable contact as he went to hob-knob with the Dads.

"Dig the fruits or *dig* the fruits," asked a voice, coming from a Dude.

"*Dig*," I said. It was he who guffawed, this man, this Dad who was somewhere in his later forties. Maybe fifty. He was at that point where he was transitioning into total comfort, in dress and body. One foot in. He wore Rod Laver's that flirted with filthy, all four end-laces knotted individually for easy on, easy off relief. His khakis were just there, old and not not baggy—if he had to hit some tennis balls or throw the football around in them, he could. Not ideal, but he could. That was how he seemed to wear himself: Not ideal, but he could. His face once had angles, a strict jawline. The juicy reds hadn't caught up with him per se, but they tailed him from a few hundred yards back. His hair was in a good zone, but it frayed and was matted in parts uncared for and unknown to him. A crew-neck Champion sweatshirt with not yet enough coffee stains on it to banish from public consumption. He had blue eyes and if not for the full head of hair I would have thought I was looking at the Ghost of Christmas Future.

"Figured," he said, but he hadn't yet looked at me directly, was just scanning the room like he was acting distracted in order to hand me the NOC list.

"Seconds of Pleasure or Seconds of Pleasure?" I asked, without conviction. I was getting greedy, pushing the envelope like this.

He snapped his attention on me, eyes boring so hard it made my eyes ache.

"...*about his hopes and ambitions, wasted through the years*," he sang, softly.

"...*the pain will be written on ev'ry page in tears*," I whisper-sang back.

We stood there, dubious but assured before he winked at me and left.

IN THE PARKING lot, I straddled my bike, scrolling through my iPod to find that record. I had to get home. I'd been gone since one and it was six-thirty. The dog was fine. I still didn't like it.

"Coach…"

I turned around to find the Croat, the Au Pair. Something skipped. My vision chattered like a short-wired ecstasy blip, like Max Headroom.

"You can call me Ryan," I said as if I were deaf and had just had a root canal. She could, though, call me that, as it was my name. I just hated saying it out loud. My R's escaped me as a kid, and I was 99.5% in the clear. But "garlic" and my own name made me want to jump out the window. That's me.

"What kind of cleats should we buy?" She looked at me both year abroad curious and like she had my number, front to back. Like she'd seen it all but only just broke through the plasma.

"You have a kid on the team?" I had to know. My age gauge was fritzy.

"Step-kid."

"Far out," I said, not knowing what this new knowledge made me feel. "Football cleats. I like a low-top but that's just me. Whatever makes your calves look their best."

"Far out," she said, smiling like she was both sharing in the groove and giving me shit.

"Who's your…step-kid."

"John."

"With the…" I wrinkled my nose in an impression that could have been anybody, but was also spot on.

"That's the one."

"He's a good athlete."

"Low-top football cleats." She smiled and spun on a heel, changing my seasons.

Just John had brand spankin' new cleats.

THERE WAS STILL a feint red-orange ember glow over the ocean when I got home. It made the rest of the sky run a spectrum, lavender-to-deep-blue, making outer space look more inviting. So Sam and I went for a run.

Late-dusk runs on the Pacific were liars, though, and that was why I was a junkie. As things turned to night and the Ferris Wheel on the Santa Monica pier lit up in the Malibu foreground, there was so much false possibility that you could burn through a pair of Nike Vomeros in a month. Misappropriated hope and confidence in rabid overdrive with each song on a curated Kings of Leon-heavy playlist shuffle. The cream rose and that email is coming and the dialogue is *that good* and people still care and that credit card debt and those back taxes are one lucky read away from this all being the adorable struggle, the adorable *past*.

But that's just the -tonins, baby. And it was always the present. And that's why I ran.

The thing that had screwed me was what I had thought, not a few years earlier, to be the best thing that had happened to me. I had optioned a script. Meaning somebody had read something that I had written and wanted exclusive rights and a set amount of time to make that script—my script—into a motion picture. I optioned a script. I optioned a script for no money, but still: my words were wanted! It was a young guy and the optioner worked for the production company that had produced *Blue Valentine* and holy shit! And, I know—when I say "no money", you think "okay, so, like, ten grand, right?" Wrong. No money. Rather, I think it was a dollar because there needed to be a monetary transaction, a currency exchange to pair with the chicken scrawled loose-leaf contract. If I could do it all over I would have written the contract on cardstock myself because I write in all caps. Instead I had this third-grade caliber squibble thumbtacked to my corkboard reminding me twice daily of what a loser I was. But it was a double edged sword, or a sword and a spoon and a set of razor blades and some comfortable voluntary restraints because I had made a deal with myself that if nothing happened, if I didn't sell anything by the time thirty years ran up behind me and whacked me on the back of the head with an Easton, it was time to Kenny Rogers right the fuck out of L.A. Thirty came quicker than I had imagined it would, as it does, and both contracts had expired: they didn't make the movie and I hadn't sold shit. Yet still. I used that Playskool contract as a means to option myself another few downs in this toolbox town. One American Dollar. That's what I was worth. That's how much I needed to not give up. It was all so fucking adorable.

The running kept me stupid, kept me a believer, if only for five or six miles, four or five times a week. There is such a thing as the "runner's high" and it is just that, a high. And most highs do what? Make you (erroneously) think things aren't as bad as they are. That's not all true, but the good ones do, the good highs, the ones that kill you, and on every one of those runs, I believed. I believed that something good was going to happen. Because I ran hard. And I wrote hard. Or hard adjacent. Or just shy of hard. This runner's high made me believe I was something that I wasn't: Due.

Now, if the erroneous math on this translated, if I used my deluded tactic for sticking around Los Angeles with these kids I was coaching; if I ran these kids into the vicinity of my deception, of my stupidity, they, too, would believe that they could do what they couldn't: Win.

FIVE

Cuthbert couldn't make practice on Friday because he had to do an open mic at the Dave & Buster's in Irvine and I was nothing if not overbearingly supportive. There was perhaps a mild rift in the coaching staff. But there was a version of it—my version—where he benefitted from my publicly club-shaming him the week prior. I was a lot nicer to him now than if I had bit my tongue, swallowed the castigation. And yes, he was all flawed molecules that were rejected for millions of years until finally the appropriator said "whatever—I don't give a shit" and let them weld themselves into a male embryo. I didn't want him to like me but I also didn't want to fucker the whole season just because I couldn't help myself. So I let him have the offense most of the time even though he over complicated things[1], and I took the defense to procure the grit, bending the ears of the offense during fundamentals, scrimmages.

Today was mine, though. And while the majority of the kids preferred me to Cuthbert, they'd seen glimmers of my unhingedness, sensed that, whatever I truly was, I diluted it

---

1) *Team Sports: Beat your man, draw the double, pass. If the double doesn't come, shoot.*

for public consumption. Without a buffer, without a grounded presence—even if it was Cuthbert's—the boys were nervy. We huddled up and Just John was the only one with the stones to look directly at me.

"Where's Cutty?" he sniggered.

"Coach...Cutty," I corrected, half a reprimand, wincing at having to say the C-word.

I said no more, just looked around, trying to get someone to crack. I bore a hole in Burt's averted eyes and he looked at me and grinned, whispered a bashful "come on," went rosy and looked away. I wanted him to remember me in twenty years.

Manassas jitterbugged like a crackhead. He blurted out: "Coach whatta you think we're gonna do today?" and bonked himself on the head for blurting. The other guys groaned at him for what he bonked himself for: the far off chance that he reminded me about my own running fetish. It was cute.

"We're gonna practice, Manassas."

We eased into it. Full field passing, a star drill, three-man weave. I limbered everyone up with some light-hearted chiding. Walked around giving positive pointers, waxed about the NBA, the previous night's games. Their stick skills hadn't gotten better, as it was still the first week. But still. It'd been almost a week. And even if they had improved drastically in that short amount of time, what I was about to do was what I was always going to do in every variation, iteration or rewrite of that day's practice, their progress notwithstanding. But they still sucked. So after a half-hour of good-natured stick work, I brought them in.

"You can take off your gear." They understood but didn't

understand. Most of them tried to calculate how long the past thirty minutes had actually been. Those who knew, walked slack shouldered over to the bench, where they whispered to each other as they took off their pads.

"From here on out make sure you pack running shoes." The ominous was too fun.

"Why?" Squeaked Manassas followed by a regretful wince, admonishing groans chorused.

"Because," I took a weary breath for the mezzanine. "We practice four days a week. For an hour and a half, hour forty-five if we hustle out here after the bell. Once we start playing games, we practice three, sometimes only two days a week. Our first game is in two weeks, right?" It was time to start asking questions. "And we've had three practices this week, correct? You had Wednesday off, am I wrong?" They warily agreed that I was not.

"So I have an hour and a half a few days a week to get a.) your guys' sticks better, b.) your brains better, c.) your bodies better. It's the rule of threes and you gotta pick two." I think it was two different ideas I married, but I was rolling. "b.) is a given because I've lived longer. And a.) is on you because I'm not gonna come out here and play catch for an hour and a half. That's not fun for me. We've had four practices, a day off and your sticks are as bad as they were on day one. Did anybody touch their sticks on the day off?" Everybody looked to everyone else. Just John raised his hand.

"I appreciate the honesty. And, listen: we're gonna run regardless. So let's just package that into our, you know, collective psyche. But I'm not just gonna come out here every day and play catch with you chuckleheads because I'm not in the business of babysitting. You guys have to get here," I measured an arbitrary height, a goal in space, "before we do...anything."

"But isn't it, like, your job to teach us, like, how to play?" said a spindly kid with braces and expensive snacks. His name was Quinn and he was certainly going to file a complaint with his parents this evening.

"Yes! Thank you, Innie." Short for Inuit → Eskimo, Quinn. "It is my job to teach you how to PLAY. Not how to catch and throw. Just John—what'd you do on your day off?"

He looked around, wondering if his answering would encroach on ass-kissing.

"Took some shots...played wall ball."

"Wall ball! Just John is now our Captain." Nobody bristled at this. And it was a smart move on my part. He was a little peckerhead but he worked hard and kids listened to him. By muscling him into a leadership role, I could head his inevitable insubordination off at the pass. Just John, my pubescent marionette.

"At lunch, recess, show-and-tell, nap-time, snack-time, free-time, all-time: Wall Time." I nodded at Just John, he nodded back. "At home, before you turn on your consoles, before you start whuppin' on innocent old ladies in Downtown Los Angeles—actually new rule: I don't want you playing that game. *Twisted Metal* or *Jimmy's Got a Gun*—whatever it's called. Only sports games." Was I a tyrant? Perhaps. But I also didn't want them virtually beating on virtual geriatrics with virtual lead pipes. "Two hundred reps each side."

"What if we don't have a wall?"

"Find one."

I walked away, grabbed a stack of cones and started arranging them around the perimeter of the field.

"Playing catch," I yelled as I threw down cones, "is not what I am here to do. I need more. I am what they call a 'Masochist'."

"Gross!" Just John bleated. I called him over.

"Don't shoot yourself in the dick right out of the gates, pal."

"What?" He was the kind of kid you could judiciously swear in front of. It grabbed his attention.

"Masochism: pleasure from pain." Give or take.

"Oh. I thought it was, like—"

"Well don't think like!" Although he wasn't wrong. We both weren't.

"Okay." I nodded for him to correct himself. He turned back to the team, seeing more clearly his role. "Sorry, Dudes, not gross!" He yelled out, jogging back over to the fellas. "Pleasure from pain or some shit: it's gonna suck."

"Language, Just!"

"Sorry Coach!"

"I enjoy suffering!" I yelled, a confessional. "I'm not PROUD of it! But it's what's on the other side of suffer. *That's* the point. Without the bitter the sweet ain't as sweet." I circled back toward them, cones set. I was feeling it and embraced whatever "it" was without a drip of cynicism, and I let myself feel, for the first time in a long while, that I was right where I was supposed to be. My Little Gentlemen were petrified. The consideration of quit hung muggily in the air.

"You can't have the funny without the sad, My Mens."

I broke us up into three groups. Two groups on one sideline at midfield, one group opposite. The first group would run around the perimeter of half the field, the first guy there would tag the other group and they would take off, tag the third group that waited where the first group had started. And we would run and wait and repeat like that untill somebody cried but keep going until the parents showed up. I didn't want to get into anything too complex, too agility or acuity focused. Just mettle testers till the sun went black. Gassers till somebody crapped.

I took the first group, put Just John in the second, and Beaker, our goalie, in the third. Beaker volunteered to play goalie because he was crazier than a shithouse rat. And if you're going to volunteer to have limestone-hard rubber balls hurled at you a hundred times a day, a lotta crazy goes a long way. He was on an array of spectrums and would make a billion dollars someday, reconfiguring and rejiggering the way future generations would digest media. He had no chin (hence, Beaker) but he had cross-country legs, which is why I placed him in the third group. Because the real bitch of these two hundred yard gassers was this: the fastest guy is tagging the next group. And if you're the last guy in your group, your rest time gets shorter and shorter, that lead dog bearing down on you, a little bit closer each time.

"We're gonna crap tears! We're gonna cry blood!" I preached like a maniac as we rounded our third or fourth or fifth sprint. "But we crap together, we cry together! Whatta we doin', Just?!?" I yelled ahead of me before I slapped his hand to *Go*.

"Crappin'!"

"Whatta we doin', Kumal?!?"

"Cryin'!"

It was stupid but it was fun. It wasn't fun for them but they'd remember it and laugh. Around and around we ran, screaming like Comanche's until the screaming tanks ran dry and all they had was each other. I think Maybelline said a Hail Mary. Burt said he couldn't see and Kumal threw him up and over his shoulder like a wounded soldier and got him to the next leg. We went around again. This was real live empathy. One more late-night drink at the kitchen table: The Bones. And again. Beaker started squealing like a stuck pig in tongues. Crothers' legs couldn't keep up with his body and then vice versa and he was Truckin'. We went around again. We were going to be a real team.

And again.

Manassas barfed and fell over. I looked up and saw a rack of parents in their Audi's and Beemers and Benzes. It was time to bring it in.

THE BOYS WANDERED in from the perimeter of the field, ten thousand yard stares like they'd just got out of Watkins Glen or the last night of Lemonwheel. Shoes missing, shirts half on or wrapped around their heads in do-rag form. I was pretty wiped. They were *twisted*.

"Good work," I said, choking on some water trying not to laugh. I didn't want to laugh at them. I now loved them.

Effusive end of practice speeches are bush league. Everyone's too tired. You lose what you just gained. Those rants were for the Cuthberts of the world. Practice was done and the last thing they or anybody wants to hear is a rambling off-the-cuff gush from the self-absorbed tramp who just made them sprint five miles.

I told them to find a wall. We agreed on our cheer, our collective mantra through the trying afternoon.

"Through the darkness…" I said.

And they yelled as best they could: "To the light!"

IF I WASN'T bipolar I was well within spitting distance of it. Or at least it's atmosphere. The fun and the purpose I had found not twenty minutes ago now seemed like a joke. *So, what? You're gonna be a middle school lacrosse coach when you grow up?* He was right. I was right. And all the people who kept saying "you're so young—you've got time!" were wrong. Yesterday, I was twenty. A week before that, ten.

Before I could slink into the night's funk, my phone buzzed, a text:

you know the lost & found

It was a question, and I did. I replied:

Chili-dog night.

I DIDN'T NEED to know who it was because I knew I could trust anyone who dug the Lost & Found. It was my favorite bar in Los Angeles. A seedy but not completely gross hole-in-the-wall in a mini strip-mall on National & Barrington, a part of town that had no idea what it was. Not Santa Monica. Kinda Mar Vista? You could call it Palms but that never felt like an actual neighborhood, just a square mile of half-shitty Spanish-ish apartment buildings kind of near the 405/I-10 nexus. It was nowhere in a city with a revolving soul door and that was what gave the Lost & Found its non-identity. It didn't have that old Hollywood charm of Chez Jay or Dan Tana's, nor the switchblade patrons of the Drawing Room. Nobody new was coming into that dump, which is why it was so lovely. There were no troupes of young, industry hungry ass-baskets crowding the place, visiting with ironical novelty. Nestled in between a New York Bagel and a Chase Bank, it opened sad and early and had loyal clientele. It had a long bar with stiff, cheap drinks and a shitty new jukebox where you could pay money to hear anything you wanted. Toni, the bartender, was somewhere between forty-two and a ninety-two and she liked me and always insisted that I help myself to another chili dog when she could tell the month was probably running tight. Another chili dog at the Lost & Found probably wasn't going to correct my course, but she was a doll for caring.

yahtzee came the next text, followed by: 7

I wrote *O'tay.* and pressed send before I could delete it. I had heard that the Little Rascals were all treated well and had had a ball on set. Still, I wasn't really in any position to throw Buckwheat's signature expression around. Too late.

I got a thumbs down emoji.

THE LOST & FOUND was just close enough to justify biking. If I was sipping, anything 3.5-4 miles and under was biking territory. I didn't want to drive because a DUI would ruin me. I had to reserve my drunk driving fortune for those rare if not regular one-eyed return trips from the East Side. It was in the early days of Über and I was still afraid to attach any of my cards to anything. The bike ride wasn't safe but I tended to boogie when my faculty, the employees of my dwindling constitution, started lining up to punch the clock. I had hurt my shoulder something awful once, but let myself off the hook because the crash was so egregiously stupid that it would have been unfair to drunken pedalers the world over to punish myself. I ran into a building.

I locked my bike around the post of a street sign and removed my lights. Should I have asked who it was that I was meeting? On the ride over I thought it was exciting, harking back to a time of spontaneity and answering machines, when you would just see people, friends, out in the world, at a place. This didn't apply at all, I realized—I was just thinking these thoughts, distracting myself with inane gibberish because I was giddy with believing that it was not *definitely not* the Croat inside. She seemed more Soho House, less Buck Hunter, but that's the beauty of not knowing.

I pushed through the swinging screen door into the bar and there sat the Dad who sang the Rockpile song—it was Crothers' Dad—in a booth with his attention on the Laker game. His eyes flitted over to me and he put a finger to his lips, shushing. I didn't know what that meant. But he was a close runner-up.

I went through the formalities, quickly caught up with Toni and ordered a tequila-soda-splash-of-grapefruit with a Heineken back. Crother's Father—Alex was his name—had his own rig, declined my offer to refresh. Toni insisted I help myself to the chili dogs.

"Smart," Alex said after I told him what I was drinking after he asked me. I didn't know what to say so I asked him if he was gonna get a chili dog.

"Outlook good," he said, like Burt Reynolds, still looking at the television. "I like to reverse base with a chili dog, though. Booze on the bottom, chili dog…" He indicated the sedimentary layers of our stomachs. "I don't want to give it a false sense of…"

I understood.

"I understand."

"You see a CHILI DOG…" he trailed off, laughing to himself, eyes on the game. I understood that, too.

There was a long silence. Kobe clanged one off the rim, a million hands in his face.

"Like Scat-Man?" Alex asked, wondering the etymology of his son's nickname.

"I think so," I said, as it was mostly that. He nodded and sipped what I gathered to be his stamp of approval.

I HAD GONE down the roster and looked up every kid's parents to see if any of this could be worth it. It didn't make me feel skanky. Not terribly skanky, at least. I was living in Weasel City and something had to give. Burt's Mom was a big-time entertainment lawyer, had Sandler and Charlize Theron as clients. Maybelline's uncle was a DP. He shot a few Alexander Payne flicks. A kid named Delta or Isthmus or something, his old man had been first AD on "Jarhead" but hadn't really done anything since. Isthmus' mom had a pretty big-time apothecary line—I think it fell under the apothecary umbrella. Homeo-what-have-you's. Lotions, butters, balms, dream catchers. There were other parents in real estate, a dentist, a husband-wife team who designed roller coasters. That one didn't seem real. I needed to believe the Germans or Japanese exclusively designed roller coasters or this whole thing was sure to collapse. And a married couple? Please.

My background checks yielded two and a half notable players, one of which happened to be the wife of the guy I was going to use alcohol to soak up a chili dog with. Marina Reese, founder and executive at Management Reese, husband of Alex Reese, Cape Codder enthusiast. Manager to the likes of many funny fuckers, young and old. Kristen Wiig, Bill Hader, Jim Rash, Shirley Temple. She could change my life. But her husband, my best friend, was also a writer and his last acknowledgeable credits were a co-write on an episode from season four of *Scrubs* and a "story by" credit on a strange indie from 1999 called "Ramona's Monkey". The movie was pretty bad but this guy was great so the plot thickened. Season four of *Scrubs* was in 2005. That's ten years. Was it a decade of misses? A dusty pile of pilots and features and specs and adaptations that never found their way? That was my nightmare. Maybe he just quit to protect himself, insulate his ego from this village of rejection. Or was his shit just stale? He couldn't take what he had, what he *was*—which was strange and terrific, sad and angry and quiet, hilarious—and put it on the page. That's how it was for most. Why should he be an exception? OR, equally probably, he cheated on his wife and she held the testicles of his career in a pickling jar with no brine. Dusty now. In the basement. Desiccated. Open the jar and the contents crumble, pfft. As usual, all of my theories had merit.

"God, shut the fuck up," was what he would later tell me. "I just got nothin' to say." I was young enough to not believe him.

As for the second notable player I found in my gumshoeing… lo and behold, as I live and breathe, by Jove-go-fuck-my-ass, none-other-than…The Croat's Husband. Turns out the Croat didn't have just any husband. No. Turns out the Croat wasn't Croatian at all and she was married to the guy who was, if not solely, then at the very least dually responsible for my illogical dream of writing for the screen. My Hero, My Liar, My Lama: Buck Tourney.

Buck Tourney created a show called *The Yips*, which aired its pilot episode in the summer of 2005. *The Yips* was about an NFL prospect who, well, gets the Yips[2]. But it's about more than that. The kid who gets the Yips—quarterback Gill Wheatley—has an astounding, if highly unlikely fall from grace. In just forty-seven minutes of flawless television, The Kid goes from being a projected late first-round pick to working as a stonemason in his hometown for his Old Man. One bad throw at the combine after a coach mutters something about his accuracy and his brain just goes AWOL. Dead ducks left and right as he's hastily diagnosed by all the NFL scouts and coaches as having weak football temerity. A scout tell him to take five, get some water, some lunch. He does,

---

2) *The Yips are a cosmo-synapse glitch. Chuck Knoblauch perhaps the most famous poster boy for the syndrome. Also known as the Steve Sax Syndrome. A routine throw from second to first, something as vanilla to him as an easy overhead is for Federer, suddenly and inexplicably…is abducted from their muscle memory. Happens to golfers on putts, receivers and tight ends on easy catches, a chef flipping an omelet. The brain is your enemy. Never let your guard down. Or never put it up. There: you now have the Yips.*

and in quite possibly my favorite five minutes of television, he has a conversation with himself in the locker room while trying to eat a turkey sandwich, trying so hard not to cry, but he knows it's fucked. It's like when Rudy reads his acceptance letter but the opposite. Rudy Ruettiger is sputtering joy, Wheatley failure, in gut-wrenching sandwich specks. If it wasn't so perfect, it'd be gross. If it wasn't so heart-breaking, there'd be too much sandwich on the mirror. But it works. Because you know, even as you hold out hope: *there's no coming back*. Wheatley bullies himself back out on the field and throws one, two, three—six more heated warblers and just. Fucking. Cries. Broken beyond repair. And then you have an ensuing season of what everybody of any age, any color, all the sexes and LGTBQs can relate to: life didn't quite turn out how you thought it would. Your stupid brain got in the way. And that was the arrival—that bathroom crying scene with a mouthful of Boar's head on a Kaiser roll—of Amory Wells, America's Dreamheart, and, ultimately, yes: Bruce Wayne, the Batman.

That first season aired the summer after I graduated from college. I had read the Times' review of the pilot the morning it was to air and the critic was so deeply awed and in love with the show that I canceled my plans of drinking ten beers in some soggy bar corner and made sure I was home to watch it. This was before Tivo, see. That show rewired my motherboard. My Wednesday nights were booked solid until the third and final season FX changed it to Tuesday nights. I used to joke that I liked that show more than I liked my friends. It's criminal that it was canceled after three seasons, but it's better that way: if you love something, let them cancel it and be indignant about it forever and look down upon those who didn't watch it in real time. Because I was Gill Wheatley. And I'm guessing so was everyone who watched the pilot on that late summer's eve and then raced home to identify with him and his strikes and gutters every Wednesday and eventually Tuesday night for the next three seasons. I love that show. And whatever I wrote, regardless of the content, that show was how I wanted it to feel. That's what I reached for. And now I was coaching its creator's Son and gullibly evening-dreaming about his Wife.

Buck Tourney went on to direct blockbuster action flicks that flopped, smaller war films that killed, produced and mentored some slick up-and-comers, directed another few two-hundred million dollar mounds that burned in the driveway. He never quite found that rough and tender pocket in which *The Yips* lived (yes, sure: said pocket can be attributed to show-runner and head writer Jason Katims, but Tourney had the foresight of compassion to hire him). Despite his duds, he was granted asylum from director's jail as a select slew of white guys who came up in the late 90's and early Aughts were—the Favreau's, Todd Phillips', Guy Richie's of the world. Not great examples as those guys have made a lot of people a LOT of money but still, there are examples. Guys who got an all-access, carte blanche, un-expire-able Hollywood pass to fuck up and not be fucked for it. The likes of which passes exist no more. In 2014, though, Tourney had the market cornered on dude's Dude entertainment. The Last Dude. He had a field-turf field on his Palisades spread and hosted an extremely VIP touch football game every Sunday morning during football season. Walhberg, Timberlake, the Rock. Jamie Foxx. Pink. I think Master P showed up. Tourney also owned a few boxing clubs around town. Had heavy shares in UFC, which gave me queasy pause. He sounded like an asshole.

"Ah, he's a fuckin' asshole," Alex griped as he spooned Hormel onto his Ball Park.

"That sucks."

"I bet he puts ketchup on his hot dog."

"That's...no." This I could not abide. The Man may have been a cocksucker and done some bawdy shit in his ascent, but this allegation was out of bounds. The Man gave me *The Yips*, for fuckssake.

"Exactly: gave YOU the Yips. You don't need to look through the glass onion on that one."

"I don't believe in the Yips," I said, whereas it was all I believed in. The Yips was my religion. I was a walking Yip. Alex gave me a spooked, patronizing look and walked back to our booth.

"I mean the life Yips," I corrected what needn't be corrected.

The Lost & Found had mismatched office chairs at the lower tables, which I loved. The barstools for the most part matched. The stuffing was coming out of the booths, half-assedly sealed up with black gaff and it made me wonder why I reveled in the mire. This was a problem. Perhaps maybe the bar needed to be set higher than my current wish list:

<u>really build out record collection</u>
<u>go to dinner and not think twice about it</u>
~~vacation?~~

I wanted the big things but glorified the chili dog. I longed for and let myself secretly believe in a small apartment in Carrol Gardens, a bungalow in Venice and a lake house in Vermont. But I got mad at my favorite bands for licensing their songs to banks or Volkswagon. I'd never borrowed money from anyone but couldn't remember a month where I wasn't in tears on the 22nd, transferring monies and scrabbling for gigs just to not go under on the 1st. It wasn't all a sham and even if it was, this artificial veracity I was clinging to like a binkie was the shammiest of them all! I wanted to live in Rome or Paris—write a couple scripts, one for me to direct, two for them to fuck up—and I'd never been to either city much less directed a movie! It wasn't this town that was killing me it was me that was killing me. I was brainwashing myself into thinking it possible, likely even, all the while hobbling attainable dreams, dragging around a fifty-pound iron ball of manufactured authenticity. And there it was again: "attainable dreams". Let it go. Get a job. Start your life.

"I actually sold a pilot laaasst—no, two years ago."

"What?"

"I don't understand—are you asking for advice?" Alex seemed to be slightly put out, although I think that was his default. I didn't know what I had said. I hoped it wasn't what I'd been thinking.

"I am." I was. "Wait. If you don't mind my asking…"

"I don't give a shit. I made, like one-fifty. Before taxes. AND they shot the thing, it just didn't get picked up. Whatever." He took a clean bite of his chili dog.

The casual "one-fifty" circuitously reverberated in my head like a Bon Iver coda. I was back to where I'd been. The dreaded hope.

"But that was one unsung win in ten years. I mean, it got so awful I was nice about it. Your wife becomes a gangster and you have no choice but to be Dad of the Decade because if you fuck that up they'll put your head on a pike."

"Who's they?"

He gestured his cranberry-vodka to the ghosts or nothing, didn't matter. I frantically did the math and if this dude was forty-eight, Crothers' sister was two years older, probably fifteen? So that meant Alex had had her when he was thirty-three? Actualized her at some point in his thirty-second year? I loathed the numbers, the clock made me so sad, so scared, so angry. They never put enough ice in my drinks at the Lost & Found.

SIX

"CITY OF ANGELS, GRUNTS!"

It was a beautiful day, which was what I assumed Cuthbert was trying to get them to appreciate. I was distracted. Across the parking lot was the track, inside it the football field where the High School lacrosse team practiced. They sucked and were poorly coached. I wasn't watching them. Beyond that was another practice field—Jack Nicholson's dusty sperm boy went to school here; there were a lot of fields, embarrassment of riches, plenty of everything. On that field were two kids—a black kid and a white kid—running wind-sprints, parachutes strapped to their waists. An older dude, who I gathered to be the football coach, as he had the affected, no-nonsense look of a real asshole, monitored their workout. I grabbed Just John by the elbow.

"Ow, Dude."

"Who are those kids?" I hissed at him. Cuthbert prattled on about his "inverted offense," which was fine because it didn't matter; we still couldn't catch and throw.

"Dude, that's Varsity."

"No, knucklehead," I twisted his facemask toward the two parachutes.

"Oh, Dude—that's Jake and DeMarcus."

"Stop calling me Dude," I said. "What grade?" They were sturdy boys, but still (hopefully) 8th grade small.

"Eighth. But, Duu—Coach: McMillan's got 'em on a leash. I've tried."

I nodded for him to pay attention to what he needn't retain and I plotted my recruit.

"Coach, you wanna run 'em?" Cuthbert asked, which was nice. I told him to let them scrimmage for the last twenty and I stalked across the lot. Truth was, I didn't like running when Cuthbert was there. My oath to run every sprint with the team was sullied because Cuthbert would line up with us and suck the crazy right out of me. I didn't want him getting in great shape; I loved looking down on his paunch. It wasn't him hamstringing the operation, it was me. The only thing that could give us a fighting chance, my scripture, the x-factor that I brought to the table was being forsaken because my priorities and intentions were completely misaligned. I was tanking our only hope because I didn't want this innocuous ass-monkey to look good naked. It was so weak. But I was already redeeming myself with my recruiting skills.

DEMARCUS LONG COMMUTED every school morning from the Westmont neighborhood of South Los Angeles to the Brentwood School, back again in the afternoon. It was twenty miles, could take hours. There were better football schools to choose from: Chaminade, Oaks Christian, Sierra Canyon. But they got you further and further out into the Valley and unless those schools paid for a nearby midweek apartment for one of the parents and their star—and the schools often did—that drive is off the table for a working class family. A lesser football team but a nicer school, Brentwood was closer to East L.A., closer to the Long family, and Coach Patrick "Patter" McMillan had years ago convinced the administration to throw some meager funds toward a nice passenger Sprinter van and a driver to pick up and drop off some underprivileged scholarship athletes from the other side of town. Mostly football players but a shortstop from Boyle Heights, twin sister tennis phenoms from Rampart Village and a speed cuber from Walnut Park. The Brentwood School didn't have a Rubik's Cube team but McMillan figured the kid could start one. Mostly it was good for optics, before that dreadful word was folded into our collective trivial lexicon. But the optics annually cuckolded the grisly badger because the tennis players, baseball studs and speed cubers all stuck around to attend the "upper" (high) school while the football saviors he recruited in their infancy headed out to the valley for the brighter lights of opportunity, the better programs, the better coaches. It was all so easily calculable for the families of potentially (and God-willingly) game-changing kids: go to the closer, nicer school while they're young, when it doesn't *really* matter who they play with or for. Save on miles and when the clock strikes Freshman, take that apartment deal out in Chatsworth or get a Prius and run yourselves ragged, Valley dashing for four years because he can probably go to Oregon. The "probably" was where I'd step in.

Dragging parachutes, DeMarcus and Jake were faster than most of the guys on our team. Both kids had the calves of champions. McMillan sensed my poacher's lust, told the boys to get a drink. They looked my way and I threw a peace sign.

"What's up?" McMillan grumped, forgoing the niceties, hating my peace. He had an old reptilian-avian look, a lizard of the sky—a pterodactyl I guess—wore a USS NeverSawAction hat, khakis and a navy blue polo. He had strength and a thin upper lip that bore his veneers, which were immaculate and imported. It was like Mr. Burns fell into the Secret of the Ooze ooze.

"Hey, Man." I was probably the first person aside from his poor wife to not address him as "coach" in twenty years. But he'd curtly "what's up"'d me. He could suck my dick.

He looked at his watch, looked at me: "What do you want?"

It took me aback and I spat out a laugh. "Whoa! We're all... what are we, the Eagles? We're all Eagles here, Man." I didn't love a confrontation—never had. And my corporate sillies had only exacerbated that a decade prior. But when it came to the world of sports, especially when it came to cocksucker coaches, I didn't give a good goddamn.

"What I WANT is to win," I said. But mostly I didn't want to lose. He didn't know me, though, and he surely didn't know my fraught relationship with competition. "And what I SEE are the two best athletes in the eighth grade playing parachute games in the *spring* to get ready for the *fall*."

"Not gonna happen."

"I'll get them in the best shape of their lives."

"Not football shape."

"Ship-shape," I quipped. "They'll be better football players for it." This I believed.

"Too risky. I don't trust that game."

"They play FOOTBALL!"

He stiffened up, felt the kids' eyes on us, sensed their intrigue.

"That kid's life depends on football," McMillan said sternly, out of their earshot.

"A plan B never hurt anybody." I was one to talk. McMillan walked away, hating me, hating lacrosse. I grinned at his back, gave the boys a Jeremiah Johnson salute and went back to my team.

OUR FIRST GAME was that Saturday, a home game. I was in bad shape, as Paul and I accidentally did a bunch of cocaine Friday night, staying up past the wee hours, unironically listening to Phish in his little house behind his house. His wife, Allie, was teaching her acting class and after we put his kids to bed I said "my cocaine guy is right around the corner" which was half true because the cocaine guy delivered but he didn't go to Venice— which was great for me because I rarely left the West side, and I didn't *really* want a cocaine guy. Paul started nervously (albeit theatrically) snacking, pacing, pointing at me saying "NO! No. Nope. Noooo. NO! NO! NO! Not like this." Before he kissed me and pressed a few hundred dollar bills into my hand. We spent the rest of the night saying things like "I don't care who you are or what your stance is on these guys: you can't hear 'A Live One"s *Hood* and say 'eh'." Allie came home and laughed at us, went to bed, and we continued to act like full-blown retards for a few more shows. Suffice it to say, I felt like quite the role model on the drive over to Brentwood. Luckily, Sam and I had slept over, and Paul had every face tonic, tincture, syrup and salve a desiccated Man-Crone like me could have asked for. That, some FOP, and a proper costume change and I looked better than the part. I just felt like Ebola on the inside.

At some point in the night, I had gotten an email from the Croat (her name being Camilla, which I had known since the night we'd met, but still, it felt too familiar or too formal). She had drawn the short straw for first post-game snack duty and was wondering what constituted proper post-lacrosse game food. Whereas I should have just responded *fruit, tacos, doesn't matter*, I panicked, waited, and then cocaine, liquor, Paul and myself unpacked it, repacked it, dissected, bisected and intersected it until a sweet YEM came on and we forgot about it. Now as I pulled out of Paul and Allie's driveway, I still didn't know, or for that matter care, what foodstuffs these kids were going to eat after the game. But I respected her place in the world, and I longed to hide behind that gross understatement. Her husband shook my tree. She shook it, too. My tree was shaking, goddamnit, and they were taking turns shaking it.

I wrote:

Egg-a-muffins?

Fifteen minutes and no response later, I turned onto Barrington and wondered if that, too, was maybe racist. "Egg-a-muffins" was what we called Egg McMuffin's growing up. It was from a National Lampoon radio sketch, a parody where Christopher Guest is Mr. Rogers and Bill Murray is a bass player and part-time piano mover, presumably black, whose diet consists, mainly, of "garbage food": tins of tuna, "chicken from a chain store," what sounds like "cheese pranish," and "egg-a-muffins". All she wanted was a straight answer and I, a coach of the whitest sport in the game, from the whitest state in the union, basically put on blackface and told her to bring fried chicken and watermelon. It was despicable. Then my dander of reassurances took over because who the fuck appropriated fried chicken and watermelon to anyone but the universal? I was sick of it. Everyone loves fried chicken, nobody doesn't like watermelon. Maybe some people don't like watermelon. But, again, I had no legs on which to stand because the low-down dirty-worst of it was that this was the exhausted debunk and diatribe rewrite which so many lily-white Obama enthusiasts before me had defended. Kumal would play the whole game. Or not at all. Or the fair amount. I wanted to retire, 0-0.

It was seventy-three and sunny, so it was yet again hard to argue that LA's a cloudier town than everyone makes it out to be. It was probably still cloudy in Venice, at least. An easterly breeze took the smog away from Brentwood, out to the valley where it hurt. I had had three seltzers and two Airborne's and I still wanted to die. It was so nice out I almost wanted to give the place a break. All the nice high schools in California had their premiere athletic fields baked into some canyon or another. And this place where I was partially employed was the premiere of the premiere, the stands etched into the steep hillside like some Hippy Whitman had cooked it up. I looked down on the field from the upper parking lot and past it, above it, I could see a sliver of ocean. It wasn't cloudy in Venice, either. The field was grass, real grass, grass so green and that pissed me off. They obviously had the funds to get FieldTurf, do the bare minimum to curb the ever-drought. Also we sucked, which bummed me out. But drought and stick skills aside, I felt lucky. To be alive. To not have died behind the wheel the times I probably should have. To not have OD'd on oxy when I was at my dumbest, before we really knew or really cared who the enemy was. I shouldn't have done all the cocaine the night before, I knew that, but heck if I wasn't going to make up for it by coaching my butt off. I took Sam out of the car, made an excited noise I had never made, knelt down in front of him, took off my Aviators and stared him right in his ice blue eyes. He licked me and shook his head, walked off. I don't think he liked the expensive lotion of Paul's I had put on my face.

"Hey, Coach." It was Just, making his way down to the field. It was the first time he'd addressed me devoid of snicker or pimply sneer and I knew that he was a gamer. He wore sandals, which was nice because I was waiting to give kids grief for walking through the parking lot in their cleats. I handed him the ball bag and we slapped hands, a silent agreement that this was more or less up to us.

I sat back in the car and finished the last of the third seltzer, made sure my mussed hair hid my recede and grabbed the football from the front seat. I didn't like lacrosse coaches who paced the sidelines with a stick in their hands, and I figured Cuthbert would be such a coach. But I needed something to occupy my own hands, and a football—an NFL regulated "Duke"—calmed me. I could point with it, futilely try to pop it in frustration, raise it in celebration. And it was also something I hadn't considered: an olive branch to McMillan.

Sam had wandered and he was near a nice car. Redundant in this parking lot, with a few exceptions, two being my '98 Subaru Outback Legacy and whatever shitbox Cuthbert rode in on. I loved my car, respected the hell out of it as it had taken me back and forth across this sad, mad and confusing nation one and a half times. I didn't want to lump it in with whatever vehicle Cuthbert had ruined. Sam was sniffing around one of those Porsche SUVs, though—they had a name. A little girl was trying to pet him, saying "hello. HELLo. Helll-O. Hello?" but his mind was elsewhere. The Croat stepped out from the driver's side, closed the door, which the girl—presumably her daughter or step—had left open.

"I think he's after the egg-a-muffins," she played in dog-talk, razzled Sam's jowls. My head already felt like a heart in a sarcophagus. Now the coffin was rusty gong parts. I got out of the Subaru and shut the door too hard and my head nearly crusted into salt, blew away in the breeze, bore a giant rust hole in one of these hundred thousand dollar cars. I walked over, mute, possibly forever.

"I didn't feel like driving all the way to McDonald's," she said, still gruffing Sam. Then she turned up at me. "So I got breakfast sandwiches from the Brentwood deli. Not cheap."

She wore a plain grey v-neck tee, over a decade worn, tight jeans and white low-top converse with no socks. Her blonde-brown hair was in a low-pony half-knot. She had blue-green-grey eyes that had a mystique which got me drunk again. There were flecks of something else in them—a galvanized amber, who knows, I liked her eyes, I liked them looking at me. Sweat dripped into my own. Whatever Paul had put on my face burned like a bastard.

"We're not in New York anymore, Mrs. Tourney," I said, not mute. Stupid. But not dumb.

CAMILLA EMERSON TOURNEY grew up in Scarsdale, New York, great-great granddaughter of St. Louis' own John Wesley Emerson, founder of the Emerson Electric Manufacturing Company. Emerson Electric being the company that made the first ceiling fan, thus making high-rise buildings livable, thus, along with many other thuses, allowing Manhattan to build UP, not OUT, unlike *some* cities.

Teddy Emerson, Camilla's Old Man, was a scrappy stickball wunderkind from out Flatbush way. Apparently he was there for "The Catch"[3], which she claimed he claimed got him so juiced up that he immediately ran all the way back to Flatbush from Washington Heights, missing Dusty Rhodes' pinch-hit three-run walk-off shot in the 10th.

Before he retired into the family business, Teddy bopped around the eastern seaboard playing single and double A baseball, meeting his wife—Fawnie Emerson nee Boswell, a gypsy of sorts who claimed Irish—then a cigarette girl at Johnson Field, during

---

3) *Willie Mays' dead-sprint, over-the-shoulder catch in the eighth inning of Game 1 of the 1954 World Series between the Giants and the Cleveland Indians at the Polo Grounds. The catch was incredible but it was the throw that makes it the "The Catch": he spun on a dime and rocketed a throw to the infield to keep the runners from advancing, keeping the score tied at 2. The Giants would go on to win the game 5-2, and, eventually, the Series.*

his time with the Binghampton Triplets. They headed back to the city to exist in those upper echelons of Manhattan Royalty. Had kids who grew up and were rich enough to take chances, and so it goes, so on and so forth.

Camilla was a prep school kid. After she graduated from Holderness, she wasn't quite drawn to college, so she set off to try it all, recreationally, professionally, usually with a dashing rich kid on her arm (or vice versa) to navigate the noise. Months long stints in Europe, Southeast Asia. Dipping a toe into the fashion world, be it modeling, styling, designing. A little acting here, photography there. "An inch deep, a mile wide" as she'd later tell me. But for those years and into her mid-twenties, that would certainly do. Then, in 2007, Teddy died suddenly of an angioblastoma while driving north on the FDR. Nobody else got hurt, he just eased the car to the shoulder, said thanks to it all and kicked. And the girl was shook.

Living in Los Angeles at the time, with hot-shot writer/director Buck Tourney (ever the status-tician) in relentless pursuit, Camilla returned from Teddy's funeral and was engaged to Tourney—whom she had kept at arm's length for years now—in two months, married in six, had a kid in twelve.

"This is Teddy," Camilla looked at me now, smiling. "Teddy, this is Coach."

"Hi, Coach."

"Hi, Teddy. That's Sam."

"Hi, Sam." Sam heard the familiar phonics and turned his attention on the little girl named Teddy. We were all getting familiar.

"You didn't really get a bunch of breakfast sandwiches, did you? I was kidding."

"Well that's your fault. I'm very literal." She stood now, hands on her hips, brow furrowed in what I gathered to be staged irritation. I gathered right because she smiled quickly—"D'you want one? You do. You look thin." She twirled back, disappeared into the Porsche. I didn't know which me she was basing that off of, but I took it as a compliment. I also desperately wanted a breakfast sandwich, my life perhaps depended on one. My feet were rooted in the asphalt, my body made up of poison and air—I felt like one of those inflatable tube dancers you see outside of car dealerships and I was deflating rapidly. Teddy stared at the Duke in my hand and I instinctually flipped it to her. My stomach clenched in regret but she deftly snatched it out of the air, then Camilla was tossing a breakfast sandwich my way and there were so many things in the air and all these nice cars and this Woman and the Kid and cocaine and my head hurt so much yet I was still grinning like the dopey Smurf. I unwrapped the sandwich, took a bite and suddenly I could bend my knees, wiggle my toes, my ballast reset. I raised the sandwich in thanks.

"It's fake bacon, but…"

"We're not in—"

"—'New York anymore, Mrs. Tourney'." Nope. Yup.

I asked Teddy if she could watch after Sam during the game. She flipped me the football, I gave her the leash. I smiled at her Mom, she smiled back and I walked down the hill to my team, not knowing how happy I'd get, how fucked I was.

THE SPOILS

WE GOT SHELLACKED. I should have called the game before the first whistle. The kids on the opposing team were massive. Full beard, O-line massive. They were terrible but we were way more terrified than they were terrible. They had two different monster varietals for our boys to be scared of. The smaller monsters had beards and trapezii; the ogres were baby-faced with breasts. And if you're a four-foot-eight seventh grader whose nuts are a distant cry from dropping, who's to say who's scarier? Cuthbert was trying to overcomplicate offensive schemes to expose their (lack of) speed but we were like lemmings running away from the ball every time it hit the ground, or, God forbid, was in the air, in an intentional pass from a teammate. It looked like a Laurel & Hardy routine. Just would fling a pass to someone, anyone, and the recipient—let's say it was Maybelline—wouldn't even attempt to lift his stick. The pass would fly past him—one such pass just hit Manassas in the facemask—and he'd just look around, look at me and mouth *was that...was that to me?*, hoping his absence of effort could masquerade the throw as shitty.

There was one silver lining, though, and one minor to major... whatever the opposite of silver lining is. Soiled lining, let's say. Soiled lining: I got kicked out of the game. Silver lining: We had another gamer. 7th grade kid, Madison Bleibtreu—we called him Mecca. He was just a great American kid, despite the phonetics of his surname. Tough, smart, perfect ratio of nerd to cool, which made his cool sneaky. You only had to tell him once. He stuck his nose in there, threw his body around with purpose, just shy of recklessly. A coach's dream. We were bad and very scared but I figured we could win a game or two if Mecca & Just got great.

My getting kicked out of the game was either an authentically blown gasket or I was trying to make up for coaching like my mind was in the upper parking lot. At halftime, Cuthbert unspooled the most artificial-pop, nonsequiturial word-soup imaginable, and I remained silent out of spite and also my hangover had roared back full-tilt. The game had started again but I was pitched forward like I had back problems, drinking everybody's Gatorade, trying to muffle the exhaustive analytics on my giddy reverberations from the earlier parking lot interaction. That's when Burt *caught* a pass behind the cage[4]. It was exciting. And then he performed a textbook roll-dodge (spin-move for the layman) and beat his guy. Fee-Fi-Fo-Fum, though, and the kid he beat—who was my height and had fifty pounds on me—swung his stick in humiliation or desperation and crushed Burt in the back and Burt buckled like Willem Dafoe in Platoon. As he starts to drop, another like-bodied colossus slides (the right play, to double) and mows Burt over, above the shoulders (kid didn't have much choice, as he's five feet taller than the little Rabbi), takes Burt's head off and lands on him, smothered in Jobba. Dead. Maybe I had some remains of the night in my olfactory, a last rush I gasped into my cortex upon seeing Burt actually catch the ball, and then, by the Grace of God, roll and push the cage...but I was on the field like a rabid terrier. I threw the kid off Burt—he was getting off, he was just big and slow—pulled him up, grabbed his and his teammate's facemasks, ranting and

---

4 *The goal (cage) sits about fifteen yards from the end line, meaning players can go behind the cage. The goal sits in a circle with a diameter of about eight feet? called the "crease" in which offensive players may not set foot.*

raving about God knows what: tact, couth, integrity of the game, Comanches, Capitalism, pocket full of rye. Their coach came out onto the field, "get your hands off my guys" this, "you and I can settle this" that. I told him to get his shit together. The ref ejected me, took pleasure in my due process, feeling I justified his day's wages. I laughed him off, questioning his resume. I didn't ground my charge till Burt grabbed my arm and said, smiling with a few hurt tears already dried:

"Coach, I'm fine. I'm good, Coach."

I finally exhaled, grew dizzy. I pulled him in, bapped his helmet.

"Just 'cause he's the Two Thousand Year Old Man doesn't mean…" Nobody laughed. I looked at Alex on the sideline and he shrugged. He was fine with it.

The kids I had accosted were shook. They were kids! They couldn't help it! They were playing a violent game and they were trapped in monster bodies and hadn't yet been given the manual!

"Sorry, Dudes," I extended both hands, they each took one, like we were gonna pray. They were wary, one eye on their coach. "I'm fucked up!" I whispered, they laughed. "I'm sorry, fellas—I know you didn't do it with malice, or whatever." I started off the field, nodded toward Burt as I walked away. "Give him a hug please."

The two child giants hugged Burt and everyone clapped.

I WATCHED THE rest of the game from the upper lot. My mania had somehow loosened everyone up; it was a friendly outing after I showed myself out. Manassas did a bit where he offered the ball to one of the monsters who demolished Burt. Everyone thought it was funny, save Just, Mecca and myself. This would not stand. I pulled back my vocal bow, ready to make someone feel bad, but Sam bound up the winding access road that led down to the field, shushing me, thank God. Teddy scampered after him. It was a steep hill. Kid could move.

"He started goin' crazy when you left," she gasped, hands on her knees.

"Thanks for watchin' him."

"Sure." She stood, checked to see if anything about me had changed, physically, since the on-field incident. "Did you get kicked out?"

"Asked to leave."

"My Dad got kicked out once."

"I believe it," I said, as Just tried to dodge through three guys, got stripped. "It's hard to stay cool."

"Yeah," Teddy agreed, convincingly, like she knew.

We watched the game for a few minutes before the world slowed down, tilted, flipped and reversed: Inception. Her Mom crested the hill, winding up the access road and as all of her came into view, for whatever reason "Dream Weaver" played in my head—*Wayne's World*, I'd later realize—and I was so stunned and appalled, I pulled the soundtrack of my mind over to the side of the road and kicked Gary Wright the hell out. I needed a song, quick, and I flew past Bruce, Bonnie, Brendan Benson, Flying Burrito Brothers, Bright Eyes—I was stuck in the B's! Fuck me! McVie! I picked her up, put her in, Fleetwood Mac's "Why" clacked on just in time. Big things needed a song. But this wasn't a big thing and the song I picked's first lines were this:

> *There's no use in crying, it's all over*
> *But I know there'll always be another day*
> *Well my heart will rise up with the morning sun*
> *And the hurt I feel will simply melt away...*

I picked a song to rise from the ashes with before I even gave the silly schoolyard crush a moment to breathe! I was completely deranged by choice! By free will! I took the super highway to devastation without even considering the pretty back roads. I hog-tied *myself* and flopped into the quarry like a feckless monk. Who cares, fuck it, get it over with, taste it all, finish the cookies, the coke, scoop the fifty dollar candle out of the jar and burn it at both ends. We're not meant for this world so stuff it all in your brain, your ass, your heart, wherever it hurts the best.

But maybe it wasn't just me and my propensity to go big. Maybe it was her, specific. Maybe she was doing something to me.

She gave a quick wave and a smile as she approached and I realized why I got so got, realized what it was about her, what shook my tree, what she was doing to me and what she was: a Perfect Transition. She was "Sing My Songs to Me"→"For Everyman." All of her. The easily identifiable parts, sure: big-toe to head-crown, proximal wrist crease to the tip of the middle digit, lilac crest to biceps femoris, biceps femoris to the gastrocnemius, platysma to nasalis, hairline to eyebrow. All pretty standard stuff. Was she the prettiest dame in the room? Subjective, but for the sake of the song, no. She *was* the most perfectly put together human I'd come across (subjective, still? Perhaps), and it wasn't limited to the physical. The way she shifted between sentences, phrases, questions to statements. How she listened, blinked her eyes while you talked, in between her talking. How she made you feel *funny →stupid→smart enough→dumb again→tired→alive*, all adagio, all with the flick of a breakfast sandwich, some sort of master class in conducting; a puppeteer, a politician; she was Jim Jones, *The Last Waltz*, drink the Kool-Aid, dish runs away with the spoon.

This had everything to do with who her husband was.

This had nothing to do with who her husband was.

"Well. I guess that's it," she said, standing next to me, watching the game. But the whistle hadn't blown. There was still a lot of time on the clock.

"I guess," I said. But I didn't know. "Wait, what's 'it'?"

"You and I!" She said, as if everything else in the world it could have been—the war in Afghanistan, the last Formosan Cloud Leopard, calling Caramel deLites "Samoas"—were obviously not it.

"What the hell are you talking about?"

"John's with his mom for a few months."

I made a "few months?" face.

"The Husband is shooting a movie."

"Ah." This explained why I hadn't seen the deadbeat. He was busy and successful. Doing what he loved *and* providing. I had just whisked his wife away to the back of my dumb-fuck mind, which is where I would have loved for a bullet to go if only guns didn't make me queasy. I was in somebody else's clothes. I felt something deep within me that I was certain had left, disintegrated with age. Striking out in little league; falling in a ski race; getting a choral part, not Mr. whatever-his-name-was who Walter Mathau played in *Hello Dolly!*. There was a mercurial uprising, a guileless emotional anarchy. My laboratory was smoking, the scientists fled, the last one out pulled the alarm as he ran for the door, his lab-coat flapping in the slipstream: I was gonna cry.

I coughed, barbled something about the defense, jammed my car-key into my leg. I relegated her to the Croat again. She had to be nameless as she listed the locations Tourney and Will Smith or whoever-the-fuck-who-gives-a-fuck were globetrotting; the places she would fly to and visit once school got out. Places like Istanbul, Singapore, Ho Chi Minh City, Hague—to which I said "Long Island?" and she laughed not knowing I was serious and I wanted to start the car and suck on the tailpipe. Sam came up to me and put his nose in my junk and I've never loved like I loved him then. He needed water. I could take care of him. We took care of each other.

"What are you working on?" She asked as I grabbed a Nalgene from the back of the Subaru. It was scalding, but it was the best we had.

"What do you mean," I said, almost snippy, wondering where I got off being snippy. It was almost admirable.

"Well you're not just a crazy lacrosse coach."

"Not that there's anything wrong with that." My indignation was insane.

"I saw the short you made!" She was already tired of pulling it out of me. *Imagine how I feel* I almost said, but it would have been too cryptic, too much work to make make sense. I wished I'd said it.

I had in fact made a short "film," which I had all but forgotten about. Or had at least forgot that anyone, people, namely Buck Tourney's wife, could click on it, watch it, judge its low-rent and forgettable hackney. I needed to make it invisible. Although it was a little late for that. I was now being placated, patronized, spayed.

"Oh. That was…just…silly…fun." I spoke in words.

"I loved it." She glanced at Teddy, who had found a tennis ball in the back of my car and was trying to get Sam to fetch. Fat chance.

The Croat whispered: "I didn't care for all the baby penis stuff."

Shit. "There wasn't *that* much baby penis stuff." I had to change the subject. The baby penis stuff was simply a barometer of just how far one (young balding man) would go to save their hair, which any balding man could understand. It wasn't for everybody. What would you do to not go bald? Punch your mother in the face? Put on a permanent seventy-five unflattering pounds? Lick a hundred baby peckers? Tap of the tongue—the babies wouldn't remember a damn thing. It was all above board. Nobody hurt, nobody scarred, save the licker. I was asking the big questions. I was fine with the bit.

She looked at but didn't examine my head. "You've got plenty of hair," she dismissed. "And if you go bald, who cares." I settled back into our life together, now with a stoic clarity. She knocked me down and around but I was better for it, always would be. It had been a long couple minutes.

"So what now?" Camilla asked, retreating to her car, keeping an eye on me because she knew how needy I was.

"I mean…a couple…scripts…collecting dust…a few…I'm working on…to sell?…a musical…with, you know, statutory…blackmail…undertones."

She returned with the breakfast sandwiches, handed them to me. "And the Woody Allen / Lena Dunham with a good body stuff?" It was semi-vague, but I knew what she was talking about. I had taken my shirt off in the baby penis piece. Or had worn a flattering tee. Either way I tried to dim my glow from the compliment. "Your Dad's great. That's him, right?" Lamenting hair-loss and accosting my Dad for being middle class was the gist of the whole thing. Life, art, snooze.

"That's him."

"Well, I think you should 'build around that' as they say."

"Who says? Who's they?"

"Send the dusty scripts." She knew when to ignore. "And the rape musical." Christ, she listened. "The Husband is always looking for promising young talent to monetize." She looked at me like it was the beginning of the end or vice versa, which it's always one or the other. Or just the end. Or just the beginning.

"Bye, Ryan."

It was the first time in my life that I loved the sound of my name.

I DIDN'T HAVE a rape script. Thirty burnable pages at best. And my sideline of scripts certainly didn't have a Robert Horry coming off the bench to throw her way. They were written by a madman devoid of interesting smarts, enviable quirks. They were just extensions of me: felt a lot but lacked direction. Buckled under pressure. I started fresh on the rape script and everything else took a back seat. "Co-coaching" with that dweeb—with anyone for that matter—was useless. I let him take the lead and I started pounding on my computer and daydreaming about my idol's wife and my idol, too. We stopped running and lost two more games the following week—one to Oaks Christian and the other to Harvard Westlake. Oaks Christian were quite bad and if I hadn't had my head up three different asses, my own ass being the main cavity, we could have beaten them. Harvard Westlake was a different story.

Harvard School for Boys as established in 1900 when Los Angeles was just orange groves or barley fields, who gives a shit, the movies weren't around. It was originally a military school, but discontinued its military and boarding factions in the 70's and people like Bridget Fonda and Jake Gyllenhaal and Mayor Garcetti eventually went there. I mention the year of establishment because there seemed to be a deep-rooted history in the air, on campus when we played them. And by deep rooted history, it seemed like an Aryan marching farm from the old country, the mean one. Yes, of course there were and are Jews at Harvard Westlake; it's Los Angeles, it is Hollywood. Maybe they just had Reich-ide in the water.

The Bears of Harvard Westlake were flashy but fundamentally sound. They moved the ball, saw the field, were unselfish and smooth. Fast breaks went: Bob-bop, *Bang*. They cleared out for one another, ran an actual offense. And their defensemen had great handles, could actually clear the ball and time their stick checks. It was a drubbing. They weren't bigger than us, they were just so much better. I phoned it in, hung it up, kept it light. We were bad, undisciplined, helpless. I figured the least I could do was stay artificially sunny.

As we shook hands with the affable Nazis, I made a few jokes at our own expense, went for some cheap yucks, trying to buddy up to the cool kids. Back on the sideline, Just stopped me in my tracks, shaking his head. He wore the disdained face of Toby Huss' son in *Jerry MaGuire*, the hockey player's kid who tells Jerry to stuff it up his ass because Jerry doesn't care about his old man's mangled brain.

"What *happened* to you?" Just asked, a hot auger to my gut.

I started to defend myself, to laugh it off, blame Cuthbert or the collective athleticism. But I felt the eyes of Crothers, Burt, Mecca and Kumal all wanting an excuse, my good reason for abandoning them. But I couldn't give them one. And if I tried it would have been worse than what I'd been doing. I walked off the field a little ashamed but mostly fine: I was just the wrong man for the job.

SEVEN

THE FOLLOWING MONDAY, KERI ASKED TO SPEAK WITH CUTHBERT AND myself in her bunker before practice. I had planned on putting in my two-hour notice that afternoon, so the timing worked out. This was all a new feeling for me: I hadn't any guilt. I'd always been wary of quit because I knew of the guilt that followed, and stumbling unremarkably through the finish line seemed preferable. Camilla's new residency in my thoughts was perhaps dumbing all of my otherwise typical anticipatory frets. However, this seemed to me a no-brainer. 1.) I had no real coaching aspirations. 2.) I was poor. 3.) I didn't want to be poor. 4.) I could count the grains in the hourglass. I had committed to the writing for the screen racket and I finally had a feasible line out. Every shot in Hollywood could be the one, the shot that slingshots you up into the hob-knobby cock-wad parties in the hills, dishing on cold plunges and diets with Dax Shepard. But, same coin, same side, a missed shot and an errant sip could be the fatal sip, the sip that casts you under a 101 underpass of your choosing, talking to yourself and comparing tents with Tricky Pete. If a shot seems even terribly wrong on an ethical level in that morally bankrupt town, you have to be willing to step on a burlap sack of puppies to get up another couple inches to get a better look at that sadistic pitch so you can take another desperate swing, one more crack to finally smack it out of this idiot park in order to taste the success that nobody really deserves. These rich kids were not my problem. My poor fucking life was my problem.

As it turned out, those rich kids were very much my problem. Furthermore, in fact: mine and mine alone. Keri informed us that the head coach of the High School varsity team—a forty-something Georgetown-scented Tate Donovan stand-in—landed a pilot that was shooting post haste in Vancouver and Keri needed one of us to take over as Varsity head coach. The assistant coach of the varsity team of course wanted to stay assistant because he was mid call-back for a CW pilot and felt more comfortable to, if duty called, let the team down in his lesser ranked role on the staff. It all came at me pretty quick, as I had walked in there, cut from the same spineless trollop cloth as those other coaches, ready to abandon my guys for a far-fetched and fleeting maybe. That's entertainment.

"It's up to you guys," she said, although she didn't really mean it, speaking it directly to Cuthbert as though it were his choice. The cahoots of the ordinary. But I could feel Cuthbert eyeing me, ready to fellate the entire spirit world in order to sway my decision in the direction he had no idea it was already firmly rooted in. I nodded. Took a deep breath for ruminative effect. I wanted the decision to seem measured and I wanted to come across gracious, although it was simple: I didn't want to coach the high school. They were dicks. And more importantly, I now *wanted* to coach my gentlemen. I could finally lop off the useless limb that was Colby "Cutty" Cuthbert. For it was he who had sucked the wind out of my leadership sails, not the Croatian paved road to Tourney. And that road was lark-paved, anyway. It was a smile, nothing more, not a penny less. Gee-whiz, I wasn't immune to the occasional fantasy whim. I wasn't above it. It was a fun part of life and if nobody gets hurt, it's actually what gets us through our frivolous, cookie cutter days. Did I love her? It's none of my business, that's what it was! She made my heart skip a beat in my thirty-first year and that's a pretty nice thing to think about. And if I was lucky, I'd remember it every few years, wonder if she did, too, or not even wonder, just smile, think: "that's pretty nice!" Or maybe it would be just a feeling, the memory flitting by in my subconscious, intangibly tickling a gland or a node we don't even really know exists. It's just pretty nice. And even knowing that that was our fate, that brought me calm. And guess what? It *was* pretty goddamned nice. But me? Oh, I was nothin' nice. I was as lunch-pail as the day was long and now I was plucking my own raw hide off the trash-heap of washed-up coaches and leaders, angling the claw of the bowling alley treasure chest and thrusting myself into its clutches in a back-door deal. I almost felt guilty for these kids, getting the gift that was Me. What a steal! I was a molder of young men. I was a sage. I was a lunatic. I could save this country if I had to. Lawrence Taylor's "let's come out like a buncha *crazed dogs!*" sound-bite sounded off in my mind. I was running through wall-studs, storming beaches and I was ready to recommit to these kids with a rabid fervor the likes of which had yet been seen, the wide world of middle school sports over. Maybe I'd start smoking crack, Sorkin style.

I respected that I was considering it.

"To be honest," I began, "Colby's coaching *techniques*, his... *schemes*, are very...they're more...how should I say..." I tried to look like I was looking for the word, fluttering my fingers in search. I was going a bit big, but I was jacked up about coming out of retirement. And I could make him feel indebted to me, which was ice cream.

"...cerebral." I laughed, finding the word I was fake looking for, like I was in awe of his prowess. I laughed such an asshole laugh I thought maybe I should get into acting. "Leagues more advanced than my meat-and-potatoes shtick," I continued before I flipped it back on him. "Do what you wanna do—I mean, we're gettin' there and we're havin' fun and I'd hate for the boys to lose you..."

Cuthbert was creeping forward in his seat like a child trying to wait patiently his turn for cake at a birthday party.

"But those dudes at the upper school need you," I said, rubbing my face for the consternation effect. "And then OUR boys can look *forward* to getting to play for *you*. A little fuel for the fire as it were. We can start a real program."

Cuthbert hid his jubilation and nodded at Keri as if this were the situation room or a real program. They nodded back and forth a few times and I wanted to clunk their heads together.

"What should we do as far as the lower school assistant coach? We'll need help down there," Keri asked as she continued to speak only to Cuthbert. I wanted to roll up a newspaper and slap her with it, tell her I'd slept with more lesbians than she had. But this one I had to play cool. I could have these kids to myself.

The successes and failures of this team would lie solely on my Quadrophenic shoulders. I had to go this alone.

"Yeah-yeah-yeah...for sure..." I nodded, mused, aped to discover the flip-side. "*Howev*er. To bring in another personality at this stage..." I looked at Cuthbert, needing him for the first and last time, ever.

"I see what you're saying," he said. I could detect an early onset authoritative role developing in him in the forty-five seconds since he loosely assumed the position as head Varsity coach. "Those kids have the bones of what I was teaching them, offensively...and I'll only be a few fields away," he chuckled. "I can keep an eye on you guys. There'll be trickle down." I barely knew what he meant by that last part but I wanted to shit in his mouth and butt-fuck his mom. I couldn't understand the brain and how it worked but understood that my misunderstanding it was what allowed the world to be so fucked up. You stutter-step and get cute, think you're manipulating a doofus, tipping the scales in your favor, but that doofus gets into office because you were too near sighted and selfish to see that it is quite possible; that the bad guys can prevail when people like me think they're the smarter ones in the room.

"Colby. We can't score any goals because nobody respects you." It had barreled through all of my blockades. I had tried so hard to not say it! The oxygen in the room turned to Boromine. Cuthbert was too confused to wonder if he got tricked into drinking the cup with the poison in it. If he rightly thought less of himself, he would have hit me.

"Dude it's from *Meatballs!*" I slapped his shoulder, laughing.

I had never seen *Meatballs*. "I think what we're saying," I said, turning my best Eddy Haskell at the rough-and-tumble woman's rugby player who had little to no respect for me, "is that we've got it covered." Cuthbert nodded, beaming the pride of the dunce following his unmerited and remarkable early ascension. I was the reason this country sucked. But this team was mine. And we were gonna kick ass.

I HUSTLED OUT of the meeting, feeble reassurances of a lone coach left hanging in the air. Coaching alone was irresponsible for a smattering of reasons, but I worked terribly with others. And even though I had been ready to quit, had sworn off the job, with Cuthbert's sudden exit, this universe I didn't believe in was on its hands and knees, begging me to reconsider.

I ran through the halls, unencumbered by the oligarchical beauty of the high school kids' dismissal. I hop-stepped, skipped, ducked around faculty and students. Through the floor to ceiling glass paned windows, I saw our hope with a gym bag slung over his shoulder, walking toward the track, flipping through his iPhone. I got through the doors and the throng thinned out. I ran to the kid, put a hand on his shoulder.

"DeMarcus," I said, my other hand out to receive. "Call your Old Man. You're playing Lacrosse."

WALTER LONG WASN'T a hard sell because I told him what I knew to be true: lacrosse could get DeMarcus a free ride to any college he wanted. Football wasn't a sure thing, but lacrosse, I assured him, was. Five million kids played high school football in this country, I stated. And even though I pulled that number out of thin air, I later looked it up and I was pretty close. One hundred thousand boys play high school lacrosse. Again, thin air. That number sounded even more ridiculous to me and I said it for effect, but that, too, was close. I'd always been terrible at guestimation and now I was coming at Walter Long like Will Hunting.

"Well then how many football schools play this la-crosse?" It was the right question.

"A good amount. And more every year. Penn State, Ohio State, Notre Dame, Michigan recently got a team…"

"Oooooh—sounds cold."

"Then let's go to fuckin' Chapel Hill, Mr. Long," I sang to him. "LT, Hakeem Nicks." Those were the only football Tar-Heels I had off the top of my head. "Julius Peppers! Carolina barbeque sauce is a little vineg-ry for me, but I can get down." I was more worried about getting my ingredients right than racially pandering like Hilary. He was a good dude who schlepped FedEx packages through the scorching neighborhoods of East L.A.—he didn't give a shit about regional sauces or my Yankee affectations. He wanted his kid to get an athletic scholarship to a major American University.

"Awright. Awright. If you think you can get him nice in a few years time, I'm with you." I shoved DeMarcus and slapped his hand twenty times in succession.

In my brief conversation with Walter, I had also promised to, regardless of which high school he landed at, be DeMarcus' Lacrosse Guru for the next four years. I didn't have any other plans.

"There's already murmurs, My Man," I went on. "'You hear about this kid from Watts—'"

"Watts?"

"Compton."

"Man, we live in Westmont. If you're looking for hard, look no further."

"Admissions at UNC doesn't know that. Westmont sounds like a goddamned country club—'Bartholomew J. Westmont'—"

"Shiiiit." I had him, he liked me, and I was at that moment probably the happiest person in the world. I had been rinsed, I could die.

"'You hear about that kid from Inglewood? Runs a four flat—'"

"Four flat!"

"'—puts up five hundred—'"

"Shiiiit."

"'—squats a grand—'"

"Man, I gotta work!"

"Works part time as a Doula—"

"A what?"

"I dunno looks good on the transcript. I'll talk to you, Walter."

"Awright."

We hung up and I handed the phone back to DeMarcus. Jake—the kid he trained with—and McMillan were making their way over to the field.

"Is homeboy gonna play?" I asked DeMarcus. He nodded absolutely. "Is McMillan gonna fuck me up?" He laughed, nodded probably. We dapped and I told him I'd get him some gear. As

I ran over to hear the last of Cuthbert's exit speech, I winked at McMillan but I had my sunglasses on so it felt leagues less ballsy.

BACK IN VENICE, as I descended back into the reality of shattered hopes and an unattainable future of the quenched, I decided to not let Tourney's wife fade in my rearview. She wanted to help. She seemed to give a shit about the underdog. Sure, it was easy for those forever at the top to find the peasant cute. But nobody's going push back if you say "*Rocky*'s the best movie ever," so who could really blame her.

The reverse statutory musical couldn't be sent in the state it was in and she was leaving for who-knew-where for who-knew-how-long pretty soon. Electronic mail made physical location not matter, but I couldn't be bothered with the particulars. The musical was sloppy in its current condition and putting lipstick on that pig wasn't the way to stay relevant in their mind-feed. Well, her mind-feed, as Tourney had no idea who I was, but she was the conduit. Thus, it was okay to stay in touch. And if I used words like "thus" it could stay surficial, entertainment clinical. Thus, I kept saying such things to myself in every translation imaginable as I sifted through scripts to send to her, as I began to panic about panicking about drafting the body of the email on which a script could be attached. All the translations and all the panicking were derived from one source, one spring: this was my shot at Buck Tourney. And if I screamed it loud enough inside my skull, and tried really, really hard to believe it, I could feel properly cheap and that other thing—Her—could be muted, forgotten noise, the extraneous din in trying to get ahead.

My resting heart rate was where it was because I was one forwarded email away from the only Man I deified.

The script I chose was the script I had optioned. I figured the option was up but I also didn't care because that shit meant nothing and if Buck Tourney wanted to get involved with it, everybody shuts up and asks how high to jump. I had written the script a few years prior, mid recession, and it was about two brothers who move back home because they're broke and sad. They start a band with their Grandmother—who lives in a nearby nursing home—because they think the, for lack of a better term, "hipsters" will eat it up. Their Mom moves back home, too—their parents being long divorced—because, well, recession I guess? There's original music, quirky Grandma stuff, drunk brother love, drunk brother fights, divorce parsley. The script was good enough. Funny, sad, drunk—all the things I liked about life. But as I re-read it, I wasn't a huge fan of the guy who wrote it, which is understandable and obvious for anyone with an iota of self-awareness who has ever seen or heard from their past selves.

My palms clammed and I felt a stye forming because you only get one shot for someone like Buck Tourney to read something you wrote.

The script needed a few small tweaks, some subtle references to bring it to present day. Other than that I was just north of ashamed of it, south of proud, and that was the best I could ask for. It was devoid of an eating disorder thread, which I felt was its strongest asset. I thought back on the starry-eyed numbskull who wrote it. The night I typed the last lines of action, I cried. I thought it was special. The camera tilted up to the Sky-Blue-Sky or some shit. And as I re-dated it and attached it to an email, I didn't look down on the dude who had cried when he finished that script. I just felt a little pang of remorse for not holding off a little while longer, giving him another season or two of hope before I became the Me I now was. The pang was just that—a pang. I moved along.

There were seven different variations on my "hey" intro in the email. "Hey," "Hey there," "Well," "Well, Shit," "Anyway," and "Hello?" were six of them. I didn't even dare attempt a subject line because that could take days. I needed a seltzer and I had had too much caffeine although it was night and I hadn't had any since morning. I smelled toast. This was because *The Yips* had changed the trajectory of the way I thought and felt—it was *Graceland* in TV form.

As I wrote the email, the Alien made its way through my breastplate. I tried to do the Nixon era paper bag breathing thing but I only had a plastic bag and thought maybe that could actually kill me. Keep it short, keep it snappy, keep it focused, send the script. I found a subject line. I tried to reread the email but the pixels of the computer oozed from my screen like a magic eye poster. I pressed send, wanting my body to go back to normal. Sent. I opened my sent mail to see what I had done. The subject line was *Egg-a-Muffins* and I hated it. My "hey" intro was "Mrs. Tourney…" and I hated it. The body was lean but still contained silly patter and I hated it.

She wasn't going to forward that email to her husband. She'd probably read the script first and decide in her own words if she wanted to pass it along.

What had been happening to my brain, my body, my organs, I now had to admit, had nothing to do with her husband.

There was newfound purpose in the drive to practice the following day. Sam wouldn't be left at home anymore because I was in charge. He was a calming presence for the fellas, mostly just wanted to be left alone, wanted to find the shade. I loved his feline hobo side.

We got to practice early and McMillan was waiting for me on our field. He had a whistle around his neck, blue Under Armour polo on, khaki shorts, mid-calf white socks and I thought "he has nice legs for an older guy" as he strode across the field at Sam and me. He didn't seem to be in the mood for compliments—mine in particular—so I shelved that ice breaker.

"Dog can't be here," he said, almost blowing the whistle on Sam.

"Okay." I didn't want to get into it with him. He hated guys like me.

"I don't know who you think you are—"

"Nobody."

"—or what you think you're doing—"

"I'm trying to not lose!"

He squared on me, pointed a stiff digit at my chest: "I don't like guys like you."

"I know that." This seemed to take some of the gas out of his tank. "But, Dude—" I tried to laugh it off, but he was ready to slap me around. He probably hadn't been called "dude" in forty years. I removed my sunglasses, hoping it would do something. "Lacrosse is tailor made for guys like you. And, believe it or not, guys like me are on your side." He clearly didn't want to be aligned, but there had to be, if not an olive branch, a meat-stick. "What I told DeMarcus' dad wasn't just something to say." He didn't speak this semi-nonsensical language. "In the far off chance that in three years, he is that good of a football player—"

"He will be if—"

"Sure. Let's say he is. And let's say he gets hurt Junior year, playing football. He's still got a full ride to play lacrosse—"

"At some little artsy-fartsy—"

"At Michigan, Ohio State, Notre Dame." Notre Dame shut him up, the racist Catholic bastard. "It's just a good plan B, Coach."

"If he gets hurt playing this pussy crap I'm gonna kill you."

"Alright."

And that was that. McMillan stalked off. He crossed DeMarcus and Jake as they made their way out to the field, Jake's voice cracking as they vied for his forgiveness. "Hey, Coach!" They sang in unison. McMillan barely nodded and they watched him go, guilty pups. Good God. Men were such babies.

WE WOULDN'T TOUCH our sticks. I was gonna prove to McMillan that I would do his job, too. Also, I had lost a lot of important days in my pathetic apathy recess. We were net zero on conditioning now, in good enough shape, a little bit better than everyone else and that would get us nowhere, fast.

I looked up at the sky, felt the wind go out of the guys who were gearing up.

"It's gettin' dark, Boys." Cacophonous moans. We hadn't started practice yet and it already sounded like a combat evacuation hospital in Da Nang.

"Coach, let it be sunny," Kumal pleaded. "Let the sun *shine*, coach." He whispered this to me, grabbing my hand like a pushy beggar.

I had explained to DeMarcus and Jake that the key to assimilating, to folding into the team, was to be clueless, humble, gracious. For the first few days act as it was: you are on somebody else's team. And after a week of that, nobody'll remember the team before DeMarcus and Jake. I watched as they let Burt and Crothers—two seventh graders, mind you—school them on what this "darkness in the day" nonsense alluded to. DeMarcus and Jake nodded along. They were perfect.

In cautious optimism, Manassas started putting on an elbow pad. I wagged a finger. He took a few quick breaths through his nose to fight the tears.

"This is our first practice alone, together. I wasn't...I was a shithead for a week or so there, and I can't blame that on anybody but myself."

"Not even Cutty?" Just added because he could never not.

"Well that would be pretty sackless of me, now wouldn't it." Some nods, but it was always hard to tell who could hear through the terror. "I'm sorry."

"It's okay, Coach," Burt said just as the silence stretched. I guess I was looking for forgiveness.

"I'm not saying we start over, but..." I looked over at DeMarcus and Jake, Just and Mecca—the four of them ready for whatever it took. There was a circuital osmosis crackling. These boys could carry that weight.

"Whatever happened up till now," I said, slapped Just on the butt. "Is Prelude."

And I started running.

By the time we got back to the field, most of the parents were waiting in their cars, wondering where their kids were. A few were unpleased with our tardiness. People have plans and schedules, and I tried to understand and respect that, but in those moments it was hard because what had happened in the ninety minutes prior was not fit for earth. Or at least not the earth we know through our human bodies. I once saw a Golden Retriever play fetch for two and a half hours straight, every toss a forty or fifty-yard bomb, that guy or gal fetching every felt Prince like it was her last. But that's a dog whose breed name is "go get it, bring it back".

As a former collegiate athlete, you have one specific practice you can go to in your mind. For the alumni of the teams in the middle—the struggling programs; the scrappy adequate—this practice has a darker tinged hue of desperation on the border of its memory than those at the top; the John's Hopkinses, the Virginias. They have it, too, their lone practice which everyone on the team cosmically agrees was the very worst time. All coaches are sometimes dicks, and coaches have shit days just like the rest of us, even if their job is secure as Quantico. But as players on the teams that were just trying to stay alive, trying to win enough so the last three games of the season still mattered, you had a coach that was trying to keep his job, going through twenty sleeves of Rolaids a day, eenie-meanie-miney-moe-ing which mid-grade muttonhead to take it out on that particular afternoon. Warming up in *practice*, stretching and everybody's shakin' like they were asked last minute to speak at the Inauguration. Conference play-off hopes still barely alive. *Barely.* You gotta win but a few other people definitely have to lose. Out of control of your own destiny, throwing and catching becomes Gladitorial. Thumbs down. For there is nothing scarier than a Meathead on the hot-seat, making in the park of 75k with a family and a mortgage and no applicable skills to the outside world. He get scared, he yell, he make run. And borne from that is a practice, a two-hour episode so terrible you carry it with you for the rest of your days. But you laugh whenever you remember it because that was the worst it ever got. All physical-spiritual misery pales in comparison. Eat too much of an edible? Just think back to that day. If that day ended and you survived, every day, every gnashing careen into psychedelia or sorrow or panic, every plunge into despair is a bowl of Kix in comparison. That day in Brentwood, I wanted to give my guys the worst it ever got. But I wasn't a Meathead on the hot-seat. I was just a selfish guy and wanted them to remember me, remember this one day for the rest of their lives. Even if they went on to play lacrosse in college, play football at LSU; attempt a marathon when they got chubby or run ultra IronMans in their forties after they sold their tech start-up; in a few years when they ate too much fungus or liquid or got their heart so mangled by a dame that not even Death Cab for Cutie could help; in their darkest hours for the rest of their days, I wanted to resurface in the Super 8's of their hearts, the stars of their souls, to where they could will a smile and say: "Okay. Okay. That was worse." I wanted to give them the gift that was the certainty that it could never be as bad as it got on that afternoon in the Spring of 2014 when they were twelve or thirteen or fourteen years old. Time was quick. I needed legacy insurance.

So we ran.

We ran a few warm up miles up the back entrance to the Getty. We found a service road, a hill so steep you could almost reach out and touch it on your way up. We ran that hill till somebody puked, I forget who. We ran till we had to walk. It was too steep. So if our legs made us walk, "Fuck You, LEGS!" I yelled and they echoed. We buddy'd up and piggy-backed for two more wobbly gusters. That would have been it for many; curtains on a hard day's work, raise a glass, call your Mom. But I wanted the worst. I wanted to tattoo their spirits in this diabolical soot. If we didn't die, it would someday make them happy.

We jogged back to campus, haphazardly crossing Sunset like drunks because our periphery was shot. Maybelline dove across the hood of a Mercedes. Kumal tried to get hit. There were honks of rage, honks of encouragement. Honks of concern.

Cuthbert and his new battalion were on the field inside the track. The track team had a meet in Palos Verdes, so the track was clear and we took to it, slapping each other's backsides, whooping call-and-response gibberish to whomever's ears happened to be around. We had the Maverick-Goose upstairs-downstairs hi-five working in synchronicity, all resonant palm connection, no clams. Cuthbert held court on another diatribe to nowhere and we were, officially, Crazed Dogs. The high school kids were envious or scared, trying to convince each other that we weren't cool. We made them question themselves, their place in the order. We were like Queers right before the AIDS crisis. We were fucking partying.

Three-man two-hundred yard relay sprints. We flew because our legs were elated to not be on the hill. I felt like I had Michael Johnson's gold slippers on, floating around each bend, exploding down the straight. I came back down to earth for a second—or back up, depending—and locked eyes with DeMarcus and I saw in them what he thought, what he felt: the good worry you only see in the movies. And that I was the craziest sonuvabitch he'd ever met. And he'd run with me forever. Jake, too. He was a happy machine. In between legs of two-hundreds, he looked at me, or where he thought I was, as everyone's rods and cones were noodling, and said "this is...*insane*...thanks, Coach."

After that I told the boys that we'd run a half-mile (two laps) and we'd move on. But everybody had to break three minutes. Which wasn't unreasonable for the bulk of them. But for five or six it was out of the question. And until everyone broke three, we'd keep running half-mile desperators. So, again, we ran.

DeMarcus, Just, Jake and Mecca came in right behind me, somewhere near the two and a half mark. I gagged. Everything was bile fire. Beaker came in at ten seconds later. Burt and Crothers came in at two-fifty. The majority made it by their chinny-chin-chins. But Innie and a hormonally transitional doughy kid we called Willow for no reason, they missed the cut by eight and ten seconds, disappointingly. Manassas missed. Kumal came in twenty seconds behind that. I lined everyone up to do it again. Kumal reassured them he could do it and when they weren't looking gave me a look that preached "No I can't!" But we tried. Again. Again he missed but by less. Innie made the cut, Willow just missed and Maybelline lost some time, missed it as well. We ran it again. Everyone lost time, but Burt and Crothers had dragged a wounded Manassas to the finish, improving his time, wrecking theirs and missing the cut but getting the point.

And there, a light had gone off. Just, Mecca, DeMarcus, Jake and Beaker huddled up. They took Innie aside. I heard desperate pleas and bribes as I counted down from thirty, to our next half mile. The Varsity team had stopped what they were doing and were cheering our guys on, those who couldn't find the time. DeMarcus, Just and Jake flanked Kumal. Kumal beat his chest and roared and cried and went through his rolodex of emotions into the sky. "THERE WILL BE LIGHT!" He shrieked. He took off his shirt and shorts, leaving just his compression shorts and running shoes. I wasn't gonna stop him. All bets were off and we were all the same. I counted down from five. And. We ran.

I hadn't said a word, they all rallied themselves. The first lap was steam-rolled. Kumal even smoked it shy of a minute fifteen. But the body starts to reject the madness and the mind has no idea who you are and things started to lag. I dug as deep as I could and finished in two-thirty-five or so, threw up, turned around. They were coming. It was, in fact, war. And they were the Good Guys. I staggered back toward them, drunk Melly Gibs playing Forest Gump. Crothers and Burt got Manassas over again. Maybelline found something and got his own self there. With each stride, Innie was gagging, a one-man-band with a kick drum and a mouth harp just out of his reach, two tambourines quaking in cut time. Fifteen seconds. Mecca and Beaker picked Willow up, *Weekend at Bernie's* style and got him across. Eight seconds. Jake, DeMarcus and Just couldn't figure out how to carry Kumal's girth. DeMarcus and Just each had a leg, Jake had his arms; they were carrying him out of the surf at Normandy. But Jake's slippery mitts kept slipping. I sprinted back and took an arm. We ran this big boy in his athlete's undies the last twenty yards as fast as we possibly could. I looked at my watch. We missed it by four seconds but I told them we did it. That we beat the clock. I wasn't a *monster*.

I wish I could say that we stopped after that. We didn't. We ran stairs. And one legged stairs. Double-leg-hop, skip-a-stair stairs. And stairs again. Shins bled. We ended on a four hundred meter beat-the-clock. I said we all had to beat a minute and fifteen seconds and I was ready to lie, fudge a few seconds for the cause. But everybody broke it. And we were bound.

I WATCHED FROM behind as they staggered back toward our own field, arms slung around each other like they were louses on Bourbon St. I was happy, wondering how long it would last, thinking of a Sierra I had in the fridge and that if I had a girlfriend or a wife I could text her to put it in the freezer, two for that matter. It was a helluva day.

"Crazy doesn't add up to smart," McMillan soft-barked from

the shadows of the equipment shed.

"Yeah, but crazy is how the dogs do, and on and on and on and on…" I was slurring. I kept walking. I wasn't going to let him ruin my imaginary girlfriend and my real Sierra.

"What?"

I turned to him. "I'm HAPPY."

"It's not about you."

"I said 'we'. They're happy. We're happy. I'm happy." I ambled off. "It's all the same. It's one in the same." Fuck him. *Fuck*. I had said *I'm happy*. I watched my guys as some of the parents hurried them along, annoyed with our punchy swagger. They didn't know we had just orbited the moon without any space gear. Kumal was still in his rudds. They were happy. And they'd remember this.

"Fuck you," I said to McMillan.

"Fuck you," I said to myself.

EIGHT

I WANTED TO HAVE OPENED AN OPTIMALLY COLD SIERRA BEFORE I LOOKED at the email. The beer was in the freezer for less than five minutes but the situation was extenuating. I was nervous because I had attached things in the email that I was excruciatingly self-conscious of: words from my brain, through my fingers, for people to read, for maybe Garret Hedlund to someday say out loud. It would always feel insane. "I want your attention!" was all any of this ever was. It made me feel like I had Crone's. The Sierra tasted so good I wanted to marry it. I was making a desperate play for this poor woman and her brawny husband's attention and it made me sick. It was how this grubby town operated but I would never get used to it. This poor woman. This poor, terribly wealthy woman. This poor, terribly wealthy, married woman. This poor, terribly wealthy, married, unsettlingly attractive woman whom I suddenly realized was occupying so much of my mind for the past month that it could end with a Wikipedia page and an option for a miniseries that never got developed. It felt good, it just didn't feel right. It felt fine when it felt foolish, when I reminded myself that it was probably nothing. I muscled myself into this fun and foolish state and opened the email:

hello. i love this script. it feels squid in the whale-y. i mean that in a good way. will forward along to husband although he won't be nearly as punctual with his read as I was. he's a little busy, in his defense.

having a small dinner thing friday if your free. a friend of mine who works at a company that produces noah baumbach's films is coming over. she's lovely (and single!) although maybe that's not good to mix the two. but your beautiful script made me think of it.

   xx Camilla

I reattached my head after stumbling around the room for it like sloppy Balboa once did a chicken. I put another Sierra in the fridge and wondered when to say yes. To the invite. My head fell off again and I accidentally kicked it close to the stove. A dinner party! With strangers! A dinner party with highfalutin strangers! This was my absolute nightmare! I'd been wrong this whole time! The darkness, the hill sprints, the *pain* had nothing on this! I was so happy with myself and I wanted nothing more than to not exist.

"Squid in the whale-y"!!!! Sure it was "and" not "in" but that aloof mishap was packaged into the most lovely front-handed compliment with a soupçon of questionable condescension—she said "i mean that in a good way," so, no, no, no condescension questionable or otherwise—that I had ever been witness to let alone received. She was forwarding it to *BUCK* MOTHER-FUCKING *TOURNEY*. No, I was *not* stung about the her maybe wanting to hook me up with her friend part and how dare I even wonder if I was? "Stung"? Get a life. This was game-changing. The nexus of Baumbach & Tourney and all I had to do was buy a bottle of rosè and not have a social stroke. And if I had infected her brain at a sixteenth of the infection rate with which she had infected mine, her mentioning her friend was simply an offensive defense mechanism, her getting out in front of it and that's the right play! We could be *friends*. We were adorably crushing and what better base from which blossoms a beautiful friendship than a crush? Right? I didn't want to speak for her. But that had to be a common cornerstone of friendship. If not completely common then semi-common. Either way, she compared me to Noah Baumbach, the one association I had ever wanted, and I was going to go over to her house to immediately, upon arrival, lose all of my already questionable charm and cognitive motor skills. A large part of me thought that *not* going would be a better career move. Let her forward the script to Tourney and he'll surely never read it and I'll find another way. If everything I ever dreamt of was a dinner and cocktails confirmation email away, something good could maybe happen by the time I hit forty-five. The wait was perhaps preferable. This seemed disastrous. Not the looming fantastical tryst—I assumed that that was out of my control. But walking into that house, bowling a turkey on spilled drinks within my opening fifteen minutes, speaking in tongues, a mishmash of fruity word-loaf cranked out through my meat grinder for their displeasure. Or, the worst scenario, as well as the most likely: the Freeze. I make the mistake of keeping quiet, quickly, and then get too deep into the mute-hole and I never find an opening and my legacy is confirmed: "remember that night with the silent guy?" I had to cancel. But I hadn't yet confirmed so all I needed was to lie or just do something else. I didn't like this and I wasn't cut out for it and I would never, ever rise to a moment. I needed to start a different life. Or I should go to that dinner. I needed counsel.

"It'll be a *heartbreaking story about love and luck…*" Alex sang, smiling, clinking my Heineken with his glass though I hadn't offered it.

In my hands were the soggy pieces of coaster I had shredded. He looked at them and shook his head, feeling sorry or put-off, took the coaster remnants, cupped them in his own hands and leaned over the bar to throw them away.

"So do I go?" I was at my wits' end with uncertainty. When would I not need someone to tell me who to be.

"Well, Pal: is this a movie you wanna see?" I was still trying to decode her email and of course I'd want to see this movie. I was the star. I was American. Also, she *xx*'d everyone: that was her signoff. And this movie Alex was talking about. Was it my getting a script to Tourney in a funny, non wife-fucking way? Or was the movie a darker comedy and I was fucking Tourney's wife whilst trying to flint start an entertainment mentorship with Tourney himself.

"Is it Nancy Meyers or…Nancy Meyers?" I didn't know what else to say and that felt insider-y. I forged ahead before Alex could make me feel stupid for trying to fit in. "I dunno. I dunno. I dunno." I didn't know. "I dunno."

"Oh, Jesus," he said as he motioned for another round.

"What?!?"

"You are troubled."

"Well, yeah." I said. Wait. "Right now or always?"

"Okay," he nodded, realizing that I did, in fact, need advice.

"I will tell you this: it doesn't end well. Ever." The bartender put a Heineken in front of me and a Bud in front of Alex. "But maybe it's worth it—I can't forecast that. That's life, though," he shrugged. "It doesn't end well. But maybe it's worth it." He was happy with himself for that. I was happy for him. "But he'll fucking kill you if he finds out."

I looked at one of the regular's legs, a guy who was never not at the Lost & Found, from what I knew, from my tenure inside. He looked pretty good up top, like a little Tim Legler. But he wore cargo shorts and his legs looked like my Grandma's. I supposed that's where all the liquor went.

"And he will find out," Alex said as if this were a voice over audition for a Liam Neeson trailer.

He looked at me and I'm guessing my face looked clingy, clinging to the fading hope that this could be all be chaste. That it could just be about the words.

"Oh Jesus: this isn't about getting him a script," Alex laughed, barbling up Budweiser for the point. He was a mensch, he read me well, even if I was an easy read. He flipped through his phone. "You want his email? We can get him the script right now."

"But maybe it's better coming from her?" I said it like I was watching a Mylar balloon float away. *Keep an eye on it? Maybe it'll pop early? I can run and grab it?*

"Yeah, Pal. You might be right. His wife gives him a script from a dashing young up-and-comer. That's the route you want."

Dashing! Up AND coming! I never wanted to see any of my other friends again.

"If it's about the script," he waggled his phone again. "We

can get it to him. But. You're gonna go to this dinner on Friday because you will convince yourself that it's rude not to and that it's good practice for your 'social anxiety' or whatever-the-millennial-fuck. But you're going into the henhouse thinking you're just gonna play a couple rounds of Boggle, and what you're doing is fucking with somebody's marriage. And even if the marriage isn't…sound…" He winced like I had drawn up a flea-flicker at a very questionable time. "Listen. I'm sure he fucks around plenty. He's a fucking asshole. Fuck him. Fuck his wife! I don't know, Man—nobody does!" Heads turned, I tried to laugh. "But. He will find out. And he'll kill you."

"What's she like?" How that was the next thing that came out of my mouth after learning that my life was in potentially grave danger, I haven't a clue. I almost coupled it with "Is she sketch?" but I could feel myself wading into the murky swamp of grown-ups and the "s" word—at least its earnest usage—had no place there.

"She's lovely. I don't know her very well, but she seems nice and funny enough and…"

"No, no—I…" I knew those things.

"Is she known to fuck around?"

To which I got embarrassed, offended, and violently defensive of her. I wanted to kill him.

"Not that I know of," he said.

I laughed at the contents of my life. "It's just not…I'm just a shithead. I have some records, a hand-me-down bed, one borrowed suit and a la Creuset I kinda stole…I eat entire meals from the Whole Foods salad bar—I almost choked the other day because I was shoveling falafel balls into my mouth like a Blue Man." I took a sip, tried to rinse out what was coming. "I've never been to Europe." It wasn't that that broke me, it was the entire assessment. I wasn't even fraudulent. I was an authentic, professional flounder. And it sucked to say out loud. Alex put his hand on my shoulder, gave it the squeeze you give to somebody who's fighting back tears at the Lost & Found.

"Pal. You don't give yourself enough credit," he said. "But that's why I like you. And that's probably why she does, too." Again, he found me a mooring. "And yet, you're still an arrogant asshole!" We laughed and got little bags of chips. He original Lay's and Fritos for me.

"And when I write the book about my love, it'll be about a Man who's torn in half..."

He had a pretty good voice.

"THE PRACTICE" DID not prepare me for the drive over. No practice could have. I wanted more traffic. The counsel at the bar had helped but that was a different era. I saw now why people joined the army or became carnies: they were running from dinner parties.

Sam was with me, as The Croat—I had resigned to calling her The Croat until further notice, a futile attempt at arm's length—had asked for him on Teddy's behalf. Nothing more obnoxious than someone who brings their dog everywhere. It's pathetic and vile, insisting your animal on others. But I was so terribly grateful for him because it gave me an opener, a shtick for these strangers who scared me more than death.

My diaphragm and pancreas—all known innards—felt cluttered with waterbugs. Little invaders zig-zagging and zapping about my guts. I could not see a version of this evening going even plain bad. Flu-like and clammy, I had no business in any business and I just wanted to be left alone, eaten by a bear or a shark or I could turn around and drive downtown, score some smack, boil up a lethal dose and set free the birds and the bugs.

Berea Pl. off Chataqua Blvd. and I needed an inhaler. I thought I saw Charlie Kaufman jogging against my grain but when I slowed to look, he was gone, if he was ever there.

I didn't die and I found a spot on the street, a few houses down. I futzed with my hair one too many times and couldn't get it back. "You greedy fuck," I said, so mad I almost chipped a tooth. I opened a second Heineken bracer and poured it down my throat. I was trying to be religious about it, Monk-like, a smooth, steady pour devoid of glugging. The rivers of Babylon, who knows. I got comfortable and choked a spout of lager onto my lap. My pants were a tan Levi, somewhere split between a chino and a jean, a bad pant for a spill.

Every pore perspired. I was a ghost pepper.

Two houses up, a basketball clanged off a rim and I saw Teddy corralling the shot, scanning the streets, maybe looking for us. I stepped out of the car and got my act together.

"I wet my pants," I told her as she ran to greet Sam.

"No," she dismissed, giggly.

"I got nervous!" I got another big laugh as I took the basketball from her. I was killing. I could text the Croat and tell her I got two early laughs and had to scram. The night could only go to hell from there. It would be a crazy yet respectable move and it would get me out of my inevitable tailspin into blunder-drunk. I handed the rosè to Teddy, pulled up from eighteen, BANG!: Mike Breen, take the wheel.

Despite my pleas to not leave, Teddy followed Sam around the corner of the house to the back deck where he heard voices, smelled a searing. She had the rosè. I wished a rattlesnake bite on Sam for leaving me lonely and afraid.

Up there on top of the world was what was wrong with this country and cognition. Because I looked around and thought "I mean…it's not *impossible*." But it was. It is. The Tourney house looked modest from the outside, aside from its commanding view of the mightiest ocean. It was a Modern/Cape Cod structure high on the hill with bluish-grey clapboard siding and white trim. Big windows, natural light. Three car garage seemed to be its biggest flaunt. Two lemon trees in front with a run of bush poppies lining the yard for privacy. Bougainvillea on a pergola. It was very nice but I wasn't a stain on the place. My dad had painted nicer houses. I laughed at the rumor that Tourney had a turf field on his property. Serfs create the myths.

I needed that bottle of rosè for my hands. I was comfortable with the property but still wasn't ready for the kind of people it welcomed. I flipped the basketball up with my foot, shook an imaginary defender and pulled up again—this time from twenty—and it clanged off the rim and I hated anyone who ever said to keep shooting. The door opened behind me and I stood there, feeling like Tom Cruise on the ledge at the end of *Vanilla Sky*.

"Square your shoulders a little more." Her voice drizzled into my ears like Tupelo honey. It belonged on toast. She wore tight white jeans and an old navy blue t-shirt whose logo was too faded to make out. Some sailboat company or a defunct literary journal. I couldn't spend too much time trying to read it because it would flirt with ogling. I wanted to plunge my head into an ice bath and kiss her chin. Her feet were bare. She held the rosè

"That's mine," I said of the wine. "I mean, it's for you, but I want the credit." The basketball had kicked back to me and I picked it up as I made my way toward her and her house. "And I didn't square my *hips*, as the shoulders follow the hips." Alex was right. I cried tears of self-loathing into my lagers yet I was arrogant as an oil baron. I hurled the ball blindly back over my shoulder, figuring if I sunk it, we'd elope. Her face went worried and I heard the hollow pop of aluminum, roof or hood of a luxury car, followed by an alarm.

"Shit." I gave her a quick Long Island hello-kiss, hand lightly on her ribs as if I knew things, had a firm grasp on the firmament, before I hustled down the driveway and across the street to get the basketball.

Somebody somewhere silenced the alarm.

INSIDE, THE HOUSE was Malibu modest. But I had nothing to compare it to, Malibu or otherwise. It was the nicest home I'd ever been in. Chic, clean, but not afraid of the slightly askew. A lot of books, some classy memorabilia, an on-set black-and-white photo of Tourney directing Ryan Leaf and Ki-Jana Carter during the filming of an episode of *The Yips*; a picture of Tourney and Wahlberg sparring in between set-ups on the set of that Jack Dempsey biopic. The place had a tasteful touch. Similar tones to the outside, the light blues and white moldings. Dining room wallpapered with Toucans in trees, a wicker liquor cart screamed at me. The art on the walls I knew nothing of but liked their look. I opened my mouth to speak on it but remembered my pedigree and made a mental note not to go my entire life being an aesthetic rube. There was flora aplenty and I made another mental note to get some flowers every once in a while. I had brought the invasive fauna and I watched him sniffing about through the enormous glass wall that accordioned itself into multi-folded French doors. Beyond the doors, the deck was perfect—ipe with dimensions too grand for me to guess upon. Five hundred square feet? Ten thousand? Seventy-five? I wanted to live there.

"Do you want some...wine?" The Croat said this from the fridge so I followed her into the kitchen where I made one last mental note to kill myself if I wasn't rich in twelve years. "Or tequila?" I wanted to play percussion on all the hanging pots, filet a dorado or a suckling pig on the butcher's block island, make a dramatic advance on her figure and face, get slapped and stick my head in the oven.

"Sure." I wanted a beer, though. A cold beer is man's only friend. Sam was outside sniffing a cheese plate, turning his back on everything we'd built. I snapped my fingers and he felt it somewhere within and backed off, spooked.

"That's a heckuva snap," she noted.

"It's all I've got."

She demurred an "Mmmhmmm," and I tried to but couldn't think of anything else I had that was as good as my snap. I liked jumping into rivers. But that wasn't funny. Nor did it require any skill.

"Tequila or wine," she asked again, as I was just saying "sure" to everything. "We don't have any beer. Husband's been out of town."

Tourney didn't have any emergency cleansers? A cold, crummy PBR to navigate the madness?! What an asshole! Wine made me converse at a fourth grade level. When nervous I tended to drink it like we drank Gatorade in the summertime 90's. If he was forcing my hand, making me guzzle liquor and wine in new company, maybe I *should* hump his wife.

"Do I have to meet those people?" I winced toward the outside but smiled at her, trying to run interference on my lurid, brazen thoughts.

"Probably."

"Tequila?" I asked. "Tequila," I said. Agave gave me a charm pocket I could work with.

She nodded, opened the freezer. "Shit! The ice thing clicked off."

"It's fine," I said, but it wasn't. No cold beers and hot tequila—we didn't stand a chance. Temperature didn't make a blip in her registrar. For me it was a non-starter, full-stop, dead-stop; we were dead before arrival. DBA. Temperature was everything. Or maybe, *maybe* she was just hosting aloof-obtuse, obtuse-aloof, which did have a sexy undertone. Jump-stop? Maybe it'd be a running joke between us. You only need one temperature guy in a relationship. I'd always make sure we had plenty of ice, that the beers were frosty. I liked my reds chilled. I'd make that face at her and she'd pinch off a "you *motherfff...*" smile and go into the other room or outside and continue the conversation she was having with whoever was over. I'd ask her to flip the record but she'd be out of earshot or pretend to be, which was cute, too. Half of the last song on the first side of the record was still left, anyway. I'd flip it in a minute. Later we'd laugh and fuck. We'd be okay. Her quirky disregard for temperature actually saved us. She now handed me an empty glass and it took everything I had not to hook her in my arm, slow-dance her and laugh the unspoken, understanding laugh of our inevitable future selves. I was sick. I helped myself to four fingers or a fist of the expensive stuff in the dining room with the Toucans and relaxed a little. I refilled in one motion so it could be mistaken for the same pour and walked back into the kitchen where Teddy was bartering dessert.

"I ate a piece THIS big," she said, outlining a piece of pizza, a square with her forearms and hands and I wondered where they made Detroit-style pizza around here or if it was frozen. "So can I have two mochis?" She asked like eating the pizza was pulling weeds for an hour.

"What're mochii's?" I asked because I didn't know. And the tequila made me care less of my ignorance.

"It's like a Japanese ice cream ball," said the Croat, signing its size, slightly bigger than a golf ball, maybe a good plum.

"They're the best," Teddy said, bar none. She looked again to her mother, growing tired of asking. "Mom, please."

"Sure," I said. I shrugged at the Croat, a non-apology for trying to get in good with the Kid. I looked down at the Croat's newly pedicured feet. Perfect biped feet on a tiled floor and I looked all the way up through limbs and exposed tissues, cartilage, flesh, bone, hair and I understood and sympathized with every fetish up and down to the fetish of the philtrum. The tequila made me feel at home. I took another sip. "Lemme get one?"

"*Yes.*" Teddy was pumped for the initiation. Her mom got a box from the freezer, handed her what I assumed was a mochii ball, which Teddy handed to me—a small act that said a lot. Teddy watched eagerly, waiting on hers to see how my experience fared. The texture was a little weird but we felt like a family.

"Pretty dank," I said, trying to diffuse my beam. Camilla and her daughter laughed the same laugh and the next bite was even better.

Ejecting from the mochii moment was hard but important. I was resentful of outside and the people there, but I had to step out and in because my presence was already suspect. Introductions were made and I was met with the kind of indifference I'd only seen from the mean high school chicks in coming-of-age movies. Perfunctorily limp-wristed hands were offered from the two women who lounged on the Arhaus sectional. The woman who acknowledged me only slightly more than the other I took to be the Baumbach connect, Rachel Hardy. The dream of cultivating the mentor of my dreams died on the deck, DNR. Rachel had blonde hair and sharp features like a witch that could go either way and wore a loose fitting white oxford and tight black jeans and she liked gold things on her neck. She seemed irritated that people like me came around, like the night could have had promise if I had salt and pepper hair and an Amex Black, a reputable client list. The other woman looked over my shoulder as I introduced myself and I could have made a generous stretch, given her the benefit of the doubt: maybe she had some Asperger's in her or weird vision, a lazy eye. But she was just a plain old, hot Bitch. She had fake breasts and a snug, flowery blouse that tied. My pants were still a little wet in the crotch but other than that I was dressed like I could make seventy-five thousand bucks a year. A chambray shirt and Red Wings. And I smelled good. Hell, I could be making eighty thousand. Then I remembered what I made and how much I'd never made and understood what they knew me to be, what I was: their friend's step-son's lacrosse coach.

I turned to the ocean and made my way to the edge of the rail-less deck, following the light plume of bar-b-que smoke. The ocean was big from up on high and it made me feel a little bit better, less so than the night sky in the middle of nowhere but it at least made me think "fuck those chicks." There was a lot going on under there. A lot of plastic, but still. Sets were rolling in, stretching from Point Dume down to Palos Verdes and I felt guilty for not surfing even if I didn't even like it that much. But I did, I just didn't like surfing in Los Angeles. Maybe I just didn't like Los Angeles. I thought of East Coast women and breakfast sandwiches and got to the edge of the deck and was walloped by the scope of what I had mistook for rich residential modesty. The house behind me and the deck I stood on, they were only the beginning. There was another story of the Tourney house—I could maybe now upgrade its category to "estate" or "manor"—angled to the right, the south I suppose, baked into the hillside. Full glass paneled master bedroom which made me queasy, made me want to stick a finger down my throat and rid myself of the stupid mochii and the boutique tequila. The deck descended into a long set of large stadium steps which led down to…a turf field. Beyond that was a vertical red cedar-paneled guest house or an office or a gym or all three probably. I saw a heavy bag through a sliding glass door and an editing bay on the opposite end, but "where Tourney goes to fuck little boys" was where my rotten, jealous mind went. Separating the field from the diddling house (I couldn't help it) were two pools; a lap pool and a casual baster with a slate border and a beautiful rainbow pebble floor. A perfect place to unselfconsciously throw around bad movie ideas with the Hollywood elite. It made me hate all the movies I ever loved.

There was a lacrosse cage on the field with a large netted backdrop. I remembered we had a game tomorrow. The field itself was probably seventy-five yards. Perfect for a game of touch. A dude at the grill by the basting pool was holding a baby in the crook of his arm, tongs in his dominant hand. He must have watched me looking at everything, stopping on every stadium step to gather more envy and disgrace. Sam helped guard the grill.

"Do you have things like this?" I asked the Dude as we shook hands, or I shook his forearm, rather, because his hands were full. I put my drink down and reached for the baby, offered my services. He handed it over, an unspoken gratefulness and trust as he rolled his shoulder and hinged his elbow a few times. The baby was a boy.

"No-no. No." He sipped a sweating bottle of Stella Artois.

"What the hell is that?"

"Beer. Stella?" His name was Will and he wore round tortoise shell eyeglasses. He had great hair and an outfit on which I imagined he had ten near identical variations of in his closet that rotated on an electrical closet rack and washed themselves. Chinos, plaid J-Crew, Clark's desert boots. He seemed about my age but the baby obviously wizened him beyond my years.

"No, I mean where." He pointed inside the smaller really nice house and I spotted a fridge in the room with the heavy bag. "*Sick.*" I made my way. "You want one?" He nodded.

He wasn't in love with me, but who could blame him? I was just some interloper his wife's friend invited over to her house while her husband was out hustling, making screen dreams. What was there to like? He didn't know that I was just a decent shithead with nothing to lose, not a shithead-shithead. I liked him, though, and felt I saw the good in people. All that self-branded misanthropic bullshit of mine was bullshit. Here was a guy, probably with a trust fund and an Ivy League degree, Manhattan rich kid married richer. But I saw the Dude in him. "Born This Way" by Lady Gaga popped into my head. If I wasn't exactly a "people person" I was at least a man, a person of all people. People deserved a chance. Not Cuthbert, but everyone else. I wondered how long it would take and how much it would cost to get my therapist's license.

An elegant woman in a lime green calf-length spring dress with a belt emerged from the house and smiled warmly at me as Will introduced us. It was his wife. Moira. She was pretty if a little tired of it all, had thick brown hair and she put her hands out in an "I'll take *that*" gesture and took back her baby as we crossed paths. She wasn't worried-worried, she just didn't want me disappearing behind closed doors with the little fucker. Even with all the natural light.

I returned with the pair of beers and Will's wife had retreated back up the steps, probably just to leave the males alone, not because of me. But the damage was done, the "probably…not because of me" had permeated my metrics. I felt a little weak, realized I had done everything wrong, body-wise, for drinking. Dehydrated. The last thing I had eaten was half a tomato and a spoonful of old bee pollen I had bought the previous year because allegedly it made your dick better and your hair less less. I pretended to have left something inside when I went to get the beers. Nothing specific, and Will didn't give a shit either way. "I left my button" I think is what came out.

In the gym area, there were cases of some new-age protein bar that Tourney had by the pallet and I tore into one, a Cro-Magnon Man awoken from hibernation by an epipen. I saw the Croat coming down the stadium steps and I tried to swallow too fast, too hard and the space paste from the bar got lodged in my throat and I thought what a funny way to die. It became very unfunny, right quick. I had no choking experience. I pressed my stomach against the corner of the refrigerator thinking it could Heimlich. It could not. I tried to casually walk out of view from the window, out of frame, out of sight to die, curl up with some dignity in this joke of a death. I caught a last glimpse of myself in the mirror as my face blued and there, in my dying hand: a Stella.

Like looking around for your cellphone when it's right there in your mitt. I poured a slow sip into the blockage and it fizzled, foamed, made the plug malleable, then fluid, and I didn't want to only drink Stella for the rest of my life, but I would drink a lot more of it than I had in the past, before it saved my life.

I caught my breath, filled my lungs and head with air and re-emerged not believing in God, but humbled and less insane. Grounded. The Croat looked at me like we hadn't seen each other in a while and she was happy I was there. I loved earth. It seemed every one of our exchanges or looks eclipsed the one before. When it can't get better but does. The middle finger to the cynical science of what you thought you knew about infatuation.

The Croat started to say something, stopped, looked closer at my face. She reached a hand over, "Sorry—you have chocolate on your face," and wiped it off. The moment of intimacy gave me a heart murmur and if it fazed Will at all, he didn't show it. He'd seen a mammal come out of his wife's crotch.

I stood there getting chocolate wiped off my face by who, at that moment, was my favorite person in the world, and I chose to lay my cards bare. I started with the drive over. Then I went back a few days to worrying about how to subject an email—a universal concern. Fast forwarded to that day, practice, making the kids run far too much, too long and too hard during a pregame practice because I had the pre-dinner-party jimmies. I talked about buying the rosè; my price point boundaries that would make me look like I wasn't trying to be something I wasn't but wasn't leaning into what I currently was. I picked back up with the drive over, likened it to bungee jumping, base jumping, skydiving. Adrenaline junkies ain't got shit on me, et cetera, etc. The Heineken meditation gone sloppy, wet pants, hitting an eighteen-foot jump shot, BANG! and I knew Will got my Mike Breen. I hit that pocket of drinks-to-storytelling where the whole game just slows down for you and you imagine this is how Roger Federer feels a lot. I gave the Croat ice grief. I talked graceful but cutting shit about her friends on the deck. The baby hand-off, bee pollen and the weakies. The protein bar and the Stella that was still in my hand. It was just what had happened but sometimes you want certain people to know why you act a certain way. It was all a lot and not much at all, my mortality just a small part, and I started to get choked up and I pointed that out, too, because it really was all, always, more-than-occasionally *heavy*, and maybe you could stop the water if you called out the clouds before it rained.

"And that's how I got chocolate on my face."

Neither of them said anything and that was okay. From where I stood it seemed they'd enjoyed themselves. The Croat broke first, happy and compassionate, hugged me, onlookers be damned. Another exchange eclipsed. And the moment I'd probably look back on when she couldn't be the Croat anymore. When she really became Camilla.

Will shook his head, giving a last chuckle of credit for the yarn I had spun. I picked up the hot tequila and took a pull, pretending to burn my mouth on it. There was a last sip and I handed it to Camilla. She pinched off a smile and shook her head at me (*"you motherffff"*) before she drank the tequila and took to the stairs.

"Can you flip the record?" I called after her.

She gave a thumb's up.

EVERYTHING WAS FINE after that. I had flirted with death and what followed was ice cream & gravy. I was on the other side. I could drink a billion beers and walk the line. Will and I slammed a couple more Stellas and pontificated on the Knicks and the Giants and the tri-tip cut, agreeing that it was a joke, a sham, a rip-off and only chicks bought it because it sounded like it should chew nice but it didn't. And we agreed that it was nice to say "only chicks do ____" around a grill with a beer and a new buddy and new buddies at this age were really rare and wild and nice, too.

"You guys are both writers," said the Baumbach woman, Rachel, when we sat down to dinner.

"I'm a lacrosse coach," I said.

"I'm a Dad," Will said.

Both were true. We didn't need her charity conduit—we were already fine. I didn't think he thought I was trying to do what I wasn't exactly sure I was trying to do yet, anyway. Tourney had come up in our grill-side chat, and Will seemed respectfully ambivalent about the guy. Tourney was fifty-two and a powerhouse, had a wife who was thirty-five who he somehow stole from me. Will was thirty-three, and, like me, trying to see how, where, and if he fit in anywhere. Him and Tourney weren't buddies but they were friendly. The age and success gap naturally thins things out. Or maybe just the success gap because Alex and I were pretty thick. Either way it seemed like Will liked me better than Tourney even if he wasn't aware of my angling for a comparison. We're all children I tried to remind myself. Or just me, forever, and there was no comparison because Tourney was a Megalodon and I was just a mercurial perch.

Don't lose your hair and always do the dishes. That's what I told my guys. If the first happens, you'll probably be better for it, but you'll never actually believe that, which is its fighting chance at truth. But always do the dishes.

"He's actually started to," Camilla said when I asked if there'd been a change in Just's household weight-carrying, if he started helping. I felt a pang of pride knowing the fellas were heeding my practical nonsense off the field. Also, Camilla and I were cleaning the kitchen together so I had geysers of other misguided happy waves happily crashing in all systems, endocrine and otherwise.

"One of these days I'm gonna walk up behind you and buzz it all off." She was talking about my hair, which apparently I had muscled into the conversation.

"I've still got four decent years! And three super sad ones after that."

"But you never shut up about it!"

I shut up and smiled at her for too long and in the eyes too deep and her left iris twitched like she thought maybe she should look away. They were witch-hazel, her eyes, emerald, flecks of lavender and Burberry and storm trooper. I grabbed a half drunk glass of water beside the sink, raised it and said: "We're having fun now."

Her eyes widened as I downed what was in the glass because

it wasn't water, it was tequila or mezcal, gasolinà. I shuddered and winced and wheezed something about drinking everybody's old waters because of the drought, climate change yet again the culprit of my demise. She handed me a slim-canned Perrier and I poured it on my Oaxacan belly-fire.

Will and his wife had left with their baby. The Baumbach woman was waiting me out outside, eyes flitting up to the window above the sink as she flicked through her phone, sending clockless Hollywood emails on the deck by the infrared fire-pit. The other woman was recklessly swiping left and right on the couch opposite.

"I should take my leave," I agreed with myself. I needed to scram before all the booze officially seeped into my system. I had maybe ten minutes and the drive was fifteen but the last five were autopilot. Camilla began to protest my driving but recognized that I was a professional and would not be dissuaded.

I poked my head out to say goodbye to Rachel and the Bitch. They waved with their phones. I started to make a dumb joke to get a smug reaction but it would have only broken even and my metamorphosis into sotty pumpkin had already begun. I had to hustle.

With Camilla behind me, I nodded to Ryan Leaf as I made my way to the door, as if to let him know that I still believed in him.

"I'd still take you over Peyton," I felt I needed to say out loud. I didn't care about Ryan Leaf. He seemed like a dick. But at fifteen years old I was certain he should go first.

I turned outside on the front landing and she stood in the threshold. We didn't want me to go.

"Tell the Kid I said goodnight," I told her.

"You already did when she went to bed."

"Tell her good morning, then."

I said thanks for having me over. Sam followed me down the steps after they said their own goodbyes. I turned back, feeling each grain fall into the dangerzone of my BAC's hourglass.

"I gotta ask you something."

It was a question I'd been avoiding. Well, not avoiding, because it was one I never knew I had to ask. But it was something I now needed to know because it could save or ruin lives, maybe mine forever, and that was the most insignificant of the possible casualties. I was the tree in the woods. But the wrong answer here and we could walk away. We could high-five and she could go to Dusseldorf, give my script to her husband to never read. He would make more movies; flops and hits, blockbusters all. They would keep inching upwards into the lower percentile of the one percent, their walking around money equivalent to sums that could change so many lives. Their marriage would bob and bite. She could introduce me to her friends, sing my praises, playing up my potential, the charm of my poor. The ones who weren't put-off by my projected bank sums I may or may not lacklusterly bang, revel in or spite the vapidity of second rate Hollywood tail. She and I would see each other at Just's games or at Erewhon or none of those things and more realistically, this funny little doodle of a Kitchenaid flirt would just fall by the wayside and fade in a blink and a smile and I'd move on with my trifling and misplaced ambitions, my half-assed, wayward life, make some money or not, meet somebody or not, die soon or later. That was the outcome of the wrong answer, but clearly what was right. The *right* answer and things would go wrong. Irrevocably wrong. I knew then that Alex was right. I knew nothing about this world of sanctity and disdain, this contract of "I do" and "you mostly gross me out" but "if one of us fucks it up, that means war." The right answer and things would go wrong—I could end up in a Guyanese Necktie or with the insurmountable age-old American Heartache. Their alright marriage would dissolve. I would be the Emancipator or the Grave Mistake.

None of that mattered though, because, adults aside, the right answer, and I was fucking with Teddy's life.

"Led Zeppelin or The Who?"

"The Who." She didn't even bat an eye.

I inhaled infatuation. I exhaled inhibition. My chin fell to my chest in beautiful defeat.

I scooped Sam up and slung him over my shoulders, walked back to our Subaru in the way of the Shepherd Boy who knew he was destined to be the Dumbest Fuck this side of the Euphrates.

"I'm singin' this note 'cause it fits in well with the chords I'm playin'," I sang. *"I can't pretend there's any meanin' here or in the things I'm sayin'…"*

The door clicked shut behind me.

"But I'm in tune. Right in tune. I'm in tu-u-une…and I'm gonna tuuuune!"

From the street I could swear I felt the door peek back open.

"Right in on you-ou-ou…"

And shut again.

NINE

The day after *The* Practice (see, also: The Day the Day Went Dark), we played Sierra Canyon, a team that had Waldorf traces, a student body with too many "old souls" in that they probably collected Pogs. We lost to a lesser team because we couldn't walk much less run. I had to lay down on my side to tie my shoe that day, the previous day's test of spirit, strength and wills having shredded every fiber in my lower half. We were a children's hospital. I had done it knowing the consequences, knowing it was arrogant and selfish to go crazy the day before a game but knowing, too, my guys didn't deserve a shit win like that. Their ceiling was too high for them to think they were any good just yet. I wasn't worried about Sierra Canyon.

But I was now quite worried about Newbury Park, who were up next. We desperately needed a win. Time was running out and we needed a before and after. We needed our *moment*. We'd be a little bit of a joke if we lost at Newbury Park, and the natural mutiny that followed would be a descent into jest. How could I continue to make them run if the only place it got us was lost? Another loss and we would only know how to lose and that would be our thing. One more loss and we'd be on the sad side of the joke, the misguided pomposity of throwing away the Sierra Canyon game biting me in the dumb ass. One more loss and it all falls apart.

"Sweet set-up you've got at your place." These were my first words to Just as we were boarding the bus to the game. Feeling good made one slip.

"What?" Luckily he was still wiping the sleep from his eyes, struggling to open a cereal bar. I opened it for him, took a bite.

"Turf field. Field-turf-field. Is it? Do you not?" I ran interference with double-talk.

"Yeah but how do you know?"

"Crothers' Dad told me."

I sat down in the front of the bus and doodled John Madden inspired football plays on a whiteboard until I figured my stupidity had passed him by. I wasn't lying—Crother's Dad had maybe told me. Plus, I didn't owe anybody anything, this greasy little whipper-snapper especially. And there, oh wow, there I discovered acidic stitches of jealousy toward Just, toward the hundreds of thousands of moments they'd had, him and his dad's second wife. I wanted to choke him, slap the milk money out of his hand but I also wanted to be around him, buddy up and get all that I could of her through second person step-son osmosis. Everything felt very out of my control. *Suppressiooooon! Suppression!!* sang forth my mind in Fiddler form.

"Jake, Just, Dee and Mecca: up front," I barked, bouncing myself back to more practical thoughts.

The night before, after the dinner party, I had started to make a "dream board." This was also, subsequently, after I had overdrawn my checking account on account of the six-pack of Heineken, pack of Trident White and Big Grab of Fritos Honey BBQ Twists from the 7-11 I was rewarding myself with for being pinch-me smitten. From a pinch to a slap which found me huckling nickels and dimes from the recesses of my car seats to complete my purchase. I agreed, then, again, to promise to be rich.

A lady I had slept with some years earlier—a "young professional"; very pretty, very smart, very driven, but, eh, a touch serious—had climbed the corporate ladder and was now a higher up at Mattel and swore she got to that higher place by what she called a "dream board." I had laughed at the time, at the astrological Palo Santo scented manifesting. But as I looked for a good piece of cardboard in the recycling bin in the alley, I felt a budding of what I could only assume was actualization. Causation and Actualization. I used my duplicate copy of *Love Stinks* as a straight edge and flipped through some magazines for visual references. My goal was simple but impossible to collage: I wanted to do whatever it took to take care of someone. Two someones. Two someones whose basic needs I couldn't fathom. Take care? These were two someones who were already very, very well taken care of. Very. Very. Very. All of those verys quintupled my exhaustion and the dream board didn't quite come together. It was an absurd, fleeting notion. How do you take care of the taken care of? *Steal Family, Make Soups!* Was that the title of my Dream? *Be Great Even if Bad, Provide.* Putz. The whole thing stunk like Honey BBQ Twists and I agreed to put myself to bed after one more glum-struck Heineken.

In the mirror I tried to worsen the mood. Shake the fist

of contempt. See the future, the past, the present, all just one forgettably superfluous, same-old-Me. Hum-Diddly Rumple the Bumpkin goes to go kick rocks. It didn't take, though. I was smiling, curiously confident, mocking my own fist. I couldn't dress myself down. It seemed the residual good she had made me feel kept me from bottom feeding, kept me out of my comfort gutter. Brushing my teeth, I saw someone else. I looked a little closer, prodded my stupid, smiling putty-face because I saw something new: I saw somebody she liked. I saw *who* she liked. *Fuck you, that's me!* I thought. It felt like a corner turned, one that would get me shot.

"Coach?" DeMarcus hooked me, reeled me in from above.

"Yeah, Buddy."

"You said 'Lambeer, Dumars...Terry Mills' and then just..." He did a good impersonation of me spacing out, losing interest, drifting between lofty thoughts. Or I guessed the impersonation was good—what did I know? *Lambeer, Dumars...*—it sounded as though I'd been likening Newbury Park to the early/mid 90's Pistons: beatable but you weren't psyched to play them. Win or lose, it was gonna hurt.

"I wanna be the Knicks," I picked up where I figured I had left off. "But the '99 Knicks. Hard but silky. Latrell and Houston. Chris Childs and LJ. Patrick as elder statesman." I loved what I wanted even if it was lost on them. Point was: Newbury Park kids were from the other side of the tracks if both sides were rich but one side had a few kids who smoked butts and rode dirt bikes.

"Just, I'm moving you to attack," I announced. He looked hurt. He wanted to run. "You've got the best stick," I reassured him. "I need you on the field as much as possible." He looked less hurt.

"But listen," I flipped the whiteboard around. "You know how defensemen can call 'middie back' so they can go into the offensive side of the field?" He nodded. What I was getting at, what this "middie back" referred to was that, as I've mentioned before, you simply need three offensive guys and three defensive guys (Goalie not included) on each half of the field at all times. So if a defensemen sees some daylight as he's carrying the ball up the field, he yells for a midfielder to hang back in his stead. Same can be said on the opposite end.

"You wanna get your defensive ya-yas out? Tell a midfielder to hang back on attack and go rough somebody up.

"Now," I said, squaring up to my fab four. "I need you guys to be *really* good." They nodded in time.

I turned to the rest of the team: "I need you guys to be capable." They were unsure if this was a test, if they needed to feel slighted. "I need you guys to be reliable. *Trustworthy*." That word at the least gave them wobbly vigor.

I turned around to watch out the windshield. We crested the hill of the 405, the Valley sprawled out below, socked in in its irreversible grey-brown exhaust.

I was tired and pulled my hat down over my eyes. I had biked up from Venice because I couldn't even have afforded a few gallons at 1999's gas prices. But I was happy. I couldn't help it. I had felt more good in a few hours the night before than I had in the past decade.

"We'll win this together," I said to my Cabinet as I faded out. For good measure, I added: "But if we lose, it's on you four."

Coaches who went through their pregame rituals stone-faced and businesslike were first-rate. I respected the hell out of the composed, but that was not me. Not that day. I was Crazed Dog. Low-fives, high-fives, Top-Guns—I even spun Manassas around by both arms in a whirly-woo like you do a four-year-old. It was a terrible decision to carry on like that because where does it all go if it's gone before the opening face-off? But it wasn't a decision, it was just who I was out there in the Valley. Somebody should have slapped me across the face or put a mongoose in my trousers—anything to expel my lunacy before I sabotaged the game, the season. But there was no mongoose in sight and by the end of the first quarter we had stormed out to a 0-5 deficit.

"Alright, well: we know we can get scored on and they know we can't score," I said in the huddle. They laughed, thank God. "I'm not a math guy, but if we just flip it," I stacked my hands in the air and quickly flipped them, for real: "I think we'll be fine."

They weren't tired. They weren't scared. They just needed some fucking *coaching*.

On the Newbury Park bench, they sucked wind, gasping as though there wasn't enough Powerade or oxygen in Simi Valley to keep this up for three more quarters. We'd be fine.

"Dudes," I leaned in, whispering so the parents couldn't hear me. "I fucked up. I think I'm in love." I locked eyes with Just and one of my eyeballs twitched, bugged out, Total Recall. "It's a weird feeling and I don't recommend it at all and I can't recommend it enough. But we'll talk about that later. Point is: I came out a little hot before." I blindly slapped Kumal. "I'm still crazier than a buckthorn in July, but I'm ready to re-enter the atmosphere if you'll have me." They nodded, and we re-coalesced. I looked around at each of them.

"They don't know what we know."

I put my hand in. They put theirs on mine.

"Through the darkness."

"To the light!"

As they went back out, I grabbed DeMarcus and Just by their facemasks.

"YOU," I ground my teeth at DeMarcus. "Pull it out and RUN PAST YOUR MAN."

"Yes, Coach," he said, knowing. DeMarcus gave the best *Yes Coach*.

One week and DeMarcus had gotten good. Sam and I stayed after practice with him every day till the late bus took him home. I was stubborn with my word to Walter and my Fuck You to McMillan. We went to work. Well, we went to repeat. Because we did one thing over and over. And over. And over. And over. And over. And overandoverandover. And again. And then ran it back.

The split-dodge. Lacrosse's equivalent to the crossover. If you're fast enough and stronger than most, offensively, there's nothing more you need to do, no other tricks to amass up your sleeve. Catch and throw and pick up ground-balls, sure. But it is a sliced-bread-and-the-wheel sport and if you can beat your man from up top and shoot before the slide comes or dish it to your teammate (the guy whose man slid), the game is pretty easy, and, as a result, pretty pretty. But you have to beat your man. And

DeMarcus Long: he was gonna beat his man.

Every evening I'd put on a helmet and gloves and he'd take a run at me from just below midfield. I'd wait just above the restraining box (halfway between the mid-line and the end-line. Again: the goal is set ten yards ABOVE the end-line), my hips closed, facing either sideline, dictating which direction he'd go. He'd drive at my up-field hip, getting the defender (myself in this case) to open up, sit back on my heels for just a hesitation and—

(*WHSHT*)

(*He gone.*)

"YOU," I put my face against Just's grill. "Put the ball in the back of the fucking net."

He smirked, nodded. They bumped fists and took their spots.

The faceoff in lacrosse looks like a hockey face-off or a jump-ball meets the start of a wrestling match. One dude from each team crouched in the middle of the field with the ball in between them. One dude from each team on each wing. Whistle blows and the dudes in the middle scrum for the loose ball and the dudes on the wing run in and try to help or hurt; a three-on-three for possession. On both offensive/defensive ends, nobody can cross the restraining line till a team has gained possession. Then it's game on.

In this instance, Mecca won the face-off on his own, ran it down and passed it to Just. Just danced in the corner for a second as I made a midfield substitution (subs take place, by and large, on the fly, mid-play). I told Just to get it to DeMarcus, he did, and DeMarcus pulled the ball out to midfield, his defender confused on whether or not to follow him out. His coach was confused as well because he gave his player no instruction ("do NOT follow the really fast black kid all the way out there!" would have been my advice) and the kid followed him out and DeMarcus blew past him. Just's defender made a confused slide at the meteor that was DeMarcus Long, DeMarcus flung the ball to Just and Just was so wide open, so alone, that he looked at me, wondering if maybe they didn't have enough guys on the field. I waved him on and he shrugged, looked back to the cage and plunked it in the bottom left corner.

Newbury Park won the next face-off but turned it over on a bungled pass. Crothers picked up the ground ball right by our bench and moved it immediately to Mecca and that alone made me well with pride. For a kid who not just a month and a half ago started playing, for him to pick up a ground-ball with a long stick and move it in one-ish motion up the field, for a coach, it's like seeing your kid take her first steps and those first steps are hop-scotch. I ditched my restraint and stepped out onto the field, hugged Crothers, wailing like he had just returned home from the Great War. I pointed at Alex in the stands, the tendons of my index finger strained with conviction.

I urged the fellas to move the ball around. Burt dropped a pass behind the cage but picked it back up after some mild harassment from his defenseman. Two more passes around the horn back up to DeMarcus, who pulled it out near midfield, same as before. This time his defenseman played way in, having learned his lesson, but that didn't matter. DeMarcus looked to me and I smiled, nodded—it was nice to be consulted—and off he went. I yelled for Just to clear through, underneath DeMarcus and in front of the cage, opening up the whole side of the field for DeMarcus. Just's defensemen didn't know who to go with—stay with his man (Just) or slide to DeMarcus—and as a result he froze. With no slide, DeMarcus let it rip, a bounce shot that bounced in front of the goalie, who dropped, and the shot bounced up over his shoulder into the upper left corner.

I turned and took a few steps across the track behind the bench, hopped up onto the guardrail of the stands where Walter was sitting and put my face two inches from his. He broke first, leaned back and cackled to the sky, shoved me back toward the sideline.

By the end of the half we were still down a goal—6-7—but we had arrived. We weren't exactly watching the money pile up but we were finally getting a taste of the good life.

"Man, I'm a fat kid and look how tired they are," Kumal chuckled as he squirted some water on his head from a green Gatorade squirt-top.

"HEY!" I snapped and he tightened up, scared, wondering what it was he'd said. "Don't you talk about You like that." He relaxed, relieved. "You're my Beautiful Boy."

We gathered on a patch of shade in the deep corner of the track. I shooed the parents away who edged toward our congregation, gave them a squinched, baffled look which hopefully made them feel stupid. There's no parents at half-time. Manassas' Mom had slipped around my field of vision and handed him a little pouch of baby food—it read "Go-Go Squeeze!"—and now, Manassas sat Indian Style, sucking on a baby sack. I watched him for a while before he capped the pouch and put it behind him. It was too strange a thing to make fun of—I felt sorry for him, for anyone who had to see it, for his Grandfathers, mostly. I had to at least go at his sitting style to lighten the air, the bummer that hung from watching that sorry display.

"Manassas, this isn't show and tell," I said and he nodded, thinking I was going at his Go-Go Squeeze. "You're not sharing about our trip to the Great Escape, eating graham crackers and drinking whole milk, Man." I was one big, dated reference. "You can't sit Indian Style at half-time!"

"It's criss-cross apple—"

"BRO!" Groaned everyone. Burt nudged him with his foot and Manassas stood.

I went back to chatting with Jake but I wasn't saying anything, just a staged conversation as I reached in my pocket for my phone and flung it through the flock of bodies at Maybelline, who dropped his Kind Bar and caught my phone like he was Bombay poor and the phone was an egg. He started to walk the phone back to me and I pointed across to Innie. Maybelline reluctantly tossed it to him, Innie caught it.

"How many of you guys have iPhones?" About one-third raised their hands. "Treat the ball with half as much care as you do your iPhone and we'll win this game."

I walked away, left them to chat. My Fab Four took control and I didn't hear what they were saying but there was command in the air. I whistled Beaker over.

"Hey, Buddy."

"Hi."

"I know *nothing* about playing goalie."

"Okay."

"Just stop the ball."

"Okay."

"Beaker. I'm kidding."

"Okay."

"I'm serious."

"Okay."

I couldn't tell if he was smarter than me or if it was the Asperger's. Either way, it was unnerving.

"Every shot they've taken has been where?"

He pointed at the ground.

"So let's assume they're gonna keep doing that. Step toward the ball," I took his stick—the goalie stick has a massive clown-sized tennis racket shaped head, the better with which to stop the ball—and stepped forward, whipped the head of the stick down like the pendulum of a Grandfather, the top of the head touching the ground in front of me. I stood back up. "And if it bounces anywhere out here or beyond," I made an imaginary marker a few feet in front of me. I really did know nothing about playing goalie. I played for a few weeks in sixth grade because of my first ACL injury and got hit a few times in the leg and was appalled that such a position existed. It felt cruel. "Step forward, but stay up." I was still slightly crouched, knees at about 150°. "And stop the ball." Made sense to me. Seemed to make sense to the both of us.

The ref blew the whistle and we huddled up.

"Whatta you got?" I looked to Just. He didn't smirk, didn't wise-acre.

"Take care of the ball. Score some goals."

I nodded. "And?"

"Let's…" We all turned to a squeaky Crothers. "…not let them score."

"I love it."

We did our cheer and took the field.

I looked over at their coaches and couldn't drum up any ire, so I gave a peace sign. Wanting to win it for us was plenty enough juice to fuel the next twenty-four minutes.

My goalie whispering days proved unfruitful when, in the opening thirty seconds of the second half a little attackman of theirs went to shoot a bounce shot but it sprayed out of his stick and he scored high.

Incredulous, Beaker flapped his arms in my direction.

I called a timeout, told everyone to stay where they were, waved Beaker over. A one-man time-out thirty seconds into the second half looked imprudent and dictatorial, which made me want to do it more often.

As Beaker sprinted over—he sprinted everywhere—he squawked: "You said that when they go like THIS, they—"

"Beaker, *shut up*." I waved blindly behind me, a half apology in case his parents had heard. "The shot went high because the kid sucks. He doesn't suck, he just…just started playing. He was trying to shoot it low. He wasn't giving you a no-look change-up up-top, for Chrissake."

"But--"

"Dude shut up and trust me."

He nodded.

"So whatta you gonna do?" I asked him.

"Shut up and trust me. You."

I had meant *anticipate a bounce shot*, but, again, he may have been fucking with me. "That's fine," I said, and bopped his helmet, sent him back to his post.

We lost the next face-off and they came down with it, barfed up a dribbler of a bounce shot that Beaker saw coming from a mile away and even if it was an easy save, he was proud and found a belief in the system. He stepped out of the crease (inside the crease, the goalie is not to be touched; once he steps out, he's fair game) and got hammered by one of their scrappy attackmen, stripped of the ball. There was a low-rent scrum for it in front of our goal. Going down three goals isn't that big of a deal in lacrosse, but I wasn't in the mood, given our absence of wins. My eyes drifted to DeMarcus out by the restraining line. I could see his mindset, being far enough away to wait it out; someone would pick up the ball before he could get there, anyway. This was the mindset of most everyone, ever. But a switch went off in him. The "fuck it—I'll do it myself" Braveheart switch and he took two long, loping triple-jump-high-jump-long-jump strides before it looked as though he were shot from a cannon. He barreled into the lazy scrum and everyone exploded like the bricks of the Kool-Aid Man. DeMarcus came out with the ball and one of their midfielders kept up with him for two, three strides before DeMarcus Twilighted into Randy Moss, 1998. He was simply moving at a different speed than everyone else. Mecca, quite fast in his own right, called for the ball but just waved him on. He did the math and DeMarcus was traveling with the ball faster than the ball could have traveled in the air by pass. The first slide came, DeMarcus flipped an ugly underhanded beginner's pass to Just. The recovery slide came to Just, he skipped it down to Burt. The goalie came out to hit Burt and Burt face-dodged the kid and buried it in the bottom corner of the net before he could allow himself to be happy for simply catching it.

And I loved Lacrosse again.

It wasn't beautiful because we still weren't good, but things started to slowly gel after that. Wrists and elbows loosened up, ground balls started to look like lacrosse, less like a drunken, improvised lawn game. Sloppy Hogwarts, Quidditch, what-have-you. The game didn't exactly slow down for us because it was already quite slow and ugly at this age, but it at least dabbled in something resembling flow. The fellas started to understand the simplicity of it all, our Fab Four especially, as they gained a sense of calm and, as good leaders do, infected their battalion with a false sense of confidence. We ran one play and any one of the four would start it. Beat your man, shoot the ball or move it. We went up a few goals toward the end of the third and I said every offensive player had to touch the ball before anyone dodged. We went up by a few more and then everybody had to touch it *twice* and I was giving their coach the invisible bird, all of us acting like we were too good to be there when we most certainly were not. But we had to start acting at least a little bit shitty if we ever wanted to get anywhere.

After the game, I briefly chatted with their coach at midfield because it was the right thing to do. He looked longingly at DeMarcus and Jake who were yucking around with Just, taking their equipment off and fielding the praise of parents.

"I wish I could get those kids to play for us." Jake, too, was in his eye-line, so I had to give the guy the benefit of the doubt, that the "those kids" he was referring to were football players, not black kids. But I doubted it.

"You think kids wanna play basketball for a year or two in *Lexington, Kentucky* because they like, like, bluegrass and horses?"

His confusion refocused him. I shook my head, answering my question.

"Calipari's the fuckin' Man."

I wondered how long it would take him to figure out that I was comparing myself to John Calipari, but I wouldn't wait around to find out. I whistled for one of the kids to go long so I could air out the football I'd been carrying, unfurl some of the pent-up aggression I'd accrued in the past hour and a half. And to show off my arm. Jake was a Stallion, hungry like a Labrador. I threw it as far as I could and high enough for him to run under it, to clean up my margins.

"Rude Boy!" sung Walter.

It was probably right around then when the Newbury Park coach figured out what a conceited peckerhead I was.

THE BUS NUMBERS were slim because a lot of the kids rode back with their parents. Just, Maybelline, Innie, and a few others lounged in back, smelling bad and giving each other grief.

After the game, Alex prodded me about the dinner party. There was nothing funny to tap into, though, no zany shenanigans, no anxious foibles of the night. All of the heightened glow seemed manufactured in my rearview. Now that the night had been processed, distilled and refracted all these hours later, I saw it for how it had gone and it had gone fine. Good. Really good, even. Or just good. I had maybe made a new Dude friend, I hadn't broken anything expensive, I told a bad story at dinner (which bummed me out but was manageable), I did the dishes, I didn't black out, the Baumbach woman wasn't a fan, the hostess laughed at my jokes and appreciated the help. Good was good enough for me. The syrupy-sweet-underdog-meets-uptown-girl colored glasses I lived the night through were lovely and I wanted to put them back on, but like every pair of sunglasses I'd ever owned, I'd lost them. I was unsure how much of the night had actually gone how I had thought it had. Did we connect, Camilla and I? Or was I just a nut or maybe a little bit of both? Was Mochii real? Did I even hit that jump shot? Yes and definitely. Looking back now, though, everything was fine—and fine was great!—and if I felt anything, maybe I felt a little bit wiser. The game of reverse telephone that the brain can play with the heart is a fun one and has its glandular merits, but it's just a phone. You gotta pay the bill.

"That's it?" He asked, let down. We were all chicks.

"Yeah. Kinda. I mean, the ride over was pretty high octane. My heart felt like it was gonna jump out of my throat and sprint down the hill to the sea." This was true. "But I kinda calmed down." Also, more or less true.

He was trying to steer me away from the trail of parents walking back to the parking lot.

"But nothing, like, nothing crazy, implied or otherwise?"

"I mean...maybe? But...not really? I almost choked. In Homeboy's pool house or gym or whatever. When I was getting a beer. I think that made the night different...bigger... existentially...in my mind, but...no, I think it was good—I didn't freak anybody out. I think it was normal?"

My whole life I'd been making a bigger deal of things that were small potatoes and vice versa. My loser extremes weren't sustainable in the land of adults. I had to force this shit into the middle.

Alex sensed this. The tactical grappling with the illogical and unpredictable muscle that is the heart. Was I wrestling something massive into the banal? Or was that where it all needed to go. The safest place. He nodded, patted me on the shoulder and said:

"You're a fuckin' good coach, Man."

I nearly cried and we agreed to meet at the Lost & Found sometime in the coming nights.

PORN SOUNDS WOKE me. It was jarring because I was dreaming about Tourney but it wasn't Tourney, it was that guy Karl-whatshisname, the whiny Norwegian prick with the endless volumes of diary. We were in some old European city I was certain I had never been to—Prague, Brussels, Dachenhoös—because I had never been to Europe. But we were getting along, rapping outside some café on the cobblestones and out of his mouth came the porn sounds of a woman, un-synched.

We were on the 101 headed east when I awoke and I looked at the bus driver in his wide rearview mirror. He was a Guatemalan dude in his 40's and he went by, well, what I heard was "Rancor" but I didn't ask him to repeat it. He shrugged.

"Technology, Man. I never liked that internet." I didn't totally hate it, but I knew what he meant. "It's gonna ruin the generation, Man. And every generation till it's gone."

"Sadly, I think it's here to stay." The porn sounds reverberated.

I looked back at the kids, all of whom were scrambling for a cover-up. Screen-tapping, hushed whispers, the shuffling of bags and gadgets and eyes. I felt like ignoring it but I didn't want to let myself off the hook, either. It was a situation.

I walked back to the gaggle of young monkeys and sat down. I eyed Just because he was one of the ones with a phone and he had the pubescent markings of a sick puppy.

"What're you watching."

"Nothing. It was just a weird pop-up."

He forked the phone over into my outstretched palm, steely but scared. The other kids looked for hiding places in their laps.

"Nobody's in *trouble,* fellas." There seemed to be a collective exhalation of relief and reassurance at this. "I just don't want you guys gettin' all spanish on the twisted world of boundless porn. Sometimes a Jewel video or a Victoria's Secret is all you need to beat the hell out of your little Bronson Arroyo. Let the mind work."

They laughed a bit and it was all fun and games and back-of-the-bus jerk-store talk until they saw me blindly open the Safari icon. They tensed up like they had early onset late-stage scleroderma.

It felt like I was getting the phone call with the news that someone close to me had died. The feeling where you know you're supposed to be feeling something, you know that that feeling is coming soon and it better come quickly because this purgatory of incoming is hell. A guttural moan escaped my throat and I slapped at the phone trying to mute it. I didn't need Rancor thinking I, too, was a deeply mangled fan of the internet. I watched for what was probably two seconds but felt like two seasons. I tossed the phone and dug the heels of my hands as deep into my eye-sockets as they would go. But tattooed on the back of my eyelids in reverse Clockwork Orange projection was the gnarliest skull-fuckery I'd ever seen, followed by a few frames of whale-spout anus gape that could make your irises peel. A porn so grubby it bummed me out, killed my appetite, drained me of humor. I was devastated.

"Dudes." Nicknameless Matt, who was just a 7th grader, was so red in the face he was purple. He looked stillborn.

"*Dudes,*" I pled. But I had nothing. "That's not…it's not even…"

I staggered back up front, sat down. Rancor must've seen it on my face.

"Never liked it," he said, and flipped his hat around backwards, as if to defy the whole internet. "Ever."

TEN

She hadn't texted and that was fine but I wasn't going to, either, which was also fine. I had written twenty different "thanks again for dinner" texts but maturely discarded each of them with theatrical pomp, placing my phone face down, patting it for good measure. I really was trying to square peg my way into the middle. *Everything was trivial*, I kept trying to mantra. It didn't have to be elation or devastation. It can all be a Tuesday. Plus, I was busy. The incident in the back of the bus had left me shook. I knew I couldn't erase their minds. I couldn't board up the infinite doors in the never-ending hall of fetishes that was the World Wide Web. But I also couldn't do *nothing*. I had to let them know that that wasn't the world. That, worry not, most dicks aren't that big, the butt is no place for a fist, and, if you're lucky, you'll maybe get *a* blow-job or two that looks like that. In your lifetime! A woman can fuck your dick with her head but not the other way around, boys! That last one I'd have to finesse the language on, but if I could distill it, it would contain the gist of my worry for these kids: You can't do that shit!

They were already robbed of so many of the things that made

the generations before them who they were, who we are. Calling the landline of a middle school crush a little late on a school night or just having to watch what's on. Only two things, but two really seminal things! And now their masturbation imaginations. When the Victoria's Secret catalogue showed up, it was sexual Christmas every month. A JC Penny catalogue was perfectly adequate. The Sports Illustrated Swimsuit Issue? You could feel the tides shift from the gravitational pull of eleven to sixteen-year-old dude hormones as we all, in synchronicity, scuttled from the mailbox to the bathroom, bedroom, basement or woodshed, little jizz-junkies, cockroaches all, every Mom in the Land, on the day that issue was released, wishing they'd had daughters.

"You want me to do what?" I had called my Old Man in the hope that he could go up into the attic and take pictures of the old Swimsuit Issues. We had backlogs all the way to Kathy Ireland.

"Nothin'," I said. He didn't have a camera on his phone and he was a guy who needed things to make *some* sense and I was asking him to do something creepy and insane. He moved on and told me about the weather, a friend who never brings beer to tennis, a few of his rotten-body injuries and the temperature of Lake Champlain. Then he screamed something about how much of a dick Sean Hannity was, said it was still bath weather, said "alright," told me he loved me and got off the phone.

Why did I want these kids beating off to pictures of the pictures I once beat off to? Was I turning into some knotted up nostalgia tsar? I didn't want to read too far into it—I knew far too much about myself already. I simply wanted to procure some tasteful material for 7th and 8th grade boys to masturbate to.

I downloaded Jewel's "You Were Meant for Me" video off of YouTube, alongside Sheryl Crow's "If It Makes You Happy" (that skirt length!) and En Vogue's "Free Your Mind." LL's "Doin' It" seemed too risqué. I amassed stills from SI's Swimsuit Issues—Laetitia Casta, Tyra and Heidi Klum. An assortment of Victoria's Secret pictures. Scantily clad Carmen Electra and Jenny Mac to show I could have fun with it. Some low-brow Maxim and Stuff shots for the cheap seats. I got a little stirred up and was about to have a pathetic yank to my curated show when my phone buzzed and worried it away.

It was She.

I was hesitant to swipe it open, to read it. It felt like a letter from admissions of a school you had no business applying to but now that the letter's here…*well, my essay was pretty sick? Hell, why NOT me?* But if I never opened it, I could say that I was maybe gonna go to Washington University, but the financial aid wasn't enough and they didn't have lacrosse back then so I went to a lesser school because of reasons not my lacking smarts.

I remembered the middle. I remembered it could all be a Tuesday. It was just a text message. I opened the text message.

well how'd it go?!?

All my shades were drawn and I hadn't even jerked off so I was fairly certain I wasn't being spied on; this was not the Truman Show. She was asking about the game.

I stood up and touched my toes, vowing yet again to stretch more. I got a beer and let Sam out. I had used too many words too many times so when I got back to the phone I wrote:

W.

It was my finest work yet. It was brilliant. I needed to bind my fingers or set a character limits in settings.

that's great!

She forced my hand. I couldn't outrun my own verbosity:

It was fun. Their raw athletic ability is being tragically undercut by the mania plaguing the coaching staff. But-But: thanks again for dinner last night. That was a nice time. What a rush. Has Will mentioned me? Actually don't answer that. Some things are better, better...

I pressed send before I could second-guess the sentimental and loopy "better, better". I'd felt stupider. But "what a rush" on second guess seemed possibly passively romantically or (fuck) sexually implicit. Perhaps explicit. But bubbles...

ha. he was mutually smitten.
leaving a thing now on your side of town.
fancy a drink?

I wrote:

Chez Jay in fifteen...

The Lost & Found would have been extreme and the new Me strove for the middle. It was just a drink and we were almost friends and it was convenient, geographically. This was the world, and it was all just a friendly drink. Manifest Destiny. I didn't say it out loud, but I thought it feebly: I am the Middle Man.

Chez Jay was a nautically themed bar with consistently mediocre and expensive food. They had help-yourself peanuts, though, and got irritable when you forgot or didn't grasp that the shells went on the floor. This made for a nice insider feel, to look at a bartender like "look at this fuckin' asshole..." as a non-regular littered the bar top or table with dusty shells.

I had gotten the shit kicked out of me there by some UFC trainer yakked out on NOS energy drinks some two years prior. He was actually on crystal and I shushed him with a wave of my hand after he interrupted me, not knowing it was his girlfriend I was talking to. He spiked my head off the bar, then his knee off my head and ran off into the Santa Monica night. I was, once again, deeply concussed. At that age I wasn't worried about my head just worried about my life and the following day I felt as bad about myself as I ever had. The guy who was bartending that night—a slender, handsome black dude named Lance (struggling actor)—tracked down my number somehow and checked in on me. He wasn't the nicest guy, so it felt extra nice.

And now, as I walked through the Dutch door and grabbed ahold of the wooden helm at the host's table, Lance gave a laugh from behind the crowded bar, pointing at me, and in my periphery I knew that she saw, too, and I loved him for that. Still do. Always will. She sat at the end of the bar, closest to the door—the west end—tucked into the corner by the Juke Box. I smiled at her, a big, genuine smile that surprised me. It hadn't occurred how happy I'd be to see her, how happy I had the capacity to be in seeing someone I'd seen not twenty-four hours prior. I gave her a "just a minute" finger and made my way to the opposite end of the bar where you help yourself to the help-yourself peanuts. I reconfirmed my confidence grade in my outfit choice (jeans, crewneck grey sweatshirt, Chuck's, a mesh-back hat from the farm of a friend of a friend) as I gathered my druthers and the peanuts and made my way back to her, where Lance was putting my Sierra, an old pro.

I took a long quaff and smiled another stupid and genuine grin before we tended to the formalities of the hello smooch. I could have just sat there looking at her, feeling my pulse, sipping in time, smiling like a court jester for at least another pint. I was where I wanted to be.

She laughed because we weren't saying anything and it was still really fun. I think that's why she laughed. I had finished my beer on the second sip because it was all too good. I started to speak but stopped, just nodded, bobbed like a lobotomized marionette in space. Lance swooped in with another Sierra and we slapped hi—I happily bumped it back in SoCal fashion, which I typically hated—and I introduced them and wondered how many times I'd need to hang out with him outside of his place of work in order for me to say without reservation that he was my friend.

"You look pretty," I said when I finally addressed her personally, privately. She looked around, wondering if it was a crazy thing to say out loud. I waved away her skepticism and had a peanut.

She did look pretty—that was an objective fact. She wore a blue knee-length dress with a faded red floral print and an army jacket.

"Can I try that?" She asked on my Sierra. After she took a sip, she looked at her vodka-soda and lemon with remorse. I took the vodka-soda, gave her the Sierra. She balked but I insisted, cracked another peanut, tossed it in my silly face.

We kept asking each other questions and answering the other's question with a question. I wanted to watch her mouth move and I wanted to hear it all. She worried that I hadn't eaten but also admired my eating peanuts and pints for dinner—rich people romanticize the pauper's resolve.

She did this thing with her eyes when I listened too hard or gazed too loopy. She would widen them and tilt her head—she'd done it at her house a time or two, a look that said *we can't do that here!*

"Did I mess up your Saturday night plans?" she offered as a pedestrian courtesy.

"No. I was going to eat Percocet, drink Heinkens, lay on the floor with Sam and listen to records. But I can still get that done." I remembered my inner Big Pharma rants and felt guilty. I was trying to sound cool although that had been my plan at one point.

"That sounds amazing."

"There's worse things to do."

She looked at me with a frustration I understood. She looked at the clock and our empty pints with a disappointment I understood as well.

"Well," I finished the vodka drink, nodded. "You're always invited."

It was a heavy throw-away. Which, by definition, meant it wasn't a throw-away at all. Whatever it was, it sat there heavy between us, the infinite "always."

"I think I have some Vicodin," she murmured before snapping herself out of it. "I should call a car."

She reached for her wallet and I rejected it, assuring her that

I was going to eat more peanuts and have another beer.

Her car arrived and we walked outside, lost on how to be normal. I protectively sized up the driver. He was awesome—a chubby, happy-as-hell Latino. It was totally out of character, the sizing up, but I had done it before I didn't and made up for it by giving him an over the top reception and a soul-shake through the passenger side.

Camilla and I stood looking at each other till it was time and I got her in the car, grabbed her hand and squeezed it before I bopped the roof twice and sent them off. I went back inside after the taillights disappeared down onto the PCH.

I RODE HOME and vacuumed the rug. It was a nice rug I had gotten from the dumpster of a Hennessy event I had worked at the year prior—white with black wing-ding symbols, medium pile. My two floor lamps were from similar dumpsters. I put on a fluorescent pressing of Ryan Adam's *Easy Tiger* and opened a Heineken. I wanted to save the Percocet I had—six or eight or ten of them—just in case. I did love pills and I hated what they'd done, yet I was cut of the cloth that didn't like to sit on life's indulgences (see: cocaine and / or brownies). My history of efficient gluttony made this Percocet restraint feel particularly distinguished.

"I got a really good heart, I just can't catch a break," I sang with my favorite sad n' whiny narcissist. But it didn't make me feel better in feeling worse like it always did. I wondered if maybe I was catching my break. On paper and to my friends it would

look like the masochistic compound fracture I'd been seeking all this time. But fuck paper and fuck friends. I felt good.

My phone buzzed, ringing, lit CAMILLA. My heart lurched.

"Hi." I didn't know how else to answer.

"Hi."

We listened to each other breathe for a few and she must have remembered that she called me.

"The Über driver said to me after we pulled away…'it's okay to tell a boy when you like him.'" She stopped herself, wondering if she'd been the one to have gone too far, first. "Isn't that strange? I mean, what did he…"

"I love Lil' big Papi."

"Yeah. It was cute."

We went quietly smitten again.

"Thanks for the drinks."

"'course."

"Bye."

"Bye."

It was the best phone call of my life. As I flopped back on the rug, my phone buzzed again and I thought it unlike her to push the envelope like this, as she was a woman of tact and grace. But the Brainheart's crazy.

It wasn't her, though. It was a text from a woman who frightened me. And with my current status as unjustifiably committed Other Man, she scared me doubly. The text read:

i'm in your hood and your lights on. want company?

How did she know I didn't already have company? Did she look in my windows? I felt triply frightened now and my thumbs froze over a response. I put my phone down and decided to wait it out. My pulse galloped, I forgot to breathe. Her name was Veronica Dresser and she was coming over.

Veronica worked at the Gagosian gallery in Beverly Hills where I had once painted some walls white, in between shows, rolling flat Bennie Moore alongside some speckle-bearded wannabe from West Virginia who wanted to keep it real but daydreamt of showing his shit on the very walls he was spite-painting. Veronica had enormous knockers. Breasts notwithstanding, she was quite attractive, but more handful than hot and not terribly interesting. Or at least our interests didn't align, because I would easily find myself uninteresting if I didn't like the stupid things I dug. She was nice and actually funny a few times and she really liked me, which made me like her even less. I wasn't very nice to her, I gave her subpar sex (I ejaculated quickly because of said knockers, but didn't make much of an effort to draw out the process) and I never saw her outside of my apartment or earlier than midnight. It sounds like I was an asshole, but sometimes that's the natural process. What makes me sound like even more of an asshole is that there were a few other women in her same seat. Women I didn't want to be with but liked enough, enough of the time, to keep at arm's (or Johnson's) length. Recurring dalliances; cyclical, low-bar, just shy of rude. I've said it before, and I've meant it a few times: being a dude is hard. And now I had a wine-soaked, cock-hungry boob-monster prowling my street, peeking in my windows. I thought of Camilla. I'd probably never know what we were but I felt guilty about where I was trying to keep my dick from going in the next few minutes.

A silhouette passed through the curtains from the front stoop. My doorknob cranked. I wished I had grown up in a dangerous place so that I locked my doors out of habit, but it was too late. I mushed my face into the rug, played dead or asleep.

Sam, ever the gracious host, greeted her with a wag and a smile of familiarity. I couldn't get mad at him. He was a stupid animal.

"Hey, buddy!" she cooed at my dog. "Oh-oh—is Dad sleeping?" It made me sick when people spoke like that, parents and pets. She took off her jacket (or so I heard) and sat next to me on the floor, did something to my hair that made me clench my toes in anger.

I knew I had to wake up—fake wake up—and deal with it. She might call an ambulance if I tried to go the distance. Or she would get the picture and leave, deem me a full-fledged asshole and delete my number. She gently shook me again, her face close to mine, the sour afterburn of Sauvignon Blanc and Narciso making my eyelids twitch. I woke as if from a *Young and the Restless* dream.

"Heyyy," I rasped. "What's up?"

I sat up, wiped the stage drool from my face. The "what's up" was meant to make her feel slightly and rightly dumb for walking into my private residence and waking me from slumber. I sat up, my back against the couch. She sipped my beer, feeling far from stupid.

"Nuuthin'. Was in the neighborhood. Did you get a little drunkie?" *Why did people put ie's and y's on things?*, I yelled in my head. Maybe I did that sometimes, too, but why did everyone insist on proving me right all the time?

I said nothing, going harder at her stupid bone. She was drunkie.

She took another sip of my beer, sipping coy in a way that annoyed the daylights out of me. She took my hand and put it on her leg, moved it up under her skirt and I was bummed out at the thought of even anger-banging her. I had evolved. I was done with this rat-race of fuckery. I was in a committed relationship with someone who had agreed to be with another person till death separated them. He could die. I didn't WANT that. But I thought it for a passing moment as this busty knucklehead moved in to kiss me.

My condescension shone through when I politely smiled with her mouth on mine. She pulled back but chose not to register my complaint, interpreting it as come-hither. She went back in and I pulled out, smug lips pursed like a proud prude. I felt a whiny tug in my briefs, but I bat the feeling away like a country maid shooing out a pest with a broom.

"I'm kinda seeing someone." I went for it. The heat of a lie didn't even burble my mercury because I believed what I was saying. I believed what I felt. If I fucked around, I'd feel awful. I'd lost my mind!

"Really?" She looked stung but she was okay. I had lain the boundaries of our association early on and every time: I was a lazy asshole and had never wavered. It was all there, black and white, clear as crystal. I wasn't proud but I was at the very least consistent. I could see processes behind her clouded, boozy eyes and the legalese I had doctored in my mind was moot. Women were tricky.

We arrived at an impasse. It seemed as though she was waiting for me to expound on the matter and even though I didn't owe her the details, she was a female and they didn't tend to go quietly without exhaustive discourse. So I began to babble.

It was a stream of guarded truths, a retelling of the past weeks with some omissions and tweaks to protect the players. It felt therapeutic, though, like taking a series of deep breaths in the Green Mountain air after you've been so long in the city. With the exception of Alex, I hadn't spoken to anyone about this, about Her, and it was a lot to feel, a lot to lug around. I pet the dog, flipped the record, got another beer, kept rambling platitudes and immediately questioning their platitudiness.

When I finally shut my mouth, I shrugged at her a friendly shrug like we'd been through some shit together and had become buddies. But buddies we were not. I wanted to never see her again and she bore the face of the disgusted.

She stood up.

"So. For…let's see…two years, you've never taken me out to—not dinner! God no. Not even a bar. Never a *drink* at a place that's not your shitty little apartment at, like, one in the morning before you get to fuck me for about thirty-six seconds, come on my tits and apologize to, like, come across as a fucking gentleman? And now you have feelings for some rich-ass married woman because her husband's some big-shot director?"

Where were the omissions and tweaks?

"That's not the reason. I said it was *confusing* because he's… he's a producer, though—not a director." I desperately tried to jam that seed in her brain. I was a shit protector.

"Whatever." She gathered her coat. "You're typical. And pathetic. And fuck you."

She showed herself out.

ELEVEN

Monday afternoon, I handed out thumb drives of my lad-mag look-book to the fellas. A seppuku ending blipped like a mirage warning in the distance of my vision, wafting up from the heatwaves of the new tar in the parking lot. The Pete Townshend door-kickers in their Bobby-hats wailing on me with billy clubs, the soccer Moms pelting me with whole rotten oranges and vitriol. I felt like Robin Hood, though. I was younger then.

"I'm not gonna get into the X's and O's of what I saw on the bus the other day," I began as I handed out the drives from a New Yorker tote, lipstick on a hippo. "But it wasn't good. And it's not your guys' fault; you're coming up in grubby times. And, times aside, a lot of you guys are about to get grubby yourselves—some of you already are." I shot Just and a few of the eighth graders a look.

"If it looks like it's uncomfortable for a woman, assume it is." This obviously had layers to it, but it was a good base. "Don't seek out the weird corners of the Internet just because they're there." Everyone reddened. "Please, just…always remember…" I drew a hard blank, because who was I? I had gotten accosted for tittie-jizzing with no dinners not forty-eight hours prior. I'd performed some pretty grisly acts in my time. Nothing that would impress the internet or get me kicked out of college, but still. But *still*. The things these kids had access to were not okay. I liked women, I liked the company of women. They scared me, made me nervous, I respected most, and right then, I *really* dug one. Woman. I thought of Her and if we ever did what we might do, how I'd want that to go or how I'd want it to be for Her. Me to be for Her. I wanted them to remember what I now knew.

"It's okay to be lovely."

I got the tee-hees and snickers I'd presumed but I smiled the unselfconscious smile of the elder. It was true.

"Coach, are you giving us porn?" Just turned the thumb-drive over in his greasy dick fingers.

"No, Pal. It's just a springboard for your imagination. But," I caveated as I tied my running shoes. "Keep it close. That could probably get me in trouble."

WE RAN THAT day but we did it in dance. It was all attitude: stag leaps, pirouettes, pliés and arabesques. Laterals and spirals. Or what I gathered to be those things. We looked like concussed fawns, flamingos on Quaaludes usurping the Rite of Spring. It was a field of giggles which made it fun to get mad at, and McMillan saw us which made it fun to do. And it was awful. Muscles in my legs I'd never met. A goofy vulnerability tethered us together in a new way. It was good to not always be chest-thumping stalwarts of the darkness. You need a little Nathan Lane.

We scrimmaged at the end and those who could stay late,

stayed, the ones whose parents had other kids to grab, other things to do, left. But I saw something in the posture of the kids who had to leave, as they slunk off the field to their parents' cars. They were bummed. They didn't want to stay, necessarily, but they didn't want to leave. At that age, we've disappointed parents, friends, siblings, teachers. But to walk away from a band of brothers. Crestfallen. Twelve or thirteen years on this inconsiderate orb and they felt a new feeling, a new consciousness of character, of honor. That was when I knew we could win. We could beat Harvard Westlake. We could beat anybody. We could beat Harvard Westlake.

I ran after the kids who were leaving, hugged them, told them what their sadness meant to me, to the team, to the cause. They laughed before they left and the rest of the kids slowly trickled out until it was just DeMarcus and I, split-dodging, waiting for the late bus.

Keri waddled out on her way to the faculty lot. I told DeMarcus to keep taking lefty shots on the run and tried greeting her brightly.

"Hey there!"

"Hey. You can't keep the kids late."

"I don't."

"I've had numerous complaints."

"Numerous?"

She tightened her messenger bag to indicate that this was not a back and forth.

"I stay with the kids whose parents are running late and we keep—"

"Practice ends at five. And you can't run it like a boot camp. They're just kids."

The term "boot camp" was insulting and cheapened what we did. And was she mad with the timing or the running? She had to narrow her grievance. And they weren't "just kids."

"We did ballet today," I tried, extending an olive branch with a clown buzzer on the end. "Pliés," I said, demonstrating.

"Five o'clock," she gruffed.

The scope of improvement in DeMarcus' stick skills was baffling. It had only been a few weeks and he was good. Not just running-back-with-a-stick good. He was a gifted-athlete-who-wanted-to-be good-at-lacrosse good.

"You been hittin' the wall?" He had to have been. We were having a regular catch and his stick was naturalized.

"Yeah. My Pops makes me hit it every morning. Behind the Ralph's around the corner. And sometimes at night. They got lights."

"My Man!"

"You definitely convinced him."

"Well I wasn't lying."

We whipped some quick-sticks back and forth.

"You having fun?" I hadn't really asked any of the kids that, which made me feel like a bad friend.

DeMarcus paused and I held the ball. He nodded, thoughtfully. "Yeaaaah. 'Fun''s not, like, the first word I would use." I laughed at that and he loosened up. "Football is this…it's everywhere, you know? It's like, life." I threw him the ball. "But this," he looked at the ball in his stick, "and, like, the running and…

and...*you*." I nodded, wondering where he was going, encouraged him to go on, even if it was going to sting.

"It's like something's going on that, like, only *we* get."

He threw the ball back and I told him to go catch the bus as I turned and sprinted to the goal behind me so he wouldn't see my eyes shimmer.

IN THE PARKING lot I checked my bank accounts, not to crucify myself but because I had to know. At Chez Jay I had put the beers (I ended up having six—including two buybacks—plus her Vodka soda) on a credit card I had many times vowed to cut up after I squared the balance. Credit cards scared me the same way gambling did—I wasn't good for it. That fear kept me out of debt, within reason. I checked the credit card first. It had a balance of $323.17 and I incredulously balked, but it actually checked out. I had gotten new running shoes, I had a phone, and, I had to concede: I was a sipper.

The checking account worried me. I had sunk below sixty bucks on my attempted Heineken and Fritos purchase and the first was coming up fast, and two days after that was the third, the day that slobs like me pay rent. I had a check for five hundred dollars coming in on direct deposit for a gig I had done a few weeks prior and that wouldn't get me even halfway there, but it would cauterize the ruthless hemorrhage. Or, rather, it would keep me from punching myself in the face or ripping off the steering wheel. And after that, hopefully before the third, I had a coaching check coming in for a whopping eight hundred bucks from a private school in one of the wealthiest neighborhoods in America, the world. Oh, inverted world.

With one eye on the screen, I opened my checking account.
CHECKING ACCT BALANCE:
$557.60

I whooped. I even yelled "hurray!" I put on *Exile on Main St.* and set out for the Venice Whole Foods to buy some beer and steal my dinner from the salad bar.

THERE WAS A figure sitting on my stoop as we walked up Horizon and all my wishful thinking nodes fired as they now did every time I saw a person with longer hair or one of those Porsche trucks. I thought I saw Her four and a half times in the Whole Foods, a half time because I thought I saw fourteen-year-old Her by the olives. Not in a creepy way, I just thought that maybe the time-space continuum got rejiggered and I had frenzied my way into chaos, time living on top of time, gobbling us both up.

I disengaged the nodes even though you can't control hope and Sam took his own hopeful few bounds forward up onto the landing and she stood, backlit, and I heard Her voice.

"What took you so long?"

SHE SAT ON the couch and I got her a beer and glass of ice, got Sam some food. I hadn't spoken yet, just smiled and welcomed her into our home. I didn't want to ruin it with the sound of my own voice. I took a thirty-eight second military shower, put on jeans and a grey pocket-tee, and when I came out she was still wondering about the ice, not yet marrying the two.

"That was quick!"

"We live in a desert."

"Is this for the beer?" She asked as I grabbed my own Heineken on ice and walked the three steps back into the part of the apartment with the couch in it.

I sat down, a whole territory between us. "Yeah. My Old Man's a big temperature guy. And the open cooler at Whole Foods. And the car ride back."

"I have to break-up with you," she said, smiling after a deep breath, half-way meaning what she said but also acknowledging we were a thing to break.

"Don't do that," I said on the heels of her "you"; my "don't" nearly a full octave above my "do," my "that" in the middle of those.

"Ryan, I'm married." I didn't love my name as the opener for the words "I'm married," but I understood its place in the line. She said it and it needed to be said. Not my name, the M-word. It was the albatross and maybe if we finally acknowledged it, it could fly the fuck away, span the Pacific while we figured this out.

"We're just listening to records!" I said and stood up to put one on. She groaned softly like she had come in clutching the long-shot chance that I'd make this easy, be the altruistic nobleman, set us free as new friends, fizzle-out, fade.

"Well I did bring the Vicodin. But we can't do them all!"

And that was that. She tried. And, also—I was right. Nothing bad had happened. Sure, it didn't look *good*. But there could be a tsunami—I had a sign right out front that pointed east and said "RUN."

The record player and the record shelves were in the part of the apartment with the bed and the refrigerator in it, the shelving and hutch built into the wall that divided the bathroom and the one-lane kitchen. I gripped the counter that held the record player and steadied myself, fighting the urge to take out my jig saw and mow off my giblets just to show her that those and that didn't matter. I respected her marriage. Okay, not exactly. But I honored its role in the Butterfly Effect.

I scanned the records. I put on *All Things Must Pass* and as I put the needle down, I worried about the title of the record, told myself to not read into it, then remembered the first song—"I'd Have You Anytime"—and was proud of myself for reading into it, shushing myself, and still being right.

I sat back down.

"Do you think we love each other?" she asked.

"Absolutely," I strolled back at her, the "r" in her "other" barely out. She giggled, and with that—the giggle, and the way she asked me if we loved each other—the brazen, elephant sized riddle that was obviously on our minds, was solved. She had this wizened whimsy about her, a put-upon, childlike innocence when she asked questions. She knew the answers but she was curious for the insight, the other point of view, and the way she looked when she asked made you think she really wanted to know. It was masterful because she already knew it all. She was an ace.

"I don't like being afraid of the word," I said, which was true but not evident in my history.

"No, I agree."

"Not that I throw it around willy-nilly."

"No!"

"But I love plenty of things."

"Me, too."

We sat there, thinking of the things we loved, her list having at the very least one and a half—she had to love Tourney a half. But. She was on a (on-paper) near stranger's couch with a fistful of opioids. Maybe she hated him half and loved him half and that's a numb net zero. From what I had gathered in the field, the nothing could be a lot worse for a decade's-long union. I didn't care much, though. She loved him one, whatever. I was fine with it. Marriage seemed thorny.

"I guess not *plenty* of things," I said. I loved Sam. And Conor Oberst. And Eli Manning. We let the Love Elephant hang out in the room, take a nap. It was just a baby.

We looked at each other for awhile, till the end of "My Sweet Lord," making sure it was real, double and triple checking in the silence in between dumbstruck smiles when it didn't get uncomfortable, even when we wanted or needed it to, when we'd shake our heads, simultaneous pantomime, the same thought, the same wonder: *Where the fuck have you been?* And that was just two songs.

We reached for the pills. Two apiece and when she went to the bathroom, I took another, because because. Something had to bring me down, put me together and I thought maybe the inverse would happen, what with all my tags and organs on the outside. It wouldn't, but that was just as well, better maybe, because you have to stop thinking *it can't get any better,* turn off the governor and let it ride. There's an invincibility, not with the drugs—she had a kid and I knew dying wasn't in my best interest—but with a feeling and a night that wasn't planned, was very not according to the plan, where everything, *everything*, was in its right place. Everything. Distill it, blitz that night with a neutron and that nuclear fission could reverse global warming. Or swallow us in a black hole. Either way, I was very, very happy my folks banged that night in '82.

By "If Not For You," the poppies had sashayed their way down my spine and up over my scalp like Shining Happy leeches with Sham-Wow bellies. I got more beers, frosty green bottles I had put in the freezer, handed them out and moved the coffee table and drizzled down onto the rug, not to make good on a previously painted image, but because that was where to be. She floated down, leveled out, and we talked, laughed, canoodled without the oodling. We had a pact, a mutual agreement from a same-time mimed look from last song that said "we probably won't, definitely shouldn't go *there*, because we're here! This is the place." And I didn't want to kiss a married broad. I wasn't gonna make the first move. Scared, respectful. Apples to apples.

All six sides of *All Things Must Pass* flew by and Bonnie's first record, too. I put on *Tunnel of Love* and we had another pill and I another-nother and we were back on the rug and I sang "Ain't Got You" like an unselfconscious bozo and then "Tougher Than the Rest" came on and the pills and lager wrapped me up in a cocoon of *There's Nothing Wrong With Love* and I crawled over to her, probably muttered "fuck it" to myself and buried my olfactory in her armpit, took a drag like she was a Winston and I was on my way to the Chair. I took another whiff, from somewhere near her collarbone and rolled over and let Max Weinberg's late 80's snare thwack and Danny Federici's Hammond wash over me like cool pudding. It was like I'd lived in a sewage slum in Mumbai my whole life and got plucked up and dunked in Lake Willoghby, dropped into Shelburne Orchards in June, whenever the apple blossoms blossom, whenever they smell their best. I loved Vermont, I realized—that was the other thing I loved.

That's an option. I let my brain think.

Teddy would love it. My brain was a bad guy.

I'm not a bad guy. My brain was on drugs.

Nobody could hear what I was thinking but I wondered a little if she was spooked. I was probably wearing my thoughts. But by the time I thought to look over, by the time I came down from the waa-waa of her nitrous, she was in my aroma-house, conducting her own sense-test. She giggled again—there was a better word for her laugh, or, silly me, there couldn't be—and that had its own smell in my ear. Her laugh smelled amazing.

She went back in and I recounted the seconds and steps of the shower I had taken. Insufficient at best. But she slowly pulled out of what I'm guessing is my lat region like Tommy getting his sense of smell back from the Acid Queen.

We went back and forth like that, trading whiffs, one-upping each other with sneak-attack huffings. We plowed through records—from Frankie Lymon to Jerry Jeff Walker (*Self-Titled*), *Imperial Bedroom*, Rickie Lee & The Glands. Steve Miller's "Circle of Love" but only that song because the rest of the record pales too hard. David + David's *Boomtown*.

> *And I'll kiss your face, attend to your aches*
> *I swear that I can make you happy*
> *And you'll rub my back, forget the past*
> *And baby, I know that that ain't so easy*

We laughed. And laughed. Her sneaky doe-eyed funny funnier each time. We talked about things so banal they don't even exist. Nobody in the world could ever give two hoots about what we were trading. Just stuffing ourselves on nothing sandwiches and saying really nice things to each other. A two-hearted narcissist playing tetherball with itself. Or two pilled-up pheromone monkey junkies in love, trying to not ruin it with, you know, sex.

TSSSSH....DNNNN....TSSSSH....*dnnnn....tssssh*

"Shit. I gotta get a car."

It was 4am. We had fallen asleep. The record was still spinning, the needle with the quiet lint skipping on the label. *Yankee Hotel Foxtrot*. "Reservations".

We never mentioned the L train. For records and hours we just rolled around inside its tracks as it circled the perimeter of my apartment, feeling as good as we could, as good as two can, letting the baby elephant sleep till dawn.

The car came and she left and I realized that that was the longest I'd gone without worrying about losing my hair in years.

SAM BARKED ME awake. My phone was dead but my clock read two o'clock and it was probably right. I just hoped it wasn't two days later. Because if it was today, we had a game in an hour and a half.

I let Sam out and grabbed a seltzer and a granny smith from the fridge. As I walked outside in last night's clothes, I looked at the two things in my hands and didn't know how to start. I knew it was with the seltzer but my communication lines were down.

There were heat-waves outside, making me nauseous. Sam had taken off, somewhere, down the back alley maybe. I wasn't worried about him—he probably needed some space. I sat down on the stoop's front ledge, opened the seltzer and mostly missed my mouth. The apple was cold and almost impossible to eat but I knew I had to get things going in my insides. I ate it like Pac-Man; core, stem, seeds and all because I had once seen a friend do that and I needed to do something I'd never done, for reasons I didn't understand. Once I got it down, I stood to look for Sam and felt systems rejecting. Sam came back around the corner as I purged and he had to dance back like "Bro!" to avoid its spatter.

Back inside, I plugged in my phone and stumbled out of my clothes. In the mirror I looked slightly deranged but I was expecting worse. I didn't know how this was going to work; how I was going to coach the game. I didn't want to, but I looked at the pills I had: four left. Who knows how many of her Vicodin we'd eaten, but it felt like all of them and that felt like so many. I knew whatever I was rationalizing was what every junkie told themselves, but this really was different. After these four, I wasn't gonna drive down to San Pedro & 5th and prowl for smack—I couldn't afford it and I knew myself really well. I might end up there for cost of living, but I'd most likely figure something else out. I had grown up friends.

I ingested the pills with an empty belly and my systems gobbled them up with relish. I hit the showers and as they hit, I felt so much better but rationalized that I'd never be a junkie because I worried too much when I didn't crap. And with that, I put it to bed.

I dried, started to feel great and put on my Super Bowl XXV shirt for good luck. My phone came to life and buzzed with a text:

i threw up

I typed back, fancy-free and meaning it:

Best night of my life.

Her:

I was waiting till you said it

Me:

I threw up, too.

Bubbles.

Good!

I put the phone in my pants pocket, the remaining pills in my breast, ready to win.

On our way out the door, Pancho—the guy who lived across the hall with his wife, Rosa (apartments in Venice are just big houses broken up into tiny apartments)—handed me a Tamale, steamed hot and all bowed up in a corn husk. He had probably heard that I'd had a late night, and perhaps saw me wretch just twenty minutes ago on our collective sidewalk. The year prior, he'd had his stroke and a few weeks after the stroke, when Rosa was out, I'd heard a bleating "Rye-een! RYE-EEEN!" and I went over to find my Man had spilled onto the floor. I hoisted the little big bowling ball back up and onto a chair and we never spoke of it again. Before the fall, Rosa occasionally gave me tamales and tupper wares of pozole. But since the spill she gave more regularly and with a deeper connection.

I kissed Pancho's head, knowing this Tamale could prove essential.

THE TAMALE PROVED disastrous. It maybe saved my life, too, sustenance-wise, but it almost got us killed on the way up to school as it crumbled and flumped all over my lap when I tried to treat it like a burrito, which was entirely on me. It's not a driving food. Sam lunged—from the back, mind you!—for a few stray clumps and knocked my arm, which was driving. I hadn't fed him, in his defense, but still. But still yet: my unforced errors were piling up early.

I cleaned the masa off my lap and, what with where the day had started (at the crack of two) and where it was headed (not good!), I resolved to go full Larry Bird the Coach on the day's game. Stoic, unflappable, vegetable-like. I wouldn't say a word. *It's a player's game*, I nodded. Let them play. I could masquerade how handicapped I was, neurologically, with a steely confidence in my squad. I didn't exactly have Chris Mullin, Reggie Miller, Mark Jackson and Rick Smits to trust in, but I had sacrificed my mind and body and I would do it all again, every time, eight days a week and twice on Sunday. That wouldn't quite jive with my gripe with the Sacklers, but the drugs weren't the point.

Hiding behind my aviators and under a Knicks hat, I clutched my football and walked toward the field, the long retired Catholic in me feeling squeamish that I should be punished for having had last night.

10-7. We won. Or the fellas won is more apt. I did a great job doing nothing, fronting as though I thought we were a mature outfit, that the fellas were up to the task of doing it themselves. Which they were. Though we should have won by eight.

Obviously, I coached a little. They're 7th and 8th grade kids. I had to run substitutions and at least gesticulate occasional frustration or befuddlement, be it palms to the sky or fingers to my temples, a mouth agape. Kids mess up a lot. But to do most of my job, I put two kids in charge. Mecca and Jake. Born captains. They weren't ass-kissers, they were rah-rah guys. The difference is substantial. Ass-kissers are back-stabbers, ladder-climbers, politicians. Rah-rah guys care about the cause, care about the team, care about the *culture*. They're the guys who keep track of how the team's doing years after they've graduated. Decades after. They're annoying to the cool guys but the cool guys just end up being pill-popping philandering losers, anyway. Rah-rah guys are the current. They're the guys you can count on.

I pulled DeMarcus aside once or twice, only because I got him into this mess, and only to say:

"Dude, it's simple. If I was pretty good at this, you better get a full ride to Virginia."

Or

"You can only use your left hand for the rest of the game."

Was it racist of me to give him more attention than the other kids? I didn't care. Because if anyone thought that, they wouldn't say a word for fear of being themselves, racist. If they wanted to accuse me of *reverse* racism, I'd let them bend my ear. It was like my Dad calling me up just to talk about a handshake Obama had given somebody:

"**I love that motherfucker.**"

"**I love him, too, but…**"

"**Oh, God. 'But' what? Tell me—'but' what?!**"

"**Criminal Justice Refor—**"

"***Shit*. Forgot those goddamned fries were in the oven. They're burned. God*damnit*.**" (*Takes a bite.*) "**Not bad, actually. I'll call you in a minute.**"

I gave DeMarcus more attention because now Walter really believed in this game. That sonuvabitch had the kid playing wallball behind the grocery store at *dawn* while his teammates were still whimpering dreams in their five-hundred thread-count sheets. And dawn down there behind a Ralph's…I don't care how much you say the city's changed or how many jobs the new stadium's going to bring—that's not where I wanna see the sun rise.

DeMarcus had three and two, Just had three and one, Burt had two assists, Mecca two and two, Jake had two and one and the other two goals were garbage.

I did feel guilty but I didn't feel bad. My life wasn't going anywhere, but for a moment I loved it. I loved those kids and I loved that Woman and I never knew how to just, for a second or a day, be happy. And there I was.

"You drank cold beers and ate painkillers till four in the morning and then coached my kid?"

Alex had only heard one part of the story, apparently.

"What? No. Not, like…" I had eaten the last two pills on the way to the bar and with a strong well cocktail and a chili-dog in front of me, I had figured I was in a safe place.

"I'm kidding that sounds amazing." He took a big bite. "You just smelled each other?" he asked, muffled with dog.

"Yeah. Nothing untoward."

"BAH!" He almost choked. "I dunno, Man. If I came in and some svelte EMO tween was sniffing my wife…I'd probably rather have her riding some Matt Dillon type."

"Why riding?"

"You can't see your wife getting fucked from behind. There's no coming back from that. If she's in control, then, whatever—it's a service. It's just a dick."

"Who's the 'tween'?"

"You. It's just 'in between' isn't it?"

I shrugged.

"You're in between adulthood and inconsequential knuckleheadhood."

This was a lot to take in, even if it had that easy bar-banter production. I was in between life stages. And sniffing somebody's wife for six to eight hours was really, really fucked up! Upon further review, not a lot to take in—these things were already in. These things I already knew.

"Why Matt Dillon?"

"He's just threatening enough to be bummed out about but

for some reason I could get over it. I don't know. I've thought about it." He ordered another round. "So where do you go from smelling?"

I didn't know. I didn't know where anywhere was after that. Luckily, she was in Santa Barbara for some eco-fundraising thing for the next few days. Preservation, conservation, getting that ocean-water distillery convertor up and running, this time for real. It felt like West Coast Nantucket with her sometimes. Lunches and meetings and jerk-circles where everybody tells each other how great they are as they pick at their vegan niçoise and glad-hand money back and forth, signing checks that somehow, this time next year, ended up back in their own pockets, under a different trust, a different cause. It was all a tax write-off. Even though I still couldn't figure that out. "Write-off your laptop." I didn't understand. I hoped adulthood would unlock such mysteries.

"Rome," I landed on, on where to go next.

"Rome's the best."

"I've never been to Europe."

"Overrated."

"I could sell a script and move to Rome." *What about Camilla?* This question followed every single thought now. *Is that a waning gibbous?* (What about Camilla?) *I should have a pair of black jeans.* (What about Camilla?) *Are squirrels everywhere?*

"Do it."

"Can your wife rep me? Or some hungry youngster at her agency…"

"She won't even represent me. Get in line."

That was the extent of my seeking representation. My

thoughts shifted to another chili-dog. Perversely, I understood it would help me tomorrow.

"What was the last thing you wrote? Why haven't you killed? You're…" Hilarious, great, smart, ornery, empathetic, condescending, curious, kind. I hoped he gathered these superlatives from the way I squinted at him, elbow slipping off the bar.

"God, shut the fuck up." He didn't look disgusted, just spent. "I got nothin' to say."

I understand now what he meant. It's the natural progression. It's randomly cyclical, the only thing you can count on are the intervals of inspirational vacuity growing longer. And longer. That's reliable, scientific. But that night I waved away his white flag, tried to cheers him for morale. He laughed at my gills so green. I didn't care—I flapped them for him, for a smile. I'd been down before; I was born jaded and maybe now I had things to say. Not about this, per se, but about my archeology as I saw it now, looking back through this new lens. Feeling things was informative and energizing; it could jumpstart dormant chambers and synapses, unearth an angle I wasn't privy to back when. Hell, my heart was going for gold on the uneven bars with the whole world rooting against me. Yes, it was small, trite, shameful, selfish. But I felt like maybe I was back for the first time.

TWELVE

That week felt right. I woke up after Chili-Dog night at the Lost & Found, ready. Sam and I went on a punishing run, spitting Kanye all over the Santa Monica bike path. I wrote every day. Not well, but I wrote, tried to limit the tri-half-hourly breaks in which I stood up and looked in my empty cupboards, muttering "Jesus" every time I allowed myself to feign surprise in finding them bare. I set a deadline for my pseudo-musical (nee "rape script"). Coached my nuggets off to make up for my past follies. One day we ran hills till I threw up and I was forced to call practice—we still had forty minutes to go. We played optional catch or wall-ball after that. The point of my running with them was to know the limits of what we were doing, what the body was capable of, could withstand. I puked. That was our Everest. Kids openly wept, Kumal howling like a fifty-five year-old black Woman after Obama got elected. They tried to carry me down on their shoulders, but it was unsafe. It was that victorious, though. I ordered a couple pizzas I couldn't afford, and we talked about video games and girls (I was a little too eager to say that not everybody likes girls, lied about a Gay uncle) till the parents came and picked them up.

Camilla had us move over to a new mode of communication,

a different app called "JellyBurger" or "TskTask." It was encrypted or unencrypted, whichever's better for a torrid affair of redolence. It didn't thrill me but it was also thrilling. Her acknowledgement and fear, keeping us out of the public domain, encrypted or otherwise, meant the things I felt were not out to lunch. The things I felt were very much home for lunch. And I'm not a big lunch guy. Things had evolved and we were (un)encrypted but out in the open with ourselves, saying some *shit*. I had never kissed this woman and there's nothing I wouldn't have done for her. She smelled that good. And she laughed that good. And she walked that good. And she said that good. And, yes: she looked that good.

WE WON ANOTHER game that Thursday against Paul Revere Middle School, which was nice because my horses didn't need to play. Innie, kids with no names, Manassas—they carried the load, got a lot of burn, absolved me of my playing time guilt which didn't really exist.

Friday we won again and I almost got into a fight with the other coach because I ran out the clock. We could have scored another pair of goals, ran it up 13-7. He was some California-bred lunk-head—probably played a year or two in high school—who didn't understand my gallantry. And I didn't feel like explaining it to him.

If my schedule and Camilla's didn't quite synch up in the days and week following OlfactoryOxyFest, well, it was not not by design. All I wanted in the world was to see her, smell her, hear her, touch her. But I was worried about two things. Well, three, for posterity's sake: 1.) I didn't want to tarnish what was, without question, the best night of my life, therefore I could implement the Jim Brown clause. 2.) Her marriage and family or whatever. 3.) (but really, 1, 2 & 3 & & & &) I was worried about my dick. So I acted busy, something I'd never been. I was ducking my hecklers.

I was worried about my dick! Johnson, rather. "Dick" feels curt. I was worried about my Johnson. Because, contrary to popular and simple-minded belief, the dick (Johnson) is an effeminate part. It's a chick. It needs attention, tending to, flattery. Buy the little bastard flowers every once in a while, for Chrissake. The dick swinging, pissing match, fuckity-doo-dah mythos of the Johnson and its porter has been aggrandized to the point where it's not birth that's the miracle, it's the miracle of sex. Actual, unfertilized intercourse.

Let's paint a hypothetical and crunch some numbers for a billion dudes on earth. If, pre-penetration, you really like someone, *really* like them, Allah forbid "love" them, the odds of your fickle dick giving you the green-light when the lights go down are one-in-fifty. And that lucky one-in-fifty requires:

#1.) the precise amount of two and a half lagers (32 oz.) or ales in the 5-5.6 ABV range.

#2.) two days (prior to consummation) of food pyramid meals, three square.

On top of those barely manageable nutritional requirements:

#3.) one must be majority-house devoid of self-doubt.

Number three is tricky because if you really like this woman or dude, you probably are, or were, near-brimming with confidence…until you realize that the next time you see her or him it's probably Go-time and the odds double against you and you start betting against yourself days in advance because it's a sure thing, a shoo-in that it's never gonna happen. It's like betting on the Expos to win the Pennant next season. They are no longer a team and while you are bad in Vegas, you're positive that Montreal couldn't come up with the resources, financial backing, front office, back office, vendors, sponsors and players, within the calendar year, to get Olympic Stadium MLB ready again.

When that little twerp Cupid skewers you with an arrow, the one thing in the world you want is to make the one person in the world feel good. Really good! And you'd really like to have something to do with that, their feeling good, and, moreover, you'd love for your Johnson to be an ardent participant.

I wanted it, I wanted *Her*, it was all I wanted, thus, it could not be. Oddly, it was not dissimilar to wanting only to NOT get a cold sore in the fourth grade. It was all I ever wanted (to not get a cold sore), ergo, tri-annually, a little boy leper was I. To worry the very worry you cannot unworry until it's ruined you is nothing short of madness. A boner for this woman of my dreams became my nightmare. The hecklers were lining up early, camping out to buy tickets. These rodents of gloom I'd known since I knew who I was, arriving in Talpid form in my formative years, when the wind would blow askance and I'd manifest that morbid, sharp tickle on my upper lip, worry myself into a cold sore like Magic Rocks in a time-lapse. They were the Boston fans of my psyche, these repellant whack-a-moles of worry or doubt. I used to have an imaginary mallet that I carried around, an old croquet mallet painted in red & blue or orange & blue, New York colors (depending on the season), ready to scrap, but knowing they would not relent until I got a coldsore and cried. Until they won. These moles, these doubts of erection were of the same ilk (see: Icelandic *moldvarpa*; the dirt tosser) and I knew their stratagem would be ruthless. They wouldn't stop until they won. Until she gripped my disappointment at room temp. They were coming, my hecklers, backwards fitted hats and chin-strap beards abound. I won't even tell you what courtside were going for.

Once this infection of doubt spread from cerebrum to cerebellum, I had trouble cajoling midday reassurance boners, basic training and there was already mutiny in the nethers. My mind would drift to dark corners, earnestly drafting mock-ups of a 9v battery defibrillator. A good hour wasted slapping the floppy bastard against my leg, yelling "c'mON…c'MON!" like Phil Connors trying to resuscitate the old man in *Groundhog Day*, giving him soup, knowing he's gonna die, but maybe this time's different. I even considered calling up Gagosian Ronnie for a pep-rallying reassurance visitation. Boners with her were easy. Boners borne of annoyance, contempt or apathy are the only boners a man can truly count on. I'm not saying it's EASY for women. I'm just saying, worst consensual case is you find yourself not attracted to the dude, so you say "I'm good" and go your separate ways or you say "ah, whatever," close your eyes, spit on everything, picture Oscar Isaacs and this will all soon be over. But if you like the Dude and he can't get a boner? Be flattered. Pour him a drink. Say something funny, then something sweet, maybe buy his dick some flowers. And in the near distant future you'll be so disgusted with the thing that you'll yearn for the days of his misty-eyed impotence. Dicks are impossible.

So there I was, at a one sided impasse, unable to even plead with the other side. Just an old, stubborn Okie in a dustbowl, fine with the horsemeat. There was no reaching across the aisle of my venereal congress; it was wholly partisan, unanimous yea's on the bill of my erectile dysfunction. I wanted to have sex with a woman who was married to a man I wanted to be. But the candle of moral dilemma got blown out with a dismissive wave when held up to what I had already seen etched on my headstone, its words heckled to me in the briniest of Boston accents...

THIRTEEN

SOUTHERN CALIFORNIA NOT EXACTLY BEING THE HOTBED OF LACROSSE meant we played only a handful of games and had to play some teams twice. One of those teams was Harvard Westlake, who we would play Saturday, which would be the final game of the regular season, a four-team play-off beginning the following week.

Friday being post and pre-game practice, I doubled down on what made us good and had weeks earlier almost ruined the season. We ran. I heard Cuthbert yell to me as we ran 200m & 400m sprints around the track around the varsity field: "Implement an inversion for tomorrow's game," he called out, thinking he was program head, my superior, implying we didn't need to be running like maniacs the day before a big game. He wasn't wrong, but his team was well below .500, a spot in the playoffs out of their control, their destiny in the hopes of other teams losing.

"What? Sorry, I can't hear you! We're too fast!" I hollered as I rounded the bend, a pack of wild kids on my heels. I had cultivated a culture of disrespect toward him, twelve-year-olds sniggering behind his back, in front of his face, across campus. It was churlish but funny and he deserved it. Plus, it brought the team closer.

My run of ducking Camilla, however, I was not fine with and it had reached its tipping point. "Fuck my stupid dick," I had resolved. It was too arrogant a reason to hide, even if its root cause was the biological antithesis of arrogance. I needed to see her. *Needed.* She occupied my all. And, hell—I could try? What if, at the perfect moment, I became re-comfortable in my body? Doc and the Clock Tower. Stars and cells align, pig takes flight. Ha-ha, no. No chance. Better yet, I could put upon a put upon act of valor, strap on a chastity belt emblazoned with an honorable crest, Ulysses S. Grant's face maybe, a shield not that of a Wuss but of compassionate virility, a sacrifice to preserve her and Tourney's matrimony. Or I could kill myself. All viable options, with the exception of consummation.

I told her to come to the Harvard-Westlake game, that Teddy should see her brother play. I insisted. I demanded, unencrypted, with my thumbs. I told her that I'd lost my sense of smell.

ALTHOUGH I VERY much needed it then, middle school coaches are not, by and large and hopefully ever, in it for the money. This season would be the one exception of my dependence on a middle school coach's salary. I wasn't too worried about job security—the season was almost over and if I was coaching middle school lacrosse again next year, well, that wasn't an option because I would be too busy grinding words and pages and scripts, providing for my new family (with maybe one on the way, inevitable boner notwithstanding) and that near-future Me wouldn't want any of Buck's alimony out of respect for him and his sorrow. He was, in this future, a relic, and I had up and came. In the seconds following these thoughts, the year seemed to be going by terribly fast.

Ah, but those really were my very own imbecilic thoughts—the year of grit and determination, the hustle, my arrival and comeuppance, a family modern—when I saw her and Teddy from across the parking lot. I broke into a trot then had to put leg brakes on, cool it and walk. It looked like I had a condition, like Clint Eastwood in a rush.

We hugged and didn't care. Inhaled for an obscene three seconds, then quickly got our realities together. But for a whiff we were like Ennis Del Mar and Jack Twist involuntarily clutching for dear life, groin-mashing through their dungarees while Michelle Williams watches from up the back stairs, through the kitchen window. Teddy took Sam and when she was out of earshot I said: "Sure, let's get married," before I ran off, not needing a reaction, because I had made up our minds.

HAVING GOTTEN SHELLACKED by Harvard-Westlake in our previous meeting, the key to this outing was to go in cool. We took our time getting gear on. I sung softly "Franklin's Tower." A nice, easy jog around the field. An even easier stretch—no obscene military counting, no jumping jacks. I even scrapped a stretching circle or lines for an abstract team stretch down in the corner of the field while I warmed up Beaker. An easy, free-wheelin' intro before the set coalesced. We yucked it up. We even yawned like we had messed up real bad the night before, drinking Barq's and playing

Baseball Stars till the wee hours in Kevin Child's basement.

"Lull 'em to sleep," I instructed my top brass before the warm-up lap as they were getting their cleats on. Off their dubious looks, I said: "They don't know our address." I had never said anything to them that made complete sense, or even, really, work-in-progress sense. But we had established a fluency in the nonsensical, a Rosetta Stone for improvised jive, our own private idiocy that only comes from crawling and clawing through the sick shit together. I was thirty-one going on fourteen and we were best friends on that field. They knew what I meant.

The kids on the other team were stealing glances at Jake and DeMarcus so I told them both to do line-drills with their off-hands. And because their off-hands had gotten good, I told them to warm-up as if they had the limbs of Pinocchio or the Tin Man—an old Stella Adler exercise.

"Got a couple new studs there, huh," their coach, Jed Prossner said to me as we shook hands at midfield. I was a stranger to him but I knew who he was. He was great in college, played at North Carolina, before that at Avon Old Farms or some such Future Secret Republicans of America breeding ground where he started his freshman year, taken under the wing of some senior who was buddies with the guy who had taken Camilla's virginity however many identical campuses over. Expanding assets, properties, portfolios; these were things he now knew, forever in denial that it took using starry-eyed, redneck-hoser scrotums like mine as gription on the road to get there.

"Yeah, Man! They're pickin' it up," I smiled and gave a tip-of-the-cap wave to his ample coaching staff; younger dudes than I but all of polished ACC or Georgetown pedigree. I clapped him on the shoulder: "Go easy on us, now."

I jogged back to our sideline, blood teemed with juice.

Teddy corralled Sam somewhere on the hill and I didn't look but saw her mother there and lightly pumped a fist of determined hope. A Confident Man.

The ref blew the whistle. We huddled up.

"What we were when we first played them…and who we are now…"

We had worked so hard and felt so much; we sucked and now we didn't. But that's not pep-talk talk. This was heavy. This had Good Vs. Evil undertones. I couldn't go with a *take dead aim at the rich kids* tip because, well, look where we were, who we were. I looked over at Prossner and the Young ACCs for inspiration and it was then that I remembered who I hated the most.

"We are the Giants and they are the Patriots." It didn't occur to me that some of these kids were three years old the first time Eli crapped in Tom Brady's Little Debbie. But they knew. The ones who didn't understand my lackadaisical pregame game-plan now understood. Even Manassas' eyes singed, his jaw tightening. It was all I had, so I said it again.

"We are the Giants and they are the Patriots." Kumal mmmhm-mm'd. "There's a bunch of little Tom Brady's over there. And we're comin'."

Even Just was all-in on this analogy, his too-cool, soon-to-be-stoner-jock sneer unable to wiggle its way out. He nodded. Punched his gloves together, clacked his helmet against DeMarcus'.

"And we're gonna run. And we're gonna keep coming. And

keep running. And keep runnin'. And run it back. And run some more." It—we, the team—hummed.

"It's time."

I looked at all of these kids and loved them. And, yes, no I did not know that love in absence of the exploding kaleidoscopic prism of Camilla which I now loved them through. But it didn't matter. That was all chicken or the egg, tree-in-the-woods conjecture. I loved them.

"I love you guys."

"Love you, too, Coach," smiled Burt, blushing. The others nodded and echoed the love.

"We run." I smacked Crothers on the helmet. "Through the darkness."

"To the light!"

The Bears of Harvard-Westlake turned to our roar, as if catching wind, an unseasonal gust, an ominous line out on the ocean's horizon as the beachside town's siren sounds.

Suddenly, it seemed, we had their attention.

IF WE WANTED to keep up with them score-wise, we had to have them desperately trying to keep up with us, conditioning-wise. So, initially to his chagrin, I put Just back at midfield.

"What? No. Why?"

"Shut up. Yes. Because I said."

He still looked confused, stung, wary, put-out. Like it was always a test with me. Good-God I loved his Step-Mom.

"You are our best player. And now I need you on both sides

of the ball. The only way we beat these guys is if we stack the midfield and run all over them."

I put Just on the first line with DeMarcus and Maybelline. Mecca and Jake and Innie on the second. I put Simply Matt down on attack with Burt and Manassas, where their only instructions were to catch the ball, move the ball, don't drop the ball too much. We had two really good midfield lines that could run forever.

In practice, I had implemented a defensive scheme that put most of our chips on Harvard-Westlake getting frazzled. They were kids. Kids get frazzled. The Nazi's got frazzled at Normandy…eventually.

"Scheme" sounds a little robust and dynamic for what our plan was. We were simply going to double early and double often. Yes, that leaves one of their guys open, often, but if we slid (doubled) fast enough, waving our sticks in the air like lepidopterists on crank, we could frazzle them into turnovers. We'd be tired, but at this point, we laughed at tired. Tired was a joke. So this would leave one of their guys open, as our second slide and defensive rotation would be a little slow (7th & 8th graders), resulting in an easy pass to a dip n' dunk one-on-one with the goalie. To get to that one-on-one, though, it required other-side-of-the-pillow-type composure from the kid who was doubled. And if, at twelve-years-old, you have a heat-seeking missile like Jake coming for you and you keep your shit together, create some space for yourself and make a calm pass over or around said missile, well: I was more than willing to live with those goals. We were out to frazzle. I had the horses to frazzle. Prossner would see what I was doing, think it low-rent and gauche. They were going to want to slow the game down. And we weren't going to let them.

JUST JUMPED THE gun on the face-off, a turnover before the game began. Their face-off guy casually picked up the dead-ball as I signed what looked like gibberish for Just to *not* drop in—dropping in the standard defensive practice—but to stay put. He caught my drift. The whistle blew, I gave him the nod and he shot out like a falcon, built like a gun, the Harvard-Westlake kid so surprised that he didn't have time for consideration, couldn't process the surprise, just stood there facing Just, stick in both hands like he was posing for a yearbook picture. Just blew him up. Ball loose, stick lost in the air, everyone tracking it like a foreboding marching band baton in the opening frame of a school shooting movie. A caterwaul from the visiting mothers echoed around the canyon. The ref went to blow the whistle, trying to compute what exactly the infraction was. But there was no penalty for a perfect hit. He dropped his whistle as DeMarcus scooped up the ground ball, ran through a series of futile stick-checks, split left-right down the alley, cocked his hips, hammered the ball into the bottom left corner of the goal.

We erupted like the Garden after LJ's three, soon-to-be four point play.

I put in the second midfield, quick blows for the horses. Mecca lost the face-off but stayed on his man, on his hip, whapping stick checks on the kid's bottom hand. Jake's man jogged idly down the sideline closest to the bench, Mecca and his man at the center of the field, running toward the opposite sideline.

"Jake, go." I barely got the words out of my mouth before he went tracking across the field like one of Obama's night drones. I yelled for Mecca to turn back his man—step in front of him and reverse his course, roll him back in the other direction—which he did just as Jake arrived. And it was like the kid had stepped on a mine. Ball, stick, Mecca all went flying. The referee inhaled to use his whistle again, gripped his flag like a stress ball, but came up empty once more. Crothers picked up the ground ball and took off, Mecca staying behind in his stead. Crothers moved it to Jake, who went left, rolled back and the defense had collapsed, leaving Burt open from seven yards. Jake moved it to Burt and Burt fired a tepid bounce shot through traffic. It bounced off somebody's leg and spat into the goal.

Our bench reacted like that of a thirteen seed in the NCAA Men's Basketball Tournament going to the sweet sixteen.

Prossner called a timeout.

Across the field, Camilla had her hands in the pockets of her slim and high-rise slate blue Gap khakis, shaking her head, fighting a smile that could break a face, fix my heart. I winked behind my sunglasses from sixty yards away.

We were only a minute into the game. I watched as Prossner pled a "c'mon" to the ref, and he wasn't wrong. He was trying to protect his kids, who were, after all, kids.

"Keep the foot on the gas," I told the fellas. "But we're not gonna get away with too many more hits like that." I added: "Two of the finest hits I've ever seen, on the record."

I tried to explain that the ref was going to start calling "unnecessary roughness" or "unsportsmanlike", something subjective to anesthetize our nuclear objective. But my guys were head-butting and fist-bumping, too juiced to hear my faint warnings. I sent them back out to get penalized for perfect hits.

As the ref made his way over to me, I put up my hands of compliance.

"I know, I know," I offered. "Pretty good hits, though." I needed him to know that I knew that he knew so we would both know going forward that he knew, too.

"Maybe in a few years," he half scolded. He took a few strides out to midfield to set up the next face-off, turned to admit: "But, yeah: pretty good hits."

I looked over at Prossner and shrugged. Not an apology, per se, but an "Ahh, whatta you gonna do?" or perhaps a "You remember me now, no? No worries, either way: get fucked, lol." Though I probably just smiled and he smiled back, two old bros not yet what they want to be, not even close, with the odds only getting worse in an impossible town.

THE REF MADE use of his whistle after that. We won the next face off, threw it away, and they came back down the field. When Just's guy crossed midfield, I hollered for him to turn his man as DeMarcus came darting across the field, clean hit, loose ball… but the ref blew the whistle, calling a "push with possession," intimating that DeMarcus had pushed him from behind. Which was untrue. He hit him cleanly, from the side, just frighteningly hard. Either way, we were man-down for thirty seconds and they made efficient use of it, scoring after each kid had touched the ball. It was crisp and pretty and it pissed me off.

They did try and slow the game down, holding onto the ball if they bested a double, running the clock down (although it was still the first half) and catching their breath if they found enough space. But we were relentless. Like a wine-drunk woman in a late-night spat. We just wouldn't leave them the fuck alone.

"They're like machines!" said a Harvard-Westlake midfielder to Prossner as he came off the field. "They won't stop!"

He had just been mugged by Just and DeMarcus while trying to clear the ball over midfield. Just came screaming in for a full body shot but stopped short and wound a clean, precise wrap-check to the kid's stick, knocking the ball loose. DeMarcus scooped it up and they motored down the field, bop-bop—BANG! to put us up 7-5 with two minutes left in the half.

Harvard-Westlake ran the clock down in the final minutes, Beaker taking a shot off the quad to end the half. It all seemed possible.

I GAVE THE team a minute alone as I jogged across the field, their minute alone a shabby veneer to my already thin veil of going to check on Sam.

"Wanna hang out tonight?" My behavior was gauche but my insides were mawkish. I wanted everybody to be happy, I swore, reconciling that celestial alignment such as this benefits all the players, the people, every creature: The Choir. Even the casualties, those sacrificed for the stellar union would eventually be happy, blessed even, to have played a role in the Impossible Love.

She quickly nodded and I scraggled Sam for the show. *You're welcome, World!* I all but screamed. I ran back across the field, boner-fret quickly countered with a long-shot hope of a Tourney-hired sniper in the trees, my head-blood pooling into the sod, dying an impoverished hero, up 7-5 to the enemy, her heart irreparably crippled for the rest of her years despite having never crossed the threshold of penetrative infidelity, the "what if" assuring me a legacy, a memoriam in void. She'd pop in at the end of the service, shed a few and leave before they played "First Day of My Life" or "Gettin' in Tune." I'd be forever missed. For all she knew, I was the Greatest Lover.

No sniper.

Prossner was talking to one of his player's parents, a guy who looked like he produced Doug Liman movies. Prossner nodded, engaged, reflective and it dawned on me: Prossner was probably working at Lakeshore or Bad Robot or HoneyBucket, being paid, nurtured and groomed to be sought after as, if not a virtuoso, an up-and-comer, a "creative producer" whom everyone would "ohmyGod, *love*" to work with. His mentor saw the Weinstein storm on the horizon, got Prossner and himself way out ahead of it to where he now garnered a rep for truly respecting women. A "Good Guy." Avon Fucking Old Farms. The Great Divide scythed my brain again and I wanted to make him squeal like a pig.

"Don't change a thing," I instructed the boys. "Keep your foot on the gas, let them try to adapt."

"What about the calls?" Just asked, referring to the penalized legal hits.

"Okay, how's this," I reasoned. "Don't head hunt. Don't try to hurt anyone. Don't hit anyone smaller than you." Fair parameters. "Don't be a dick," I summarized. "But…" We were up 7-5 and this whole thing, I wanted them to know, was just a fleeting imperfect endeavor in a quick trip of selfish mistakes. So if something like this comes along, well, catch it if you can and get it while the gettin's good. Don't rape Ned Beatty. But fuck somebody's wife.

"It's a contact sport."

They nodded, yanked their helmets down on their heads.

"Through the darkness."

THE FUZZY GNATS cleared in time for me to see him walking away. No blood pooled on the lawn but it dribbled in my eye as I got to a knee, the immediate, un-articulable but wholly intimate invasion of being punched in the face slowly making its way to my processor.

Cars slowed down to watch, to check that he (I, me) was okay; at least moving. A tap on the brakes, slowing their automobiles a few measly miles-per-hour for a stricken fellow man plenty charitable for them, above and beyond, really, in this Star-Bellied Sneetch infested town.

He had called me over across Barrington Avenue so that he didn't hit me on school grounds. I followed him, knowing he'd maybe hit me, his clenched fists and general menace the obvious hints. But I wanted to take my medicine. Pay the piper. If hitting me would make him feel better, he could have at it, because the coals I would rake myself over for what had happened earlier would make his right cross pale as a tickle, EMDR to my brow.

With his back to me, he apoplectically muttered to himself as I approached. I inhaled to speak with nothing to say as he turned and summonsed up all his old man strength and knocked out every one of my lights.

Turns out McMillan was a lefty.

WE CAME OUT in the second half the same way we started the first. Our brawn bullied their beauty. We traded two goals with them, and in the final minutes of the third, it was still a two-goal game in our favor when Mecca put a bounce-shot off a split dodge in the back of the net. Up three goals, I looked over at Prossner and saw a pre-emptive panic.

He called a timeout.

Our defensive mania hadn't let up and they couldn't figure out how to anesthetize it. We were measured dervishes, frustrating the opposition to the point where Prossner would have to make a bush-league adjustment or we'd most certainly win. I saw it on his face as they huddled up. He was not proud but he could write it off on the account that we were playing a different style; convince himself and the team that I had taken tact and grace off the table, had secretly visualized toothlessly ass-plowing him against his will in Appalachia. He'd claim that I'd forced his hand. He was going to turn this into a soccer game. They were going to flop.

On the face-off, DeMarcus nudged one of their midfielders on a ground ball and the kid lurched forward, splaying out like a bad actor playing drunk. Loose-ball push. They picked up the ball and as I sent Just on a double, DeMarcus went to turn his guy and before Just arrived, the kid threw himself on the ground, a distressed damsel in the square. Push with possession, thirty-seconds.

I laughed a bellicose laugh, letting Prossner and this now noodle-spined ref know that this new tactic was for dishonorable pussies of the lowest regard.

They scored quickly.

I put the second unit in. Harvard-Westlake won the face-off and drew another penalty, another flop. They scored on their man-up and I called a timeout, giving the ref my best disappointed and fraternal "*Bro…*".

The chatter in our huddle bordered on whiny.

"No-no. *No.* Crying about it is just as bad. They're flopping because they're freaked out. These are the Flops of Desperation. Keep. Foot. On. Gas."

I sent them back out but couldn't relieve them their confused reluctance.

Just won the face-off and got checked as he tried to move it to DeMarcus. The ball died in the air and landed on the ground near our bench, still in play. The Harvard-Westlake attackman closest to the ball ran parallel to the sideline, upfield, toward the groundball, perpendicular to DeMarcus' plane. The attackman looked up and saw DeMarcus tracking the ball full-speed and the kid panicked, terrified, enacting his Prossner-issued choreographed flop entirely too early, throwing himself on the ground between DeMarcus and the ball. In his panic, the kid flopped wrong—if there is such a thing—and the world slowed to bullet-time Matrix-speed and I knew the game-tape of this moment would be forever kept at the perfect temperature in the archives of my guilt. The flopper laughed on the ground, trying to make funny his bungled flop and I wanted to stomp his little nuts in. Time and space were not on DeMarcus' side, and for a moment, this Athletic Pythagoras didn't have an answer. Moving too fast and not wanting to trample this rich imp, DeMarcus straightened up out of his ground-ball lean, his brakes locking as he tried to avoid the huddled mass before him and I saw it in his eyes seconds before it happened, one last hope that the body can correct its course before...*pop*! goes the ACL.

The next moments and minutes are hazy. But the cause of guilt, immediate and lifelong, were not because I had gotten DeMarcus Long to play lacrosse and then subsequently injure his knee, ergo putting a stick in the spokes of his football career. No-no. That I could, can, do live with—that's sports, Man. It wasn't my fault. He didn't tear his knee up because we ran too much, although that wan argument could be made, but not to me. DeMarcus was on the field playing the game, a game that he would go on to play in college, yes, in no small thanks to me. I don't feel guilt about his knee because that shit, when properly digested, can make you stronger, and, again: that's sports, baby. No, the reason I felt guilt is because after I heard his knee pop and saw his eyes go wide with The Fear, the first thing that went through my moonstruck-mind was: *Is this gonna fuck up my plans tonight?*

And, listen: immediately after feeling that thought, I overcompensated ten-fold in my Pacino-like theatrical reaction to the play. I made everyone—Prossner, the Ref, the Flopper, God—feel eyes-on-their-shoes guilty about the events leading to the injury. But even as I seethed and danced, the thought was still there. I *did* feel awful for the kid and I *was* angry at the way it had happened. I just really, *really* wanted to hang out with Her. 9/11 could have happened again. Long Island could have just snapped off and sank into the Atlantic like the Titanic—I love Long Island and have a lot of friends and family there—we all do! Or I can one-up all of it: my *Mom* could have died. My MOTHER. She who made all possible. Every feeling. Every stupid beautiful feeling. Connected through a tube, floating in the tropic of her fluids for nine months. I could have gotten the call that afternoon and I would have bluffed a crackling, a bad connection, not dismissing what I heard, but postponing...*let's bump this to tomorrow...this could DEFinitely fuck up my plans tonight.* She'd be dead forever!

That's Love on the Brain, though.

We got DeMarcus over to the sideline, where he sat on the ground. Somebody got him a bag of ice.

I grabbed his hand, looked him in the eye but had nothing to say. I tried to sing "don't you worry 'bout a thing" but my voice was spent and it sounded dismal.

"But that sound," he said, looking into the unknown. He looked up at me. "Did you hear that?"

"Knees are weird, Man. It could be nothin'." Luckily I was wearing pants because my mangled knee would have been a stormy forecast for him at eye level.

DeMarcus was a great kid. He was black, a gifted athlete and he looked up to and trusted me and I, in turn, favored him on a team which that year, saved my life. He stood up and could hobble about, giving him a false hope I remembered once having, and I forgot, for at least a shabby second, about my night's plans and felt bad for him and him alone.

The game resumed and I called off the doubles, the game-plan, the crazed dogs. Their flopping had gotten one of our guys hurt. They flopped because I sent a lot of doubles. So it was on me or whatever. We didn't throw in the towel, we just stopped doing the things that had us winning. The fellas were bummed out, and I understood. This was just the biggest and best "fuck you" to Prossner and the Ref that I had access to. The boys didn't know it yet, but that's life's currency.

We lost by a pair of goals.

While the kids glumly milled about post-loss, Walter helped his son limp across the field to the parking lot, toward the mirage of "sprain," and I think he felt my eyes on him. I had been avoiding eye contact with the man, and maybe he wasn't searching for mine, but we both knew, as men, that we needed the moment.

We stood looking at each other from twenty-five yards. I gave him my hangdog. He brushed it aside with a shake of the head and a fist out, an invisible bump in the space between us that I returned, a bump which I took the liberty of taking to mean, in the most understanding of ways: *you go on ahead with your plans.*

Camilla had left unseen, given Teddy's care of Sam over to Crothers' younger brother, my phone a vacant machine, cold to the touch, hands turning it over and over, trying to will a minor buzz from it, the night's plans I had felt bad about prioritizing over my Mom's life in flux while I sat with my driver's side door open in the parking lot, one foot on the ground, all the players and parents having long gone home.

"Get over here, maggot." I think it was "maggot."

McMillan strode across the parking lot all khaki shorts and New Balance. He assumed I was joining him because he never looked back as he pressed the pedestrian crossing button that triggered the blinking yellow lights to cross Barrington.

She was leaving tomorrow and probably left the game because the tealeaves of DeMarcus' Anterior Cruciate Ligament steeped danger. I fought hard to ignore the leaves and continued to hold the night's plan in its haloed light of armor while DeMarcus was maybe receiving terrible news. This made me worse than most of the Me's I'd been and, quite frankly, possibly a sociopath. Although nobody really knows what that means. What I did know was that it was time for me to get punched in the face.

"You good?" a man asked from his Range Rover, a thumbs up out the window as he rolled past.

I gathered, in full, where I was when I saw McMillan trotting back across Barrington and down the winding access road to the faculty lot like Dabo Sweeny jogging into the tunnel after he got away with another ethically questionable win.

"Meester? Meester, you okay?"

A small Latina woman gently guided me to my feet. My

faculties had reacclimatized, but I leaned into the gesture as gently as she had given it, trying to do whatever small part I could in completing the human connection. I looked down at her Caramelo-brown hand on my elbow, looked at her plump, worried face of forty-plus years and I weighed and reasoned a career change to full-time Coyote. She pulled a few Subway napkins from her tote, which muddied my experience, but they smelled like a taco truck so it broke even. I dabbed at my left brow and she grabbed my hand, took the napkins and wetted them with water from a single use water bottle. I cursed myself for deducting humanitarian points from this Belizean Saint just because I thought Subway was for the lessers and Kirkland plastics the gross, but how dense! How shortsighted. The napkins and the Kirkland had more likely than not come from the place of her employer, the family she *nannied* for! The blind footprints of the well-to-do. She wiped most of the right side of my face—more blood than I had thought—and gestured for me to splash some water in my eye, wash out the blood. Cars drove past, cars that probably cost more money than either of us would ever have at any given time in our lifetimes. People talking, people texting; even on a Saturday, people scrabbling to get to the next thing. *This* gets me *that*. But everybody forgets about This. And This alone.

"Gracias, gracias," I muttered, trying to show her I cared, but also asking her with my wince at the world around us: *Why would you want to be here if people as lovely as yourself are where you're from? This country is a can of Red Bull.*

Correction: Reverse Coyote. Roam the Sonoran hills, the Chihuahuan Desert on steed, stopping immigrants before they make the biggest mistake of their lives. Wave to them from atop the final hill they're set to climb and yell: "It's not worth it!! This place sucks! There's a couple good restaurants but you'll never get to go!! Just go back and make where you're from better!!!"

My phone buzzed. A wall went up. My blinders back on. A little green icon, encrypted or un- was Joaquin Phoenix's thumb in *Gladiator*.

whatcha doin?

Horns sounded and I found myself in the middle of Barrington, apparently having reacted to the text by running blinding into the road, a headless horseman. I stopped, turned back to my Latina Saint who stood there confused if not entertained. "Let it make you *better*!" I may have yelled aloud, urging myself to use this beautiful feeling—this In LovedNess—to spread *good*, spread love. I ran back to her, grabbed her face in my hands and kissed her on the forehead and hugged her, saying over and over three of the fifty or twenty-five words I knew in Spanish:

"Todo bien, todo amor. Todo bien, todo amor…"

I held her by the shoulders and said it again. She laughed and repeated this mantra from the bloodied crackpot, thinking he may need medical attention or thinking nothing of it, having seen much, much worse where she's from. Her hand still held the diluted blood napkin, and I put both of my hands around hers—our little miracle, our moment, our napkin—kissed the hands collective and took our napkin, holding it high in the air like an Olympian as I leapt back across Barrington.

I ran into the school to get an ice pack and found Sam padding through the halls.

"What's your problem?" I asked him.

Keri came out from an administrative looking room, her energy harried. Before she could give me grief about the dog, she saw my face.

"Whoa, what happened?" I hadn't yet seen the damage, but judging by the near caring reaction of someone who didn't care for me, I imagined it wasn't great.

"Jake and I were taking shots after the game and he fired one into my brain—how bad is it?"

I wasn't in the business of upending someone's life because of a waivable infraction. Was McMillan an asshole, a bully, a mishmash of -phobes? Sure. But getting the guy axed just because he probably shouldn't have hit me seemed ridiculous. I wasn't being Jesus-like about it. I wasn't taking the high road or turning the other cheek or, God Forbid, letting a bad guy off the hook. I was on the punchable side of punchable; I knew that. And if he was Sandusky-ing around I would have hacked and cauterized him a Barbie Doll crotch and drove him to Sing-Sing myself. But he was just a lonely codger and this was his lifeblood. Or he was a happily married husband and father of three, day-lighting as an angry codger and this was something he loved. Either way, he could go to hell. But he could go there while still coaching high school football. All of that notwithstanding, telling the truth would have probably meant paperwork, forms, aggravated assault. I didn't have time for that shit. I had plans.

"Pretty bad," Keri winced before she remembered she didn't like me and that my dog was in the building. "He can't be in here."

"How do you know he's a 'he'?" I was unsure of my motive

here. It seemed like a strange remark given her own androgynous structure and panache.

"Because of his penis."

"You call that a penis!?" I lunged at Sam to make a show of his furry hidden member but he knew I was playing my usual nowhere games and side-stepped me. Cuthbert emerged from the side-hatch, the same office where Keri had been. A dimly lit office buried in an empty corridor of a sleepy school on the later side of a Saturday afternoon. He was flushed, looking like he'd been smearing offal with the skate-shoed butcher. She was unfazed, though. This all made fine sense, and I loved it. At the very least, it made them both a lot more interesting.

"Bro!" he looked at Keri, I think to make sure being nice to me was okay. "You got fucked up!"

"Kinda," I smiled at both of them—not to humiliate, but to encourage. "I'm just tryin' to get an ice pack."

"Dude—I think you need stitches."

"No way…" I couldn't. Insurance. I'd glue it. I hadn't even responded to the encryption! I took out my phone.

"You have to get him out of here," Keri said, back to her old self.

"Dude, chill the fuck out!" I snapped, typing into my phone. "Who gives a shit?" There was nobody in the building and they'd just been playing Ren & Stimpy in the nurse's office. And if I did need stitches-stitches, I'd have to throw McMillan under the bus. Or maybe they'd pay for it because the fabricated lacrosse shot incident happened on campus. I didn't have time for this shit! I'd get some butterflies.

"Excuse me?"

> *I'll be home in an hour. Come over.*

I didn't press send because it was too plain and these people had me flustered.

"You can't talk to me like that."

"Dude, you can't talk to her like that."

"GUYS," I pled with them.

My phone pulsated with regular. I added:

> *If you don't I'll kick your rotten teeth in.*

Sent, received, seen, all of it, everything.

"Alright," I put my phone down. "We're going."

Keri gave Cuthbert another look that said *go on, Pussy...*

To which he said, off of her look, looking at only her: "While you're here—we'll get you an ice-pack in a second, but..."

Bzzz-Bzzz

> *rude! but tempting. see you soon.*

Cuthbert was stammering on and I hadn't caught any of it. "What?"

"Just, you know, moving forward, I think you guys, going into the playoffs, you're in good enough shape, so I would cut back on the conditioning..."

"Oh, would you?" I beamed, blinking my eyes like a doll.

"Yeah." He started to stiffen up, what with my acting like a smart aleck. "You have to put in some different looks, different offenses and man-ups." He was gathering steam, forgetting that I hadn't remembered asking him a goddamn thing. "You're in good enough shape."

"Yes," I said, sending up Andy Kaufman.

"I'm serious."

"Yes."

"I'm not asking."

"Yes."

"You ran those kids into the ground all season and that leads to injuries—look what happened to DeMarcus. You have any idea how much shit McMillan's already giving us?"

My eye twitched or the cut above my eye blinked. They both saw an irrevocable nerve had been struck.

"Here's what I'm gonna do," I said, smarmy dander-boosters Houston ready. "I'll forgive you the DeMarcus comment because that's a rat-fink thing to say and I gotta believe you're better than that."

"Just—"

"I don't," I said, "and you're not. But I'll forgive the comment anyway because I actually really have to go. I have to get this DOG out of here before he…"

Sam looked up at me drolly then glanced past at what I assume was a clock. I finger snapped and he hopped-to as we started back down the hall. But, of course, I was not finished.

"Are you guys in the play-offs?" I asked Cuthbert, my back to them.

Nothing. I turned.

"Sorry?"

He shook his head.

"Well. Maybe if you guys were in better shape, you'd still be alive."

I skipped, hopped, clicked my heels in the air like Dick Van

Dyke.

"Maybe next year!"

Once we rounded the corner and I could feel we'd cleared their line of vision, me and my dog took off like jackrabbits. Sam fed off of my manic fervor and kept pace. We got to the Subaru and hopped in. My eye didn't look that bad. Well, if I'm being honest, it looked pretty bad, needed a couple to five stitches. I just never remembered how bad it looked for such a long time after that—months, years—because all I ever remembered was how excited I was.

FOURTEEN

At the Whole Foods, I had the fishmonger throw some shaved ice in a produce bag for me and I bought a six-pack of Sierra, a six-pack of Heineken and stole a box of butterflies. In the car I opened a Sierra and looked to where the sun had been, now disappeared behind the Dollar Store, and the colors above made me think of a sailing saying that made me think of The Sugar Hill Gang. Three times—was it only three?!—this woman and I had hung out and it felt like we'd been together since the discovery of fire, witnessed the discovery together and were both equal parts disappointed and relieved when the world didn't develop and evolve fast enough thereafter. The human (nee American) conundrum condition. *Hurry up. Wait, hold up: let's enjoy this.*

Three times. Never been kissed.

I put some chill in my tank, the ice on my eye, and tried to remember what a disappointment I was, figuring that was the crow's flight to stasis. It worked, not in that I felt bad about myself, but it brought my heart rate down, slowed my jitterbug. Maybe this was meditating. It seemed like only successful people meditated; people who could afford to meditate, to take twenty to thirty minutes off from freaking the *FUCKOUT*! White people.

If I ever tasted success, this would be my meditation: a Sierra Nevada, a parking lot (any parking lot will do) and the repeated mantra: *Never Forget, You Piece of Shit. Never Forget, You Piece of Shit.*

I took another sip and turned the car over, feeling the furthest one can feel from *Piece of Shit*. It was working. It was all working. Sadness *was* my luxury. And this was one man's harmony.

Many colors and creeds practiced meditation, I reminded myself and shifted into first gear. With the opening chords, the syncopated strumming of Fruit Bat's "When You Love Somebody" propelling me home, I reminded myself: you know what I meant.

SHE CAME INTO my apartment as I was trying to cinch my wound, applying a butterfly in the bathroom mirror. It was proving harder than I had thought, and I had already wasted two.

"OhMyGod, what *happened*?"

She made her way through the small big room that was my apartment and I started to tell her the same story I had told Keri and Cuthbert—*shooting…Jake…behind the cage…brain*—because I was stun-gunned by her outfit, or, rather, her Her-ness. She wore a pale yellow vintage dress, cut just above the knees, its print containing a small blue bird. A Hermit Thrush. Over that she wore an army coat which I had seen before, and on her feet, a suede high-heeled ankle boot. Her hair was did. She liked silver, not gold.

"I like your dress." *That's it?!* I almost thunked myself in the head.

I leaned in the bathroom doorway to take her in and recalibrate.

"You...god*damn*, you are...devastatingly attractive."

That got her. Her eyes went wide for a moment. But she never stayed in one place too long.

"Thank you," she said, with a genuineness you get from someone to whom you just gave a very inconvenient ride to the airport. "I just got it a couple minutes ago," she referred to the dress and took a rolled-up pair of jeans from one pocket of her army coat, a t-shirt from the other, tossed them both on my bed and I watched her move, watching like a puppy on dope. "What?!" she said, justifying freely: "I wanted to wear a dress for you."

She moved into the bathroom with me and took over the reins on the butterflies. I redacted the account of my eye, told her that, actually, I had been decked by an old man, not a lacrosse ball, and that I had told her the initial story not because I was ashamed or afraid of him but that it was her dress and her legs and her hair and her face and neck, you see? I asked her how the rest of her day was and if she was all packed and if she was looking forward to going to Istanbul—Istanbul, correct? She wanted to hear more about the punch as she better cleaned the cut, began to dress it, cinched it with a butterfly, bacitracin dab, cinch with another, bacitracin dab, and so on. I told her it was fine, that McMillan was a fucker but whatever; I both didn't want to get him canned and wanted to see her sooner than tattling on him would have allowed. I told her I also felt fine about getting punched as penance for my mind's amoral impulse upon hearing DeMarcus' cherry-bomb ligament. I asked her what time her flight was tomorrow, if she took a car here: afternoon and, yes, she took an Über. She said that she had seen DeMarcus get hurt and that she had to scoot directly after the game because she had to get Teddy to a buddy's house and that she was sorry, so sorry, about his knee and the game and the punch and she finished the last butterfly, took my face in her hands, assessed her work, nodded, approved, kissed me on the wound she had mended. My blood on her lips.

She buried her head in the pocket above my collarbone, sighed.

"I'm sorry I'm married, Ryan."

A Corkscrew to the Heart.

"No-no," I protested. But who can say anything after that? I wanted to Temple of Doom my own self, hand her my heart with the bill, a receipt that says *Just Kidding—On the House xoxo*. I tried to articulate anyhow, because, you know, aforementioned Butterfly Effect; if some young Grecian boy wasn't raped on one very specific afternoon in, you know, Ancient Greece, her and I are not here, then. We are not There. Her marriage was our forcibly sodomized Grecian boy.

"Without that, there's no…and we wouldn'tve…so it can't… don't be sorry." I felt for the girl, the woman who would have said she's the last girl in the world anyone should feel sorry for. I felt for her. I felt for us. How redundant, how pedestrian, how selfish, how silly: Yes, it and we were all of those things. But. There's certainty in the exception.

"Don't be sorry," I re-upped. "It's all part of God's plan."

We laughed. In my little bathroom we looked into each other's sad, untimely eyes. We could have sat there till boarding time. But she had put on a dress.

"I'm not huge fan of eating but apparently getting punched in the face makes you really hungry." I figured she was a fan of lite eating-disorder humor. "You wanna get something to eat?"

"Yeah," she said, widening her eyes to keep the water away. "I'm sad enough to eat."

When I was a young boy
My Momma said to me:
"there's only one girl in this world for you —
and she probably lives in Tahiti..."
I go the whole wide world
I go the whole wide world
Just to find her...

Or maybe she's in the Bahamas
Where the Caribbean sea is blue
Weepin' in a tropical moonlit night
Because nobody's thought about you...

I took a left onto Venice Boulevard, turned Wreckless Eric up even louder. I wanted to blow a speaker on the chorus.

I go the whole wide world
I go the whole wide world
Just to find her...
I go the whole wide world
I go the whole wide world
To find out where they hide her...

On the passenger side, Camilla had her head in her hands,

shaking it in defiance, in denial of reality, stealing glances at me from between her fingers. I gave her a horse-bite. I gave her two. Were we special? Yes. Of course not. It didn't matter, nobody's equipped. This woman in my car, married to a blow-hard older Dude, a woman unaccustomed to feeling much of anything for, for safety's sake, six years? Reading and re-reading scripts, watching cut after cut after cut, knowing just the right notes to hit when giving notes, supporting and cultivating and protecting the ego of a touchy Hollywood blunderbuss. A good, bright, whip-smart Hollywood wife, a conversationalist supreme no matter who she's seated next to at a dinner party—Steve McQueen, Kathryn Bigelow, Damien Hirst. That's a job in and of itself—the parties! But. She gets numb. Comfortably. Shrugs-off having never really sank her teeth in but sinks them deep into the Kid, her Dad's namesake. Out there she fades, blessed, a Hollywood Wife on auto-pilot. Happy enough! Which is kinda sad, but still. It's fine. It's okay. It's *fine*. But. Then. This dithering East Coast Gentile-schlemiel comes teetering through the saloon doors and his features, his configuration—they charge her tides; he's got good shoulders and a funny way of navigating the world and this town, and something about him, something about him, something about him…he's scrappy and *pure*—that was the word she kept seeing. Not pure-pure, not in the clinical sense, not in its purest form, but a higher, lower, grittier purity; somewhere better than this place, and she sees, feels and hears that he smells exactly like what she's been waiting her whole life for; waiting for him to stomp through this trap door and flip the trip on its monotonous head.

Anyway. That's what I saw in her eyes between her fingers as she stole glances at me in the car. She had said or would say the thing about my being "pure," which I always half-took as an insult, an indictment of my Hollywood shortcomings. But she had been hamster-wheeling in this micro-town of suckle-cells, so any distinction from that lot was okay by me. It didn't matter anyhow when, now, her hand was on the back of my head, in my hair, reading the brail of my face, trying to decode our reality, this fantasy, and again and again with each swipe of her hand I was Pinocchio'd; I was a real boy.

I was a Man.

I go the whole wide world…

DEAR JOHN'S WAS a charming dump. It got bought a few years ago, refurbished, made-over to honor what it used to be, allegedly, in the Rat Pack days. I prefer the dump days.

In the (charming) dump days, the crowd was thin and strange, even on weekends. Prime Rib was the special every night. They served that "Italian Bread" that was just an alternately shaped Wonderbread with the colors of the Italian flag on the packaging. Their butter was cold and it ripped right through the bread and you had to either put it aside or chew on butter; either way, off to a bad start. Which was the best.

An older Chinese gentleman tended bar. His martinis weren't cold enough but he kicked ass nonetheless, kept the pretzels and peanuts replenished until you had to beg him to cut you off. When we walked in, he acted like he knew me and moved a pair of dudes down a few seats to make room for us. He kicked ass.

"Cocktails with Zimmy" nights were my favorite nights at Dear John's. Tuesdays and Saturdays from 5pm-8pm. Zimmy, a one man Casio keyboard act, had custom coasters printed with a picture of him dressed in a purple satin shirt and black vest, one elbow atop his Casio, "Cocktails with Zimmy" emblazoned across the bottom of the coaster. I couldn't name another coaster but it's my favorite coaster. Zimmy looked like a mustache-less Jeffrey Jones and used his loop effect wisely and once played "If I Only Had a Brain" → "If I Only Had a Heart" → "If I Only Had the Nerve." It was eleven or twelve minutes in total and they're the same song so I likened it to when I saw Leo Kottke play "Desolation Row" but Leo Kottke didn't have the lyrics in front of him and Zimmy did. I mention the two together for no other reason than seeing Leo Kottke play that song stuck with me (one of the greatest performances I've ever seen) as did Zimmy's decision to play all three Wizard songs (one of the most lawless decisions I've ever seen). For eleven and a half minutes, two performances that could not have been more different, yet both performances had me looking around wondering "is anybody else *hearing* this?!?" They made me feel special.

I gave Zimmy a point and a thumb's up when we sat down, praying he wouldn't play the full trifecta. If he did, it would make his long ago decision less important to me (*oh, this is just what he does*), thus undermining the arguably life-changing Leo Kottke performance of "Desolation Row," double-thus making me question what was happening here, with her. The consequences would be tragic. Fatal, even. I needed Zimmy's Brain, Heart & Courage to be special, for they were Me. I needed to be special.

Because not twenty-four hours ago I had stopped second-guessing my merits, stopped wondering if this was what adults did, stopped asking all the right questions: does everyone cheat? Was this a Los Angeles thing or a marriage thing? Were they doing this in Tucson? Limestone, Maine? I had never really hung out with adults before or even those who were married to adults. Not really, anyway. Was I special or just a peg in the Plinko board of a married person's mortal amoral roustabout?

The second-guessing recommenced and our fate rested in the chubby fingers of a lounge singer who looked like Madison, Wisconsin.

We ordered a dirty Stoli martini and a Heineken to split. We didn't speak much, just sipped and smiled into our shared drinks, both demure on our first night out since things had taken a turn for the berserk.

Okay, fine: Why, you ask, was she seemingly comfortable in public? I wouldn't say she was *comfortable*, per se, but: fair question. First, I can only speculate here, but it seems to me that you can reach a point in a marriage where you stop caring. "If I'm seen, I'm seen. If I'm caught, I'm caught: it's either a way out or a way to something, *something*; a defibrillator or a fist fight, either one sounds better than this." Second theory: Even though we had crossed lines of the most insidious offenses, lines subjectively much worse than a one-off roll in the hay at a high school reunion or a Moen conference in Cedar Rapids, we could still find warmth under the fire blanket of "we haven't *done* anything." Perhaps she was under the fire blanket. Third: We weren't going to places where people knew her. My apartment and a few dingy pockets of the West Side. Chez Jay was different because at that time we weren't aware we would be aroma-raping one another in the near future. Fourth: Fuck you, she loved me and nothing else mattered.

And then, as if on cue:

> *I could while away the hours,*
> *Conferrin' with the flowers,*
> *Consulting with the rain...*

I took a quick deep sip of the martini, trying not to wear myself like the (Pre-Brunson) New York Knicks fan that I was. There was hope. He could just play one of them. They could be good this year. Only *Brain*? Only *Brain* was fine! More than fine! Only *Brain* would make his decision to play all three on that long-ago Tuesday evening all the more special!

> *Oh, I could tell you why*
> *the ocean's near the shore...*

Crap! cursed my mind. These songs were short! Really short! My memory fucked me! These weren't four-minute ballads; they were lean. They were in a movie and they got to the *point*. That was their *job*. There was no anomaly here, it wasn't crazy to play all three. As a lounge singer like Zimmy you had to fill three hours—three hours!—how could you *not* play all three?!?

> *I would not be just a nuffin'*
> *My head all full of stuffin'*
> *My heart all full of pain...*

Well it was fucked and I would be exposed as the piddling day player that I was. Sure I liked *Serendipity* as much as the next guy, but Kate Beckinsale was incredibly annoying in the opening twenty minutes, so cosmically desperate, so disposable, and here I was acting just like her. I looked at myself in the mirror across the bar, my big, stupid head, punched because it's what it deserved. This beautifully bored woman next to me killing time till the next truck driver she could find. I wasn't special. I was a scarecrow.

Maybe she felt me giving up, because she sought out and found my hand somewhere below the bar. She locked our fingers and put her head on my shoulder and looked at me in the mirror across, between the bottles, and *zap,* **clack**, a make believe Polaroid snap, an electric shock. There were no truck drivers in queue. It was just me. And that's the only picture I have of the two of us.

> *...and perhaps I'd deserve you*
> *and be even worthy of you*
> *if I only had a brai--*

I shot up out of my seat in applause.

"Alright, ZIM! Alright, Pal! Love it. *Love it!*" I couldn't chance it. Zimmy was *not* going to be the one to dictate our fate. "You know 'Desolation Row'?" I yackled, scared and relieved. "Kiddin', kiddin'—play whatever you want."

He started playing "Up on the Roof" and I sat back down, Camilla slightly startled by my sudden outburst from our intimate mind's eye snap-shot in the mirror.

"Sorry-sorry—I had a lot riding on the next song," I tried.

"How so?"

"It's at once both really stupid and really, really stupid."

But she wanted to hear. I wanted to talk about her, she wanted to talk about me and we always ended up talking about Us, even though we'd only just breached the middle teens in hours logged together, a quarter or a third of those being in group settings.

We ordered more drinks and, both being aspiring part-time vegetarians who could take or leave eating as a practice, split a burger and fries, our agreed upon rationale being that it's just a garbage meat sandwich; it doesn't really count. You can't reinvent the wheel.

She found the Zimmy story funny but rational, given the logic of Us, the crossing of streams and sensibilities, cognition and the fantastical abyss.

I pressed her on her, but with grace and tact she batted most of it away. It wasn't the "so where do you see yourself in five years?" type questioning—she had already done it; she had a kid and what does any of it matter, anyway? She was the sneakiest ace I'd ever met and I was just curious about her brain. She was knowledgeable on all fronts, could kick it around and keep up in talks with every sector, be it creative, financial, religious, taxidermic (not a fan). Unintentionally, she made me feel dumb. Which wasn't hard, but still.

"Inch deep, mile wide," as I said she'd say when I wanted to know where it all went. "I dunno," she shrugged, taking a wry sip of Heineken. "I've just always been good at having a man take care of me." She split the difference between self-deprecating and boastful, became a matter of fact. She just was. And she was a wonder.

We finished the sandwich, the drinks, and I paid the check, a new old credit card dusted off, excited to get back to work and take money from me for at least a few years because interest rates always struck me as the boring fine print. She offered but

I would have rather taken money from the Klan. In a good way. Plus, it felt like things were going to work out.

LEAVING A PLACE together proved more exciting than entering it. There was a covert op, mission accomplishment in leaving—"we did it! Holy shit that was crazy!"—the night taking on a new hue, a dangerous and sexy appeal; a secret Los Angeles revealed, a candlestick beside a bookcase. Raymond Chandler cracking his knuckles from the underworld.

We drove around the corner to the Cinema Bar and I let Wreckless Eric play at a low volume, from featured to background. The song played itself back because no other song would even dare. I parked across the street, in front of a little strip mall that contained a Papa Johns and a Donut King. It was early on a Saturday night but nobody was around, nobody was out. I wanted to smoke a million cigarettes but I knew it would make me dizzy, putz-up my charm and perhaps stalemate the boner I might need, hadn't really thought about untiiiiiiii...

Oh, no. Nono. NO! FUCK!FUCK!FUCK!

The china on the walls of my brain started to rattle; that old gray cat had kept close to the wall. Security was breached. They were coming.

I cracked the first worry on top of the skull with my old mallet. It shook him (or her), this heckler, this *terrorist* in a Wes Welker jersey. It wore a sadistic smile and I couldn't kill it, I well knew, but maybe I could concuss the hecklers and buy time, think happy thoughts, there's no place like home. Another—this one with a backwards Red Sox hat and a goatee—started to crown, to peek, but he saw his buddy bleeding from the ears in the parking lot of a Donut King and went back from whence he came.

Few cars, if any, were on Sepulveda. But I reached my hand back nonetheless as she joined me in front of the Subaru and we set out to cross the boulevard. Everything was a new milestone; the cleats, the first email, egg-a-muffins, Chrissie McVie, mochi, the Who or Zepp, transition text → future accursed (un)encrypted app, no longer the Croat, the Über driver, trying to break up before we burned it all down, the first whiff in the Greatest Night, kissing the mended wound, driving in a car with Wreckless Eric, Zimmy, an imaginary portrait in the barroom mirror. And now; our hands as we crossed the street. There was a charge when we touched, when her hand hit mine, like a stick of dynamite dropped into a pond, a livewire hit the ground and all my vermin thoughts of penile misgivings that were slobbering up from Ballona Creek, popping up out of sewer drains and from the tailpipes of Civics; they got shocked into the night, levitated and sucked eastward, back toward Boston where they belonged.

The red, white and green fluorescents from Papa Johns spilled onto the pavement before us and I passed into them, her next, and she pulled back on my hand, pulled me back to her on the double yellow lines in the Papa John's light, was serious then smiled, tilted her head and said:

"Let's just see how it feels…"

I don't know how long we kissed in the middle of Sepulveda Boulevard. I opened my eyes to check on her and she me and we smiled in the kiss, kept kissing, the whites behind my eyes melting into my brain, my brain into hers, our mouths, the penultimate milestone in a traditionalist's sense. A Green cab flew buy, fluttering her dress and we stopped, smelled the new smell, and got out of the road.

Inside, a mal-practiced band played "Pale Blue Eyes." I got two PBRs, paid in cash and the cash register sprang open and with it a worry, a straggling heckler in mole form slurring "No-MAHH" as I cracked it on the head, bedding it back in with the dirty currency. They had procreated, as I knew they would. Litters in the night. The kiss had only made clear the reality of where this evening was headed, the electric shock only pissing them off as they now spawned like seahorses—the Dudes were giving birth. My groin prematurely drained of any blood, preparation of the defeatist.

Camilla smiled at me and I had to fight. I ushered her out to the back patio to see how close together we could stand.

Two dudes were outside, George Lucas' Theologians, and we found a dark corner beyond them and fell into a motionless dance of cheek-to-cheek respiring. In the back of the Cinema Bar, we listened to each other breathe, listened to each other listening to these two beautiful nerds, caricatures of crew, ACs no doubt, going deep into the ideology of Episodes I, II & III, but who's to say, really, we ourselves were in a Galaxy far, far away and we were lucky to hear them. They tethered us to earth and Los Angeles and we listened to one another's synched up, syncopated stifled laughs like we were in the back pews and her breath ran cool, her cheek hot and I kissed her nose. She took a sip of PBR and my knees wobbled and she kissed me harder than she had on the street and I knew we were leaving. I followed her out and I looked at the Theologians as I finished my beer, nodded, wanting to reassure them, let them know just how hard it was being cool; how being a nerd was a gift. But I left wordless, worried, mallet in hand, and they went back to their Clone Wars.

We drove home in silence. It was better than songs. She rested her head on my arm as I shifted gears. I took a left on Venice and the two lane straight shot gave me the autonomy to crane my head down and kiss her like the movies. I'd been passive up till now, not wanting to force something that wasn't really up to me. My second, third and fourth guessings had always preceded me, as had the roiling self-conscious milieu of my mind, but we'd crossed the threshold and now it was kiss and be kissed. I was in love. Was it bigger than that? Yes. But was it as simple as that? Yes. When we kissed in the Papa Johns light, my mind was devoid of everything but the unfiltered rapture of simply being. It happened in real time, in waltz time and there was nothing else and everything prologue was just a blended fade-out, a fuzzy, beautiful part of this slapdash fated chaos trip. Beyond that, in that light, there was no next. No future. No thoughts. No hecklers.

And here in the car, as I kissed her like *Drive*, each revolution of the tires carried us closer to my sexual demise. We threw our tongues at each other and I steered the car with my knee and swung the mallet blindly, desperately fending off the doubts, the vermin, the city of Boston; I was whacking the moles but they had gained traction. They came out of the vents, from under the seats; from the taquerias and the place where they filmed *The 40 Year-Old Virgin*. From inside and out. Three of them in jerseys of the original Big Three—Paul Pierce, Ray Allen & KG—pounded on the roof of the Subaru.

You have to fuck her, faggot!

WHACK!

I give it ten to one—

WHACK!

You're-a-druu-uunk, you're a druu-uunk!

WHACK!

She's wicked HAWT, you pussy!

WHACK!

It's gonna be like shovin' a rah oystah in a paaakin' metah.

WHACK!

Son…

I put down my mallet. This mole looked wise. He was an old black man in mole-form, come up in the most racist city in America. He was reading the paper from a rocking chair on the dashboard, his young brethren battered about, silent for the time being, retreating to their respective holes. He wore no jersey.

Son…

He looked up over his newspaper, oddly the St. Louis Post-Dispatch.

Son, I'm afraid you don't stand a chance.

He muttered something about Pumpsie Green but I bopped him off his rocker with a nudge from the broad side of the mallet. I squeezed her hand, happy for how happy she seemed, how happy she was. I looked out my window and I prayed. I fought the tears—I still had a chance, the Knicks are gonna be great this year—but hoped that if she saw me crying she'd think it was because I, too, was so happy. Because I was. I was so happy. But I'd never been more scared.

DEAD MAN WALKING.

Let me be clear, though: I was still having a mind-bendingly lovely time. She had all of my attention, she had all of *me*, and, yes, I will say it: I wanted to take care of her.

I was the fool sufferer. She was married to a man with successes and picture deals I could only dream of. She had family coffers that could dwarf my richest acquaintances' trusts and I went to a college populated by a LOT of prep school kids AND I lived in Los Angeles where nobody works!

But I wanted to take care of her. Like that and like *this*. It's the caveman bone, Man, and there, between the moles and me, my manhood was withering on the vine.

One whiff, though, and it was all again possible. The Knicks… this year.

She walked in front of me, led me to my place. I left the mallet in the car because violence wasn't going to win. I had to capitulate. Also, they were probably right. My blood flow was dammed, damned, damn. I could eat her buttcheeks, run a mouth-train on her vulva. There were workarounds.

This redirection of game-plans didn't silence the hecklers like I thought it would. They picked up on my last-ditch effort, the phony attempt at reverse psychology. Now they came in droves, like mop splinters from the Sorcerer's Apprentice, following us up my front steps, dipping Mint Skoal as they set up stadium seats outside the windows to my apartment.

I unlocked the door and grabbed her butt, torturing myself. Sam bounded past us, out from the apartment and down onto the sidewalk, a slight snarl in his mug as he paced, casing the block before he took a leak. It wasn't his style, but he was prone to surprising bits.

We got inside and I went to distract myself in the light of the fridge, tapping the top of the door like there was anything in there other than the two different types of beer and some carrots. I grabbed a Heineken and turned back to the room. Her dress was on the floor by the bed and she was under the covers, on her side, propped up by her elbow, smiling at me. I smiled back, sung "okay-alright, okay-alright" and handed her the Heineken with a kiss before I moved to the stereo, aimless, lost, my brain a fuzzy warbler.

Who could I hear? Could Frank Ocean sexy me into fruition? Sam Cooke? Who fucked? Who could I hear?

They're selling postcards of the hanging...

Casanova is just being punished for going to...Desolation row.

Casanova, hardly. But the song made me smile, and it had been a player in the night. I turned and leaned back against the shelving, took a sip and appreciated how lucky I was. And, yes-yes, very lucky, but god*damn*, was I pretty good. I was *nothing* to shake a stick at, game-wise. *You ol' rascal,* I thought to myself. *Good fucking job, Pal. Good fucking work.*

I kicked my boots off and yanked off my shirt. If I was gonna go down, I was gonna go down swingin'.

I climbed on top of her, pinned her down with the covers, trapping her underneath at the shoulders like a straight jacket and kissed her. I kissed her ear and smelled her hair, covered every inch of her face, neck and chin before I moved onto the clavicle, loosened up the straight jacket and moved to her breasts, which had rebounded from Teddy's use years prior but still had some wear which made me love them more. I flipped her over and kissed between her shoulder blades, because I wanted to see her back. I half-gently pushed my thumbs into her lumbar before she turned back over and we tussled like that for a few verses, infinity dolphins doing laps till we were tangled in the sheets. I collected her thick hair in my right hand and tightened my grip, a light tug from the back of her skull.

And then I kissed her. Not just kissed her, because as a kisser I'd always been historically reserved, perhaps even prude. I don't entertain sloppy kissing. But I kissed her like the dickens. A free-form, interpretive Chatsworth-style kissing where we tried to taste each other's tonsils. I cleaned the backs of her teeth, paused for a cheek-swab, speed-bagged her uvula then went for the guts, the dark stuff, and with that material we saturated one another's philtrums' to where we looked like runny-nosed kids coming home from sledding. We looked sick.

Her hands explored my topography, too, and I was thankful for my long-standing body image issues. I gave myself another pat on the back—*it's not easy, buddy! You did the work!*—my internal glad-handing foreign and welcome like an exotic food sample at a Bazaar.

Her breathing became short and gaspier and I hadn't received any encouraging messages from downstairs but I hadn't heard a white flag flapping, either; hadn't been issued an SOS, and, plus: we were having a gas.

She was a few inches shorter and we fit together like the Origin of Love.

She then breathed into me, fingers urgent on my back and I knew it was time but she said it anyway:

"Let's just see how it feels."

I looked at her and she glowed. She was what was in Marcellus Wallace's briefcase. But I was not, as it turned out, Marcellus Wallace. I soldiered on, though; I Sally'd forth. I kissed down to her navel, not to buy time but to cover her map, put a pin in every territory, her body my bucket list. I leapfrogged the honey pot, gave her hamstings a scrunch, her quads a bite. The backs of her knees, calves, full transition down to her toes—everything I had envisioned that day light-years ago in the parking lot, it all checked out.

Maybe...we just see how it feels.

Oh, to be a Woman!

She leaned up, grabbed me from both arms, and pulled me on top of her. This was a war that would not be won with my tongue.

I let my weight fall on top of her, propped myself up to have a look, readied a sheepish smile of apology and self-reproach for the man downstairs. I kissed her first, though: I wasn't ready to go.

They're spoon-feeding Casanova
to get him to feel more assured...

Her hands went to my dangerzone and I arched, twitched

my hips, Barry Sanders between the sheets. I looked at her again, took a deep breath, this time buying time. I looked down the vertical of our horizontal bodies, under the covers, in the glow, and I thumbed the band of her Gap undies, ran that thumb around and in front. The rest of my fingers followed, ever-so-slow (still buying, still buying), ever-so-gently, peeling her undie-band back like a late-level Cat's Cradle design and as my middle and index fingers hovered, pulsed millimeters before parts unknown, her eyes closed and I looked up at Sam, who had lain down at the base of the front door, his back jammed against the crack of the sill; something he often did, as that was where the draft flowed. But his body twitched and his front lip was curled, an annoyed yet fierce snarl and I realized: I hadn't heard a peep, hadn't seen hide nor hair since he bounded out the door and paced the sidewalk threateningly. My Best Friend had done the impossible. He made Boston shut the fuck up. And now he was fighting tooth and nail to protect me from their last ditch effort, their fourth and forever shot down the field to win it all.

Fingers still hovering, I kissed her again and heard the air go out of Sam. I could see in my periphery that he had gotten pushed back; he had lost the battle at the line. From the crack beneath the door, their last heckler squeezed. Fistful of dirt in his forepaw, he wore a Tom Brady jersey and stood on his hind legs, filled up his lungs to hurl the last heckling dagger-of-doubt, the final insult. But Sam lunged; My Dog the Giant, a Patriot Killer… and bit its head right the fuck off.

I looked back at Camilla as my fingers landed like a pair of butterflies on her golden bog. Her eyes twitched beneath her lids.

I felt my own eyes dilate, the hair on the back of my neck not just stand but multiply, thicken, coarse and black. My trap muscles hulked and my breathing suddenly sounded like I had smoked a carton of Winston's but didn't feel the least bit labored. I gently sunk my fingers, swirled come-hither, and my motherboard started to short wire. I felt a canine grow and sharpen in my gums.

Camilla opened her eyes, her own carnality actualized, and she went hard-charging for my Johnson, and I let her, for what will be will be. She got ahold, her eyes going wide, having realized what had formed before I—it was like the pain delay, the pleasure delay—but having no earthly clue what mountains we had climbed, what battles we had fought: the war we won to get there. I yanked down her undies and she mine and as my eyes followed down our bodies I saw what Sam had fought so hard for me to procure: The Greatest Boner Ever Told.

She took me in, primed, and she moaned a moan that made it seem like us having sex was the only thing anyone should ever do. I thrust further, not fully, and her eyes went lambent in her head. I wanted to high-five myself but both hands were occupied, and although the hard work—the impossible—was done, the rest was a race against the clock. I needed to breathe because if this GBET popped off on the inside, it didn't matter where she was on her cycle, these fellas were gonna find an egg and gang rape it.

I slowed my pace and we moved in time. I grabbed her thigh and she wrapped it around my flank. I rolled my hips, as pumping could prove disastrous, and we gyrated a mamba, a samba, a fuck-waltz. We could have stayed right there, forever in time; a clip, a GIF, a whiff of perfect sex. But, alas, we had to Wabi-Sabi.

She dug her nails into my back, bared a flash of her teeth, nodded to me like it was time to give them the high heat or a flea flicker—the Throwback Special. Like it was Go Time. *Sure, sure.* I took her signal. I heaved forward to see if that's indeed what she wanted—it was—and we could throw numbers around till the cows come home but they're home and it was thirteen seconds if it was an hour. *Desolation Row* was still playing, so that's a clue.

Hips back, slip, heave, ***pop!***

Well that's not right.

My teeth felt sweaty. I heard the sound of flat-lining. A beep. A beep. And then I heard Yoko Ono screaming.

A SLIP N' SPIKE is a laughable interlude during sex: *Oo-ooh—you okay?* she asks. *Yeah-yeah,* you say as you take a breath and slide back in.

But this. This was not that.

Camilla performed her line to a tee:

"Oo-ooh—you okay?"

I opened my mouth, I knew my line, but the words just wouldn't come out. My salivary glands responded first, the opening act for the wave of nausea, the shock that would headline. It happened quick and I knew IT had happened, but what *it* was, I did not know. I had not yet assessed the damage and I let my brain err on the side of "how bad could it be? We've slipped before; we've spiked before."

I blinked and the opening sequence in *Tree of Life* shown on the projection screen of my eyelids. Yoko was still screaming. It occurred then that that this was not, in fact, your Grandaddy's slip n' spike.

The way my vision tunneled as I watched Camilla, still in it, still in the throes, in the grips of what we had created, which was, indeed, supernatural; the way my hearing slowly went as she arched her back, beckoned me back, back in. But she was a silent movie.

Camilla propped herself on her elbows and she was smiling now and now not smiling but smiling concern, her distant voice that of Charlie Brown's teacher on the rotary phone under water.

I scooted to the foot of the bed, still not ready to look, and crouch-walked like Encino Man into the closet to source a pair of sweats.

Camilla was sitting up in bed and I returned, sweats on, and sat down next to her, my vision and hearing still disabled. I put my hand in her hair and kissed her and said what I think was: "I don't know. I'm sorry. I don't know."

I stood up and went to the bathroom to meet my Man.

TRUTH WAS, UPON first glance, I was relieved. Prior to having a visual, I had pictured compound fracture, assumed there was a bone sticking out, nonexistent dick-bones be damned. But, thank God, everything was contained. Just below the tip (of my circumcised Johnson, for accurate visuals) on the left (my left) side, it looked like Ali's jaw after the first Norton fight. It wasn't yet "OhMyGOD!" but…it *wasn't quite right*.

It went slowly—but quickly in dick-time—from not *quite right* to *reallywrong-reallywrong*. My faculties were still handicapped but I watched Ali's jaw slowly fill with fluid to where I couldn't call it Ali's jaw anymore. As it gave rise, it reminded me of something awful, something shameful from my past, something to which many would say: "well that's what you get." And those who say that are all chicks and they can go fuck themselves.

This doesn't need a flowery anecdote and I don't need to disclaim my actions with a gutless pre-internet pedestal, that late 80's/early 90's Oregon-Trail-Gen holier-than-thou bullshit: "we had to occupy *ourselves* and we only had MTV and TGIF and we had to masturbate with *FastOrange*—you know what *FastOrange* is, kid?" I'm not going to do it. So: I played baseball with a frog with Pat Shea in the summer of one of those years. Frog Baseball. It may have been a Beavis and Butthead episode, now that I think about it. I don't know who pitched and who swung but the frog got hit and when we went to field it, well, there was a bubble, a hematoma swelling from its neck-belly, and, well, sure: I got mine. Mike Judge broke my dick.

Camilla knocked on the bathroom door. I waisted my sweatpants.

She came in and I could see in her eyes that a two-thirds majority of her thought my drunk body had squandered our boner. And that was understandable! That's what I would have thought, too. That's certainly what I was *wishing* had happened.

"It's okay." She handed me a Heineken. The votes were in and it was clearly her seven-eighths majority who thought my boner got dunk and died. An eighth of her—I saw it in one of her eyes—thought that maybe something that we didn't know could happen, happened. Her pelvic bone had to have had registered that blunt stabbing. She had put on my Super Bowl Twenty-Five tee and had her undies back on, and her hand unconsciously grazed the jousted area as if trying to recount the incident. But she let the thought evaporate and I handed her back the beer.

"I don't think so," I sing-sang, spooky like a stuffed animal in a horror movie. I moved past her, to the fridge; I needed a Sierra, something earthier to keep me grounded.

I felt bad for her. I did. She finally got the nerve to adulter-ize—yes, yes: it's not a noble practice but at the very least the impudent act takes some gall—and all she got was the second to last verse of "Desolation Row."

I sat down, tried to focus on anything but the two words that kept repeating themselves over the intercom in my head. Five words, but the two that mattered:

(you don't have) **HEALTH INSURANCE**

She put her arm around me, her head on my shoulder and I could feel her go all in on thinking that my boner had waned. And I wanted her to believe that. I *needed* her to believe that. A deflation was ice cream compared to the darkness in the barrel of the gun I was looking down. A deflation—that's fixable. Hell, I could fix that tonight. But this. This could be the "sign" that what we were doing was kinda fucked up and we (I) got bit. She would get on a flight to Bucharest or wherever the fuck to see her husband blow shit up with one of the Ryans and I'd stay here, one in a million'd dick in hand, good night and good luck.

But maybe she was right? I mean, partially right? It could still be in the vicinity of no-big-deal. Hell, it's a *slip n' spike*! It's *trivial*! Little Jimmy capillary went to market, eating his curds and whey, he came tumbling down, pop goes the weasel, swells up for a minute or two just to keep you on your toes.

I hopped up and went to the bathroom, peeked gingerly, peeked with one eye…it was not better, it was not the same, it was worse. And worse, in dick-years, well, let me tell you: it's a lot worse than ankle-years. This was not little Jimmy Capillary by any stretch of the imagination. This was little Jimmy Pulmonary. This was Little Jimmy Superior fuckin' Vena Cava.

The romantic in me wanted her to think the boner died, that the wind-sock lost its gusts. The Man in me wanted to tell her that something bad had happened; that the Greatest Boner Ever Told was maybe just…*too Great?*

(you don't have) **HEALTH INSURANCE**

She was putting on her clothes. She wasn't harried, she was accepting. She wasn't like me; she didn't live in the extremes. It wasn't only everything and nothing. We were fine, as far as she was concerned. She had a flight to catch, a kid to pack, and she'd be gone for a while and we had had one of the finest nights in the history of Night, abbreviated, penetratively, but that can't be how you measure a time.

"It's fine!" she said off of my ashen spook.

I took a breath. All of it could seem like I had an ego bruised in the company of a love who was leaving the next day. I could try and play that part, looking like I was making a big deal out of *losing a boner*. But I hadn't lost it and this wasn't another stage for my fine acting. No. I hadn't lost a boner. I had bashed its brains in.

She sat back down on the bed and looked at me, possibly

entertaining the idea that something, something *else* had happened. I paced a little, put on a shirt, sipped my Sierra. I couldn't sit down. I could feel my dick getting bigger. In what I then now knew to be the bad way.

"I don't think, um…I don't think eeeeeeeeeehhhhhh…I'm not so sure…something is…" I sat down.

"What is wrong?" she half-laughed.

"I fucked something up."

"Like," she pointed toward the frog. I nodded. She did some replays, calculations. Maybe wanted a recount. "Can I see?"

"Oohh, no, I don't think that's a good idea."

She went back to thinking it was probably an emasculation deflation. She looked toward her phone, toward an app that could come pick her up.

"I'll give you a ride."

"No."

"Yes."

IT WAS PAST midnight, approaching one when I dropped her off a few houses down the street from her house.

"Whatever it is, I'm sure it'll be fine," was what she said when she saw my thoughts wander into the worst case. She was spinning variations on that theme "it's not as bad as you think," leaving interpretive wiggle room for the implication that I was still probably just bumming over a silly boner lost, a butterfingered pass that I took my eye off of because there was nothing between me and the end-zone. Part of me wanted to show her the freak show in my pants or at least scream that it, in fact, was bad and I, truly, was scared. I had *great* hands. But I didn't want to scare her off, either, throw up this meatball of a pitch to the opposition, the anti-adulterous. Plus I hadn't looked at it in a while. Maybe it had resumed its normal semblance. I was lousy with a grave and desperate hope.

"I'm gonna miss you," she offered.

"Yeah," I said with feeling, but I was limited. This good-bye deserved more. I pulled her in close. It was the first time I'd ever thought "I need a hug." I tried to squeeze into her the gravity of my mind. From where I sat, I was too fucked to cry.

She kissed me and was gone.

I looked in my pants and drove to the hospital.

FIFTEEN

UCLA SEEMED TO ME A GOOD ENOUGH HOSPITAL. JOHN WOODEN AND ALL. Lou Alcindor. I loved the O'Bannon brothers. Being an unblessed member of the uninsured, I could pick any hospital, really, in which to plunge myself into unconscionable debt. Maybe my unethical sums would find their way to the bottomless basketball program pockets of UCLA. If you don't have good dreams, you got nightmares.

On the walk from my car to the ER I looked to the layperson like a hapless Joe in an okay rom-com hyping himself up with potential opening lines on a first date, lines I would use on reception.

"Hey-O! Um. So here's the thing about me..." **or** *"Good morrow. I could be wrong, but I believe I'm experiencing, what they call, a 'watershed moment'."* **or** *"Hello. How is everyone? Good, good—You guys see 'Tree of Life'?"*

The automatic doors opened and everyone in the lobby of the emergency room looked at me. It was only four people—the two receptionists, both Latina, and two white women—but the sixteen female eyeballs felt oppressive.

"Ladies..." I nodded, like a dip-shit. In times of trauma or distress, I don't know how to behave. I get scared, I get cute, it's usually not funny, oft times annoying, always further distressing. When something serious rears its head, I go for laughs because I am juvenile and I don't know how to handle real things in a real world. And the most serious of things was happening and I walked into the UCLA emergency room like Jake Lamotta. The comedian, not the boxer.

I thumbed some pamphlets on the reception desk, the receptionist waiting to hear why I was there.

"So," I began. "How you guys doin'?"

It was two in the morning. They were as good as they could be.

"I have...a *prob*lem."

The woman behind the adjoining desk—Angela would be her name—squinted, looked at my eye.

"Looks okay to me," she said. "Whoever fly'd it did a fine job."

"Holy *shit*, I forgot about that," I guffawed, touching my eye, the memory of getting punched so many lifetimes ago. "Oh, my problem is MUCH more of a problem," I assured them. "Completely unrelated incidents, though," I added, needing their sympathies, not wanting this to look domestic. "I got punched by an angry football coach. But, again, least of my problems."

I was a mess. But this got their attention.

I took the stack of pamphlets, smacked the counter with it and put it back.

"See...I've been trying to figure out how to...okay, when a man and a woman..."

Now I had their full attention and I was talking at a volume that got the whole room involved. The two receptionists exchanged glances, pursed smirks.

"And they're having a great night—the greatest of nights—and the night, culminates, as it were," I was losing them. "I bashed my Johnson," I summated. "And I don't know what to do." It took a second to register, but the estrogenic care that filled the room after I laid bare my cards was overwhelming. Women love a vulnerable man, love to see a man scared, the patriarchy a cute and sorry force when you come busted dick in hand.

They gave me reassuring looks and papers to start filling out. Before I took a seat, I had to know:

"Does this happen? Does this happen?" I don't know why I started talking like Jimmy Two-Times.

"Yes," offered Mina, the equally lovely and pretty of the two. "Not a lot, but…"

"More than you'd think," Angela chimed in.

"I love you guys," I said. They rolled their eyes, but I meant it—they were exactly who I needed to fish me out of the mire. Just the reassurance that things like this happened, that I perhaps wasn't the frog-dicked pariah my worst-case brain had allowed me to maybe be.

As I walked back to my seat, I noticed a sizable "insurance" section on the form below me. I returned to Mina, tapping the pen on the clipboard, trying to convey with my best Keystone Bitter Beer face that we had reached an early impasse in my road to recovery.

"Yes," she asked, tending to other things, too, as she was still at work.

"Insurance-wise," I began and ended.

"Yup?" She waited but I gave her nothing more. "Do you have your insurance card?"

I nodded, mumbled "Blue Cross / Blue Shield?"

"Sorry?"

"I think we had Blue Cross / Blue Shield...back in the 90's."

"Who?"

"Geico?"

"Do you have insurance?"

"Yes," I laughed to her and the room, suggesting in my tone that she not be ridiculous. I didn't want her to know the real me yet.

"Medicare? Medicaid?"

"Yes."

She sat back in her chair and looked at me. I looked at Angela.

"I don't have insurance," I confessed. Angela gave a "yikes"-like look as she swiveled, fetching more papers. Mina pinched the bridge of her nose as I had done so many times in dealing with myself. "I didn't want to disappoint you guys!" I whined.

Mina drummed her fingers on the desk, thought fast. "You live here? In Los Angeles?"

"Yeah. Yes."

She clicked a few things.

"I'm just always supposed to have more money than I do," I admitted, pouring the sincerity of the un-proud into the confessional. "I'm always broke." I didn't expect this hard-working Latina woman to feel bad for me, but it looked like she almost did.

"Just fill out everything else."

"Thanks, Mina."

By the time the ultrasound technician arrived at my curtained-off plot, it was four in the morning. By four in the morning my dick was fully purpled, massive, terrifying. It looked more and more like the bad guy in *Little Monsters*.

One of the few great things about being in a hospital is that everyone who works there has seen worse than what you're coming in with. Or, if they haven't, they're trained to hide their surprise. It's one of the oaths. The ultrasound tech—a black dude named Ronnie—took my eggplanted member in stride.

"Ah, Man, it's all good," he reassured me when my jokes fell flat. "They'll take care of you, Man. That's what they go to all that school for."

Ronnie was right. That *was* why they went to all that school. The cool gel he applied with his ultrasound wand to my Johnson actually felt okay if you removed everyone from the situation, the situation from the situation. But the concentric rhythm calmed me. That is, until I realized how much real estate he was working with. I couldn't see below my gown, but my dick should have long ago run out of area—he was using his whole shoulder to cover the aggrieved terrain. This was the ebb and flow of every minute between my dick injury and me. I still clung to the hope that this thing would deflate, take care of itself. Maybe I just had to say the words: *Cut me, Mick,* and it would drain, naturally.

"Cut me, Mick," I whispered. Ronnie didn't hear me over the whirr of the machines. And my Johnson didn't magically drain.

A NURSE CAME by and asked me if I wanted something for the pain.

"Sure!" I replied, as if she were offering complimentary bread or a promotional tasting of a new spirit.

She popped it into my I.V. before I asked: "Wait, does this cost money?" The nurse shrugged, implying, I believe, that it depended on my insurance? The morphine had entered my bloodstream so I couldn't return it, and I did feel better. "Mina's gonna kill me," I told the nurse, who wasn't there anymore.

At some point in the sea of minutes after my costly dripping, a young Persian woman pulled back the curtains of my sad little area, looking at papers, the ultrasound results, seemingly peeved by my condition. In her defense, she had been on a long shift. Some white dude's dick problems were not her problem, even if they kinda were.

"I'm actually done in twenty minutes," she said, looking at her watch. This was what tipped me off to the source of her agitation. "But these look okay," she said, referring to the ultrasound results. "The urologist will be down shortly, but my guess is they'll discharge you after he checks in." She looked at me for the first time, a phony smile that made me feel like she was my teen-age daughter and I had made her come to the Hildebrandt's holiday party on a valuable Friday night.

She hurried off, billowing the curtain as she left.

Wait, I thought. *Wait-wait.* I stood up, pulled back the curtain.

"Ha!" I yelped, slapped the mobile bed I'd been sitting on. "Well, I'll be!"

I looked around for someone, anyone to share my good

news with. Nobody was interested, but that was fine with me. "Sonuva *bitch*," I hit the bed now with a happy fist. I bruised the bastard. No more no less. Deep, deep, deep bruise. But it would right itself. I had played lacrosse against some very sturdy rich boys and had gotten my bicep walloped and it swelled up like a balloon animal, a chubby groundhog. But it subsided within a few hours. And now, the Johnson. It was as resilient as the greater body around it, no more no lesser, another piece of the miracle mystery machine that is the Human Body. The biological universe of impossible alignment. The checks and balances, one system picking up the slack if one of their constituents sleeps late (e.g., endocrine for immune). And the things the body puts up with! Go to, well, anywhere, USA, and see all the fat people whose bodies just *deal*. Smoking and eating butter burgers by the by and *I'm* worried about the miraculous system figuring out an answer to a banged up pecker? C'mon. I appreciated my worst-case mentality, though. Set the expectations on the floor and things will be just fine. Hot-*damn*.

I sat back down, happy that I didn't have to call anyone. Happy I didn't have to tell Camilla. Happy and lonely. Happy that I didn't have to call my Mom.

A normal sadness fell on and around me and I wasn't grateful for it, but the normalcy was relieving. I relived the events of the night before. *What can you do?* I tried to get myself to laugh when the weight of regret made my chest soggy. I had fumbled the ball. I was B-Rabbit with my one shot, Mom's Spaghetti, and I pulled a hammy and had to take myself out of the game. That was the impression of me she was left with. And I had to live with that.

A meatier David Hyde Pierce looking M.D. approached my pen. He introduced himself as "Doctor Rob Frost" which looked about right. He pulled the curtain shut to give us privacy.

He looked at a chart, then at something on his phone.

"O.R. won't free up until..." he bopped his head back and forth in an approximating give-or-take fashion. "Early afternoon? Earliest."

I looked at him, wondering if he had the wrong patient.

"O.R. for what?" I asked.

"'For what?'" He asked like I had asked.

"What does O.R...how does that have to do with anything?"

This gave him pause, but he was no-nonsense.

"Has anyone come to speak with you?"

"Yeah, some angry, you know, pretty attractive"—I don't know why—"younger woman told me that I'd be fine? I'd be discharged?"

He nodded, a man of swift efficiency realizing he couldn't waste time letting the mistakes of others slow his game.

"May I?" He gestured to my nethers, moved to check them out before I had even given him clearance. He took one look and stood back up.

"You fractured your penis."

"Ouch. Ee."

He went on to explain that when we, as men, get erections, two chambers—and here he put his forearms together, parallel, elbows pinched in, to give a scaled visual of said chambers—fill up with blood. And if you hit it hard enough—and here he judo-chopped one of his wrists with the other hand and explained that, with the right boner density—my words, not his—one of those chambers can rupture and fill with blood and...well, exhibit A.

"Uh-huh."

He then explained the surgery they'd perform. On my penis. He said it was a good thing I was circumcised, this way, they would cut around my O.G. circumcision, pull down the dick skin, "de-sheath" the penis—his words, not mine—suture up the rupture, sheath that puppy back up and zip-zap, dick-fixed. If I opted out of the surgery, I'd be left with a hard dog-leg left. I didn't have the club to dog-leg. I agreed to let Dr. Frost straighten me out.

It's not something one understands immediately; the severity of the news came in like the tide. He left and I sat on the bed, dejected I guess, looking like I'd been left at the altar. *Why had that Persian doctor said that?* I wondered. *Because she wasn't Persian and had assumed I would silently assign her a false ethnicity and she was punishing me just in case?* No way. She was tired and she sucked. It wasn't like I had called to make a reservation at a highly coveted new restaurant and she said "there'll be plenty of tables. You'll be fine." And then I showed up definitely needing a reservation. Not cool, but manageable. We could wait for a spot at the bar or eat anywhere else. But this? There's only one restaurant here and that's My Life. This was My Life she was flippant with. My vitality, my brio. My livelihood. This was MY Johnson! It was so reckless and unprofessional that I had to respect it. What a bitch.

The morphine wore off and the fear came cascading in; it wasn't tidal, it was just dammed up with opium, you dumbass. They were to cut open my Johnson! An organ when tapped weird can bring one to their knees. They were going to cut it open with a knife to try and *fix* it. What if one of the surgeons said something funny as they were de-sheathing and Dr. Frost slipped the scalpel and trimmed a pair of very important nerves? What if there comes an earthquake and he cuts the bastard right off? What if they just plain fuck it up like humans do?

In my hand, my phone was calling: *Mom.*

"Happy birthday, Bud," she answered.

Happy birthday to me.

"I was going to call you this afternoon," she steamrolled. "What time is it there? I never know what time it is where you are. Have you even been to bed?"

That she encapsulated herself in those few lines was a little feat in itself. It was indeed my birthday, something I hadn't quite forgotten but chose to not remember. And her "Happy Birthday" was actually a nice reminder; unadulterated and sweet, pure Mom. Then, upon realizing that I had called *her*, she grew slightly offended, as if I were making a point to call before she did, undercutting her motherly prowess. Without skipping a beat or taking a breath she played deliberately obtuse in asking the West Coast time when she could simply subtract three from the hour she was living in. "I never know what time it is where you are" was so perfectly her, sharp notes of baseless reverse-classism, an underlying implication "well excuuuuuuuse ME, Mr. Hollywood!" as if, for all she knew, I was having a Sancerre and snook lunch on Lake Como with the Cloon-ster or tea-time with Helen Mirren in Kensington Square. That she thought I had money was flattering and offensive, entirely hilarious. "Have you even been to bed?"

was a last little sprinkle of lye on your favorite sweater. A seat pulled out from underneath you in social studies. She somehow emphasized every word. So much contradiction, so little empathy.

"Hi, Mom," I exhaled. When you're in the state I was in, it's hard to drum up the indignation otherwise so readily accessible when talking to one's mother. "Thank you," I began, regarding her birthday wishes. "It's all good—I wasn't calling about my birthday. It's seven a.m. I'm always three hours behind you unless I'm no hours behind you. But usually three. And, no," I closed, "I have not been to bed."

"Don't be smart."

"Funny you should say that," I foreboded. "So…I…I'm okay. I'm…o…kay." My ominous tone commanded all of her maternal fiber. "But I'm in the hospital."

I gave her a version of the story, a jolly-morose retelling of the night before, not giving her all of my fear and solitude, protecting her from my dire straits with an interference of laughs. Being a nurse, she prodded for some technical details about the surgery, anesthesia, if I'd have to stay the night. I mother-proofed my answers, rubber bumpers on their corners, gave her enough information to feel apprised and involved, told her I'd call her when I knew what time I was going under, and we got off the phone.

Even my Mom had to laugh. I had *finally* done it. It was all too perfect, too good: Something for virtually everyone in the world to laugh about, outside of myself.

Sometime during the call with my Mom, Camilla had written.

we okay?

There was a lot in those two words. Granted, things were augmented and warped through the viewfinder of a fractured penis. Everything was illuminated, everything was consequential. Were she and I okay? Were we cool, our cosmic alliance? Or was our collective physical body okay? Our Johnson. Or *we okay?* meaning "are we good here?" meaning "let's call it, if you walk away I'll walk away, nothing ravaged, nothing burned, nobody cuckolded, nobody spurned"?

It was too big a question. I held off on replying.

They transferred me upstairs to a room of my own where I would wait until they wheeled me to the de-sheathing block. I called my Brother, then my Dad—both laughed but I cried to my Brother. My friend Jeff brought by some clothes and the Times after he had initially come into the ER convinced I was putting him on.

"I got Starbucks! I took my time! I didn't think you were serious! I'm sorry!" He pled with me, his laughter sympathetic as I sobbed into his chest. I hadn't seen him in weeks or months—however long I'd been in the Camilla vortex—and it all somehow became very real when I saw the face of a friend. He moved my car into a garage, went to my place to let Sam out and grab my sundries. When you're in love, you forget about your friends.

Upstairs in my new room, I tried to do the crossword, tried to rest in the science of my situation, tried to remember that that was why they went to all that school.

I laid down and closed my eyes, not tired but knowing I

should be. The sun baked my face through the window, but it felt nice or I was too lazy to pull the shade, ho-hum or zen, I was very close to feeling nothing. I had felt all I could feel. I treaded in this plasma for a minute or an hour and when I opened my eyes, Camilla was curled up next to me in the hospital bed.

"I'm sorry," she said, kissing my face.

"Am I dead?" I wondered aloud, the sun bouncing alpenglow across her features.

She shook her head and buried her face into me. We were okay.

"I didn't know that could happen!"

"You and me both, sister."

"How did it happen?"

"You made my boner explode."

She giggled at the thought of such power.

"We need to make a PSA," she declared. "People need to know!"

There was a knock on the door and we sat up before I gave clearance to whoever it was. Dr. Frost poked his head in, introduced himself to Camilla and her to him and my throat started to constrict with affection, cotton candy pride dissolving in my esophagus. She was here, consequences of justified paranoia be damned. She took this fracture not as a moribund sign, but as a sign of resilience and vigor, something that would bind us; something to build upon. I was hers, she was mine.

"We've got an opening at noon, so somebody'll be up to wheel you down within the next half hour," he said. Camilla asked about recovery time. "Six to eight weeks before he can resume any sexual activity," the doctor replied, again, no-nonsense. It felt a little rigid, but I reminded myself that nonsense had no place in the field of urology. Or any of the fields, really.

Dr. Frost left and Camilla turned to me, her put upon guilelessness in full shimmer. "Do you think my witchy powers," she leaned in and whispered, although the door was shut, *"broke your Johnson?"*

I thought about it.

"No."

"But that's exactly how long I'll be gone!"

It was curious timing. But it was a curious time.

"Well. Either way," she said. "We're gonna take such good care of that Johnson, Wilson."

She blew my mind, every time.

"Should I look at it?" she asked, asking and wondering aloud if this were the next step, the next benchmark, the next block in our cornerstone.

"No," I said, nicely. It was not for seeing.

There was another knock and behind this knock was an older nurse—short and stout, smiling and Latina—at the helm of a wheelchair, my ride to the O.R.

Camilla gathered her things, edged toward the door, the old Angel Bird nurse in the doorway, hovering, beaming goodness.

I grabbed Camilla.

"I love you," I said.

"I love you," she said.

The Angel Bird beamed more of her goodness our way, unaware that we were maybe a little bad, maybe more than a little, but also unaware that what she was witness to that day was Easter Island, it was Giza. How bad could it be if it was Impossible?

Camilla set off down the hall toward the elevator, pressed the button as I sat down in the wheelchair. The doors opened. I didn't like that lasting image; me in a hospital gown being wheeled in a wheelchair by a seventy-year-old Guatemalan woman. I stood up and gingerly wobbled after the elevator, put my hand between the doors before they closed.

"Last night, before…" I gestured at our fracture.

"Yes…" she coaxed, to go on.

"Was it okay?"

She looked at me, smiled, eyes fluttering slightly toward the back of her head.

"*Fuck*," she exhaled as I let the doors close.

FROM THE OPERATING table I watched helplessly as the team readied themselves, disappearing behind masks, hands up as they were helped into gowns and gloves. More valium dripped in and I made the unremarkable jokes, the low-hanging bits at my own expense: "While you're in there, if you guys have a shim lyin' around, maybe you could bump me up a half inch? Fuck it—three quarters."

The anesthesiologist shot another something into my IV and told me to count down from ten or a hundred but I wasn't ready to go yet, I needed a word, please, with my Johnson and I desperately clung to consciousness to remember the good times and the bad, remember our life in shaky camcorder. I wanted my buddy to know that it was all love and there is no me without him—

Ten...nine...

....Summertime 80's, two or three years-old, chocolate, blood or barbeque sauce on my mouth, naked little animal, arms flexed in an effete strongman pose, little jimmy featured, happy and proud and pure were we—good lookin' tip—and who out there from an 80's childhood didn't receive a second, third, fourth searing briss from the footsie jammies, our collective protective first foray at four-years-old thinking "we must protect this *house*!"

...eight...seven...

...awareness, murmurs in the school yard, on the train tracks, kids' dicks are getting bigger, sooner than yours, later than yours, but you got an eye on those dicks! there's dicks everywhere, dicksdicksdicksdicksdicks, and Kyle Charbineaux can wrap his dick around his wrist twice or once, whatever, I wanna make a dickwatch! but you don't know yet that you don't really wanna make a dickwatch, there is such thing as too much dick, too much, and when your undercarriage fruits in its own form you forget about the watch because everything's changed, there is plutonium in them hills, and you begin an aggressive and some-may-argue non-consensual (who wants to be handled like that and so often?!?) relationship with your Johnson and there's Sheryl Crow and Claudia Schiffer, En Vogue, Jewel, Silk Stalkings, a Barbie Doll...

...six...five...

...then one day a girl touches it and consider it a game, changed, butbutbutbut, holy moly, as I live and breath, with their *mouths* while studio YEM plays on CD?!? and soon, GoodGodAlmighty, with their *south mouths*!?!?!! That's nature's way, Kid, nature's way of receiving you, makes perfect sense, you've been to science, but on the road and along the way you get brutal reminders of its fragility, last night, for example, the example ultimate...

...*four...three...*

...but once you get inside, it's a bag of Lay's out there! so begins the decades plus portion where you throw it around, on and in, over, under and through, whoever, wherever, left to the miscreants, used and neglected like Woody in *Toy Story II* and along the way, in the hands of the wrong handlers, familiarity, it breeds contempt or apathy, finger pointing when things go wrong, ownership when things go right, the dark times, the happy times, the times, but remember this because you always forget: this is your *Guy*. You are his body and mind, who he's attached to, vice versa to a degree and it's okay to love him. It's okay to tell him. Yes, it's funny to make fun of him, sure it's funny to say "maybe it'd be easier if I just cut the damn thing off!" but like weaning off the suicide jokes, it's time to stop making our old friend, our Johnson the butt of jokes, the dunce capped Eeyore that he ain't because it's a happy romp with plenty of women to vouch—more than plenty to veto, too, but that's your fault or their fault, not his—and the good times *FAR* outweigh the bad, the funny outweigh the bad, and the good outweigh the funny! It's an oft-fraught relationship but what relationships worth their salt aren't? And last night was a perfect example. Deck stacked against us, backs against the wall, white flag balled up in a hapless fist...But...Man, Dog and Johnson prevail.

"I love you, Pal," I said through the curtain at my waist.

...two...

"Wait," I lolled. "You guys didn't ask what I was doin' last night." I gave them a second. Dr. Frost entertained me while he put the final touches on readying the process.

"What were you doing last night?"

"Bangin' my Dream Girl, motherffffuuuuggggrrrrrsssss...."

BLACKNESS GAVE WAY to a few seconds of groggy and then it was back to life, back to reality. Dr. Frost came around and said success, that things looked good, leave the dressing on for a week, wash gently with warm water and soap, stitches will dissolve in time and we should schedule a follow-up in eight weeks.

"Oh. And the erections will be excruciating," Dr. Frost added. "For, perhaps, months," Dr. Frost added again. Until the interior stitches he used to darn the hole in my left chamber dissolved—that was my timeline of pain. He shook my hand and went on with his workday.

"Hey, Doc," I said, emotions bypassing the defuzzing drugs. "Thanks, Man," I croaked, fist clenched, double-bopping my heart in salute.

He nodded and walked off. That was his job, his nod told me. Nothing more, nothing less. Momma...there goes that Man.

BY TWO-THIRTY IN the afternoon I was walking around, requisite urination completed by three. I looked at the Angel-Bird and she knew I had to leave.

"You have ride?" she asked, miming a steering wheel.

"Yeah-yeah," I reassured her. "He's in the lobby."

"You pee?"

I had.

We hugged, she laughed—we had gotten close over the last few hours. I took the elevator down and started to sneak out of the hospital but it was clear nobody cared, so I just walked out into the day.

The sky was bluer than I'd ever seen it. I walked a block south on 15th toward Santa Monica Blvd. to see if I could look west and see the ocean. Everybody was going about their Sunday. The day drinkers, beach cruisers, young parents, older parents, young grandparents, hobos.

I could see the ocean and it looked different. I wasn't meddling in hyperbole, I had simply crossed over—everything would look different now. When the dick breaks, the eyes change, the perspective shifts, your receptors soften. It's like losing a father; something no one can understand until they lose theirs and are inducted into that somber, stoic fraternity. But this was a fraternity of one.

I had to get back to Sam but I had to eat something or I was going to die. As I stood on the sidewalk shoveling two taco-truck tacos into my mouth, a whoosh of aloneness ushered me down onto the edge of a flowerbed, fastened itself on my shoulders, a marine-layered yoke on the prettiest day of the year. I wasn't *lonely*, for she had robbed me of my loneliness, and I happily let her. My cup was a love-geyser, our Care Bear stare of mutually assured destruction shined like aurora borealis. She loved me like the dickens. Hell, I'd never felt so loved. But. I was alone. A new alone, however, one I wasn't versed in. I crammed a taco in my face, tried to remember how to chew. People walked by, rode by, drove by, but I was locked up in my new small cell, and I understood that I had entered the solitary confinement of the Other Man. The one everybody in the audience wants dead or at the very least deeply humiliated. My penis throbbed with humiliation—what's more humiliating than that? She was getting on a plane to be with her husband as I sat on Santa Monica Boulevard, taco grease dribbling down my chin, counting all the people in the audience who wouldn't feel sorry for, would probably be laughing at, me and my darned dick.

SIXTEEN

THE SUN WAS STILL HIGH IN THE SKY AS I MERGED ONTO THE 405-SOUTH from the 90. I had gone home but couldn't stay there, sulking and bumbling around ground zero. So I gave myself a weird and sorry sponge bath, fed Sam, packed a cooler and we got the heck out. I first took a minute or two to smell the sheets that smelled not of her or me, but of Us. I rolled around the sheets for a few verses and got creamed by the happiest sadness, so heavy, so hard, so I excused myself back to any world I was welcome to. The Sunday afternoon traffic wasn't great but manageable—I only screamed "FUCK!!!" once on the thirty-minute drive to the Westmont section of South Los Angeles. The Fracture had reasoned with my usual instincts.

"This isn't technically Westmont," I said to Walter Long as I got out of the Subaru, across the street from their cute little Spanish ranch on Ruthelen, a U-shaped street with back yards butting up against a recreational park—baseball fields, tennis courts, playground and the like. I had been sitting in my car nervously drinking a Heineken, waiting for a sign that I had made the right decision. I started to pull away, but Walter had walked out from the back yard with a bag of bottles to transfer into the large blue recycling bin.

"Whatta you doin' here?" Walter asked me, eyes narrowed, tendons in his jaw tightening, ignoring my "technically Westmont." Not the sign I was looking for.

"Oh, I was just..." I wasn't just. I was anything but just.

"Just *what*, nigga?"

WHAT? Whoa!

"Walter, I...shit, I..."

This was a new rock bottom. Who did I think I was, John Brown, for fuckssake? I was *white*—still am—and I hate white people but all my friends are white? And I'm just gonna cruise down, uninvited to Inglewood because why? A ditzy post-op Sunday gamble? I hated myself with a fervor and was now quite scared, the embarrassment and shame making me sweat, the sweat getting in my eyes, my eyes already ready to cry.

But. But wait. It didn't make any sense. This didn't make any goddamned sense. Not that anybody should be happy to see me, but Walter shouldn't be *angry* to see me. Right? He didn't think I was to blame for his son's knee—I saw it in our exchange after the game. Didn't I? It was what I thought it was, wasn't it? We were who I thought we were, were we not? Was I truly deluded and out of touch with our actual nation state? I was checking in on his son, one of my *guys*.

I stood and looked at him, confused, deflated, scared and sillied, unable to walk back to my car with my sad little Coleman cooler of healing racial beers. But *fuck* that. I had broken my dick. I glowered back at the angry Black man.

Walter pursed his lips, his face contorted in what I could only take to be a deep Black hatred I could obviously never know, but as I considered my escape, I realized he was laughing.

"Oh-oh-oh-OHHHHMaGOT-DAMN, Bruh! No-no, NOWAY! GOTT-damn, goddamn," he howled, doubled over, knee-slapping, holding himself up by the mail box, feigning hyperventilation. He staggered over to me and used me as his next crutch.

"'Just *what*, nigga?'," he impersonated himself. "'Walter, I... shit, Walter, I...well, Walter,'" he impersonated Dave Chappelle impersonating me.

"That was fucked up," I told him. "That was fucked up." It was fucked up.

"I'm sorry, Coach—I couldn't help that shit," he clapped and gripped my shoulder in apology.

"You didn't see it but I was about to flex."

"I saw, I saw, I saw. For sure. Flex." He choked on another laugh. "You hungry?"

"Sure."

"'Sure'? What the fuck is that, 'sure'?" he gave me a friendly shove toward the house and my swaddled member swayed wrong and I hitched my step, grimaced. "Shit, my bad—you okay? Hey, what happened to your eye, Coach? You're all hurt up—I didn't mean to fuck with you."

He stopped me, making his apology official, but I assured him it was fine; I was to be fucked with. It wasn't that.

"What is it?"

"It's a been a heavy twenty-four, Walter," I conceded. "Where's DeMarcus?"

"He's in the park back there, icing his knee. We got a bar-b-que going on."

"How bad is it?"

"Not good, Coach! Shit...I'm no orthopedist but it certainly stinks like an ACL. We gonna see tomorrow, I guess."

"Yeah. I did mine when I was his age. But that was during Medieval times. Now they crank out ACLs like..." I trailed off, couldn't come up with bagels or donuts or widgets. "Just make sure they don't give him Oxy," I said, and for some reason this broke me, reminded me of the severity, the hazards, and my part in the injury. "Just high octane ibu...profen," my voice up two octaves on the "profen".

"I'm sorry, Man," I tried to grumble, pinching my temples to reprimand the wimp in me.

"Shit—I can't just have white dudes cryin' in my driveway, Bro! Listen," he said. "My sophomore year in high school I broke my wrist at the start of basketball season. Not because I was going up for a rebound and got under cut and fuckin'...*No!*" He grabbed me by my shoulders and cuffed me on the back of the head to get my full attention. "I was on stilts. Stilts! Just high as shit and my boy's dad was a dry-waller and shit and I'm like 'yo, lemme try them stilts.' Stilts, bro."

"Yeah, that's pretty dumb," I said, laughing, tears transitioning.

"At least he was playin' a *sport*. And that's all it is, Man. That happens. That's sports." We were right, we agreed: that was sports.

A dude in a crisp white pocket tee, razor-shaved head, slim-straight black jeans and white Chucks came out from between the garage and the house.

"Shit. I turn my back and BAM! there's another white dude

cryin' in the driveway."

"Fuck you, already made that joke," Walter snapped. "Dude thinks he's a comedian," he said to me, sorrowfully, like the guy was a lost cause. Turns out Dude *was* a comedian, or at least aspiring—Walter's cousin Bobby, who had moved out a year ago from Chicago to try and make it.

"Why not just try and make it in Chicago?" I couldn't help myself. "This place sucks."

"Yes, Robert," Walter cocked his head, slapped my shoulder in thanks. "Why *not* just try and make it in Chicago?"

"I'm tryna get that pilot," he said, rubbing his hands together like it was his favorite meal he'd been waiting all week for. "And that place is cold as shit why you cryin' white boy?"

Everybody trying to be funny, a couple people trying to make it—it applied everywhere, and that was reassuring.

"I broke my dick imagine if I called you 'black boy,'" I batted it back to him in his slammed together running-on cadence.

"WaitWaitWait run that back," Bobby said. "'Black Boy' can wait."

A young family showed up; husband, wife, two daughters hovering around ten years old with their hair beaded like the young Williams' sisters, a look not likely to go out of style in this part of town, ever. Walter introduced me as "Coach," a nickname I was fine with. The wife was buxom and pretty—"hot" being a word I would use if I used that word freely—and she wore some sort of tan, flowing overall, a crisp Dodgers cap and had a covered casserole dish and said hello to me as she made her way, following her daughters, toward where everybody was, where these guys had come from. The patriarch—"Stacks" was what Walter introduced him as—hung back. Once his wife and daughters had disappeared, he threw his head back and let out a sigh that only a husband and dad with two daughters knows. He was just another guy in clothes. I popped open a beer and handed it to him. They were cold.

"ThankFuckin'God," he said.

"I should say hey to the kid," I figured.

"Whoa-whoa," Bobby called a timeout, his hands tapping his shoulders as I edged toward the gathering behind the house.

"Yeah—you can't go back there all Tears of a Clown and shit," Walter said. "You don't want him to see you like that."

I took some ice from the cooler and swiped it on my face, dried it with my shirt.

"I was cryin'," I admitted to Stacks.

"*Shit*," he said. "I cried today. Straight up. Just in the shower, like," he clutched something make-believe under his chin; a loofah, washcloth or a blankie: "*Whyyyeee!!!*"

I started crying again we laughed so hard.

"ShutTheFuckUp!" Bobby stamped. "You can't just 'I broke my dick' and walk away. You can't just leave that shit on my doorstep."

"'Broke-a-dick', what?" Stacks was behind.

All three turned to me, conceding the floor, the mic, the stage.

I went into the Coleman and grabbed beers for Bobby, Walter and myself.

"Well..." I began, and launched into it. I played with time, glossed over some characters, and the story really started when

DeMarcus tore up his knee.

"Nooo, *Maan*," Stacks lamented. When McMillan punched me, nobody could blame him but Walter was pissed. He took a closer look at my eye, cursed McMillan.

I didn't tell them whose wife it was, although Bobby wouldn't stop asking for the rest of the evening. I let on that it was my hero's wife, the reason I moved to this soulless cesspool in the first place. I moved the story through the events of the night before, boner terrors and all.

"Once it's in the brain…" Stacks mourned for me.

"Shit, before Shani, shit was *bad*," Walter remembered. "I needed some voodoo or some shit—but then she came around and I was like, *what?!*" He looked at his junk, surprised like his dog came back after being lost for a month. "Twenty-four years old and I said 'fuck it—I ain't goin back there' and got that bitch pregnant. Rock hard ever since." A flash of terror passed over his face after he said "bitch" but he smiled, toasting his wife, wherever she was.

Bobby marshaled me along, getting the story back on the rails. I picked up where all was lost. And upon vulval→finger contact, Werewolf in Venice…

They erupted in celebration, spilling their beers and shoving each other and me and then I was having *sex* and these three dudes were dancing in the driveway and I leaned into it before dropping them off the cliff.

"Slip, spike, POP." Yoko screams.

"No."

"Uh-uh."

"Nope...nope."

"Yup."

I motored through the next part, the shock and the white noise, *Tree of Life*, got to the hospital and let the rest tell itself. They watched with palmed faces, eyes peeking out, checking in to see if it was okay to look yet.

"I woke up, left the hospital, got my dog and came down here," I said as I walked over to the car to let Sam out.

"Shit! A wolf!"

I returned and Bobby was sizing me up, trying to fact check things that were out of his jurisdiction.

"They really cut it up?" he asked, warily, not necessarily not a believer, just not knowing if he wanted to be.

I looked around, made sure the coast was clear, unbuttoned my pants—

"Shit, naw."

"No-no."

"C'mon, Man—kids!"

—and gave them a quick flash. There was nothing gross or terribly untoward to see—it looked like any other ace'd appendage, a fully swaddled pre-premature pre-mee baby—but it was the coup de grâce, the dark affirmation to make it *reallyreal, reallyreal*...

Walter took off running down the street. Bobby jumped six feet high and rising.

Stacks just stood there, un-tucked his shirt, finished his beer. He dipped his head toward the cooler. I nodded and winked.

THERE WERE TWENTY or so people hanging around in the park behind the Long's house, drinking beer, wine, eating burgers and chicken, coleslaw—all standard fare—and I added my thinking that it was going to be a brisket and ribs and collards spread to the pile of discardable semi-racist thoughts I'd had and would have throughout the evening.

Walter was out of his mind. He was hilarious. He was boisterous and big, but also didn't hog the air; he was a selfless director, allocator, made sure everybody got theirs. He was a different guy down here, at home. It made sense now, his reserve up in Brentwood, his terse "mmhmm"'s and one word replies—"okay. okay."—in that sea of starched vanilla. Hell, Brentwood was so white *I* felt a little black up there.

Down here I was definitely not a little black. None black. With the exception of my one man, one act performance in the driveway, I was a meeker version of me, like I was walking into a new school in the seventh grade—old enough to have *some* swagger. But I kept it real close to the vest. I wasn't quite Walter-In-Brentwood different, but I hung back, took a plate of food when it was offered up, pleases and thank-yous. I checked the I.D. of everything that sought to come out of my mouth, let most pass, turned a couple away. I mostly talked to the women because I love women and black women more and black women seemed to love me and I flicked that thought into the discard pile, let it pass through my easy mind—my Johnson had started to throb and I had taken two of the Vicodins I had been prescribed—and watched as Bobby kept telling people what had happened, Stacks threatening to knock him out each time. It occurred to me that maybe black women didn't love me per se (they did), but it was the broken dick effect as seen in the E.R. reception area: Women love a Man down. Plus their men had grown tiresome.

DeMarcus was sitting on a camp chair playing a hand-held PlayStation of sorts, his leg resting on a cooler in front of him, an ice pack aced around his knee. Who I gathered to be his younger sister hovered over his shoulder, a spectator to his game play.

"Fuck outta here," he said to her, swatting, as I approached.

"Whoa, Dude!" He looked up, confused like...well, like when you see your coach or a teacher out in the world. "Apologize—is this your sister?"

"Sorry, coach—yeah, that's my...that's Brie—Brianna—Brie, coach, coach, Brie."

"Is he nice to you?"

"Yeah, he's nice," she reassured me, seeing I needed to be reassured.

"Okay, cool," I said, giving him a threatening side eye. "How old are you?"

"Ten."

"Oh, ten's the best. All downhill from here. Although, isn't downhill easier?"

She agreed that it was.

"All uphill from here." She laughed and I motioned for her to give me the junior sized football she was holding. She needed something to do, so we threw the ball around while I talked to DeMarcus.

"How is it?"

"Feels fine. Pops is going a little overboard on the icing. I can kinda run."

"Yeah, no. He's right. Knees are weird like that."

"Like what?"

"They feel fine, but…" I pulled up my pant leg. "I had two ACL surgeries on this knee."

"But you said yesterday 'knees are weird'—"

"Yeah I just said that."

"But yesterday you said 'It could be nothin'.'"

Why only the dumb shit I say does everyone hear, I again wondered.

"Yes…no, listen." I had his sister go long and threw it even further. "It's probably not good." He shifted, not liking that half empty option. "Assume that it's bad. Assume surgery."

He hadn't even considered that.

"But," I leveled with him. "But. And I'm not saying that it's my *fault* but I am saying that I AM part Irish Catholic so I'm going to feel guilt either way. But I got you to play and you got hurt. So I will make sure that you come back bigger, faster, stronger, smarter, funnier, better dressed, much, much, MUCH better looking and just more fun in general to be around."

I slapped the Playstation out of his hand, offered my own and he took it.

"I'm sorry, Pal."

"It's okay, Coach."

His sister and Sam had found each other in the outfield.

"But, like you said—maybe it's nothin'."

"Dude…"

"Coach—I'm kiddin'."

I picked up his Playstation for him and went to get another beer and talk to his Mom.

The sun had gone down and people had gone home but Walter and I kept having another beer on their back porch. I ate another pair of Vicodin and offered Walter one or two and he said:

"Fuck it, I'll have one," and popped it so fast I didn't even know if it had happened.

"What was that?" Shani, his wife, said from somewhere, from Omnipresence.

"What? Altoid," Walter said into the air before mouthing to me *what the fuck?*

"You guys can crash here if you shouldn't drive," he offered.

"No—I mean, I'm terribly alone and I want to." I did. "But that's probably against code or conduct. Not a good look." Also, I had talked to his wife too much throughout the evening, and, although he was totally fine with it—probably took it as a compliment—he knew I had a recent history with wives. Wife.

"When's the next game?" He asked.

"*Shit.* I forgot about that."

"What?"

"I forgot that was still a thing." He didn't understand how my forgetting it was a thing could be a thing. "Tuesday? Wednesday. Shit—it's a playoff game."

"Well, alright."

"We're fucked, though."

He was unimpressed with that outlook.

"Motherfucker, you guys beat Harvard-Westlake!"

"We lost, but—"

"You won."

"Fine."

"Bro, he just started playing this year! You got all them other boys who are full fuckin' steam ahead right now and you're gonna throw it in because of a broken ass dick and a tore-up ACL?"

"I mean...still could be nothin'. Knees are weird."

"Man," he shook his head, pissed now. "Why you even coachin' if you gonna be a bitch?"

"Mouth," said its Omnipotence.

"Yup, sorry," he said, and leaned into me, whispered: "Don't be a *bitch*. Those kids'll run through a...fuckin'...tunnel of shit-fire for you, *Man*. Because YOU made them think it was possible!"

He sipped his Heineken, shook his head.

"You made them believe, Man," he nodded. "So don't be a bitch."

"Mouth."

"No, he's right," I said to the Omniscience. "I mean, he shouldn't use that word, but..." I clinked my beer to Walter's. "He's right."

HE WAS RIGHT! DeMarcus was, as seen in the pudding, invaluable. But. We had a team. A damn fine team. And the measure of a good *team* is that when somebody goes down, the *team* steps up. DeMarcus played a crucial role in helping us get to where we were. Now we just had to figure out how to get to where we all wanted to go, which was a much shorter distance than how far we'd come. We all remember Jeff Hostetler but we forget that Phil Simms marched the 1990 New York Football Giants out to a 10-0 record, 11-2 when he went down for the season with a broken foot. AND he had the highest Quarterback rating in the NFC! They lost their best (offensive) player, the best quarterback in the league (at the time, on paper) and still they went on to win the Super Bowl. Because the defense stayed the course (one of the better D's of all time) and Jeff Hostetler played good enough.

At dawn, I laid in bed thinking about Camilla and Lawrence Taylor and Leonard Marshall when the words of Dr. Robert Frost came searing through my nervous system. So horrific was the pain, so nauseatingly acidic that the shriek of Daniel Stern scattering birds for country miles could only scratch the surface. I opened my mouth to scream but out flew John Coffey's fruit flies of injury and evil. I clutched and writhed in bed like a comic book villain in withdrawal. I'd never said "Mommy" before—I danced right out the womb sayin' "Hey, Ma." "Mommy" bums me out. I think it's bad parenting. That morning, though—and I will say this, too: my morning boners had been evading me for months. I thought I had prematurely aged to forty-eight years old. But that morning, in my swaddling, a boner came with such fervor, with so much to say, I was convinced all the stitches had ruptured and it was just a pulsing ram-rod of venison, spotted in pieces of dressing and skin like the tattered garb on the little Incredible Hulk. I clutched the bedspread, curled up on my side and rasped for dear life the word that made me want to swat children: *"Mommy..."*

SEVENTEEN

Practice would prove tricky as running for me was dangerous. In my apartment, I tried various methods of securing the injured appendage, but running is running and jostling is inevitable. Telling the kids would be doubly tricky and equally dangerous. There were conditioning workarounds.

We took to the hill and did lunges up, lunges down, backward lunges up backwards down, slow side shuffle up, etc., etc., etc., until we were all walking like Team America. It was terrible. A little jostling seemed preferable, which made me think I should have broken my dick a week earlier. God's plan, though.

We did light stick work to close practice; helmets and gloves on wobbly legs. I was even going to wrap early but Cuthbert jogged over from his pointless practice (their team mathematically out of the play-offs) to fuck with my meaningful one.

"Fellas, circle up, take a knee!" He meant huddle up.

"What the fuck," I heard but pretended not to hear Just mutter.

"Everybody in front of me, in front of me," Cuthbert barked, waving them in front of him like he was doing a Tracy Anderson arm workout.

"Well, you told them to cir…" I trailed off—wasn't worth it.

"Adversity, gentleman," he began and I ended, turning off my receiver.

I moseyed around, picking up balls and cones, cleaning up the practice. DeMarcus, my new assistant, sidled up next to me, doing the same.

"You good, Coach?" he asked, delicately. He was the only one who really knew, although he wasn't asking after that.

"Me? Yeah, Man," I reassured him. But I wanted his take—he was on my staff. "Why?"

"I mean..." He looked over at Cuthbert and back at me like he wanted my take on his sandwich that had Miracle Whip, not Hellman's on it. "It's pretty weird."

"Yeah," I shrugged. "You ever heard of Ram Dass?"

"No."

"I'll get you some literature."

"DeMarcus! Yo, DeMarcus!" Cuthbert was calling him over to incorporate the tangible adversity.

DeMarcus looked at me and I shrugged. He took two jogging strides toward the huddle and stopped, wincing at his knee, put his hands up to Cuthbert in apology, resumed shagging balls with me.

"That was *fucked up!*" I ventriloquisted. "Don't swear, though," I added, through a normal mouth.

Cuthbert tried to install a man-up offense in the final few minutes but the absence of respect for him made it tough. I told everyone to go home

As I got Sam into the Subaru, Cuthbert jogged us down.

"Yo," he began, curt and businesslike, undercut by his newly dyed-pink Zippy-Hawk. "Do you have a problem with my coming to practice?"

"Oh," I pretended to ponder. "Well, I think that's a question you should have asked me before…coming to my practice."

"You need the help."

"I don't. But if I did," I looked at him now, calm, centered. "That's something you could have asked me, in question form, before practice. 'Hey—you need a hand?'"

"And what would you have said?"

"We'll never know."

I closed the back hatch and made my way to the driver's side, Cuthbert with one foot sort of in my way, one foot scared.

"I want you to work on that man-up tomorrow and I'll be over at the end of—"

I shut the door, started the car and drove home.

CAMILLA WAS NOW nine hours ahead, so our communication lines were hamstrung and abbreviated, which was nice because without that time difference it would have been nine to five (8am to Midnight) of incessant, relentless message firing both scandalous and trivial, stupid and delicious, everything in between. "Listen to this song" or "I walked on a street" to "I identify with Buffalo Bill, as I want to skin you and wear you, maybe re-swaddle my Johnson in your hide." That sort of thing. I wanna bite your teeth out, one-by-one. She said she wanted to fuck me; her with a, you know, a Johnson of her own and myself with, you know, a vagina? She wanted to fuck me in a genital swap, a fantasy I didn't quite know what to do with. I told her to listen to a different song.

It was bananas, if bananas were a dangerous and addictive food that you would burn villages and cities just to taste, one more taste. Just One Thing. It went on like this for months, daily, hourly, till she returned. It was so far out and fucked and I never resented her while she was over there, never woe'd my position, my villainous role. I mean of course I did but I also reminded myself: the real villains are never *this* broke.

But I was walking on sunshine, very positive, all things considered, and I brought that into practice, which made the fellas slightly skeptical, Sunny Me.

"Can't you just tell him not to come?" Crothers asked after I broke the terrible news that Cuthbert would be sucking around practice. It wasn't even not broken—they all saw, understood and articulated this in their stunted ways—so why try and fix something that's thriving? Why throw some line cook from the Ground Round in this Michelin star kitchen? I appreciated their concern.

"I could," I agreed with Crothers. "But. See: he's like a really stupid child." I had grown positive but I didn't magically become not myself. "If I tell him 'no', he'll come back with 'but why, but why, but why,' and I don't want to have to tell him: 'because everybody thinks you're a jack-ass!'" It wasn't the grown-up way to get boys to capitulate, but it was a way.

I tried to end practice a little early to box Cuthbert out, but he slithered his little weird-bellied self into our midst as we were cleaning up.

"Yo, we got fifteen minutes left!" He clapped as he got to the field. The fellas looked around like they were having a sleepover and Cuthbert showed up.

He called the offensive guys in and began to set up a new set offense that involved an inverted pick with a skip pass, tap your head and rub your belly. I stopped him and pulled him aside, almost nicely.

"My Man. We have a semi-final game *tomorrow*. Not the time for a new offense. Do your man-up." I was fine with him running the man-up. My man-up sucked.

"I will, I will—this is just for fun."

For "fun" he tried to walk them through an overly complicated play and named it "Cutty," after, um, yes: himself.

I told everyone to go home—I didn't want to force the kids through a stilted huddle and cheer with him. It would have zapped our juice.

As I walked off the field, I put a fist in the air.

"Through the darkness!"

And from wherever they were I heard every one of their voices:

"To the light!"

I WAS CALLED into Keri's office after we beat Newbury Park 10-4. Yes: it was only a four team play-off. But also yes: we were now in the Championship game. The parents were out-of-their-minds ecstatic, every parent of every kid attended the game—some of the parents I had never seen—and Alex tried to hoist me up on his shoulders but he tweaked his back and it was just as well, my Johnson didn't need hoisting. We agreed to meet at the Lost &

Found in a few hours, when the dust settled. We got confirmation that Harvard-Westlake had won their game shortly after ours.

The win was smooth, not without its hiccups, the score didn't accurately reflect the game (we beat them worse than it showed), if we're going to have a shot against Harvard-Westlake, we gotta tighten up, yadayadayada.

I coached with very little of my manic fanfare. Coached like this was a game we were expected to win but would still have to work hard in order to do so. I congratulated the other coaches on a fine season. Just dumped a Gatorade on my head. I was pumped. The fellas were over the moon. DeMarcus was proud and understood and believed it when I told him that this was not possible without him.

The 'Ship.

But.

But.

There was just a slight Cuthbert sized staff infection on the hull. It wasn't gangrene, yet, but it was shaving off knots.

It started during warm-ups. Since the second Harvard-Westlake game, we had taken to warming up in groove-collective form. Free and easy, stretch on your own, some leg swings while you shoot the breeze before it's time to throw down. Cuthbert wanted the militaristic phony order of the little dicks, tight lines and the barking ten counts, and instead of setting him straight, I just said "whatever you want, Man." Picking my battles or whatever.

When the ref blew the whistle and we huddled up, Cuthbert came over like he was a speed freak at a Black Flag show, shoving and slam-dancing and smacking kids on their helmets and I should have calmly said something there but I laughed it off and told the starters to take the field.

I should have said something in the first quarter when he was screaming like a banshee for kids to do simple, fundamental things that they were already well in control of, sometimes in the middle of doing. Muscle memory stuff. I should have said something then.

I did say something, however, when he called out "Cutty!" on one of our offensive possessions.

"Colby," I said, Baba Ram Dass. "You said you weren't—"

"It's *simple*. They're not *stupid*. They need to *execute*. If we're gonna beat Harvard-Westlake—"

There was so much wrong with every part of what he said. For one, it was still the first quarter and the game was tied. Mostly it was the "we" that got my belly roiling. But, I didn't want to cause a scene, so I communicated with the fellas through unspoken looks the language we'd developed over the course of a very hard fought, hard earned, and at so many times, emotional season.

At halftime it was still tied, now at 3-3.

I wasn't a great coach. If we were going to win the game it would be thanks to Walter Long for telling me to stop being a bitch. But Cuthbert was behaving like Bobby Knight and Buddy Ryan's retarded fetal alcohol syndrome ass-baby. And that's being nice because Bobby Knight's Bobby Knight—he's had a point.

I tried to pull Cuthbert aside, a coaches pow-wow while the team talked amongst themselves in the corner, in the shade, giving them some autonomy to try and figure out what was wrong (it was clearly Cuthbert, but they deserved some privacy to air that grievance). He stormed over to the fellas like a pit-bull in a brioche bun costume and started laying into them, delivering high octane platitudes about effort and heart, kicking at the turf like a Single A baseball manager who just got "you're outta here"'d. I looked at Alex and he gave me a "the *fuck*?" look and the other parents' eyes bore into me imploringly, like orphans.

"Whatta you gonna do?" DeMarcus asked me was we watched Cuthbert bluster.

"Well," I clapped him on the shoulder. "I should probably do something or we're fucked, huh?" I started across the field, added, "Don't swear."

"Colby," I called but he didn't hear. "COLBY," I said again. He registered and gave me a "yeah-yeah, just a minute" hand.

"NOW!" I sounded like my dad. It spooked me. The idle conversation in the stands went silent.

I fluttered my hand, instructing the boys to figure it out themselves and Cuthbert followed me behind the goal, out of earshot. I didn't know what I was going to say, but it had to land, it had to penetrate: there could be no wiggle room for his slippery return to our sideline. I had to fuck him up.

"What's up?" he said as I smiled, waved to the parents like a politician.

"You are the least funny person I have ever met and it makes me sad. I get sad. I don't think anyone is going to but if some desperately meek girl with a ticking biological clock does marry you because her dad was so grease-trap terrible, I want you to tell her, for me, that I am so…so, sorry…that I didn't kill you today. I'm not going to. I can't go to prison. But I cannot think of one redeemable thing about you, not one, and I think it's a tragic mistake and, quite frankly, rude to mankind that you're alive."

He was confused but he fully understood that I was not being collaborative. He started to speak but I put my hand amicably on his shoulder, for show.

"Now you're gonna walk. And you can talk to these kids after we win the Championship Game."

I squeezed his shoulder quite hard and he started toward our sideline but thought better of it, or worse, and walked in the other direction, past the team and down toward the school. He threw a couple shadow-box punches which were both completely crazy and oddly redeeming.

I didn't say anything to the fellas. Just and Jake gave a half-time speech and cheered them onto the field when the ref blew the whistle. I didn't even run the box for the game—DeMarcus handled substitutions. I made sure they had water. I gave them the gift of a Cuthbert-less second half. And in those two quarters they trampled a pretty good team 7-1.

We were throwing the ball around and taking shots after the game, relishing in the win and hyping for Saturday's 'Ship game when Keri lumbered out quick-like, a little ogre on No-Doz, and told me they needed to see me in her office. I took "they" to mean herself and Cuthbert, which was a drag because I had held out hope that I would never have to see him again, that the universe would agree with me and he'd combust into smog after our little half-time chat.

I gave a courtesy knock on the door jamb, leaned my head in and there he was, in a chair in front of her desk, not really in the mind-space to offer me eye contact. I went to sit in the chair next to him and before my butt hit the seat, Keri said: "Today was your last day at Brentwood."

I bounced off the chair to stay standing.

"Is that right."

"That's right," Keri said. Cuthbert was smirking to himself.

"Okay," I said. "And the parents are cool with this?"

"I don't need the permission of player parents."

"Oh, you most certainly do," I corrected her. "It's a really expensive private school—you work for them, Sweetheart."

She pushed a small magnet or a lighter across the desk.

"And you don't," she said, releasing her hand off the item, and it wasn't a magnet or a lighter or a desktop work-time fiddle-dee-doo.

It was a thumb drive.

"Fuck me."

Cuthbert snickered and I got the hell out of there. I heard him quote her back to her: "and YOU don't" followed by a "boom!" which I assumed was him giving her a celebratory pound and then exploding it.

I hustled out to the car and Burt stopped me, his eye-black smeared, gloves still on, stick in hand.

"Hey, Coach," he said.

"Hey, buddy," I said, trying to breathe.

"Thanks."

"For what?" I was on a tilt-a-whirl.

He shrugged. "Bein' Coach."

The tear ducts in my stomach lurched. I started for my car, stopped.

"Hey, Dude, you know that thumb drive I gave you guys a while back?"

"Yeah?"

"That was really dumb," I said. "I'm sorry, Burt."

"Oh, Coach," he said, laughing a nervous little laugh at my sincerity and contrition, smiling, blushing, waving off my apology. "You know we can get all that stuff online anyway."

"I see that now."

"See you tomorrow, Coach."

I GOT TO the Lost & Found thinking it would be the only place to rack my brain for a way out of this mess. But it was the one time—other than when I slept with my buddy's girlfriend in high school—that I didn't have even a pathetic excuse. I messed up. It was selfish and stupid and there was nothing I could do to make it okay.

I ordered a Jack Daniels and a Bud, medicine for the dumb.

"You did *what?!?*" Alex exploded when I told him. "Wait, I don't understand."

I told him again.

"What the fuck is *wrong* with you?!?"

It was loud in there but still, everyone turned.

"I dunno."

"You gave them *porn?* Whatta you mean a 'thumb drive'?"

"No, not porn." This was difficult. "What I saw them watching, like, on a kid's phone in the back of the bus was so gnarly...like, this chick was getting, like, a loose sleeping back crammed into her ass, like she was the stuff-sack." I took a sip, tried to shudder for effect. Nobody would be on my side. "It was fucked up. And I was like 'remember the old days? Victoria's Secrets and...'" He was pissed. "So I...compiled some...En Vogue videos and..."

"Can't they just get that on YouTube?"

I nodded, sipped my beer.

He took a second to compile his thoughts. I could tell they weren't going to make me feel better.

"I like you, Dude. I do." But. "But. You're just your own worst enemy, Man. How shortsighted, how *selfish* do you have to be—and listen: I understand. Hell, NOBODY understands like I do. This thing is *hard*, Man, it's so...fucking hard." He was starting to get emotional. I didn't know if he was talking about this town and this entertainment racket or this life or, specifically, being us. He took a sip of his beer to compose. "And we gotta find a smile where we can get it. We *gotta* find a smile. And you thought 'I'm gonna give these guys a BETA copy of *Debbie Does Dallas* 'cause that's what I used to rub out to.'" I wasn't going to correct him. "And that's funny and that's kitschy and tickles your I'm untraditionally-cool bone. But that's all for you. And it's all about you. If you were *really* shook by what these kids were watching, you would have said something to the parents, said 'hey, listen—I think you should look into some restrictive-whateverthefuck-ware for little Billy's phone-porn problem', or, fuck!, say something to me, your friend who happens to be a parent and then *I* can talk to…" He sipped, laughed sadly at my sophomoric tendencies.

"But no. You wanted to do you. You wanted to get cute. Do something that looks good on the page or CRAZY when you tell it to the bartender at the Other Room. 'You're so crazy'," he said, the lowest, most puerile I could feel. "And it's not even bad! What you did isn't *bad*—it's not malicious or mean. You didn't fuck MY wife. But you did what *you* wanted to do. Because you thought it was funny. And you thought it was cute. Good for the story. Thought it was even kinda sweet. Or you thought people would think it was. And, you know what? Most everybody in the world will probably agree: awww, sweet in that *cool* and CRAZY and OUT THERE way."

He was doing things with his hands, emphasizing those words in a way that made me want to break the bottle of 99 Bananas and slit both of our throats. He got gravely serious and I shamefully thought it was a shame he didn't give acting a go.

"Everybody but those twenty kids who fucking *worship* you," he said, to the bone. "Worship you."

He swiped the corner of his eye, finished his beer and stood.

"You fucked 'em."

I started and stopped. He was right, obviously. I felt the same way.

"I guess you don't wanna hear about my broken dick—"

"Nope," he said over his shoulder as he walked out.

EIGHTEEN

I HAD MADE A PACT TO STAY IN BED AND WALLOW FOR MOST OF the day—a few hours at the very least—but the blinding alarm of my morningside boner had me too wide-awake and scared to lay around and risk falling back asleep, risk napping into another boner. Plus, I'd never been a big bed wallower. It's one of the things I admire most about women—big bed wallowers. Don't get me wrong: I wallow. I wallow with the best of 'em. But I wallow on the go.

The Injury provided me a terrific excuse to not go surfing, which I was grateful for. Sam and I walked to the water anyway, to wallow and look at the waves I would have let everybody else have. We sat on our usual bench on the grass by the breakwater. A filthy tent tramp accosted early coffee walkers, and I tried to remember what had been going through my mind when I handed out those thumb drives. Did I have a Robin Hood complex without the, you know, charitable, selfless ethos? I think I thought I was doing the right thing? But it wasn't very well thought-out because, yes, of course, as everyone would continue to point out: you can find that stuff on the internet. Why, then? Why? Why would I push the things that I had beaten-off to when I was their age onto them? Now that I had sat and thought about it I felt like I should probably go door to door, just a fair warning that I'm arguably a mild sex-offender. Not *really*, just pedo-lite. Not even the P word, though. Something different for me. And here I was, at it again, trying to come up with a noble, singular name for my creepy indiscretions, gnashing at my own tail—I was The King of Pop, I was Robin Hood—see?!? I couldn't stop! (*Don't stop till you get enough!*)

"Whatta you lookin' at, *faggot*?"

I had been staring at the tent mongrel—actually it was just a tarp: the tarp mongrel—muttering to myself. He reminded me of somebody I disliked back east. He was in his forties, sun-chapped and wind-chapped, life-chapped, but he had that look about him where you didn't feel any ounce of sympathy for him or his situation whatsoever. He looked like a guy who would call me a faggot. I hated him.

"What?"

"Nice hat, faggot."

"I like this hat," I said and I did. It was pink. It was a sweet hat. I think it was a Squaw Valley hat.

"You would," he said, walking toward me, thinking that he could clear me out as he had cleared out the other suckers before me. He was testing me simply for his own entertainment. Or he had severe mental problems, tossed aside and forgotten by our slimy Nation of Hedonism. I didn't care. I was not in the mood and I was no such sucker.

"Stop lookin' at me, faggot!" He was approaching the bench. "You and your faggot dog! Faggot hat!"

"Dude. Back the fuck up," I said, low and slow, unable to imagine being a woman, reimagining Camilla's fantasy of fucking me.

"Why? What're you gonna do?" he snarled. "You're starin' at me—you wanna fuck me? Faggot?!"

Our thoughts were all crossed up. I did not want to fuck him, but I knew that already. Now he was encroaching on my personal space and my alarms were sounding. I shot up, fist cocked, before he could stand over me.

"The FUCK outta—"

"HELLLP! HELLP!" He screamed, cowering back to his tarp. "HELLLLLP!"

I sat back down, feigned settling back in, but he had dropped a toaster in the bathtub of my morning's reflection.

A guy in a loose v-neck tee, a bunch of bracelets and one of those hats I could never pull off, had been watching the scene unfold with a girl who looked like she was made in an Abbot Kinney test tube. I looked to them for support, to share in the bizarre pugnacity of the event.

"Bro, that guy's, like, severely mentally ill," said the guy with the hat.

"So?" I said, though I wanted to say more. Maybe: *but he was getting his hobo spittle on my FACE!* My ears were still thrumming and burning from the interaction so "so" was all I could muster. *My dog's gay, a), and, like, just because that homophobic troll lives under a tarp makes it not a hate crime?* I didn't say that either, and the guy walked over and gave my accoster the rest of his spinach and cheddar scone. I gave him the finger behind his back, thinking that if the girl he was with was cool, she'd think it was funny and maybe I'd have sex with her somewhere down the road if I ever fell out of love with Camilla. She shook her head, disgusted, but she was young and stupid. She'd find it funny some day and finally start enjoying her life.

Around the five o'clock hour my phone started ringing. First it was Jake. Then Mecca. Burt. Maybelline. Mecca again. Innie. Even Manassas—I honestly didn't think he was a fan. I told them all the same thing: I was stupid and I was sorry. They made me swear I'd be at the game on Saturday. I promised them that I would be. But in my mind I wasn't so sure if that was a good idea.

"Dude…" Just drawled when I answered the phone.

"Yeah," I agreed.

"Dude."

"I know."

"Do you know who did it?"

"I don't," I did. "And I don't care—it doesn't matter." Cuthbert had been giving private lessons to one of our defensemen who didn't play much—a chubby kid in the throes of puberty who smelled like Dungeons & Dragons. We called him "Dubs". He and Cuthbert were tight and I wasn't all that nice to Dubs—he didn't really want to be there plus he gave me the willies. Also, I semi-openly talked shit about Cuthbert. So I could only assume that the kid remembered the thumb-drive when he saw the contention between his own Cutty Cuthbert and myself.

"The better question," I declared. "Is why on *earth* would you let me hand out weird lad-mag compilation drives? You know how stupid I am! I need help, Just! Christ."

We had a laugh.

"Dude, you should have seen practice today. Like, we didn't do *any*thing. Stood around and watched Cutty walk around, talking about 'Del Burton' or whatever, and he lets us go and Jake and me and Mecca are like 'we're gonna do some sprints' so we all like line up to do some gassers, you know, and he's fucki—sorry—he's yellin' at us 'you gotta rest your legs! I'm ordering you to rest your legs!' and he tries to step in front of Kumal and Kumal—"

Just had to catch his breath because he was laughing so violently and he squeaked that second Kumal and I muted my end of the phone because that's what did it, I was trying to stay smiley for the fellas but that knocked me in the dirt where I belonged. I had abandoned my boys.

"—I mean he didn't mean to but he didn't, like, not mean to, but he just barreled over Cutty, Dude, and just *laid* him out..." he was in tears on the other end so I unmuted my phone because I could at least make my tears laugh for him. It was quite a picture he had painted.

"That's pretty good."

"It was probably the funniest thing I've ever seen."

"I bet."

"So, you coming to the game? You can just coach from the other sideline—who cares?" Seemed simple enough.

"I'm gonna try—"

"Coach…"

"Yes, Pal: I'll do my best. It's a little tricky, as you can imagine."

"But it's the 'Ship. You have to be there."

"Okay. Yeah. I'll be there."

"Cool."

"Alright, Pal."

"See you Saturday."

"Hey, Just."

"Yeah, Coach?"

"I'm sorry I fucked up."

"I'm sorry I let you."

I laughed, groaned.

"It's all good, Coach. Just be at the game."

It was an emotional series of phone calls, so I set back out to wallow by the sea, hopefully without being attacked by the less fortunate. As I left my apartment, my phone rang again, probably Beaker or Crothers.

"Hello?"

"This is Keri."

I waited.

"A lot of the players are going to ask you to come to the game on Saturday. I am strongly urging you to not attend."

"Okay. It's at Harvard-Westlake, thou—"

"And I have spoken to their AD and their security at the game will be made aware of—"

"Jesus Christ. Alright." I could hear Cuthbert's Crunch n' Munch mouth-breathing mouth in the seat across from her desk.

"If you care about the kids, you'll stay away."

She hung up and I was now certain it was a good idea to go to the game.

The Marine Layer cast its web from the sea to where the 10 met the 405. The ride underneath had an ominous current, the grey belly of the sky hanging low on the Subaru, making me wonder how bad of an idea this was. Was I the bad guy? I was the Other Guy, and that was bad enough. But was I a bad guy to *kids*? Would *I* root against me?!

But we hit the 405-North and I broke with the sun, remembering, howling with laughter, yelling to the windshield: "IT'S MIDDLE SCHOOL LACROSSE!" I gave Sam a playful shove in the passenger seat. I put on "If It Makes You Happy" and turned it up real loud. "What a bozo," I laughed while wondering what kind of security they were going to have there, if he or she would have a taser.

The game was at noon and we pulled into the school just after 11:45. The campus was on Cold Water Canyon behind some tall "keep-out" hedges, a lot of stucco and cement shoved into the mountainside. Nice, but relatively charmless. They hadn't taken me on a recruiting tour, but

I got the gist from my two visits to the field.

Eleven-forty-five was proper as I didn't want to make a huge distraction, wanted them to get properly warmed up, but also didn't want to show up after the game had begun. Let them get seeing me over with, then we get to work. *'They'd'* get to work, I corrected in my head, but corrected back But *'we'*.

I was not the least bit comfortable as a nervous titter was looping in my chest and I tried to remember my sunshine mantra that it was just a middle school lacrosse game. There was only one way to the field from the parking lot and it was through an entrance pavilion, past their training room(s) and down a set of stadium steps which descended to the back of one of the end zones. The stadium seating was to the right, where both teams' parents and fans would be sitting, behind their respective team's bench. Nobody was to the left, so Sam and I put our heads down, and went to the lone sideline as I tried to squeeze the air out of the football that I was holding onto for dear life.

From across the field, I heard the chorus of my adolescents, the whole range from soprano to squeaky tenor with a stray and unexpected baritone filling out the bottom.

"COACH!"

"YO, COACH!"

"It's Coach! DUDE—Coach!"

My doubts were quelled. That little hobgoblin couldn't have me kicked out. Not after that glee club greeting from the Boys. It was on. This was fine. I wasn't a Bad Guy. I was just a moron.

Sam and I stood near midfield and I thanked God for the football in my hands. All eyes from the stands across the field were on me and I stood there concentrating on the football and its shapely perfection as I spun it in the air and caught it, spun it up and caught it, a metronome, something to pace my jangled rhythms.

Warm-ups ended and the teams lined up and removed their helmets for the anthem. All of my guys (Dubs aside) were throwing out Arsenio Hall fists at me. I tried to wave them off like a disagreeable pitch call, but they didn't give a shit.

The Anthem started, heads were bowed or raised, hands on hearts or behind their backs. All eyes on the flag that flew high above us all. All eyes but DeMarcus'. He was near midfield, looking at me, and I could see him in indecision. He looked down the line of his teammates, looked at Cuthbert next to him, made his decision and started walking, a slight limp in his gait, across the field. He got to me as the anthem ended, home of the brave and all, and he put out his hand and we slapped it away and gave each other a hug and I thought *this kid's gonna be President*.

"Hey, Coach."

"Hey, DeMarcus."

I flipped him the football.

"How's the knee?"

"It's fine, I guess," he said. "How's the dick?"

"It's fine," I laughed. "I hope." He smiled, nodded,

understanding, caring. There wasn't any disrespect about him. He was asking out of genuine concern and I know he kept it close to the vest. He liked being on the inside, knowing something about me the other kids didn't. "Thanks for asking," I added, and he flipped back the Duke.

The teams took the field. Just motored over to me for a pound before he took his spot behind the restraining line at attack. Mecca, who was playing on the wing, popped over and stuck out a glove.

"Hey, Coach."

"Hey, Buddy."

The game began and I had taken a vow of silence with Cuthbert being his usual self, yelling a barrage of redundancies and malapropisms so the air would know who was the coach.

Harvard-Westlake came down, moved the ball around the horn and their attackman took a dodge from the wing, fired a hip-high side-armed shot that Beaker saved and moved out wide to Crothers, who moved it to Just, just beyond midfield—he had worked back toward the ball like a good boy, a hustler with a chip on his shoulder. Just caught it, rolled, and blew past his defender and side-stepped the double and it was just him and the goalie and he faked low, got the goalie down, shot high: Yahtzee. The dip n' dunk was something we had worked on, a very sweet, ShowTime finish that brought the milkshake to the yard. After Just buried the goal, he kept on running, arms out in airplane fashion and didn't stop till he was in front of DeMarcus and myself. He got about three inches from my face and just stared at me, a dumb grin across his mouth, blinking his eyes like a ventriloquist dummy, head cocked as the fellas mobbed him. The ref called an excessive celebration penalty. It was worth it.

The game went back and forth for the first half. Cuthbert called "Cutty" a few times only to be widely ignored, not out of insubordination but because I don't think any of the fellas knew the play and I'm not sure he did, either. A few times they scored within forty-five seconds of him yelling it and I could sense him accrediting the goal to a play that didn't really exist which he had named after himself.

On defense, midfielders and long-poles alike would look at me when they were the back-side adjacent slide—the double we had used to pretty good effect in the last bout. So as to stay true to my silence vow, I had DeMarcus sending them on those kamikaze doubles. I'd say "yut" under my breath and he'd yell "GO!"

At half the game was tied at five. Cuthbert took them behind the stands, out of sight and as far away from me as he could.

I located Keri in the bleachers, walking down one of the aisles looking like a used Lego.

Alex hopped down from the stands, onto the track and strode directly across the field in our direction, followed by another dad—Brian Bylsma—and another, and another, and Mecca's Dad, Greg Bleibtreu. Alex got to me first, a shake and a hug.

"You dumb shit."

And the rest of them, the same. I saw Keri clock all of this in the stands, video game smoke coming out of her ears.

These were good guys, good dads who liked me and knew that I had tried for their sons. And that their sons loved me and that that couldn't be erased by a silly thumb-drive with Tyra Banks' big ol' '96 bikini boobs on it.

We ignored the trouble and shot the shit, tossed the football around till the teams got back on the field and limbered up for the second half.

Maybelline swiped the face-off out to the wing, to Jake, who scooped up the ball and barreled in, no slide, and fired a high bounce shot that went over the goalie's shoulder and in the back of the net as he went low.

As they reset, I felt a tap on my shoulder. Behind me was a stout little guy of about forty-five in a red hat and red polo, khakis, a walkie-talkie on his hip. I detected no taser. He was sweating.

"Um, sir, I, we have to, I have to ask you to leave." He was freaked out. Who knows what they had told him about me and who knows what his brain ran with. They probably said "restraining order" and he probably thought I had roofied somebody's sister or made the boys play water polo one too many times for a lacrosse team. The poor guy was trembling.

"Oh, man—I'm not. First, you don't have to worry. Whatever it is you think, well," I assured him. "It's not."

"Hey, Buddy," Brian, Innie's dad tried. "He's their coach.

He's not doin' anything."

"Okay, that's. I'm sorry. I'm sure it's…I was told…I'm just doing my job and I've been told that you…"

He started to understand that he had, well, not exactly the wrong guy, but not the guy they said I was. Everyone was watching, though, and he had to see this through. "I'm sorry," he said, and seemed it.

"It's all good. You're fine. We'll get outta here."

The Dads started to protest, feeling that the mojo would be infected, extracted if I left.

But I left.

I looked up and Keri wasn't in the stands.

When Sam and I got to the parking lot, I heard the crowd erupt and the roar of a bear on the loudspeaker, goal Harvard-Westlake. A few minutes later, as we drove through the parking lot, passing back by the entrance to the field, I slowed down and we heard another bear's roar. I took a left on Cold Water to take the long way home and I swear I heard another roar behind us, back down the canyon.

Harvard-Westlake won the game 13-7.

I WOULDN'T COACH lacrosse again. Not because I was scarred from the experience but because in a year I'd be in my middle thirties and doing it for the pocket money would have been too demoralizing. I agreed that if I were to coach again, it would be in volunteer form, somewhere far less fortunate, after and if I sold a script.

Years later I went to see the Brentwood School's Varsity team play down in Palos Verdes. The eighth graders were now seniors. Men. Many of the kids had dispersed to different high schools, however. Just went to Beverly Hills High because they had a better hockey team—he still played lacrosse, though, and was one of the better players in the greater Los Angeles area, all of California for that matter. Jake went somewhere with a better football team. DeMarcus I kept up with because I helped him in his knee rehab—we got in dangerously good shape—and he went to high school at Oaks Christian and would go on to play football and lacrosse at Virginia. President, mark my words.

At the game in PV, as they were warming up, Mecca spotted me along the fence in the far corner of the field, standing under a palm. He was a happy monster, had found the weight room.

"Oh my GOD," he beamed, jogging over. "Coach!" He looked to my side, looked around. "Where's Sam?"

"He's good he's good," I glossed. Truth was that I had shipped him back east to live with my Old Man years prior, shortly after that fateful season had ended and the ruins of my financial ruin were actualized.

We hugged—Mecca had taken to wearing John Randle eye-black that covered most of his cheeks. We caught up quick and I urged him to get back out there. Cuthbert was still the coach and he wasn't as bad as he used to be, Mecca said, indicating that he had had nowhere to go but up.

"Do you remember that?" he asked.

"What?" I wondered, as it was a pretty vague question.

"That year. That season."

"I do."

"That was crazy."

"It was."

"Best time of my life," he smiled and gave me a light shove as he jogged back to the field. "Through the darkness," he called to me, over his shoulder.

"To the light."

NINETEEN

After the Harvard-Westlake game, the dominoes of my life started to rapidly turn to dust. As we wound our way up the Canyon, the bear's roar in our wake, my check engine light came on, my temperature gauge needle threatening to snap. I don't speak car, but under the hood I saw that I had a cracked coolant tube and I bought a new one and actually replaced it myself in the parking lot of an AutoZone. The temperature leveled out and as we made our way back to Venice, other things under the hood sounded crazy and a rear brake or a caliper felt weird and when I brought it to my mechanic (or, rather, *a* mechanic), he said "where do you want me to start?" And, again, I don't speak car, but that sounded expensive.

He properly readjusted the tube or pipe or whatever that I thought I had fixed and said he could replace the rear driver's side caliper for cheap. I believed him: he looked at me like he knew I had nothing. It was still almost three hundred bucks. The credit card was now not nearly as fun or funny as it had been on my first last night out with Camilla. I left the car at the mechanic's and Sam walked me home.

That same day (or one of the identical bled-together days

that followed, days that consisted of me staring at my computer screen, writing for five minutes, checking my bank account for two, emailing people for work, any work, for ten, standing up and wondering what I could sell for fifteen, repeat) an envelope slid under my door and I saw my landlord—a lanky high-panted dweeb named Brent—scurry away, and, again, something felt expensive.

They were raising the rent, as they did annually, by a minimal amount, the maximum allowed by the state. Minimal, maximum—it was all devastating. There was a way to put this month's rent on that unfunny credit card I had, but that would have to be it. I would have to live somewhere else; couches, back houses, spare rooms. It was so very late in the game to fall back on a lifestyle which, in one's mid-twenties is excusable, but still a far cry from endearing. I was thirty-two! My dad had an eight-year-old, a three-year-old, and a piece of shit six-year-old (Me!) at my age. I was soon very appreciative of the excruciating erections I had in the morning because without them, the tears I'd wake up with would be all on account of my little mountain of failures.

And the worst part was that I wasn't even that sad about any of it. Because I was tap-tap-tappin' the pixels fandango on my stupid pocket lobotomizer. I couldn't write, I couldn't reconcile, I couldn't loathe and use the me that had gotten me there because I was glad-handing the me that had gotten *her*!—the her that was, yes, in Budapest or some one-off city or volcanic island for the long weekend to get that ten second snow-boarding/sky-diving shot, watching her husband be a man, the Man, as I tee-hee-hee'd with her in secret, under the covers in the closet, chocolate and graham crusted on the corners of my mouth, sucking down an Ecto-Cooler like a putz. I was a "this is your brain on iPhone" campaign. But we were all too far gone by then, anyway.

The day I unwrapped my Johnson was the day I decided to ship Sam back east. I had waited a few extra days—past the eight to ten day period—keeping the dressing on, convinced one of the bad morning boners had ruptured the sutures.

I stood in the bathroom and thought about pushing another day but figured infection would only worsen the damage done, only further deform the potential freak-show in my pants. Breaking it, walking into the hospital, going under, leaving the hospital, the morning boners—all of that was fine, a mere backstory to what I would have to live with for the rest of my life. This was it, this was what was, what would be. With each layer of unraveling, the fear and the possibility, probability, that I was uncovering a little one-eyed Frankenstein grew in spades.

I closed my eyes for the last few unwraps, revolutions, the bandage catching, matted in old blood. I cracked my eyes and blurred them, a slow, fade-in of postponement. The last of the gauze separated from skin; a final yanked, pinched pain. I opened my eyes to look at myself in the mirror before I assessed our future. Whatever was there, was ours, I nodded. I looked down, and it was…totally fine. Totally fine. Some of the stitches had yet to fall away or dissolve. The affected area was contained on the collar of my original circumcision. There were some small ferret-like teeth marks, blood-scabbed but far from scary. They weren't scars I could live with; they were scars I would love.

I leaned back against the wall of the bathroom, sat down

and wept and laughed, thanked my lucky stars. Sam nudged the door open with his face, came in to celebrate, console, be my Best Friend. He was trying to nuzzle me, trying to share in the groove, but he was itching like a bastard—as he had been for the past week—because I had been feeding him the horse's ass-meat, Pedigree or Alpo because I couldn't afford the grain-free stuff and my friend at the dog food company had left to work for something else. He licked me, smiled, tried to scratch an itch he couldn't reach. He couldn't properly celebrate with me because I had bought him bad food. I held him close on the floor of the bathroom while I booked him a flight before I could change my mind.

THERE'S A SEPARATE terminal for dogs at LAX, much better, traffic-wise. I had read somewhere that flying isn't good for dogs, especially not in cargo or wherever they stowed them on these flights. But it was a small price to pay for the good life that awaited him on the other side.

I got him checked in, weighed, lined his crate with a NY Giants blanket and my baby blanket that I still had because that's what we do. I guess I called it my "mine-o" when I was a kid. I put my mine-o in there for him. He was Mine-O. I was His-O. He had snow-dog in him. He was better than Los Angeles. And my Dad needed a friend.

The woman reassured me three or four or ten times that he'd be okay, dogs do this all the time, every day.

I told him I'd probably see him at Thanksgiving or Christmas or some other time when the flights were cheaper—but soon—and I started to walk out.

I was doing the right thing, I kept telling myself, as the world spun. I'd cry later, I thought, I couldn't let him see me like that, in a place like this.

I got out of the hangar and he barked. He wasn't a barker but he also hadn't been in a crate in many years and had never really been in an airport setting.

I sprinted back in and hollered "hold up!" to the two guys who were putting his crate on a big set of wheels. They had been anticipating this, as one of the gentlemen was cutting the zip-tie they had used to fasten the gate of his crate. He unlatched it as I approached. They gave me space as I crawled into the crate with my Dog.

I remember what he smells like.

"We took care of each other, didn't we?" I asked him, my face buried in the fur of his neck. "Didn't we?"

He licked my face.

I backed out of the crate, closed the latch, thanked the two guys for handling him, jogged out of the hangar to my car and cried so hard I threw up.

GETTING RID OF stuff was easy. I gave everything away or sold it for very cheap. I kept all of my CDs, which took up a lot of space but figured that when I sold a script and had a nice apartment or a house they'd be good to have.

I moved in with Jeff. He had an extra bedroom in his Marina

Del Ray condo. Jeff had started a design/build company years ago that went belly-up or chapter nine or eleven, the chapter where a lot of people tie the noose. But he had the fastest brain in the west and a scrappy New Jersey resolve and within months of going bankrupt, was soon making hand-over-fist in the consulting game. He believed in me, his one dumb streak, and saved my life or at least kept me from being another scabby tarp minstrel, which is one and the same.

I pieced together work, as I always did. Had a months-long gig driving a Winnebago for EA Sports, stopping at baseball stadiums all across this sad land to let clueless, eager people try the new baseball videogame. I wound up back in Marina Del Ray in the nice condo with the high ceilings owned by a friend of mine who traveled for work twenty-two days out of the month. I could have used my situation—rock bottom, thumb drive, leaving the boys on a boat without paddles or a compass, dog on a plane, cabana boy to the Hero's wife, professional leech, full-time nobody, part-time wannabe—as my sturdy, sad flint with which to spark the feeling, the bedrock of *something*, the thing that could translate to the page. But, I had her to look forward to. I had nothing to get mad at, nothing to get sad at. I had a carrot on a stick, the rabbit on the tease pole at the dog track. She was coming back and we had our scheduled rehabilitation of ecstasy. I was runnin'.

She landed at LAX as I watched 1-877-KARS-4-KIDS tow the Subaru away down Glencoe Ave. I stood and waved with the plates in my hand, upset with myself for not being more upset, not tending to this moment of penitence—that car had seen me everywhere. But, she had just landed, and all of my systems were buzzing, lit up like the Midway.

We had run it into the ground, on the phone. Said everything that could possibly be said and then doubled back, found old phrases and lines, the effusive run-on idiom of the heart, dusted off the been-said, shuffled it, shot it with Botox, put a red dress on it and did its hair up pretty, said it all anew.

We were too familiar on the phone, through our thumbs, waiting on each new cavalcade of endorphins from the base and pathetic *delivered...seen* from overseas, up to space, and down to me. As I paced, waiting for her that evening—Jeff was in San Francisco for a few days—I got a jolt, the dime-stop redirection of the naïve gone suddenly and brutally self-aware: we couldn't live up to what we had done, who we had become in that little green icon.

There was a knock on the door. I opened it.

And I was wrong.

The plan was to get my Johnson back on its feet, back in fighting shape—"take such good care of that Johnson, Wilson"—and then we would take the leap, the plunge, into a magical mythical place where nobody would get hurt and everybody was cool, a place we dubbed "Friendship Lake." That was the plan.

That was the plan. Mend what we broke, on the great and beautiful drive to the Lake.

I wish I could say that we wanted the best for everyone.

I wish I could say that we started driving.

But when I opened the door, I saw and felt that the lake was a little farther away than our original mock-up map had suggested.

And when I laid her on the bed, took off her jeans, put my face between her legs and felt her climax without any earthly contact, just taking in the air down there, well, I knew the lake was on a different map.

And then, when I made my way back up her body, kissed her and put myself back where it had pined nonstop to return to, for eight to ten weeks, the only place to be...well, somebody had spilled grog all over the map and it was going to be hard to salvage, nearly impossible to retrace.

And that was how it went. All consuming, every thought, every synapse and fiber, waiting for the next time. Days in between were excruciating, blinding, and that was the only saving grace: I acquired the New Sad. The Other Guy starter kit I received outside the hospital was fully formed and operational. I would resent Jeff if he was in town, in the very nice condo that he paid for which he so graciously, so generously, so *brotherly*-ly, let me live in for free. And, thank God, I began to *loathe* myself for the waiting. I didn't say a goddamn word about it, though; she never received even a whisper of the ire and resentment building in me. We went on for weeks, months, speaking of the lake only after we'd come down from the third or fourth serial bang of the day. The lake and its waters, so cleansing in the theoretical horizon because we did love each other, it would be for the best. But could we be together-together? I had to get my estate in order. Well, I had to formulate an estate, but also I loved her husband (or so I told myself, told the air) because we were bound through her so the lake is the place but if I were to accrue some assets...

This was the dance. Over a pint and a garbage meat sandwich where it was guaranteed nobody knew our names; over a shared Parliament after a midday hump of clutching and clawing and clasping together so hard we fused.

"You can do whatever you want to me," she whispered through the panting of crazed lust, on Jeff's rug in front of me on all fours as I let the seconds, minutes tick by, poised behind her, drawing it out, not teasing or testing but seeing, seeing just how far we could take it, stretching it out, how long could we make our moment last.

"What does it feel like?" she asked after another, another, another one on a day as impossibly beautiful as the others.

"You first," I suggested, as she was the one who asked and probably had her answer.

"It makes me feel closer to God," she said.

She was not the religious type.

"And you?"

"Feels like..." I thought about it, and I obviously knew. "For the first time: I'm Home."

"I was gonna say that, too."

I GOT MAD at her once. Which, looking back on it, was a blessing. She was at a party one Friday night at Mr. Chow's or Jimmy Biggs', Chinese Laundry. She rang, asked me to pick her up, rescue her from the vapid din of her Hollywood night and I hopped in Jeff's Prius—he was in a Texas town for a few—and buzzed up to Hollywood like a little prissy-pawn on call, a pleated, bleating yes-man. Her husband was still finishing the movie, re-shoots or working on a different thing, in an editing bay somewhere or maybe just at home watching college basketball. I didn't know and I didn't ask.

But I scampered up to Hollywood in the low-purr of my friend's electric car and I parked around the corner from Dr. Scholl's Lounge and I waited. And waited. And waited. Called, it rang. Called again, her phone was off or dead. I went home, pretty torn up, and for the first time thought, and then said out loud: "Fuck that *fuck*in' bitch."

We talked the next day and she apologized and said that she had been drunk and her phone died and she had tried to charge it but, and, you know. I told her that it was no big deal. But it was. It was a big deal. She had used me, tossed it aside, forgotten, and I had called her a bitch. It was a very big deal. We should have been celebrating.

But we carried on as idiots do, no end in sight, summer became fall, fall crept into the holidays, flights were too expensive and we were still bending the spoon, sexually. The lake was not a mirage but a ghost, a reminder of when we strived to be better; a vast, cracked clay bed, long past saving, destroyed by us, two humans.

One day on the shaggy dream-carpet of Jeff's living room (he was in New York), we post-coitally ranked our top five. Conversation never dried up because if it threatened to, we could always talk about the thing we had gotten quite good at, the thing which, still, every time—and the times were many—melted our collective face.

My phone buzzed as she recalled a time on the rocks on a reservoir or quarry in Ojai, and I agreed: that was pretty cool. She remembered a wood-floor somewhere and a bathroom somewhere else, or the first time back, plucking me off the trash heap, off the injured reserve, easing back in, the Ginger Baker sessions. I nodded, tried to add to the list, but the security alarm of my Pentagon had sounded and it was deafening:

Tourney, Buck

Those were two of the words in the banner of my Gmail alert, the ones that got my attention. I wanted to put the phone down and never look and never have a phone but I had to read what was there before I alerted our party. I opened the email from Tourney as his wife continued on with the greatest hits of our tryst.

i read your script. i laughed, out loud, four times. i never laugh out loud. one thing i would say is that a lot of the characters speak in the same way. work on that. otherwise, i enjoyed it. john says that you can throw a football. i'm having some friends over for a touch football game saturday at 10. in the a.m. if you were confused. address is below.

buck

also, it seems like you were a helluva coach. i never got to thank you. see you saturday.

I put my phone down, lay back on the carpet, let the color drain back into my face. I disabled my alarms.

"Who was that?" she asked.

"Your husband."

"That's not funny."

"I know."

She bolted upright, threw her t-shirt across her chest as if a SWAT team were descending from the sky.

"I think we're fine," I said, my mind rereading the email.

"What? NO! Are you serious? You can't joke about this stuff!"

She gathered her other things as if they could right the past.

"I guess he read my script."

"Really? What an asshole—I gave it to him so long ago. Typical." She got angry, not at the slight on my behalf, but as a wife. Which was cool and cute and it hurt but it showed me something I'd been hiding from or she'd kept from me: they had solids. There was geology there.

"I guess he liked it," I sat up. "He said he laughed out loud."

"He never laughs out loud. Or at least he always says he doesn't."

I stopped her from scrambling about for her wares. She was antsy. I palmed the back of her skull.

"I coached his kid—we were gonna have cross-over at some point."

"Oh, I know. It just…" She took the deep breath we both needed.

I laid back down, put her head on my chest, balance and peace not something you can force, but I had to try.

"He wants me to play touch football this weekend."

"*Really*," I felt her smiling, mocking, protecting herself.

"Yeah."

"That's a very Hollywood game."

"Yeah."

"You play that game, there's no turning back."

"Yeah."

"No more you and Tupac against the world."

"Yeah."

"And you're not so pure anymore."

"Yeah."

She sat up on an elbow, pulled my hand off my face.

"You should play," she kissed me, forcing herself to be selfless. "But. If you do," she smiled, sadly, not as a threat, as a lament: "We can't do this anymore."

"Yeah."

I rolled on top of her and we lamented ourselves on Jeff's rug one last time.

Oh, but I was very not so sure I wanted to quit that game. My own private masochistic adulterous hamster-wheel in a vacuum. A resentment was forming and I wanted to splash in it for a bit, wade through it and use it to my advantage. I wanted to see how sad I could get, how empty and used I could feel, turn that on its head and squeeze it, see if it was zircon encrusted for the page. And, of course: part of me wanted to bang her in secret for the rest of my days.

But I also didn't want to, knew that we couldn't. And if I played in the football game, maybe, fingers crossed, we'd have gotten away with it, cracked the code, floated our hot air balloon close enough to the sun to get eternally kissed but not burnt, the nylon singed and prettier, come back down to earth and on the way down light our effigy, cast it out to the Pacific, our secret of the sea.

TWENTY

ALL MY LIES ARE ALWAYS WISHES...

A young Jeff Tweedy sang into my headphones as I biked north on the bike path. It was hard, it was easy, it was impossible. Camilla and I weren't sustainable even if my body, all my stupid nodes and lobes disagreed. This game, that lake, our lives.

I know I would die if I could come back new...

It was my chance. It was a touch football game—one of the one things I'd ever been really good at—with people I had dreamed of meeting since I moved to this awful place all those years ago. It could finally be worth it.

The downside was the letdown. Which would be quite the whipping straw. Rub elbows, nothing comes of it because I have the follow-through of a newt. And that's probably discrediting the resilience and tenacity of the newt.

But did I even want to meet these people? Who was I without the chip on my shoulder? I imagined that Hollywood chip fills in pretty quick when you start hitting dawn patrol with McConaughey.

I continued to pour over my cost-benefit analyses but it became pretty clear that I had made up my mind as my bike didn't exactly turn itself onto their street.

I WENT AROUND the side, following the narrow path between the hedges and the house, my breathing in controlled hysterics as I reminded myself that we were playing *touch football!* and that *silly had NO place here, on the field*. But there silly was, cacophonous in my belly. Among other sentiments.

Teddy came running around the corner as I cleared the narrow path, a little lunatic with dread locks in her wake.

"Hey, Coach!" she called out, ducking into the path, on a mission to somewhere.

"Hey, Kid," I said.

I took the steps up to the deck I had once stood on and looked out at the view, trying to look puzzled, impressed, unfamiliar. Down on the field there were nine people—I'd be the tenth. A game of five on five, good numbers for touch. Anthony Kiedis was there—just a little guy, surprisingly. Or not so surprisingly. Matty Mac was down there, rowdy, cranking the Texas up to eleven. Timberlake had a cannon, which I had already accredited him with, in my mind. He was throwing outs to Pink, who had good hands. Some guys I didn't recognize, agents or managers. Johnny Knoxville was throwing fade routes to Michael B. Jordan. Tourney was near midfield, on his back, one leg draped over the other, stretching his lumbar.

I walked down the stadium steps to the field, smiled at no one, nodded a "nice to meet you" to the air. Figuring I should introduce myself to the host, I went right to Tourney.

"Hey, Man," I said. "I'm, ah, I coached Just. John, I mean. Just John."

He hopped up, gave me a Man's handshake.

"Great to meet you. I'm Buck."

"Yeah," I laughed. "It's really nice to meet you." And it was.

He looked up to the deck and I followed his eyes, and there she was, Camilla, in her grey t-shirt and jeans, looking down at us. She put a hand up and we both waved back. Tourney looked at me, a back wheel hydroplaning in his recess. We looked back up at Camilla, who smiled as she walked back toward the house, shaking her head.

Tourney quietly narrowed his eyes at me, a faint gristle at the back of his throat. I clapped him on the arm.

"Awright," I said, and hooted for Timberlake to hit me on a flag.

TOURNEY SPLIT THE teams up. It was Timberlake, Knoxville, Pink, Kiedis and me. Pink and McConaughey shot it out to see who started with the ball and we won. No kick-off, started at the twenty, four downs, one rusher one blocker.

We huddled up, Timberlake assuming the role of quarterback, which was fine by me.

"Hey, Man," he said—nice guy.

"Hey, Dude," I said.

He began to draw up a play, and I stopped him.

"Hey, how you doin'—my name's Ryan," I said, introducing myself to Kiedis and Pink. "Listen, I got the jimmies." I showed them my leg, which was shaking. "And I know this," I gestured to my heart and whatever else was inside, "this machine of mine—I know it well—and the only way out is through, if you know what I mean." They seemed to. "I'm gonna do an out n' up on the left."

"Big dog wanna eat," JT said, amused or impressed.

"Just float it out—I'll run it down." I looked around, felt a little self-conscious and selfish. "Is that okay? I didn't mean to make this about me," I tried to laugh. "It's been a funny year."

They all gave it the okay, slapped me on the back reassuringly. We were a team.

We got to the line and Timberlake counted it down, theatrically. "OmaHA! OmaHA!" he yelled, having a smile, raising his leg like they do, setting things in motion.

They were playing soft; Michael B. on me, Tourney on the other side of the field, giving our other wide-out—Knoxville—a deep cushion.

Teddy yelled something from up on the porch and Camilla was back out, curiosity getting the best of her. Looking at her hurt but it was for the best. It would hurt less, eventually, down the road when somebody I'd love would suffer, picking up the pieces, gathering up my stuffing and stitching me back together. But it would hurt less…and less…and it would all be okay because it had no choice.

I could feel Tourney's eyes on me as I let go of his wife. Pink snapped the ball to Timberlake and I shot off the line, surprising Michael B. with my first step and he stumbled backwards but regained his footing. Timberlake looked it off, eyes on Kiedis in the slot, before he whipped to me as I planted, made a hard out twelve yards up the field. Michael B. had given me that cushion and slipped, so when I made my out and he had some field to make up, he hoped maybe his missteps were fortunate and he could time Timberlake's throw. But yes, but no, Timberlake pumped and Michael B. bit hard, thinking pick-six as I took off up the field trying not to trap myself on the sideline.

From the snap, Tourney knew it was coming to me. He played deep off of Knoxville and shifted over to the middle as I made my out. By the time Timberlake floated the ball up the line, Tourney was already heat seeking across the field. We were playing touch but he was targeting, and who could blame him? Timberlake threw the ball too high, not enough float, but I timed it right, left my feet right in tune. I reached up and up and as Tourney prepared to meet me in the air, I figured it would be one of two things: a heartbreaking drop or the greatest catch of all time. I knew it would be the latter because I was going to catch that ball even if it killed me. I was still young. Still rife with that good stupid. I still wanted it all. And maybe, just maybe, this was only the beginning.